"A seductive debut filled with ... and espionage."

—RITA Award–winning author Sophia Nash

Sealing the Deal

"I agree to the arrangement."

"Excellent. I suggest we seal the pact with—"

"A handshake?" she offered helpfully.

His gaze tracked down to her lips. "I was thinking of something a bit more binding."

"A blood oath?" she tried.

"What? No, a kiss. Where do you get these ideas? You'd prefer a blood letting over kissing me?" he asked in bemusement.

"A minor pin prick would suffice," she pointed out reasonably. "I have a hat pin in my reticule that will do nicely." Sophie reached into her bag and withdrew her weapon with a flourish.

He dropped her hand. "You have succeeded in ruining the moment. Put the pin away, Sophie, we're about to arrive at your front door."

"Oh!" She began making futile attempts to straighten her disheveled appearance. "Thank you for everything, Alex," she said sincerely, if a bit distractedly. She crammed her mostly crushed bonnet atop her head and tied the ribbons in a limp bow beneath her chin. "How do I look?"

Bedraggled, wrinkled, dirty, mussed and heart-wrenchingly beautiful.

Alex took her face in his hands and kissed her. He didn't have time for anything more than a brief but passionate pressing of his lips to hers. But it was enough to heat his blood and render her breathless. He nipped her bottom lip playfully, then kissed her gently on the brow.

"I thought you said I had ruined the moment," she whispered.

"You had," he replied, "but only for a moment."

As Luck
Would Have It

Alissa
Johnson

LEISURE BOOKS NEW YORK CITY

For Katherine Jane Johnson,
because you were the first to believe.

A LEISURE BOOK®

October 2008

Published by

Dorchester Publishing Co., Inc.
200 Madison Avenue
New York, NY 10016

ISBN 10: 0-8439-6155-4
ISBN 13: 978-0-8439-6155-3

The name "Leisure Books" and the stylized "L" with design are trademarks of Dorchester Publishing Co., Inc.

Printed in the United States of America.

10 9 8 7 6 5 4 3 2

Visit us on the web at www.dorchesterpub.com.

ACKNOWLEDGMENTS

My sincere thanks to my agent, Emmanuelle Alspaugh, and editor, Leah Hultenschmidt, without whom this book would not have been possible.

As Luck
Would Have It

❈ Prologue ❈

1796

*I*n the years to come, it would be said that the Duke of Rockeforte had died well. Very well indeed.

At the moment, however, His Grace was far less concerned with the manner of his death than with the notion that he was, as yet, still dying—as opposed to being fully dead—which indicated he might have the time for a few final words. And because his dear friend, the sole witness to his untimely demise, looked so damnably glum, one last spot of fun as well.

"A good run we had, old man, a good run."

A warm hand covered his own. "Save your strength, Rockeforte."

"I have been, and for this very bit."

"Which bit?"

"The bit where the dying man wrings . . . tremendously inconvenient promises from . . . whomever happens to be nearest."

His friend smiled at that. "Tell me what to do."

"My children . . . look after them." He paused and gave a weak laugh. "The look on your face, old man. . . . Don't worry, I know I have but one son. . . . Not hearing harps yet."

"Alexander."

Rockeforte's face twisted with a pain that had nothing to do with his wounds. "Yes, Alex. . . . He'll be alone now. . . . He's already . . . too serious by half. . . . See he takes the time to enjoy life, to be happy."

"It's done."

"The others . . ." He coughed and wiped away a bubble of blood. "Not children of my flesh and blood . . . but of my heart."

"The Coles, you mean, and Miss Browning?"

Rockeforte gave a small nod. "Whit must look after his family. . . . He'll never forgive himself if he . . . ends up like his father. And little Kate . . . needs to follow her gift . . . for music."

"I'll see to it."

"Their cousin Evie . . . life will not be easy for her."

"I will do my best to smooth her path."

"That little imp Mirabelle . . . sharp tongue, but . . ."

"I know. I'll watch out for all of them."

"I know you will. . . . Thank you. . . . No men left in the family. . . . Whit's father . . . doesn't count."

A stream of blood trickled from Rockeforte's nose. His breathing became more erratic, his voice softer.

"Rest now," his friend urged.

"One last thing. . . . Promise me . . ."

"Promise you what?"

"Promise me . . ."

"You've only to ask, my friend. I give you my word, I will see it done."

"Promise me . . ."

His friend leaned down to catch the whispered words.

Then straightened so fast his head spun. "You want me to *what?*"

Rockeforte smiled weakly and winked. "Too late . . . you promised, old man."

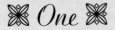

❈ One ❈

1811, off the coast of England

*I*t was the general opinion of those who had the pleasure of her acquaintance for more than a fortnight that Miss Sophie Everton had the most extraordinary luck of any human being in living memory.

It was also agreed to be a shame, really, that said luck did not limit itself to being of the beneficial variety, but was remarkable instead by its consistency and balance.

Sophie's experiences with providence ranged from the mundane to the miraculous to the catastrophic. But without fail every windfall was paid for with disaster, and every misfortune was tempered with a boon.

By four-and-twenty, Sophie had nearly become someone's seventh wife, been lost in a South American jungle, and been shot straight through the arm with an arrow launched by a drunken hunter.

In return, she had been saved from unwilling participation in matrimony by the unexpected death of the presiding wise man (her betrothed could not help thinking this was something of a bad omen and gave her half a dozen healthy goats just to go away), had inadvertently stumbled across a previously unknown—and fortuitously friendly—tribe in the jungle, and had inherited a rather lovely town house in a fashionable London neighborhood—deeded to her upon death by the childless and remorseful archer.

Such an existence would likely reduce most young women to a state of perpetual hysteria. Being of sound mind, reasonable intelligence, and, oh very well, *slightly* reckless nature, Sophie considered it a wondrous, if occasionally messy, life of adventure. It was also, she was wont to point out, wholly unavoidable. As such, she found it advantageous to keep a smile on her face and a wary eye on the world.

Much as she was now smiling warily at the gentleman sitting next to her on the deck of *The Sailing Diamond*. Easily in his late sixties, with endearing gray eyes and a mass of white hair tied at the nape of his neck in a style two decades out of fashion, the man reminded Sophie of her father.

It was to be noted, however, that her father was *not* currently onboard the ship that would, in two hours' time, deliver his daughter to English soil for her first visit in nearly twelve years.

This man of the kind eyes and unfortunate hair had been a complete stranger until five minutes ago.

And a very strange five minutes it had been, she mused. She'd snuck out from under the nose of her much loved, but often exhausting, chaperone in the hope of finding a moment of solitude. Before she'd had the chance to so much as fully settle herself comfortably on a bench, this odd little man had sat down and pressed a letter into her hand. A letter bearing the seal of the Prince Regent. Then he'd gone on to introduce himself as Mr. Smith and asked her, in the name of the Crown, to please accept a mission of colossal national import. To which she now replied:

"Hmm."

Mr. Smith waited patiently for additional comment. When none appeared forthcoming, he tugged at his wrinkled waistcoat and narrowed his wrinkled eyes.

"I say, Miss Everton," he began, "you seem to be taking this all rather well. I hardly expected a swoon, mind you, or some sort of fit, but I find myself surprised you're not a bit more . . . well . . ."

"Surprised?" she offered helpfully.

"Rather."

Sophie cocked her head in interest. "You must have done some research into my background before approaching me," she pointed out reasonably.

"As it happens, I did hear a great many stories about you," Mr. Smith chuckled. "They were so unlikely, however, that I attributed them to someone's overzealous imagination."

"It's possible they were," she conceded, "but the truth has proved interesting enough in the past to negate the necessity of dramatic embellishments."

He gave her a humoring smile. "Really? Were you truly cornered just last year in an open-air market by a Bengal tiger?"

It was Sophie's turn to laugh. People rarely believed the tales of her adventures, but she did so enjoy telling them. There was a curious sense of satisfaction to be obtained from their reactions, which generally ranged from delighted to horrified. Never was there a doubt, however, that the listener was entertained.

"Oh, yes," she replied with no small amount of relish. "And if you had any desire to see me surprised, you should have been there. After Mr. Wang distracted the beast with some raw meat and a great deal of noise, I indulged in a rather embarrassing display of hysterics. Have you ever seen a tiger, sir?" she inquired. "They really are enormous."

Mr. Smith blinked rapidly for a few moments—which she found gratifying—then coughed and peered at her as if he had just noticed something that intrigued him.

"Do you know," he said finally, relaxing his gaze and actually smiling at her, "I rather think you're perfect for this mission. You should do quite well. Quite well indeed."

"Well," she responded, suddenly feeling a little lost. "I'm happy to have your good opinion of course, but I must remind you that I have absolutely no idea what this mission entails or whether I shall agree to undertake it."

Mr. Smith patted her hand congenially. "Nothing to it, my dear. Nothing to it. You will, I presume, be residing at your cousin's town house upon arrival?"

"It's my town house, actually, but yes, I will be residing there with Lord Loudor."

"Excellent. Excellent. And are you very well acquainted with His Lordship?"

Sophie narrowed her eyes in suspicion. "We've kept up a fairly regular correspondence. He's been responsible for the management of my father's estate since we left England."

"Indeed. You'll be reviewing his ledgers when you arrive, no doubt. Well, try not to put him off, if you can help it. Lord Loudor has a wide circle of friends and acquaintances. He's rather popular amongst the *ton*. In particular, with a select group of gentlemen who garner no respect from me or my employer"—he motioned to the envelope—"and with whom we would like you to develop a better acquaintance."

"You want me to spy on my family?"

If the gentleman had been hoping earlier for surprised outrage, he was no longer disappointed.

"Miss Everton," he drawled with exaggerated courtesy. "The king, as you well know, is mad. Napoleon is ever at our gates, and two-thirds of our army is at his. England, at present, is in a most insecure state, threatened from inside our borders—"

"From my cousin?" she demanded.

"Actually, Loudor is not currently a suspect. He simply has the misfortune of naming several unsavory gentlemen among his friends."

Sophie blew out a long breath and made a conscious effort to ease the grip she'd had on the folds of her skirt. "That's not misfortune, that's poor judgment," she grumbled.

"Be that as it may, we would like for you to further your acquaintances with these gentlemen. Find a way into their studies, their libraries—"

"Find a way into their studies?" Was he mad? "Are you mad? Good Lord, I'd get myself caught or injured. I've no experience with that sort of thing." Well, perhaps a *very* little. "There must be someone, anyone, who would better suit."

Mr. Smith shook his head. "No one so much as you. You are, for all intents and purposes, new to London, without known sympathies or loyalties. That, combined with your rank as a viscount's daughter, means no ballroom or parlor will be closed to you. There is also the matter of your possessing some unusual skills, courtesy of your Mr. Wang, I believe. Lock picking, knife throwing, some form of eastern combat—"

"I'm only a novice," she interrupted. Mostly.

He continued as if she hadn't spoken. "There is also the fact that we, Miss Everton, have something you need—money."

She stared at him in bafflement, unsure of how to respond to that outrageous statement. Did he honestly believe she was greedy enough to quite literally jump through windows for a few coins? Perhaps he wasn't mad quite so much as dullwitted. Maybe if she spoke slowly and very carefully . . . "I understand my family's finances are less stable than they have been in the past, but I have every faith that will turn about. And we're hardly impoverished—"

"Your father's coffers are very nearly empty. He stands to lose Whitefield within six months, a year at best."

Sophie was stunned into speechlessness, a rare and unpleasant occurrence for her. After much mental groping she managed, and then only poorly, "I . . . we . . . you must be mistaken."

"There's no point in my exaggerating the case, is there? You'd find out the truth as soon as you reached London. I'm sorry to be the bearer of bad news, but we are in a position to help you. We are offering a considerable sum."

For a dull-witted madman, Mr. Smith was annoyingly sensible.

Dear God, why was she only now hearing of this? And from a stranger? In his last letter, her cousin had mentioned a few minor difficulties with the estate, but nothing she "need worry over."

Taking him at his word, she'd made plans to travel halfway across the world to indulge in an expensive London season. How mortifyingly stupid.

And now they stood to lose Whitefield. Though it had long been the family home and the only consistently profitable estate, it wasn't entailed. Whitefield could be sold, taken, lost. The means of their survival and the home of her lost mother and sister . . . gone.

Unacceptable.

Straightening her shoulders, Sophie turned to give Mr. Smith her best businesslike stare.

"You are not directly interested in any member of my family, is that correct?"

"It is."

"How much?" she asked coolly.

"I'm sorry?"

"How much money are you willing to offer for my services?"

"Ah, right. Well, upon arrival, you'll be given access to a small sum available through a solicitor, pin money as it were. You'll also have an open account at all the best shops in London. You'll be able to purchase any necessary items associated with a young lady's first season in London. Upon completion of the mission, you shall receive fifteen thousand. Well invested, it should be enough to restore your family's financial security."

Sophie glanced at the envelope. "And if they're innocent? Will I still receive the money, or is payment contingent upon finding proof of guilt?"

"If you find no proof, you'll receive five thousand pounds, a third of the original fee."

Sophie shook her head. "Half," she insisted, "of twenty-five thousand."

"Half," Mr. Smith countered, "of twenty thousand. That is as high an offer as I am authorized to give."

Sophie thought hard.

But not too long.

"Explain then, please, *exactly* what I have to do."

"You want me to seduce a virgin? Have you gone mad?"

Alexander Durmant, the Duke of Rockeforte, looked thoroughly disgusted. Slouched miserably in a chair by the fire and not so much sipping as gulping his brandy, His Grace looked ready to whimper.

Across from him, William Fletcher smiled pleasantly. It occurred to William that he might be smiling just a hair more pleasantly than was strictly necessary under the circumstances, but as head of England's vast and currently very active War Department, William found it expedient to obtain his amusements when and where he could.

And, holy hell, but this was going to be amusing.

"I don't recall having mentioned the word 'seduce,'" he replied congenially. "Nor 'virgin' for that matter, although I've no reason to believe she isn't. Your task is simply to keep close to the girl."

To mask an outright laugh at Alex's horrified expression, William drew out his handkerchief and blew his bulbous nose loudly and extensively. He knew full well there wasn't a single matter involving a debutante that could be reasonably described as simple. They were a thoroughly complicated and enormously terrifying lot.

If Alex were any other man, William might have worried over gaining his cooperation, but for more than four hundred years, the Rockeforte line had served the nation's interests in whatever capacity was required. Soldiers, spies, ambassadors, whatever the War Department or its earlier counterparts asked, the Rockeforte men answered without question, complaint, or demand. It was a quiet honor ingrained in every male of the family. Alex, honorable to the bone, would rather die than fail to live up to that legacy. He would even forsake his usual pursuit of actresses and courtesans and enter the dreaded world of ambitious debutantes and their title-hungry mamas.

For a time. And not without first ascertaining if it might be avoidable.

"There are limits, William."

"I'm not asking you to wed the chit," he argued reasonably. "Just make nice."

"I have no experience making nice."

"Nonsense, I've seen you perfectly amiable on at least two occasions." William shoved his handkerchief back in his pocket and leaned back in his seat to savor the experience of watching his friend squirm. "I need a man on the inside, and a courtship of Loudor's cousin will provide ample opportunities for you to be in his company, in his home."

"We could just as easily arrange for the two of us to be introduced—"

"And have him wonder why the generally reclusive Duke of Rockeforte has taken a sudden interest?" William shook his head. "Woo the girl, Alex, and woo Loudor in the process. Find out what he and his cronies are about."

Alex scowled, swore, squirmed.

Then, as William had expected, capitulated. "Bloody hell, very well. What do we know about this woman, this Miss . . . ?"

"Everton. Miss Sophie Everton. Her father owns the estate of Whitefield. I believe Miss Everton holds the place in particular regard, as did the girl's mother."

"Deceased?"

"Yes, as well as her sister, both killed in a carriage accident. The viscount left England with his daughter shortly thereafter, and gave over the business of running the estate to his cousin."

Alex nodded absently. "Loudor. How long ago was that?"

William reluctantly set down his drink, licked a bit of brandy off his fingers, and shuffled through the mountain of papers on his desk before finding what he needed. "Twelve years this past February."

"And how old was Miss Everton at the time?" Alex asked suspiciously.

"Twelve."

"Excellent," Alex grumbled, "a spinster."

It wasn't a complaint, per se, more a statement of dread.

"Come now, man," William chided. "Have a heart. She's spent the last decade continent-hopping with her father. There hasn't been an opportunity for the poor girl to make a suitable match."

"She'll be husband hunting."

Setting the paper aside, William once again relaxed in his chair and smiled. "Is that fear I'm hearing, Your Grace?"

"Yes." Alex took a gratifyingly large drink before continuing. "What else do we know?"

Chuckling, William dug through his papers again. It was a pointless exercise (he'd long since memorized them) except in that it provided an opportunity to draw out the moment. "Ah, here we are. Hmm . . . Seems she's a bit of an oddity, actually. . . . Speaks a number of languages, of which only English and Latin can be counted as civilized. . . . Raised by her father and a governess turned chaperone by the name of Mrs. Mary Summers, and an English-educated Chinese man—old friend of the family. The latter two are traveling with Miss Everton, although Mr. Wang will be journeying on to Wales. As for the young woman herself, she has a reputation for being somewhat outspoken, shares her father's interest in antiquities with no material value, and has had a rather alarming series of mishaps."

Alex digested that information for a moment before speaking.

"Any indication she's traveling to London to aid Loudor?"

"None, but that doesn't negate the possibility that she is, or will be, sympathetic to his cause. They've been in contact by post regarding her father's estate, but it's hardly uncommon for a young woman to keep up regular correspondence."

"Hmm. Have any of these missives been intercepted?"

"A few, wouldn't do to have them become suspicious."

"And were they useful?"

"They were positively benign. He asked after her welfare, hoped her father's spirits were improved." William waved his hand around. "That sort of thing. Chatty letters."

Alex frowned into his brandy and William imagined he was currently thinking of all the reasons, some of them possibly even legitimate, not to accept the assignment. All the excuses he could use to politely extricate himself from what he knew was his duty. But he was a Rockeforte, and in the end he asked only, "What does she look like?"

"Beg your pardon?"

"Miss Everton, what does she look like?"

"Oh, well . . ." William mumbled the rest of the sentence into his drink.

Alex leaned forward in his chair. "What's that?"

"Ahem . . . well, I'm not entirely sure." He grimaced, mentally congratulated himself for the affectation, and hurried his explanation. "My man in China, he didn't give a description exactly. He mentioned something vague . . . something about 'unusual.'"

"*Unusual?*"

"Likely the word was lost in translation."

Alex swore, squirmed a little more, then took a deep breath and a deeper drink.

"For Crown and country then," he finally grunted, clearly unimpressed with either institution. "I suppose I ought to find a way to have myself introduced to our unusual old maid."

"No need. I've arranged to have Loudor's carriage delayed en route to the docks. Miss Everton will be taking a delightful trick hack one of our engineers designed. Very clever young man. Just be at the corner of Firth and Whitelow at five o'clock this evening. Bring Whittaker if you like. He's likely already met Loudor and can help smooth the way, so to speak."

Alex shook his head. "I don't want Whit to go. He should never have gotten involved with your department to begin with."

"Too late on both accounts. We needed his connections on that last bit of business, and he already knows you're meeting with me today. There'll be no avoiding him. Best to give him something useful to do or he'll take it into his head to do so on his own."

Alex jerked a nod and handed his empty glass back to William. "You're certain Prinny knows nothing of this?"

"Quite sure. Our illustrious Prince Regent is entirely in the dark on this matter."

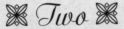

❋ *Two* ❋

*T*hree hours after her interview with Mr. Smith, Sophie found herself standing on her homeland for the first time in twelve years.

It's possible she would have been a bit more excited by the notion if she wasn't still standing on the dock, in a drizzle, pressed tightly between the overprotective persons of Mrs. Summers and Mr. Wang. Their luggage had been piled neatly off to one side and Sophie fought the urge to sit down on one of the sturdy trunks. Where was Lord Loudor, or, if he had been unavoidably detained, then where was his carriage? The other passengers had long since made their way into the city.

She let out a long, exaggerated sigh. She'd been pressing her companions to hire a public hackney, but Mrs. Summers insisted on waiting.

"Lord Loudor will be along any minute now with a reasonable excuse and apologies for his tardiness," Mrs. Summers had explained. "A public hack is *not* a suitable means of conveyance for a young lady."

After forty-five minutes of listening to these and an assortment of other excuses, Sophie stopped asking, and took up making varied sounds of disgruntlement. She sighed, she grumbled, she even *hmphed* for good measure.

Finally, after listening to Sophie tap her foot loudly for several minutes, Mrs. Summers caved. "Oh, for heaven's sake, Sophie! Have it your way!"

Sophie beamed at her friend as Mr. Wang took off to enlist the help of a dock worker. In a surprisingly short time, the three were comfortably installed in the hack.

"This is so much better," Sophie sighed. "How fortunate we were able to secure a hack so quickly. It makes up, I suppose, for Lord Loudor's absence."

Her chaperone frowned disapprovingly. Tall, rail thin, and with striking angular features, Mrs. Summers had all the appearances of a hawk, a look she occasionally enhanced by affecting a matching demeanor. Sophie knew her too long and too well, however, to be fooled. Mrs. Summers's stern countenance hid an open mind and a generous heart.

Perfectly comfortable with her chaperone's censure, Sophie returned the scowl with a smile. "Roomy," she commented, "and decidedly well padded."

The brown leather on the benches extended up all four walls and even onto the ceiling. Glancing down, she noticed even the floor held a thin layer of cushion.

"How very odd."

The carriage started with a jerk, and soon she was too entranced by the passing scenery to dwell on the unusual interior of her transportation. Street after street rolled by. London was loud, dirty, overcrowded, and positively wonderful.

She was vaguely aware of Mrs. Summers speaking, but it was several minutes before she could pull her attention from the window long enough to focus on what was being said.

". . . We've left the waterfront district, which, young lady, you shall not under any circumstances venture into again. In a moment, if you look out to your left, we'll pass . . . Well, for . . . Why on earth are we turning here?"

Mr. Wang craned his neck slightly to peer out the window. "Where, exactly, is 'here'?"

"I have no idea," Mrs. Summers stated, sounding more surprised than alarmed. "Our driver should have continued straight for several more blocks. Whatever is our man thinking taking such a shortcut through such a squalid section of town?"

Mr. Wang raised his walking stick in preparation of pounding on the roof. "Shall I speak with him?"

"And have him stop in this area? Heavens no. We'll take it up with him when we arrive." Mrs. Summers turned again to the window and wrinkled her long nose. "You are not allowed here either, Sophie."

Sophie didn't think she'd have any problem obeying that command. The neighborhood reminded her of some of the poorer sections of Peking. Too many dilapidated buildings likely crammed with too many hungry people. She felt helpless in places like these, and a little ashamed. She watched as they passed a small chapel she might have described as having seen better days, if she'd thought there was any chance at all that the church had, in fact, ever seen a good day. She rather doubted it, and settled for describing it as "glum" instead. Perhaps she could take some of the money set aside for her purchases and make a donation.

The loud report of snapping wood followed by the unpleasant sensation of the carriage tilting precariously to one side immediately erased Sophie's altruistic thoughts. She watched in horror as an unlit iron lantern slid dangerously close to the edge of the shelf over Mrs. Summers's head.

The last thing Sophie remembered was bounding off the seat with her arms stretched outward in a grasping motion.

The next thing she heard was a man's voice telling her to open her eyes. Low, soft, and just a little bit gravelly, it washed over her like a soothing lullaby.

Maybe she'd sleep a little while longer.

The soothing voice was promptly replaced by an annoying one. Mrs. Summers was demanding she wake up immediately. And she was doing it in *that* tone. That horrible, insistent, I-am-quite-out-of-patience-with-you tone every child despises.

And Sophie was going back to sleep. Absolutely.

A hand prodded the side of her head.

"Ouch!"

Sophie's eyes flew open, and she was immediately rewarded for the effort with Mr. Wang's soft chuckle, a painful eyeful of light, and the realization that whatever mattress she was currently lying on was astoundingly hard. Groaning, she squeezed her eyelids shut again.

"She'll be fine," Mr. Wang announced.

Mrs. Summers clucked her tongue (a noise Sophie found excruciating in her current state) and said, "Two square inches of unpadded space in the whole carriage and your head finds it, of course."

The carriage. London! She tried squinting against the sun, which was peeking through the clouds now, when a large figure crouched in front of her and blocked out the light.

"Better?"

"Hmm, thank you." It took a few moments for her eyes to adjust, and when they did she was forced to blink several times in disbelief.

Here was the man with the soothing voice, and good heavens but he was handsome. Without a doubt, the most attractive Englishman she had ever seen. To be fair, she really hadn't seen very many Englishmen in her travels, but she had certainly run across enough to know that this one was not typical. Groggily, she wondered if perhaps she had hit her head harder than she realized and when her eyes regained their focus she would find he had enormous teeth and several chins.

If that were the case, she hoped she wouldn't recover too quickly. He was quite pleasant to look at for the moment, with the chiseled features one rarely found outside of Greek sculpture, deep-set eyes that looked to be possibly green, full lips, and a strong jaw. His aristocratic nose certainly could have been lopped off some poor unsuspecting statue.

Michelangelo's *David,* that's what he reminded her of.

Only taller. Much taller. And with better hair. She watched as one coffee-colored lock fell across his brow. *Lovely.* She could just stare at him all day.

"Miss? Miss. . . ."

"Hmm . . . Everton."

"You can let go of the lantern now, Miss Everton."

Ignoring the pain to her head, she craned her neck up slightly to look at herself. She was lying flat on her back in the middle of the road and held the lantern in a death grip on her stomach. If it had been a bunch of lilies, she might have been mistaken for a corpse.

"I caught it," she said stupidly before laying her head back down.

"So you did," replied Mr. Wang. She turned her gaze to find him standing next to Mrs. Summers. "You were quicker than that tiger, I'd say."

"Let go now, Miss Everton," said the stranger.

"Sorry?"

"The lantern. Let go of the lantern now."

She tried, she really did, but her fingers were cramped in place. "I can't seem to . . ."

Large warm hands covered her own and gently pried her stiff fingers from the lantern. She flexed them experimentally and felt the first painful tingling of returning feeling.

"Whatever . . . ?"

"We lost a wheel," Mrs. Summers explained.

Looking down past her toes, Sophie saw the hack resting awkwardly on three wheels against the road. The horses had been unhitched and tied with two saddled mounts she didn't recognize.

"Yes, well . . . that can happen."

"You're fortunate the whole carriage didn't turn over."

Sophie couldn't help noticing the stranger sounded a touch angry. If she were feeling more confident in her ability to hold a coherent conversation, she might have asked him why.

"Driver's gone! Another hack's coming 'round."

She stared bewildered as yet another strange man walked forward and knelt beside her. He too appeared uncommonly tall and handsome (although not, in her opinion, quite as handsome as the first) but with slightly fairer features. "It's fortunate Alex and I decided on this shortcut. How are you feeling, Miss . . . ?"

"Everton," Mrs. Summers supplied.

Then, to Sophie's complete astonishment, her governess launched into a round of formal introductions and general pleasantries, for all the world as if their little group were meeting for the first time at a lovely afternoon picnic.

And didn't little Sophie just look *charming* spread out on the cobblestone blanket?

Good Lord.

"I'm better, much better," she mumbled, sounding anything but better. "I'd like to sit up now."

She pushed herself up with her elbows before anyone could stop her. The quick movement was a mistake. She knew it would be. Really, anyone would think this was the first time she had been knocked unconscious.

Her head swam, her vision blurred, her stomach lurched, and then finally, and quite suddenly, she went back to sleep.

Alex's first thought upon pulling the insensible Miss Everton from the disabled carriage had been—

Dear God. Something had most certainly been lost in translation.

His second thought had been that Miss Everton's unconsciousness was a disturbing but undeniably convenient opportunity to study her appearance in detail.

She was beautiful.

In the manner of Greek goddesses and Rubens portraits, she was beautiful. A heart-shaped face, full lips that seemed to curve up naturally at the corners, an endearing sprinkling of freckles across the bridge of her pert little nose, all framed by a cloud of thick hair the color of sable.

Alex's next thought had been to wonder about the color of her eyes. Would they be a golden brown or darker like her hair?

When her lids finally fluttered open Alex was hard-pressed not to gape like a green boy.

They were blue. A crisp, dark blue that practically crackled. He had never in his life seen eyes that color. Hard upon that realization came the less rational notion that he was going to tear William limb from limb.

And when she passed out the second time, Alex decided he would do it slowly. At the very least, William's trick hack would be scrap by morning.

Picking up Miss Everton carefully, he carried her to the newly arrived hack. "Whit, you and Mr. Wang see to our mounts. I'll assist Mrs. Summers and Miss Everton home."

Alex ignored Whit's knowing grin and wink. Likewise, he pretended not to hear his friend's quiet comment about having all the fun, deciding it would be better to concentrate instead on getting both himself and Miss Everton inside the carriage without mishap—no easy feat since he refused to set her down first.

Eventually, he managed to settle himself in a seat with her in his lap. He really ought to put her on the bench beside him. He really should. It wasn't at all proper to be holding her as he was, but for some inexplicable reason he couldn't bring himself to perform the task.

She was so very small, not much over five feet, he guessed, and the side of her forehead was beginning to show signs of swelling. She'd have a nasty bruise in a few more hours, and if it wasn't directly his fault, he was, at the very least, partially to blame for her injury.

Reluctantly, he pulled his eyes away from the woman in his arms to peer at the older woman sitting across from him. He was surprised and, for some unaccountable reason, a little annoyed that Mrs. Summers had not insisted he set her charge down at once. Wasn't she responsible for the girl?

She didn't appear particularly concerned. In fact, she was eyeing him steadily with unabashed interest in a way that immediately put him on edge. He could practically hear the wheels turning in her head.

"Will she be all right?" he asked to distract her from her current train of thoughts.

Mrs. Summers blinked once before answering. "Oh, she'll recover. The injury is not serious, leastwise not for her."

Alex would have liked to ask what she meant, but the carriage was coming to a stop in front of a small but stylish town house.

"Ah, we were closer than I realized," Mrs. Summers remarked. "If you will be so kind as to set Sophie on the cushions now, I'm sure one of Lord Loudor's men can see to her."

Apparently, by this particular chaperone's standards at any rate, what was acceptable behavior in a public hackney was not permissible in the general public.

Alex relinquished his hold on the girl with some reluctance. He assisted Mrs. Summers down and watched her follow Mr. Wang into the house before turning a skeptical eye on the servants as they came forward. There were several able-bodied men in the group; one of them was actually quite massive. But then, large men could be clumsy, or worse, stupid.

He looked back at the unconscious Miss Everton. Maybe he should just . . .

"It's no good, Alex."

Whit walked the few remaining steps from the stables to lean against the carriage and offered Alex the lopsided grin that had made him the darling of the *ton* and the bane of Alex's existence.

"You can't very well endear yourself to Loudor by entangling his cousin in a scandal her first day in London, now can you?"

Alex nearly groaned. Whit was right, of course; he was behaving like an idiot. What the devil was wrong with him? He shot his friend a nasty scowl for the sake of principle—no good ever came from telling Whit he was right about something—and gave an order to one of the footmen to care for Miss Everton.

Three

A thin older man with a sour expression, which Alex guessed had more to do with the man's nature than the day's unfortunate events, ushered Alex and Whit into the front parlor and furnished them with drinks.

"His Lordship left several hours ago to meet Miss Everton and her party at the docks. Four men have been dispatched to ascertain his whereabouts. I shall inform him of your presence upon his arrival." With that, the butler excused himself and closed the parlor doors behind him.

"Friendly, isn't he?" Alex remarked, taking a drink of his brandy and looking over their surroundings. With dark ugly colors, the scent of old cigars, and an astounding amount of leather, the room positively screamed of bachelorhood. More, it screamed of a bachelor with exceedingly poor taste.

Whit was likewise eyeing the decor. "Good Lord, if this is the front parlor, what do you suppose the study looks like?"

"With any luck, we'll find out."

"At the moment, I'm a little tempted to botch the mission on purpose. This room is dreadful."

"It smells like a third-rate club," Alex added.

"By God, you're right. I was wondering why the stench seemed familiar. Reminds me of our salad days." Whit thought about this for a moment. "Believe I'll open a window." He set down his drink and held back the thick gray drapes while eyeing the window frame dubiously. "Shouldn't there be some sort of hook or tieback for these things?"

"One would think," Alex remarked casually.

With his free hand Whit unlocked the window and attempted to push it up and open. It wouldn't budge. From his seat, Alex watched with increasing amusement. Whittaker Cole, the Earl of Thurston, was struggling mightily with a set of wool curtains and a parlor window.

"Why am I the only one who witnesses these things?" Alex mused aloud before standing up to lend his poor beleaguered friend a hand. "Would you like some help?"

"Bugger off," Whit snapped, taking a step back from the window.

Alex didn't feel the need to respond, mostly because he wasn't sure whether it was directed at him or the window. Stepping over, he took the drapes with both hands and held them off to the side. He motioned Whit forward. "Perhaps, if you use two hands. . . ."

Whit just grunted and took his place in front of the window. After several minutes of groaning and swearing, it finally slid up a meager two inches.

Whit eyed the gap resentfully. "Splendid."

Alex gave him a jovial clap on the back. "Well done. Care to have a go at the other?"

"I don't think my pride could take it," Whit grumbled, still glaring at the window. "Do you know I'm actually winded? How humiliating."

They stared at the window for a while in silence. Finally, without turning his head, Whit quietly said, "If you are a true and loyal friend, Alex, you will keep this little episode to yourself."

Alex nodded somberly. "If I were a true and loyal friend, I would indeed."

"A *good* man, a *decent* man—"

"Would keep his mouth closed. I'm almost sure of it."

Their conversation was cut short by a commotion in the front hall accompanied by a loud, angry male voice.

"Loudor," Alex supplied.

Instantly serious, both men found their respective drinks and chairs in time to see a rather disheveled looking man in his midfifties enter through the French doors. Alex estimated him to be of average height and build, with muscular arms but a slightly rounded belly that spoke of overindulgence and too much time sitting in clubs and card halls.

Whit made the introductions, while Loudor shrugged off his coat and loosened his cravat. "Don't mind, do you? Had a devil of a time just now. Accident outside Hyde Park. Some nasty business with a fruit vendor. Traffic backed up for blocks and my driver tremendously stupid. I missed Miss Everton at the docks and had to come all the way back here. Perfectly horrid way to spend the afternoon."

Loudor poured himself a drink and dispensed with half the glass in one long and rather loud swallow. Alex half expected him to smack his lips and wipe them across the back of his sleeve. He couldn't help noticing that Loudor had not yet asked after the welfare of his cousin.

"Chit's upstairs is she? Heard she took a bit of a tumble."

That, Alex decided, did not count. He cleared his throat in an effort to hide his annoyance. "Miss Everton's carriage lost a wheel on the way here. Whit and I were fortunate enough to be nearby and able to offer some assistance."

"Awful good of you. In your debt. . . ." Loudor waved the remainder of the sentence away with a flourish of his hand, polished off his drink, then poured another. "Both in town for the season?"

"We are," Alex answered in a tone he hoped sounded casual. Really, the man was an ass. "The country can get a bit dull this time of year with everyone in London. I believe Whit has some family business that will keep him in town for at least several weeks."

"Quite so," Whit replied.

"Nothing serious, I hope?"

"Not at all. Just an annoying tangle of paperwork. Shouldn't take too much effort actually, but I intend to drag it out as long as possible. I mean to spend an appalling amount of time at the clubs and races."

"That's the spirit." Loudor toasted Whit's entirely fabricated speech with another long drink. "But what of the rest of London's attractions?"

Alex shrugged. "Certainly duty requires attendance to some of the more staid events. Wouldn't care to insult the wives of our old school chums."

"Or my mother," Whit offered.

"Or your mother's friends," finished Alex with a genuine wince.

Loudor chuckled—an oddly tittering sort of sound that tore at Alex's nerves. "Not looking to be leg shackled then?"

Since his mission was to woo Miss Everton, Alex's immediate inclination was to reply that he was indeed on the lookout for a Duchess of Rockeforte, but something in the way Loudor had asked the question gave him pause. The man looked too concerned, too hopeful by half, and Alex went with his instincts.

"I'm determined to remain a bachelor for several more years at the very least, and Whit has decided to postpone matrimonial bliss until the age of four-and-thirty."

Loudor turned to Whit, looking well pleased. "An excellent decision. Why relinquish freedom while you're still young enough to enjoy it, eh? Chose the age of forty myself. Now I keep the wife and heir tucked neatly away up north."

Alex smothered a smile. Whit had never voiced such an absurd notion. He seemed to be enjoying the interchange with Loudor, however . . . nodding his head sagely and stroking his chin. "Forty you say? I had considered that myself. A sound age. Young enough to sire an heir but old enough to have sowed one's share of wild oats. I settled for four-and-thirty with the thought that it might take a couple of years to find a suitable wife, but now that you mention it. . . . Hell, this is a damnably odd conversation to be having in a front parlor. What say you we retire to White's?"

By three o'clock the next morning Alex and Whit had deposited a very drunk Lord Loudor back at his town house and were proceeding soberly through the streets of London in a hired hack.

Whit chuckled softly and turned to his friend. "Four-and-thirty? Where on earth did you come up with that?"

"It is the age I once chose for my own foray into matrimony." Alex shrugged. "Seemed reasonable at the time."

"When was that?"

"We were twenty. I was in love with that opera singer."

Whit thought about that for a moment before his eyes lit up. "Marian! I had quite forgotten about her."

"She'd be sorely disappointed to hear it. She was besotted with you, you know."

"Was she really? I hadn't realized. . . . A shame, she was a lovely girl. Whatever became of her?"

"Married a wealthy tradesman some years back, I believe."

"Good for her."

"Hmm." Alex's mind wasn't on the lovely Marian but on the mission, and Whit, and the fact that he'd prefer to have the latter completely removed from the former.

Alex had been eight when his mother succumbed to lung fever. It had been agreed that, with a father so often abroad, it would be best for Alex to spend the majority of his time at the Coles' family estate of Haldon Hall, where the late duchess's dearest friend, Lady Thurston, could properly supervise his rearing.

He and Whit, already fast friends, had become brothers in everything but name, and Lady Thurston had dealt with Alex accordingly, rejoicing in his accomplishments, encouraging him through failures, fussing over his appearance, scolding him for his transgressions. In short, he had been treated as a well-loved son. He would not repay her kindness now by getting Whit further involved in the miserable business of treachery and espionage.

"I want you to stay out of this," he said succinctly.

Whit gave him a rueful smile. "You know I won't. Besides it's a bit late for that, don't you think?"

"No, you've introduced me to Lord Loudor and some of his acquaintances and that's enough. There's no reason for your continued involvement."

"Except, of course, that I want to be involved. In fact, I insist upon it."

"You have other responsibilities." Alex insisted. "You're the head of the family and the Thurston estate requires attention—"

"Do you know much about our earldom?" Whit cut in.

Alex blinked in surprise. "Only that you've done a remarkable job thus far, cleaning up the mess your father left."

"Thank you, but I'm referring to its history. Are you familiar with it at all?"

"No . . . I can't say as I've ever given it much thought, now that you mention it."

"Let me enlighten you. We are a pack of liars, thieves, and wastrels, the lot of us."

Alex thought that unlikely, but held his tongue. The late Lord Thurston certainly fit that description well enough. Whit had spent the four years since his father's death battling to secure the family's finances, as well as the family name.

"Do you recall the summer my mother forced me to stay a fortnight at my uncle's home?" Whit asked.

Alex smiled at the memory. "We were thirteen and you offered your mother every imaginable incentive to let you stay at Haldon Hall. I believe you even made a list."

"I did, and it was cleverly done, for all the good it did me. Fortunately, Uncle Henry was as pleased to have me for company as I was to be there. He let me spend the entire two weeks hidden away in the library. That is where I discovered a most detailed and disturbing account of my family's history—no doubt why the recounting was there and not at Haldon. There is not an honestly gained parcel of land in the whole earldom. Every acre, every village was stolen through one reprehensible manner or another. Deceit, blackmail, extortion, all of it. It's disgusting."

Alex waited a moment to make sure Whit was quite through before asking, "How long ago?"

"Did we steal the land, do you mean?"

Alex nodded.

"Up until about a hundred years ago, then the wastrels took over."

"I see."

"It's important that you do," Whit said somberly. "Because I am determined not to add another chapter to that book. I will leave my family a legacy they can be proud of, something they can carry on. I don't know if it will be akin to your own Rockeforte legacy but . . . I'll not let this opportunity pass."

Alex wanted to argue further. He wanted to point out all the holes in Whit's logic, all the reasons it was an exceedingly bad idea for him to continue working for the War Department, but he knew it would come to nothing. There were few people who could match Whit for sheer mulishness, and like most stubborn individuals, the more one argued with them, the more determined they became to do as they pleased.

"Your mother will kill me if anything happens to you," Alex grumbled.

Whit grinned. "Mother loves you too much to kill you. Kate, on the other hand, would surely slit your throat, loyal little sister that she is."

"God help me."

Whit chuckled softly for a moment before taking on a more serious expression. "To business," he insisted. "What do you make of our new friend?"

Alex decided to let the matter of Whit's involvement drop, for now. "He's an ass," he replied.

"Certainly, but do you think he'll prove an accommodating sort of ass?"

"Loudor gives the appearance of being an overindulgent fop, stupid and conceited enough to brag about his ventures if plied with enough liquor. But if he's been playing the traitor's game, then he's been at it for a while and he hasn't slipped up yet. Either he has more sense than he lets on, or he's innocent."

"I can't say it's easy to reconcile myself to either of those options. Perhaps he's just been lucky."

"Perhaps."

"How are you planning to handle Miss Everton?"

Alex ignored his friend's accentuated use of the word "handle."

"Loudor made it rather clear this evening that he didn't want to be bothered by his cousin's suitors, but I imagine I can find a way around that. I suppose I'll have to pay her some attention. If Loudor proves tight-lipped, she may be of some use to us."

"How noble of you," Whit drawled. "The chit's a beauty, Alex. Quite stunning, really. If you'd rather, I might be agreeable—"

"You'll keep a respectable distance," Alex snapped. "She's my concern."

In the face of Whit's knowing smirk, Alex was forced to admit he'd been concerning himself over Miss Everton a great deal that night. "Bloody hell. Just stick to orders, Whit. Keep your eye on Loudor's friends, Calmaton and Forent. Loudor, too, when you can. And if your mother gets wind of this, it's on your head."

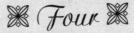

Four

$\mathcal{S}$ophie rose the next morning feeling stiff and sore, but otherwise much her usual self. Once during the night, she had awoken long enough to read the contents of the envelope Mr. Smith had given her. It contained a list of gentlemen she was to "keep her eye trained upon," as well as the name of the solicitor who would serve as her contact and provide her with any needed funds.

After memorizing the names, she had burned the papers in the fireplace and gone back to bed. Personal experience had taught her that rest was the best medicine for a blow to the head. Or so Mrs. Summers was in the habit of insisting. Having taken a considerably stout blow, she would now have to spend the remainder of the day resting. Sophie heaved a disappointed sigh. Resting was dull under normal circumstances—on her first full day back in England, it was going to be positively torturous. She wondered if she could manage to sneak outside. She wouldn't go far, of course, and it'd only be for a bit.

Mentally planning her escape, she pulled the bell cord and went to the window to wait for a response. It had been too dark last night to see much beyond shadows. In the light of day, Sophie saw that her bedroom afforded a view of a small but well-kept garden complete with a gravel walking path, several benches, and a garish, oversized fountain she guessed to be a new addition.

A knock at the door signaled the arrival of a plump girl

with a head of brilliant red hair neatly tucked up in a chignon. With her freckles, bright blue eyes, and an endearing smile, the girl looked as though she belonged on a three-legged stool in front of a cow. Not that Sophie had ever seen a dairymaid before, mind you, she was just certain the girl fit the bill.

"Morning, miss. I hope you're feeling better, if you don't mind my saying so."

"Of course not, ah . . ."

"Penny, miss."

Penny. It suited. "Thank you, Penny, I am much recovered. If it's not too much bother, could I have a bath made ready and some food brought up? I seem to have overslept and missed breakfast."

"No bother at all, but you haven't missed breakfast. It's only eleven, and breakfast is served at quarter to twelve."

"So late?"

"We keep town hours here, miss."

"Oh, right, of course." She had no idea what the girl was talking about, but she smiled anyway, and made a mental note to quiz Mrs. Summers later on the peculiar eating habits of Londoners. Mrs. Summers had spent an inordinate amount of time tutoring Sophie on the ways of the *ton,* but obviously she had overlooked a few things.

"That footman of yours, he left a note for you, miss."

"Footman?"

"That Chinese man, Mr. Wang."

"Oh, he's not a footman, Penny. He's more of a friend . . . family really."

Sophie opened the letter, already knowing its contents. Mr. Wang had left to visit friends in Wales after seeing Mrs. Summers and herself comfortably settled. He would see her again in a few months.

"I really wish I could have said good-bye in person," she sighed.

"Nothing for it, miss. Mr. Wang wouldn't let us wake you, said you needed to rest after your accident."

Sophie snorted to herself. Mr. Wang hadn't been concerned for her health. He wouldn't have left if there were any question of her quick recovery. What he had no doubt wanted was to avoid a scene like the one that occurred the last time he left for an extended holiday. Sophie had cried so hard she had cast up her accounts on his trunk and Mr. Wang had been obliged to postpone his visit until he could calm Sophie down. And repack.

"I was thirteen," Sophie grumbled. "One would think he'd have forgiven me by now."

"Beg your pardon, miss?"

"Nothing, Penny."

Sophie gave herself one more minute to mourn the temporary loss of her friend before dressing and setting out to find Mrs. Summers and breakfast.

She found the former already at the latter. She asked for scones, sat down across from her companion, and poured a cup of tea. "Will Lord Loudor be joining us this morning?"

"No." Mrs. Summers replied. "I believe his lordship had a rather late night and is not feeling quite the thing this morning."

"Oh, I do hope it's nothing serious."

"It is not." Mrs. Summers took a dainty sip from her cup. "As I said, he had a late night . . . at White's, a gentlemen's club, with the Duke of Rockeforte and Lord Thurston."

"I see." Somehow, from their correspondence, Sophie had gotten the impression that her cousin was not the type of man to overindulge in drink, but then there was really only so much you could learn about someone from a letter. Still, it would have been nice if he had taken her arrival into consideration before becoming so foxed he could not greet her properly the next day.

"The Duke of Rockeforte called this morning," Mrs. Summers chimed pleasantly.

Sophie's mental rebuke of her cousin's behavior was immediately forgotten. In its stead a rather heady feeling of excitement washed over her. Silly. She had spoken only a few words to the man and those in only a semiconscious state. She schooled her face into a disinterested expression.

"Did he?"

"Yes, he came to inquire after your health."

Sophie took a hurried drink of tea and blanched when she realized she hadn't yet added milk or sugar. "Good of him," she mumbled.

"He left his card and mentioned he would be at the Calmaton ball this Saturday," Mrs. Summers continued causally. "He looks forward to seeing you there."

Lord Calmaton, Sophie remembered, was on the list Mr. Smith had given her.

She piled sugar into her cup hastily. "And I him. I should like to thank him properly for his assistance yesterday—and Lord Thurston's, of course."

"Of course. You should be flattered, you know. I'm told Rockeforte very rarely goes into society . . . or good society at any rate. He usually spends the season at one of his country estates."

"I don't see what that has to do with me."

Mrs. Summers narrowed her sharp eyes. "Don't be deliberately obtuse, dear. It's obvious he means to attend the ball for a chance to further his acquaintance with you."

Sophie was inordinately pleased that her food arrived just then. Grabbing a scone, she took the very largest bite she could manage without embarrassing herself, or choking. Mrs. Summers set down her teacup and waited quite pointedly for a response. And waited . . . and waited . . .

"Eventually, Sophie, you will have to swallow."

Sophie made a variety of hand gestures that could have conveyed any number of things. But she knew her companion was right. The topic of Rockeforte couldn't be avoided forever, and certainly not just because it made her unaccountably jumpy. And the scone *had* taken on a rather unpleasant consistency.

She swallowed.

Then reached for a sip of tea.

Which was *not* an act of cowardice. She had, after all, taken that bite without first adding some preserves or even a little butter, and if Mrs. Summers thought differently, well—

"Thirsty, dear?"

Sophie realized she had just gulped her entire cup of tea without pausing for breath and was now making unattractive slurping noises. She set her cup down.

"Very," she offered lamely.

"We were speaking of the Duke of Rockeforte."

"Were we?"

"Yes. I had just explained that His Grace might have an interest in you."

Damn. Evasive tactics had never worked well on Mrs. Summers. Sophie tried reasoning with her instead. "I think you read far too much into the duke's behavior," she argued. "He was merely being polite."

"If you say so, dear."

Oh, Sophie did, but thought it best to change the subject all the same. "I'd like to visit a dress shop tomorrow."

Mrs. Summers eyebrows went up. "Do you want a new ball gown, dear?"

"No! I mean yes." She glared at her companion. "I would like to purchase several new dresses, for a number of different occasions."

"You detest fittings."

"I know," Sophie groaned, "but I thought it might be best to get them over and done with. When it comes to pain, the anticipation is often worse than the deed."

Mrs. Summers smiled at that. "Certainly, we shall have to stop by your father's solicitors for the funds."

"As to that . . ."

If Sophie were any other girl, Mrs. Summers never would have believed the story that she had been saving a portion of her pin money for some time and had sent funds in advance to her own private solicitor in London. But after two decades in Sophie's company, very little would surprise the worldly Mrs. Summers. If Sophie had told her she had found the money under a rock in the garden, Mrs. Summers wouldn't have batted an eye.

The next three days were spent in a whirl of fittings, shopping, and desperately trying to pin down the elusive Lord Loudor. The blasted man was never at home when he should be. The few times Sophie managed to catch him coming in or out of the house, he parried her requests for a few moments of his time with vague references to meetings, business, and appointments. When she demanded outright to know when she might see her father's ledgers, he mumbled something about a misunderstanding with the solicitor and hurried away.

He was avoiding her—there was nothing else for it—but he couldn't keep it up forever. He was, after all, required to escort her to the ball Saturday night. That event required a carriage ride, which would guarantee his undivided attention for a minimum of twenty minutes.

On Saturday afternoon, one of Sophie's new ball gowns arrived, and she spent the two hours preceding the grand event under the less-than-gentle ministrations of Penny and Mrs. Summers. She was cinched, pulled, wrapped, curled, primped, and primed. Only at the end of that ordeal was she finally given leave to view the finished product in the bedroom's cheval mirror.

Sophie gulped. The gown was gorgeous to be sure, layer upon layer of pale blue silk so lightweight it appeared almost translucent. The cut was simple and elegant without frills or adornments. It was cut with a high waist as fashion demanded, but the design was such that it avoided the appearance of having one's breasts upon a shelf. It flowed as naturally and gracefully as if it were an extension of Sophie herself. She tugged awkwardly at the front of the dress.

"I really can't understand how I can be positively blanketed in cloth and still feel naked."

"It's the dress, miss." Penny giggled. "That silk is light as butterfly wings, and all ball gowns are cut lower in front like that."

Mrs. Summers slapped Sophie's hands away impatiently. "Stop that, you look lovely. I wouldn't let you out of the house if your attire was anything but perfectly modest."

Sophie sighed in resignation. She knew Mrs. Summers was right. Still . . .

"I said stop that! You will *not* be pulling at your gown tonight. It is most indecent."

"Couldn't we just—"

"No."

"What if I—"

"No."

"May I at least—"

"*No!*"

"I was only going to ask for my cloak."

"Oh. Well, I believe it's in the front hall, along with your gloves, your fan, and undoubtedly your cousin who is very likely annoyed at your tardiness, so move along."

"I do wish you were attending tonight," Sophie said wistfully.

"As do I, but if I don't take care of this head cold now, I shall become too sick to be of any use to you for the remainder of our trip."

"I know. I'd just feel better knowing you were there."

Mrs. Summers bent down and kissed Sophie's cheek. "That's very sweet of you, dear, but you needn't worry. Your cousin and Lady Margaret are perfectly acceptable chaperones."

Sophie nodded but in truth, she had certain misgivings about her cousin's chaperoning skills. He had managed to leave her waiting at the docks, after all. As for Lady Margaret, she was an old friend of Mrs. Summers who had agreed by note to attend to Sophie in Mrs. Summers's absence. Sophie had never met her, nor even heard of her until this afternoon.

"You're woolgathering, Sophie. Run along and fetch your things."

The cloak was indeed in the front hall, but Lord Loudor was not. In his stead was a note explaining that he was unable to ride with her to the ball, but he would meet her carriage on the drive of Lord Calmaton's home.

Damn.

She couldn't very well bring up the ledgers at the ball.

Sophie headed for the door with a decidedly grim expression.

Blast.

She couldn't very well travel to the ball alone, either. Resigned, she sent the footman for Penny with a request that the maid be quick, and if at all possible, quiet. No point in giving Mrs. Summers a chance to insist on taking a carriage ride on a damp night.

Penny managed to accomplish both speed and stealth, and the girls were comfortably ensconced in the carriage in less than ten minutes.

"Sorry to have inconvenienced you, Penny," Sophie said, pulling on her bodice.

"You really shouldn't fuss with that, miss, and I'm happy to be here. Not every day I get to take a night ride in such a fancy carriage as this."

Sophie believed her, the bit about the happiness at least. Penny's face was positively glowing with excitement. She held her head almost completely out the window and was watching the passing scenery with obvious delight. Sophie supposed there were few occurrences that would allow for a servant, even a lady's maid, to view London after nightfall from the security of a nobleman's carriage. "It's like a whole other world," Penny whispered reverently. "Brighter than I would have guessed."

Sophie glanced out the window. "It is, isn't it?"

Thank God.

Sophie was very much of the opinion that there was little more inherently frightening than the unknown, and nothing altered the familiar into the unfamiliar quite so effectively as a pitch-black night. In shorter and less flattering terms, Sophie was afraid of the dark.

Very little was needed to keep that fear at bay—a single candle left burning, the light of a bright moon, or, as in this case, the well-kept streetlamps found in the neighborhoods inhabited by people of means. Any and all would suffice in making Sophie, if not comfortable, at least functional. Without them . . . she would be lost.

❋ *Five* ❋

"Miss Everton, I am pleased to see you so well recovered."

Recovered, Alex thought, didn't nearly do her justice. Miss Everton looked nothing short of delectable in her frothy pale blue gown, her thick sable hair pulled up into an intricate mass of curls that had him itching to slowly pull out the pins so he could watch each glossy lock unwind. His blood had heated the moment he caught sight of her standing off to the side of the ballroom with Mirabelle Browning. Apparently, Loudor had escorted his cousin inside and promptly abandoned her to attend to his cards, the cad.

Alex had intended to approach both women, but the sound of Mirabelle's delighted laughter had given him a better idea. Skirting along the edge of the room, he had stepped unseen into a small alcove and shamelessly eavesdropped on their conversation. Within minutes Alex had realized that his original, and begrudging, resolution to charm Miss Everton in the usual manner of pretty flowers and flowery words would have been useless. She would have been bored to tears.

He had only partially overheard the tale she related to

Mirabelle, but Alex was fairly certain it involved wine, a suitor, and an angry herd of elephants.

Miss Everton, it seemed, liked danger.

He had waited for Mirabelle to leave before approaching Miss Everton with something akin to actual anticipation.

Dangerous was something he could do.

"Your Grace, thank you. I've quite mended, as you can see."

Sophie was surprised and relieved when she managed to squeak out an entire sentence. The man had literally appeared out of nowhere. One moment she'd been watching her new acquaintance, Miss Browning, be escorted onto the dance floor and the next thing she knew, the duke was standing at her side looking remarkably like an oversized panther.

His dress black was a bit more severe than some of the other gentlemen present, but it suited him. It suited him *very* well. The color contrasted sharply with his eyes, which, she noticed quickly, were definitely green and brought out the faintest hint of auburn in his hair. The fabric fit perfectly across his broad shoulders, around his lean waist, and the breeches outlined his muscled thighs . . . almost indecently so, and . . .

Good Lord, had she just looked at his thighs?

Had he seen her look at his thighs?

Sophie felt her stomach do an agonizingly slow descent to her toes while all the blood in her body crept steadily toward her cheeks. How mortifying. To hide her embarrassment, she curtsied. To save her pride, she forced herself to meet his gaze when she straightened.

"I am very pleased to see you again, of course," she managed with a credibly even voice. "I've been anxious to thank you properly for your assistance earlier this week, and Lord Thurston's as well. I fear I made a mess of it the first time."

"It was a pleasure," Alex replied. Good Lord, she'd just looked him over. Miss Everton had just given him a visual appraisal with all the brashness of an *houri,* and all the finesse of a schoolroom chit. Fascinating.

"You're very kind, I'm sure," she mumbled.

Alex leaned against a nearby pillar and crossed his legs casually at the ankles. "Bored already, Miss Everton?" he asked, looking pointedly at her waist where her fingers were busily working at the folds of her skirt.

She looked down and winced before quickly fisting her hands behind her back. "Sorry, it's a bad habit, I'm afraid. I didn't—"

"Please, don't trouble yourself," he insisted. "And call me Alex."

Sophie's eyebrows shot up in surprise. "I couldn't. I can't. We've only just met."

"Nonsense, we've known each other for almost a week."

Her stance relaxed notably at his teasing tone. "We've known *of* each other for a total of four days," she said dryly. "That hardly qualifies as a long-term affiliation."

Alex shrugged. "People have wed with less."

"I don't doubt the truth of that, just the advisability."

"I don't know," Alex replied thoughtfully. "I rather like knowing I could haul you off to the altar should I so desire. There's a certain power in having had you in a compromising position."

She gaped at him for a moment before finding her voice. "There was nothing compromising about it!"

"You were in my arms," he replied with a wicked grin.

"I was injured!" she hissed. "Rather seriously!"

He grinned broader and leaned closer. "You were also in my lap."

"What? I . . . you . . . this conversation is absurd. I was *unconscious.*"

He was having far too much fun. Miss Everton was quite a sight when wound up, with flashing eyes and quickened breath that caused her bust to move up and down in a slightly indecent, and therefore *very* alluring manner. But it wouldn't do to push things too far too quickly. Straightening, he gave her a playful wink.

"You are altogether too charming when in a temper, Miss Everton. I shall have to remember that."

"So you can bait me?" she asked incredulously.

"So I'll know what to expect when I do."

She arched an eyebrow at him. "Have me figured out then?"

"I'm not so presumptuous as to assume I have grasped the whole of your character from a single conversation," he returned, stubbornly ignoring the fact that he had done just that several days ago in William's office—only without the benefit of actually conversing with her first. "Merely one small facet of which I am sure there are many. For example, I have no idea how well you dance. Would you do me the honor of enlightening me?"

It occurred to Sophie that she should probably decline. He was clearly a rake. When she took his proffered arm anyway, she *knew* she should have said no. She could feel the heat of his arm through his coat, it seeped up through her fingers, spread across her chest, and did the strangest thing to her legs—they suddenly felt heavy.

Fortunately, the dance was a country reel; it afforded little chance of conversing and even less for touching. Nonetheless, she was breathless and a little light-headed when he led her off the floor toward the lemonade table, and she knew it wasn't from physical exertion. She accepted a glass from him gratefully and drank nearly half of it in just a few swallows. Alex took a glass for himself and led her away from the crowd around the table.

"You are a well-traveled woman of the world, Sophie, and unless I'm much mistaken, this is your first London ball." He waved his glass in a sweeping motion. "What do you make of all this?"

Ever conscious of how sensitive people could be to a guest's opinion, Sophie instinctively paused before answering. "It's very different from what I am used to," she finally replied. "And not quite what I had expected."

The remark earned a smile from Alex. "That was a decidedly neutral statement."

"I suppose it was," she conceded. "It's too bad women aren't allowed to be diplomats."

"It's a pity women are denied a great many opportunities," he stated in all honesty. Then, not even remotely in earnest, added, "But you're right, I think, they would make excellent ambassadors. Most of them are exceedingly crafty by nature, forever arguing, sniping, meaning one thing and saying another, saying one thing and doing another, distracting their enemies with a pretty smile while they slip their dagger in the back."

She narrowed her eyes. "You have a very low opinion of women, Your Grace."

"I believed we agreed on 'Alex,' and I do hope I haven't offended you."

"Well, then your hopes are foolishly misplaced, aren't they? You just insulted me."

"I most certainly did not. If you will recall, I said 'most' women, not 'all.' Naturally, you were not included in my description of feminine artifices." God, but she was fun to tease.

"Oh . . . well, I believe I retain the right to be offended on behalf of the women who are not here to defend themselves."

Alex rocked back on his heels and looked down at her with exaggerated interest. "Let me see if I understand you correctly. Are you proclaiming yourself a representative of females the world over?"

"Don't be silly. There is too much difference between cultures." She took a delicate sip from her glass. "Just the British ones."

"Ah, excellent. You won't mind shedding some light on a few mysteries surrounding the fairer sex then, will you, Miss Ambassador?"

"I shall endeavor to answer your questions regarding *British* women, Your Grace," she said pertly, then, after another sip added, "of a certain age."

"Alex."

"Oh, very well, Alex, but only while no one else is listening."

Alex grinned at her stipulation. "Fair enough. I can scarce believe I have been handed this opportunity. Do you know that there are men who would commit murder to be in my shoes at this moment?"

"Ask your question, if you please," Sophie replied, rolling her eyes, but smiling nonetheless.

"Very well. My first question is this: Whatever do ladies, British ladies, discuss when they retire to the drawing room after dinner?"

Sophie had absolutely no idea. For the life of her, she couldn't recall ever having taken part in that particular ritual. Representative of British women? What on earth had she been thinking? In the last twelve years, she had known exactly four British women—three officers' wives and Mrs. Summers. Sophie had to be the least qualified ambassador in . . . in the history of ambassadors. Not that she was willing to admit to it, of course.

"Oh, well . . . this and that," she began, badly. "We talk of the weather . . . and our families, of course, and er . . . major events like births, deaths, and weddings." That sounded mind-numbingly dull. "And politics, naturally, and . . . literature." It was the best she could do.

"Ah, I know a great many gentlemen who shall be relieved to hear it. Most are convinced the ladies spend the time verbally dissecting every male at the party."

As his guess was likely closer to the truth than her own, "Hmm," was really the most eloquent response she could come up with.

"Next question, do you see that young woman over there in the pink gown?"

Sophie narrowed her eyes in search. "There are a great many pink gowns in this room tonight. You'll need to be more specific."

"The blonde standing next to the lemonade table with the pearl necklace and—"

"Ah, yes, what of her?"

"She is the younger sister of an old school chum, and I happen to know that she is a girl of uncommon good sense and generally a splendid conversationalist. Yet when I stopped by their town house today, she spent no less than three-quarters of an hour discussing the very gown she is wearing tonight. No other topic could interest her but the event at which we are now present. And she is even now making the most syrupy smile I have seen outside of a lunatic asylum. So, my question is this: how is it that an otherwise perfectly sensible young woman can be transformed into a deranged simpleton by the mere mention of a ball?"

Sophie thought about that for a moment. "I think, Your Grace . . . er, Alex, that you might take the time to look about the room and take note of the cut of the gowns the young women are wearing."

Alex grinned mischievously at her. "I have been looking, Sophie. I have most definitely been looking."

"Then you must have noticed that ball gowns are cut considerably lower and slimmer than day gowns. The answer to your question is . . . inadequate air supply."

Alex laughed outright. "I believe there is something to that theory, but I'll admit I only noticed the lower and quite neglected the slimmer."

"I'm sure you did. Have you any other questions?"

"Just one. Will you attend the opera with me this Saturday?"

"I . . . that's a personal question."

"So it is," Alex remarked, "but it stands."

She floundered for a moment, looking about the room as if help might be on the way. "Well, I . . . well, I suppose I might be agreeable, if . . . if you'll answer a question for me."

"Ask away," he invited, intrigued.

She cleared her throat nervously. "The thing is . . . well

earlier, you said I . . ." She cleared her throat again. "Before, when we were . . . you mentioned . . ."

"Out with it."

"Was I *really* in your lap?"

Alex was still laughing when he collected his coat to leave. He was to meet Whit at White's in a half hour. All things considered, it was turning out to be a much more enjoyable evening than he had anticipated.

"Rockeforte!"

Alex felt his muscles tense unpleasantly at the sound of Loudor's voice, but he hid his displeasure with a nod. "Loudor."

"Didn't expect to see you here. I wasn't aware you were friends with the viscount."

Alex began putting his arms through his coat. "I am not, but I've been hearing intriguing things about the man recently. I thought perhaps an association might be overdue."

"Indeed! And what is your opinion now that you've had a chance to better your acquaintance?"

Alex would have bet that the viscount had broken all Ten Commandments at least once, and probably indulged in the seven deadly sins on a regular basis.

"I can understand why you count him as your friend."

"Excellent, excellent," Loudor declared, as if bestowing congratulations. "And you're quite right, of course. He is a man of rare abilities."

"Hmm," was the best Alex could offer.

"Speaking of rarities, what do you make of my fair cousin?"

Alex followed Loudor's gaze to rest on Sophie, standing at the far end of the room, and once more laughing with Mirabelle.

"She is a charming girl." That, at least, was not a lie.

"She is, and not at all unpleasant to look at. Shame we're so closely related, she's the most refreshing views on marriage."

"Is that so?" Alex heard the edge to his voice, but apparently Loudor did not because the man was still babbling like an idiot.

"Quite refreshing. Suppose it's an effect of all those years in exotic countries, but she's quite managed to escape becoming a prim and proper British miss. None of this silly marriage business for her, you know. Told me so herself. She wants only to *enjoy* herself while in London."

Good Lord, the man was encouraging him to have a dalliance with his cousin. Alex wasn't deluded enough to deny he'd like nothing better, but anyone could see Sophie Everton was an innocent. Certainly, she was considerably more plainspoken than most gently bred women of his acquaintance and perhaps a little more liberal in her politics, but *clearly* she wasn't in the habit of "enjoying herself." Any reasonably intelligent man who spent more than a few minutes in her company would know she was untouched, and Alex made a point to never dally with virgins. There were rules about that sort of thing.

Was Loudor going about telling every male in the room that Sophie was interested in a liaison? Alex felt an uncomfortable combination of jealousy, anger, and revulsion. There was nothing he would have liked better, in that moment, than to drag Loudor to an empty room and pummel him until he spilled the name of every rake, bounder, and libertine he had spoken with. Then pummel him again just on principle. Sadly, there were rules about that sort of thing too.

Alex took a moment to leash his anger before turning his best rakish grin on Loudor. "Freshness is all well and good, but what I require in a woman is fidelity. I don't share."

"Ah, I am in full agreement. Believe we understand each other, Rockeforte."

Alex pictured his hands around Loudor's neck. He smiled at the image, and nodded.

Loudor finished off his drink and looked back at Sophie. "I'm having a little dinner party tomorrow night. Sophie has a bizarre notion that her companion should dine with the family. Need another man to even out the numbers." Without taking his eyes from Sophie, Loudor produced the most sickening smirk Alex was sure he had ever seen. "Up to the task?"

Another throttling. Another smile. "I look forward to it."

The second-to-last dance was a waltz. Fortunately, Sophie had yet to receive permission to waltz from the matrons of Almacks and was thus afforded the perfect excuse to decline the young gentlemen vying for her regard.

There seemed to be a great many of them, she realized with a mixture of pride and unease. They had appeared almost the moment Alex left her side. Apparently, the Duke of Rockeforte's attention had immediately marked her as a person of consequence.

It had all been very exciting, of course, but it was time to get to work. She had the space of two dances to get into and out of Lord Calmaton's study.

Sophie excused herself to visit the ladies' retiring room. She'd gone twice earlier in the evening, peeking into rooms and poking behind paintings in the hope she might find a hidden safe, and cautiously testing the doors along the hallway. The fourth room on the right had been locked, and Sophie hoped that meant she'd found the study.

Pausing in a darkened recess, she pulled up her skirts and retrieved a long pick from the strap around her ankle. She would have to be quick. The room was located far enough down the hall for there to be little traffic, but she had no intention of drawing attention to herself by loitering.

It took her nearly a minute to open the door. She was usually much faster, but her hands were shaking badly, and the blood pounding in her ears made it difficult to hear the clicks and taps of the inner workings of the lock.

Finally she succeeded and was thrilled to find that she had chosen the correct room. Her eyes scanned the interior. It was too dark. She crossed over to the windows and pulled back the drapes, relieved to find the moon shining brightly on her face. She quickly opened the curtains on the remaining windows. It was still too dark for her taste, but there was enough light to keep her fear in check and for her to see what she was about.

She started with the desk. The top was littered with papers; she couldn't possibly read them all. She fumbled through the stacks, hoping something would catch her eye. She had an absurd vision of finding some triple-sealed envelope with the word SECRET written across the front, possibly in blood.

When her search turned up nothing more nefarious than a delivery notice for some expensive jewelry to a woman who was not the viscountess, Sophie moved behind the desk and began opening the drawers. The first three held supplies, a ledger, and more paperwork detailing the running of the estate. The fourth was locked. Swearing under her breath, Sophie pulled her pick back out and went to work. This was taking too much time. The waltz was already finished and the last song well under way.

With a whispered plea to her Maker she pried the drawer open and almost groaned at the sight of more letters, but caught herself before the sound reached her throat. The letters were in French, every last one of them. She rifled through the pile anxiously. They could be anything! For the first time, Sophie was sorry she had chosen to learn Mandarin and Hindi over the much more popular French. She grabbed one of the letters and looked over the meaningless words. What if they were from a relative, or a lover? Her eyes reached the bottom of the page and she blinked in surprise. It wasn't signed. She looked back at the others still in the drawer. None of them were signed. Surely a loved one would sign the letters.

She pocketed the paper and then, digging through the remainder, found an envelope and took that too. She hoped they were worth something. At any rate, the music was winding down and in a few minutes people would begin streaming out of the ballroom. She was out of time.

She relocked the drawer and pulled the drapes shut once again, then paused at the door to listen for footsteps in the hall. Finding everything silent, she crept out of the study, locked the door behind her, and headed straight for the ladies' retiring room.

❋ *Six* ❋

*T*he next day promised, if nothing else, to be an exceedingly busy time for Sophie. She rose early out of habit, doing her best to ignore the fact that she had gone to bed a mere four hours earlier. She washed and dressed quickly and had just enough time for breakfast before a fabricated sightseeing trip to drop off the papers she had stolen from the viscount's study. Then on to a final fitting with the *modiste,* tea with Mirabelle Browning and her friend Lady Kate Cole, and then home to prepare for Loudor's dinner party.

Her business with the solicitor was more quickly accomplished than Sophie had anticipated. She had rather expected to be interrogated for any additional information, or perhaps given some insight as to the content of the letter she delivered. But the solicitor, a stocky middle-aged man with a large, round nose, had simply taken the plain brown parcel in which she had wrapped her stolen goods, and made some comment on the inadvisability of a young gentlewoman visiting business offices without a proper escort.

Sophie was hard-pressed not to laugh outright at that absurdity. She was being paid to spy, steal, and commit any number of behaviors that were inadvisable for a person of any gender or social standing. She opened her mouth to relate this, then thought better of it. His expression was one of earnest concern. Apparently, he had no idea who she was, what she was doing, or what was in the parcel. She offered him a sweet smile and the assurance that she would take all necessary precautions on her way home.

The solicitor remained standing until Sophie left. Then with a chuckle, he resumed both his seat and the glass of brandy he had stashed in his bottom desk drawer upon her arrival.

He wiped the sides of the glass and licked his fingers with a little smack. Ahhh. Thank God for honest free traders, the ones who didn't try their hands at weapons smuggling. Setting the glass aside, he picked up the brown parcel Sophie had left and eyed it with something akin to surprised suspicion.

"Well, well, well, Calmaton. Just what have we been up to?"

He read her note first, which made him smile. Then he took a close look at the contents, and laughed like a madman.

Sophie felt uncomfortable for all of five minutes. That was, give or take thirty seconds, all the time it took for Lady Kate and Mirabelle Browning to sit her down and ply her with copious amounts of tea, biscuits, and questions about her travels.

"Did Whit and Alex really rescue you on your first day in London?" Kate asked eagerly, leaning forward in her chair.

"They certainly were of assistance," Sophie replied.

Kate was an exceptionally beautiful girl with pale blonde hair, light blue eyes, alabaster skin, and perfect, absolutely perfect, facial features. Truly, Sophie didn't think she had ever met someone whose face and form so well matched the current standard of beauty. It would be unnerving if the girl were not so genuinely pleasant.

Kate sighed wistfully and her face took on a dreamy expression. "That's so romantic." Then she frowned. "Or it would be, if it weren't Whit and Alex. Do you have any brothers, Sophie?"

"No, I'm afraid I've never had that pleasure," she replied.

"The pleasure of it is debatable. They're unbearably meddlesome creatures, but in this case, at least, their intervention was fortunate."

"How odd, though," Mirabelle commented, "that your driver chose such an unusual route, and then disappeared."

At first glance Mirabelle was a mousy little thing, lacking the shining beauty of her friend. Her brown hair was pulled back tightly and secured in an unflattering knot at the back of her head. Her dress, made of a rather shabby gray material, did little for her complexion or figure. Her features were pleasant, adequate, and in all other ways unexceptional. Until she smiled. Mirabelle's smile reached all the way up to light her chocolate eyes, which suddenly seemed quite large and brilliant.

"He must have thought to cut some time off the trip and then panicked when his scheme turned sour," Kate offered quietly. She appeared lost in thought as she spoke, which probably explained why she missed setting her teacup on the table by at least twelve inches.

"Oh dear." Kate picked up the fallen cup and looked ruefully at the wet stain on the carpet. "I do so hope that will come out."

Mirabelle patted her shoulder kindly and poured Kate another cup of tea.

Sophie couldn't help be surprised at the girl's calm reaction to what many would consider a major social misstep.

"You're quite all right, aren't you?" Sophie asked. "You're not burned?"

Kate shook her head. "Oh no, the carpet took the worst of it. I suppose I should have warned you earlier, but I'm dreadfully clumsy. It's become something of a family joke, only it's not particularly funny."

"I'm sure it's not as bad as all that."

Kate quirked a little smile. "I'm positively ungainly. There's no accounting for it and nothing to be done. I've caused some perfectly awful mishaps."

Sophie laughed softly. "I know a little something about mishaps," she told the girls. And then with a little cajoling— a *very* little—Sophie spent the remainder of the afternoon entertaining her new friends with tales from some of her more outrageous adventures.

Sophie had never felt so uncomfortable in all her life.

Last night, her gown had drawn the appraising stares of men and the covetous glances of women, but none of her other new dresses were yet completed, and Sophie felt hopelessly provincial standing next to several elegant women in one of her more rustic pieces from home.

Perhaps she was being oversensitive. Probably, she was the only one paying attention to what she was wearing. No, she knew that wasn't true. Alex had been staring at her quite openly all evening. She felt his eyes on her even when her back was turned. It made the hair stand up on the back of her neck and all the color rise to her cheeks.

Good Lord, a bad dress and a red face. Now all she needed was to say something in truly poor taste to make the evening complete.

"I say, Miss Everton, your dress this evening is quite unlike any I've seen here in town. Wherever did you have it made?" Lady Wellinghoff punctuated the question with a thin smile.

"China," Sophie replied. There was no point in lying, and she didn't really feel like being polite to Lady Wellinghoff. The woman had insulted Mrs. Summers within minutes of arrival, commenting under her breath about the evils of overly familiar employees.

"Do you mean it? Oh, but how silly of me, of course you do. You've only just come to London, haven't you? I'd forgotten. Well, the silk is lovely, dear. Tell us, how does our fair city compare to some of the more exotic locales of your experience?"

Sophie swallowed nervously. She had never been a shrinking violet, but then she had rarely been subjected to such unnerving stares. The least unpleasant of the guests were the rather serious Colonel and Mrs. Peabody. Mr. and Mrs. Jarles were officious snobs. The Earl and Countess of Wellinghoff clearly also considered themselves superior to those of the assembly, but their disdain was of a more subtle, though no less cutting, variety. Viscount Barrows was already too drunk to be insulting; his viscountess too dim-witted to know how. Alex's presence set her nerves on edge, and her cousin, she had recently decided, was simply an ass.

She gave the group what she hoped was a patronizing smile and said, "You must understand that cultures vary so greatly from one continent to the next, and even from country to country and city to city, that I cannot possibly compare one civilization with another in any qualitative sense, but I will say that London has been all that I expected." She topped off her speech with a shrug that hinted at indifference.

"But surely after having spent some time in England, you cannot continue to regard your previous residences as truly civilized," Lady Barrows whispered dramatically, as if Sophie had uttered the most shocking statement heard this last century.

Her husband just hiccupped.

"Oh, but they are," Sophie insisted. "They—"

"But they're heathens!" Mrs. Jarles cut in.

"True, but—"

"Some of their practices are most barbaric," Lady Wellinghoff told the group with relish. "I have heard that in China, young women have their feet bound to keep them from growing and it makes it quite impossible for them to move more than the tiniest step at a time."

Sophie nodded. "I agree, it's a distasteful practice, but we British are slaves to our own fashions. I dare say none of us look overly comfortable tonight in our respective bindings and tight cravats."

Sophie's statement was met with muted gasps from the women, while several of the gentlemen cleared their throats uncomfortably. Apparently, the mention of women's undergarments was not an acceptable topic of conversation at a formal dinner party. Belatedly, Sophie entertained the thought that perhaps that was why they were referred to as "unmentionables."

Only Alex and Mrs. Summers appeared not to be shocked. He was grinning at her with unabashed amusement while she looked disgruntled but resigned.

Sophie was spared having to break the awkward silence by Mrs. Summers' tactful change of subject. "I understand, Mrs. Peabody, you have done some extensive traveling yourself."

"A lifetime of following the drum," Mrs. Peabody replied to the group in general. "I've had the opportunity to see much more of this world than most young ladies."

"Have you been to the Americas?" Sophie inquired, with genuine interest.

"I have," Mrs. Peabody replied. "I lived for several years in both Boston and Philadelphia as a small child. We left some five years before that unfortunate revolution."

"*Hmph,* and good riddance to that godless country, I say," Mr. Jarles snorted.

Lord Barrows hiccupped and raised his glass in salute.

Sophie fought the urge to roll her eyes.

Mrs. Peabody calmly raised one eyebrow. "I presume by the strength of your opinion, Mr. Jarles, that you've traveled to that country yourself?"

Sophie was surprised to hear the hint of mockery in Mrs. Peabody's voice. She had expected Mrs. Peabody to be of the same mind as the nasty Mr. Jarles.

"One doesn't need to visit to know it's populated with traitors and savages," Mr. Jarles said.

"History is written by the victors," Mrs. Peabody replied. "And according to history there are no traitors in America, only brave patriots willing to fight for what they believed in, or at the very worse, rebels who opposed a tyrannical monarch."

"That's treason, Mrs. Peabody."

She appeared unmoved. "One can only commit treason against one's own country," she retorted calmly.

The colonel leveled his best commanding-officer stare at Mr. Jarles. "I do hope you were referring to the Americans when you spoke of treason, sir, and not my wife."

"Of course, of course," Mr. Jarles sputtered. "The thought never occurred."

To accuse Mrs. Peabody of treason—a woman married to a celebrated colonel and who had spent her whole life serving her country in a capacity as close to soldiering as a woman was allowed—would not only be idiotic, but suicidal. Mr. Jarles was certainly the former, but not—and Sophie couldn't help but think it was something of a pity—the latter.

The colonel nodded once in a supremely military sort of way that had Sophie smiling. It was something of a wonder to see the unmistakable glow of respect in Mr. Peabody's eyes when he turned to look at his wife. He wasn't just tolerant of her opinion, he was proud of it. A rare man indeed. And by the look she favored him with in return, a rare match.

For some reason Sophie glanced at Alex to see his reaction, only to discover he was already watching her, his emerald eyes unreadable. Sophie wasn't certain if he had been paying attention to the Peabodys at all.

His intense gaze made her feel tingly all over, her lungs tight, her heart racing. In an effort to distract herself, she quickly turned back to Mrs. Peabody.

"Did you have a chance to meet any natives, ma'am?" she inquired, not at all certain she had spoken in a voice loud enough to be heard. It was terribly difficult to determine what might be an appropriate volume with her blood rushing in her ears.

Mrs. Peabody didn't seem to notice her distress, and Sophie dearly hoped she wasn't alone in that. "I did, my dear. But only a few, and there are a great many Indian tribes. And they are as diverse as any nations could be. Some of their customs I find appalling, others fascinating. Did you know, for instance, that in some tribes, a woman can be trained as a warrior along with the men?"

"Female warriors." Mr. Jarles snorted with disgust. "Savages, just as I said. Lacking even the sense to keep their women at home as nature intended."

"How is it that you are so sure that is what nature intended, Mr. Jarles, and not man?" Sophie asked.

"Don't be daft, girl. I'll not insult the ladies by speaking of indelicate topics, but suffice it to say, females are referred to as the weaker sex for a reason."

"Quite right, husband," Mrs. Jarles chirped.

Sophie ignored her and spoke directly to Mr. Jarles. "It is my understanding that every soldier has his own strengths and weaknesses. True, my arms are not as muscular as a man's, but I'll wager my fingers are a good deal more nimble."

Mr. Jarles snorted for what seemed like the dozenth time, and Sophie began to wonder if the man was capable of making conversation without the porcine sound effects. "Exactly my point," he scoffed. "Nimble fingers indeed! What good is that, I ask you? A fine hem won't keep Napoleon from knocking at our gates, now will it? Civilization depends on the strength of our men. War cannot be waged with nimble fingers, my girl. We need soldiers strong of body, and leaders strong of mind."

"Here, here!" some idiot cried. She was too annoyed to bother discovering who.

"I question the strength of anyone's mind who would insist that war is a more civilized pursuit than embroidery," she returned.

Mr. Jarles turned an unfortunate shade of red, but whether it was from embarrassment or temper, she would never know.

"Dinner is served."

Alex, pointedly ignoring the still fuming Mr. Jarles, stepped forward to take Sophie's arm. There would be a wait. Like all dinner parties, the procession into the dining room held all the pomp and circumstance of a military parade, and the ritual appeared to be a new one for Sophie. He could see she was trying to hide a smile. And failing miserably. She faced studiously ahead, but her eyes darted furtively about the room and her lips kept quirking in the most adorable fashion. Or perhaps adorable wasn't the right word.

He had watched the unfolding scene with more interest than he had felt at a dinner party since . . . well, since ever, that he could recall. Oh, once or twice he'd been angry enough at Mr. Jarles to seriously consider planting the man a facer, but he suspected the chivalry of the act would be lost on Sophie. What's more, it had become readily apparent that she didn't require defending. Sophie Everton, he realized, was an extraordinary lady indeed. She didn't know it, but two of the gentlemen present were considered eloquent speakers, often in demand for dinner parties and soirees. Rarely, if ever, were they gainsaid, and never by a young unmarried woman.

And yet here she was, trading barbs with men and women of means and rank. And winning. For some inexplicable reason, he felt like crowing at her victory. As if he were somehow responsible for her cleverness. For her. It was a ridiculous notion to be sure. He was there to discover Loudor's secrets, and she was nothing more than a means to that end. He would do well to remember that.

And God knew he was trying, but it was so easy to become lost in her every expression. The lilt of her voice, the curve of her neck, the way she wrinkled her nose when she was annoyed.

And then there were her lips.

Never had he seen a woman so adept at expressing her emotions with her lips. She twisted them, pursed them, parted them, licked them. And Alex found each contortion more erotic than the last. He caught himself wondering what it would be like to press his own mouth over hers and feel those delightful movements with his lips, his tongue—

"Is something wrong?" she inquired softly.

"Hmm? Wrong?" he responded, only half hearing her.

"Yes, wrong. You're looking at me most peculiarly."

"Sorry, was I?"

"Yes, you *are*."

"How peculiar."

"So I believe I said. Peculiar. Are you unwell?"

He snapped back with alarming speed. *Unwell?* Good Lord, is that what he looked like when consumed with desire? Unwell?

"I'm quite all right," he stated with a little more conviction than was probably necessary. "Merely lost in thought."

"Oh, what about?"

"About? Well, I . . . er . . ."

Think, man, think.

I'd very much like to nibble on the corner of your mouth.

"The gardens are rather splendid for this time of year."

Oh, brilliant.

Sophie glanced around as if confirming something. "We're indoors."

"So we are."

"At my town house."

"Also true."

"And you were looking at me."

"So I was, but you are right in front of me, and the gardens are not. As I said, I was lost in thought."

"I see," she said slowly, clearly *not* seeing, because she was looking at him as if she still expected he might be feverish.

Alex was vastly relieved to finally make it through the French doors and into the dining room. He was even happier to discover that Sophie had been seated next to him rather than across the table. Given half the opportunity—and he rather thought facing her for the next two or three hours would certainly be that—he'd gaze at her like some pathetic love-struck loon all evening. As it was, he was bound to have a sore neck tomorrow from turning his head to the side so often. If nothing else, the seating required that he look away if he wanted to eat without dribbling food on himself—which he most certainly did. And in the end, he managed not to disgrace himself.

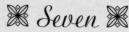

❈ Seven ❈

*A*lex had intended to spend the time in his opera box wooing the lovely Sophie. In fact, he had spent the two days since the dinner party carefully calculating his plan of attack. It was, after all, his mission to find a way into her good favor. He would whisper, wink, manage a few light but well-placed touches, and otherwise be on his best rogue's behavior. The combination of music, excitement, and his attentions had never failed to secure his conquests.

Five minutes into the first act, Alex realized he would have to change tactics.

Sophie appeared completely enraptured by the performance. She was ignoring him entirely, her eyes never leaving the proceedings on stage.

Alex was at a complete loss as how to proceed. No one came to the opera to actually *watch* the opera. They came to see and be seen, to gossip, to flirt. That's what he had the damn box for! He didn't even like the opera.

He groaned inwardly and tried to get more comfortable in his seat. At least his view of the stage required that he look past Sophie's profile. He could stare to his heart's content and no one, including her esteemed chaperone Mrs. Summers, would be the wiser. And she *was* nice to stare at. His eyes slid from the thick mass of sable hair he knew to feel like silk from the briefest of touches after the carriage accident, down to her ear, which was perfectly adorable, small, and slightly pointed at the tip. His gaze continued down to her elegant neck and then her bared shoulder. Alex wondered if her skin would taste as creamy as it looked. He followed the curve of her collarbone as it slid around to the front where he could make out the most tantalizing hint of cleavage.

He shifted in his seat again, stared at her hair for awhile, then gave up and spent the rest of the evening trying very, very hard to develop an interest in the performing arts.

Sophie, on the other hand, had planned to spend the time in Alex's box soaking in every blessed note of the opera and completely ignoring the man who inexplicably turned her mind into mush. Her original plan had been to cry off with a headache, but Mrs. Summers wouldn't hear of it. So Sophie had devised the backup plan of actually enjoying herself, but that too seemed in immediate danger of failing.

The evening had started well enough. Alex had behaved as a perfect gentleman on the ride over. At least she thought he had been—she was still a little uncertain about some of the finer requirements of that particular station. He certainly had been more subdued in his choice of conversation topics, and, more importantly, he'd been unfailingly respectful to Mrs. Summers, which had raised him several notches in Sophie's esteem. By the time they had reached the opera house, she had been confident her plan would be a resounding success.

That changed once they entered the box. It was too small for one thing, and for some reason he seemed to take up more than his fair share of the available space. He continued making polite conversation, but she had the hardest time overcoming the sensation that she had been cornered like so much prey. It wasn't that she was typically uncomfortable in small spaces. In fact, if the box were half the size with twice as many people, it wouldn't have mattered in the least. Small boned, and at barely over five feet and two inches, Sophie was accustomed to looking up to people, to feeling petite. Alex's size, although impressive, wasn't what overwhelmed her. It was everything else about him—his laughing green eyes, his gravelly voice, the way that one errant coffee-colored lock of hair kept slipping down his forehead the same way it had the first time she'd seen him. It was, simply put, *him*. He made her feel trapped. She didn't like it. And yet she did. It was positively maddening.

When the music started and she realized he intended to stare at her all evening, Sophie knew she desperately needed a backup plan for her backup plan. After some consideration, she came to the conclusion that she might not actually enjoy the opera tonight, but she could damn well *pretend* she did.

It was a draw as to who was more relieved when the curtains closed for intermission. Alex escorted her out of the box for some refreshments and fresh air. She felt better immediately.

"Will you be attending the Wycotts' musicale next Friday?" Alex asked casually, after escorting her out of the box and fetching her a glass of lemonade.

"I believe we've another engagement—the Patton ball," she responded. "It's the Wycotts themselves performing, isn't it? Kate says they're rather good."

"Kate would know, she has a gift for music. Have you had a chance to hear her play the pianoforte yet?"

Sophie shook her head and took a sip of her overly tart lemonade, not because she was thirsty, but because it gave her something to do.

"Next time you see her, you really must insist. She is a wonder."

"I'll make a point of it," Sophie mumbled. She had never been anything less than completely inept at the pianoforte. And the harp. And the flute. Was that the sort of women Alex preferred? Perfect ladies who played a musical instrument and took up watercolors? Not that it was any of her concern. Really.

"Do you play?" he inquired.

Oh, *of course* he would ask.

"Er . . . no, I'm afraid I lack the talent," she admitted.

"Thank God."

"I beg your pardon?"

"I'm relieved to hear that you lack the talent and therefore do not play. There are too many young ladies of my acquaintance who seem incapable of grasping that the latter should be employed once the former is recognized."

Sophie laughed, once more sliding into a more comfortable ease at his teasing tone. "Surely, it is not just the young ladies who exhibit this flawed reasoning."

"As concerns my experience with the pianoforte, yes," Alex stated. "Men have their own unique set of vices."

"Oh, and what might those be?"

"The usual . . . horses, cards, drink and," he gave her a wicked little grin, "women of course."

"Of course," Sophie said, or squeaked really, if one wanted to be annoyingly precise about it. So much for feeling at ease, and so much for his gentlemanly behavior. She wished Mrs. Summers hadn't insisted on staying in the box. For the life of her, Sophie could not understand why Alex's plain speaking should make her so uncomfortable. Generally, she preferred an open dialogue between friends and yet, whenever Alex spoke to her in a way that would send most young debutantes screaming to their mama's side, Sophie couldn't help but feel, for some unaccountable reason, a little disappointed.

Alex laughed at her expression.

"What's so amusing, Your Grace?"

"It's Alex, as well you know, and *you*, my dear Sophie, are very amusing. Or rather I should say, intriguing."

"Oh?"

"Fishing for compliments, are we?"

"I have no idea what *you're* doing, besides aggravating me, but *I* am trying to understand what the devil you're laughing at."

"Your language for one thing," he chuckled. "Tsk, tsk, my dear, what if someone hears you? People are looking, you know."

"Likely there are one or two ladies in the crowd who would be tempted to applaud, given that I'm swearing at you."

"Oh now, more than two surely. My reputation as a rake is more impressive than that."

She raised two mocking eyebrows. "You just *tsked* at me. I have serious doubts concerning your claim to rakedom."

"I could rid you of those doubts if you like," he said softly.

She downed the rest of her lemonade in two large gulps and handed him the empty glass. "That is generous of you, I'm sure, but I think it's time you returned me to my chaperone."

"Are you certain?" He let his hand linger over hers when he took the glass and he watched, enthralled, when she bit her bottom lip nervously. "I can be very persuasive when I set my mind to it, and I promise you'd enjoy the debate."

He was practically purring at her and, God help her, she was more than a little tempted to take him up on his offer. She didn't have a problem with kissing a man out of wedlock, not in theory. And she certainly wasn't adverse to the idea of kissing a very attractive man. It was one of a dozen new experiences she had hoped to enjoy while visiting London.

She just didn't want to kiss *him*.

She wasn't entirely certain why that was. Her body was plainly enthusiastic about the idea. But she had the unsettling suspicion that Alex would view a kiss with her as something other than what she intended it to be. As if he had captured a prize. To Alex, it would signify a battle won, a challenge conquered, and the thought made her a little sick at heart. Enough so that she was able to squash the rising rebellion in that part of her brain that demanded she sneak off behind the nearest potted palm and listen to his argument, and instead, meet his laughing eyes squarely.

"My chaperone, if you please," she insisted smartly.

Still laughing, he executed a smart bow and offered his elbow. "That, my dear, is what I find so intriguing. The warring of the outspoken world traveler with the proper British miss. I can hardly wait to see who will emerge the victor."

Sophie couldn't help but smile a little at his insight.

"I believe this battle goes to the British miss," she said taking his arm.

"She does seem a formidable little general," he admitted with exaggerated respect. "But my money is on the world traveler."

"Wishful thinking."

"Not if I send in reinforcements."

"In the form of . . . ?"

He turned and winked at her. "Temptation."

Lord Loudor lounged comfortably, if rather inelegantly, in a large dining chair in front of an enormous plate of food at his favorite club. Which, incidentally, was not White's—an establishment where he sometimes enjoyed himself, but often only patronized because it was what a gentleman of his standing was expected to do.

He was at Barney's, where the food, if not better, was a good deal cheaper. Where he could shrug off his waistcoat and loosen his cravat. And where he was always the highest-ranking member of nobility in attendance. Indeed, he was, as a general rule, the only member of nobility to grace the club with his presence. A circumstance that garnered a great deal of bowing and scraping by the employees, which was enough to set any man at ease.

He was not the only man, however, to receive such superior treatment this morning, or afternoon really since it was already well past one. Loudor made it a point never to rise before noon, and for his own convenience, he referred to the two hours following that momentous occasion as "the morning," whether it be one in the afternoon or ten at night.

And so it was "this morning" when Loudor welcomed Lord Heransly to dine with him. Loudor had known the man since Oxford. He had never particularly liked him, but then Loudor didn't particularly like anyone of his acquaintance, and the man was sometimes useful, so Loudor considered him a friend despite his personal feelings of distaste.

"Gad, man, what is this place?" Heransly pulled out a chair and sat, all the while eyeing their surroundings with disgust.

"Gentlemen's club," Loudor replied, or gurgled really, as his mouth was full.

"It's a club, I'll grant. I can see the game tables. But there's a definite lack of gentlemen."

"We're here," Loudor offered.

"Yes, and I'd like to know why exactly. Why wouldn't you meet me at White's?"

"Bloody sick of it," Loudor grunted. "All those earls and dukes, each hell-bent on being more dignified than the next." Loudor pulled a face at the thought.

"I was under the impression you aspired to those very ranks."

"Just the trappings, Heransly, just the trappings."

"Which brings me to the reason I wanted to meet with you," Heransly said. "I've heard you've been spending quite a bit of time with Rockeforte these last few days, and he's been enjoying the company of your lovely young cousin."

"What of it?"

"You know very well what," Heransly snapped. "She can't marry, Loudor."

"You think Rockeforte's likely to marry the chit?"

Heransly said nothing, so Loudor set down his fork and continued. "Said it yourself, my cousin's a lovely girl, indeed. She's also the daughter of a viscount and a bit of an original. Can't keep the young bucks away from bait like that. Now Rockeforte, on the other hand . . ." Loudor let his sentence trail off dramatically.

Heransly almost bounded out of his chair. "You've enlisted Rockeforte? Are you mad! My father will—"

"Don't be an ass. And keep your voice down. I don't think anyone here gives a damn what you say, but the noise grates on my nerves. I couldn't recruit Rockeforte if I tried. He's a bit more fun than most of his ilk, I'll grant, but he's still too honorable for human tolerance. I don't care how many women he's managed to bed. I've merely made myself agreeable to his pursuit of Sophie, *after* he mentioned he had no intentions of marriage."

"That would be a clever plan, if you hadn't just expounded on how honorable the man is."

Loudor waved the argument away. "I said he was honorable, not a eunuch. He wants the chit. Made it clear as day."

"I know a little about Rockeforte. I don't think he's the type to bed an innocent."

"Maybe he just wants to know he could." Loudor shrugged and heaped a pile of food onto his fork. "Who cares? His very presence keeps the real threats at bay. He doesn't like to share. And he certainly isn't going to marry her. Made that clear too."

"He won't take kindly to having been manipulated," Heransly pointed out uneasily.

"He won't ever know."

"He's not an idiot."

"In my experience, all men are idiots when it comes to lust."

Heransly watched in disgust as Loudor crammed food into his mouth. "As I'm certain that experience is limited to you, I won't argue the point."

❈ Eight ❈

The Patton ball was, to Sophie's mind, very nearly indistinguishable from Lord Calmaton's affair. Right down to both hosts being on the list Mr. Smith had given her. There were too many people; a frightening number of candles; too much silk, jewelry, and food; and not nearly enough air. And God forgive her, but she loved every dazzling bit of it.

"Sophie! There you are!" Mirabelle battled her way through the surrounding crowd to reach Sophie's side. "Heavens, what a crush," she breathed.

Sophie gave her friend a bright smile. "It is, isn't it?"

Mirabelle smiled back, then, craning her neck to peer around Sophie's shoulder, frowned and asked, "Where is your cousin?"

Sophie shrugged. "In the card room, I imagine."

"Already? I didn't realize the gentlemen began so early."

"No doubt my cousin, in the distance between here and the doors, convinced a sufficient number of men to join him."

Mirabelle twisted her mouth into a disapproving grimace. "I know he's your family, Sophie, and I'm sure he has a great many fine qualities, but he really is an appallingly bad escort."

Sophie sighed. "I know, and to be honest, his performance in the role of cousin has left something to be desired as well. But as you said, he is family."

Mirabelle nodded sympathetically. "I have family like that. My uncle is a complete boor. Unfortunately, he is also my guardian."

"That *is* unfortunate."

"Isn't it? I'm very lucky to have Lady Thurston. She's been uncommonly kind to me since earliest childhood. She positively insists on sponsoring my seasons here in London."

"I'd be willing to wager that she finds the endeavor no great sacrifice," Sophie stated, watching Lady Thurston speak with a rather handsome older man, a pretty blush lighting her face.

"Which is precisely why I continue to agree to the arrangement, and also why I don't feel particularly guilty about being a flop on the marriage mart."

"Flop?" Sophie asked incredulously. "The night we met, you sat out only two dances that I saw."

"Be that as it may, I am an acknowledged wallflower." Mirabelle stated the fact quite pleasantly for one admitting to a social standing regarded only very slightly above that of the dreaded "spinster."

"I find it difficult to reconcile my experience with your statement," Sophie murmured thoughtfully.

"Do you see that girl over there?" Mirabelle began by way of explanation. "The blonde in the charming ivory dress absolutely drowning in young men?"

Mirabelle waited for Sophie's nod before continuing. "Her name is Elizabeth Tellijohn and she is what's known as a diamond of the first water. She is beautiful, accomplished, well connected, well behaved, and enormously dowered. Men dance with her because they want either to seduce her or marry her or both. Men dance with *me* because they *have* to, which is a situation I am quite pleased with."

"You wouldn't care to be married or seduced?" Sophie asked.

"By the right man I might, but if I had to go searching for him in a mess like that . . ." Mirabelle waved her hand in the general direction of the young men surrounding Miss Tellijohn. "I think I might go mad."

"What's wrong with those gentlemen?"

Mirabelle shrugged. "Perhaps nothing. Perhaps everything.

I don't know, I've only ever danced with one of them, so I couldn't say with certainty. I do know, however, that it says a good deal about a man if he is only willing to dance with a woman like Miss Tellijohn and not with a wallflower."

"I suppose that makes a kind of sense."

"It makes every kind of sense." Mirabelle paused for a moment in thought before continuing. "If ever you happen to find yourself in search of a husband—and I do hope you're not offended, but I rather gathered you're not at the moment—I suggest you look closely at the gentlemen who dance with the wallflowers."

Sophie's expression must have asked her question, because Mirabelle nodded and continued. "Men who dance with the least popular girls do so for one of two reasons. The first being that they are compassionate enough to realize that every young girl longs to dance, even if she is trying her utmost to appear disinterested. Those are the very best and sadly, rarest, of gentlemen. The second reason gentlemen dance with wallflowers is because their mothers have pressured them into that particular act of chivalry, and there is much to be said for a young gentleman who will dance with a wallflower just to please his mama."

"And from which of these two groups do your bevy of admirers stem?" Sophie inquired. "For a self-described wallflower you seem remarkably in demand."

Mirabelle laughed. "Oh indeed. I have the rather dubious distinction of being London's most popular wallflower."

"I hadn't realized that was even an option."

Mirabelle leaned forward as if imparting a great secret. "The trick, you see, is to be the least of all evils," she said with a small smile. "My group comes from those who must dance to make their mothers happy. In my first season, I made a point to refrain from simpering, flirting, or stepping on toes. If possible, and it generally was, I made them laugh. In short, I helped them discharge their duty in the most pleasant manner possible, and at the next ball when their mothers began demanding they dance with one of 'those poor plain girls,' they remembered that. In exchange for my efforts, I get to dance with some of the nicest gentlemen in the room and even have the pleasure of naming a few of them as friends."

Sophie stared at her friend for a moment before shaking her head and smiling. "I'm not sure if I should be impressed with your cleverness, or horrified by your scheming."

"Oh, impressed, without question."

Sophie was denied a retort by the approach of an attractive young man who executed a proper, if somewhat uncomfortable, bow to Mirabelle.

"Miss Browning."

"Mr. Abner. May I present Miss Sophie Everton?"

Sophie curtsied her hello.

"Miss Everton has just returned from extensive travel," Mirabelle informed him. "Most recently from China."

"Indeed," Mr. Abner commented. "Excellent, excellent. . . . And are you enjoying your season in London?"

"Very much, thank you." Sophie replied.

"Excellent." He tugged once on his cravat, then seemed to think better of it and gripped his hands behind his back.

Mirabelle favored him with a kind smile "Mr. Abner is quite famous for his fencing skill."

Mr. Abner beamed, shot a quick glance at a formidable-looking woman who was staring at him pointedly from several yards away, turned back and asked, "Miss Browning, will you do me the honor of dancing with me?"

"I'd be delighted," Mirabelle replied gracefully, taking his arm.

It took all Sophie's self-control to keep a straight face. She thought she was safe once the couple turned their backs to leave, but then Mirabelle shot a look over her shoulder of such exaggerated innocence that Sophie was forced to make for the nearest balcony doors.

It was a convenient escape, and one she might need to utilize later in the night. She'd already made the prerequisite trip to the washroom, and discovered the only locked door in the main hall was, unfortunately, directly across from the billiards room. It was safe to bet that the room was already packed with gentlemen seeking a respite from the ballroom. There was no way she could sneak into the study through the door.

There were also Mrs. Summers and the other chaperones to contend with. They had claimed a strategic corner of the room that allowed their charges free range of the ballroom, but left no chance of one of them sneaking down the hall or out the patio doors into the garden without being seen. The chaperones' view of the dance floor was somewhat limited, but they definitely had both exits covered.

Sophie sighed and peered over the edge of the balcony. It wasn't more than a six-foot drop to the ground. She could manage that well enough. Of course, it might be easier to enter the garden from the other side of the ballroom and work her way around, but it was dark out and some of these larger homes had hedge mazes. The possibility of becoming lost in a dark maze was too nightmarish to consider.

Besides, it was a private little balcony, and she was less likely to be spotted than if she had to trudge through God only knew how many well-lit garden paths.

Sophie peeked back into the ballroom. The orchestra had moved on to a new dance, and Mirabelle had moved on to another partner. Beyond that, little had changed. Which, to Sophie's mind—and absolute disgust, translated neatly into this: a certain gentleman had yet to arrive.

She really—really and truly—needed to stop concerning herself over Lord Rockeforte. She ought to be giving her full attention to saving Whitefield. She was being paid by the Prince Regent himself after all, or at least on his behalf, and here she was fretting, not over her newly acquired position as spy, and not over her tenuous grip on her ancestral home, but over a man. A man who, no doubt, viewed her as just another conquest.

Sophie straightened her shoulders, hauled up her skirts, and began maneuvering over the balcony railing. She was going to break into Lord Patton's study, and then she was going to go home.

The prospect of wasting a perfectly good evening in an over-crowded room making inane conversation with people he generally disliked usually caused Alex to break out in a mental cold sweat. But after Sophie said she'd planned to be at the Patton ball, Alex had immediately sent his regrets to the Wycotts for their musicale.

He hated balls. Well and truly hated them.

There may have been a time in his youth when he looked forward to such an event, to dance and flirt with all the pretty young misses, to tease and shock all the staid matrons, but whatever joy he might have once found in such activities had disappeared long ago under the onslaught of matchmaking mamas, simpering debutantes, and toad-eating idiots, each and every one of them enthralled with his title and wealth without having the slightest idea of who he was or what he did.

Having people trip over themselves to please you is a grand thing indeed at the age of ten; at twenty, it's amusing; by thirty, it's embarrassing and offensive. Admittedly, there were some exceptions to the rule. There were people, like Mrs. Peabody, who remained singularly unimpressed with the notion that an individual's finest attributes could be accomplished at birth. Alex's close friends were similarly uninterested in his title, unless they could somehow work it into a joke at his expense.

And now Sophie. The British miss in her automatically relied on proper decorum when dealing with a peer of the realm, but with the right encouragement, that facade slipped away to reveal an opinionated and, he rather fancied, passionate woman.

Tonight, he was actually looking forward to a ball, and she was the reason. He wanted to see that woman emerge again. And again . . . and again. And he wanted to be the one who brought her to light.

He arrived at the ball fashionably late. It would have been a fair bit past fashionable if he had been anyone other than a duke. First, he had been required to change his cravat after dribbling some port on it in a very unducal manner, then change his shoes after stepping in a puddle on the way to his carriage, and finally to wait for a change of carriage after the first was discovered to have cracked a wheel.

He *was* a duke, however, and therefore quite fashionable regardless of the time he might deem to arrive. Arrive, he eventually did, and with a smile on his face. Even the evening's misadventures had failed to dampen his good mood.

After a half hour of trying and failing, however, to locate Sophie, Alex's smile had descended to a grimace. If one more bloody fool asked him where he had gotten his cravat pin . . .

"Why do you come to these events, then stand there looking as if the effort has caused you physical pain?"

The sound of Whit's voice brought him out of his musings. He was behaving irrationally. Probably the girl had gone to the ladies' retiring room and gotten caught up in a bit of gossip. He'd find her eventually. He just needed to exercise a little patience. He could do that.

Surely, he could do that.

"Ah, much better," Whit commented in an exceedingly jovial, and therefore exceedingly annoying manner. "You were starting to upset the young ladies, you know."

"Not nearly enough to keep their mamas away."

Whit continued as if he hadn't heard him. "I was beginning to fear you might go for someone's throat."

Alex threw his friend a quelling glance. "Don't tempt me, Whit."

"Speaking of throats, is that a new pin?"

To hell with patience. "Have you seen Sophie?"

Whit shrugged. "Not recently. I saw her step onto that balcony a while ago. Alone, in case you're interested, but I'm sure she's gone by now. Have you seen the imp?"

"Mirabelle? No, why?"

Whit grimaced. "I promised my mother I'd dance at least once with the little hellion tonight."

"Don't you think it's time you put aside your grudge?"

Whit looked genuinely surprised at the notion. "Whatever for?"

Alex resisted the urge to slap the back of his friend's head. "She's an unmarried female with a drunken uncle for a guardian, Whit. She needs a champion."

Whit looked at him as if he were a complete stranger. A completely insane complete stranger. "Are we speaking of the same girl? Brown hair, brown eyes, tongue of an adder? Because she *has* a champion—I believe he goes by the name Lucifer."

Alex knew he wasn't going to win this argument.

"Go dance, Whit."

"Determined to find fair Sophie, are you?"

Alex nodded curtly. If she'd been in the ladies' retiring room, she should be done by now.

"Happy hunting," Whit chimed jovially. "I'm off to slay a dragon myself."

Alex headed toward the balcony without bothering to reply. Whit's little joke had struck a nerve. His obsession with Sophie was becoming absurd. It was one thing to look forward to seeing her, but chasing her like a hound after a fox was another thing altogether. It was ridiculous, laughable. Damned humiliating. And he fervently hoped no one else would notice, because he had no intention of stopping until he ran her to ground.

It wasn't going to happen on the balcony. Just as Whit predicted, Sophie had already abandoned that sanctuary. In his frustration, Alex began making wild plans to storm the retiring room—most of which would have involved taking out his temper on the door—but eventually the cool night air managed to clear his head, and he decided on the more tactful, and infinitely less embarrassing, approach of asking Mirabelle to go in and have a look.

Alex turned to leave, but a movement in the darkness below him stopped him short.

Sophie. Alone in the garden and looking rather lost. Alex smiled slowly and wondered if he looked anywhere near as predatory as he felt.

"Tallyho," he whispered. Then with the grace of a large cat, he slipped over the side.

Sophie heard the whoosh of air just before Alex hit the ground not three feet in front of her.

"Good Lord almighty!"

"Hush, someone will hear you."

At the moment, that possibility seemed much less important than willing her heart back to its natural rhythm. It took several moments to accomplish this. Her next priority was to beat the laughing man standing before her to a bloody pulp.

"Ouch! Stop that!"

"Stop that?" *Whack.* "Stop that!" *Thump.* "That's all you can say?" *Whack.* "Hush and stop that?" *Thu—*

"Enough," Alex laughed, grabbing her flailing wrists in his hands.

"You nearly scared me to death!"

"I don't think that's possible. Unless you have a weak heart. You don't, do you?" He didn't look overly concerned by the notion. Amused was more like it. And tidy, the bastard. He had landed on his feet as if jumping off balconies were routine exercise. She had rolled right into the hedge grove.

And all for what, exactly? She hadn't found a blasted thing in Mr. Patton's study. She had climbed through the window, gone through every drawer and cabinet, and come up empty-handed. Then, she'd had to climb back out the window only to discover the two service entrances at the back of the house had actual servants milling about on the other side. And that had forced her to come all the way back around—

"Sophie?"

She glanced up. Alex looked a little anxious now. Good. She should let him stew a bit, it would serve him right. She stifled a sigh. No, it wouldn't. For all she knew, his mother might have died of heart failure.

"Soph—"

"No," she snapped, pulling her wrists free, "I do not have a weak heart. Although you should have considered the possibility before leaping out at me like some sort of crazed orangutan."

"Crazed what?"

"Orang—"

"I heard you actually. I was just surprised. Most young ladies have never even heard of an orangutan, let alone used one in a simile."

"I am not 'most young ladies.'"

"So I've noticed," he said, rubbing his chest ruefully. "Who taught you how to throw a punch?"

"Mr. Wang."

"He must be a quite an instructor. That thing you did with your knuckles . . . impressive."

"He's a master, and he had a dedicated pupil. If I had really wanted to hurt you," she sniffed, "I could have."

Alex grinned at her. "I don't doubt it."

It took considerable effort to force her face into a scowl.

Now that the shock of his dramatic appearance was wearing off, it was becoming difficult to stay mad at him. There was something delightfully wicked in being alone in a garden with a known rake. Especially when that rake was doing his best to charm her.

And she *was* rather proud of the skills Mr. Wang had taught her.

"So, tell me, my little pugilist, what were you doing all alone in the garden?"

A little devil whispered in her ear at just that second, and it must have been persuasive because she schooled her face into a slightly haughty expression and, in an uncharacteristically coy voice, said, "How do you know I was all alone?"

Alex's grin was gone in a flash. "Weren't you?"

She shrugged nonchalantly and, turning her back to him, walked a bit away to inspect a rose bush. It was a silly affectation in a silly game, but it garnered the most interesting results.

"Answer my question, Sophie," he snapped.

Ooh, but this was fun.

She shrugged again and bent down to smell one of the blooms. "Maybe I was, and maybe I wasn't. What concern is it of yours?"

She thought she heard him growl something that sounded like "good question," but she was too intent on acting disinterested to insist he speak up.

She did hear him swear though.

"Who is he, Sophie?" he barked from behind her. "One of those ridiculous fops, or that libertine Lord— *Stop* shrugging your shoulders at me!"

He was upon her in two quick strides. She hadn't even time to fully straighten before he grabbed her by the shoulders, spun her around, and pulled her roughly against him.

"Who?" he demanded.

"Um . . ." Although the game was still interesting, she wasn't certain it still qualified as fun.

"You are not, I repeat, *not* to meet men, *any* man, in *any* garden alone," he ordered with a high-handedness that almost equaled his temper. "Do I—"

"Except you, of course," she pointed out. Any sensible girl would have known that now was a good time to keep her mouth firmly shut and simply nod in agreement. Sophie had always thought herself a reasonably sensible girl, but at the moment she was willing to reconsider. Alex's fingers tightened on her upper arms. His head bent until their faces were inches apart and she could see the outline of her reflection in his green eyes.

"Do I make myself clear?" he ground out.

She swallowed, or tried to, as her mouth had suddenly gone rather dry. "Yes," she rasped.

"Good. I forbid it."

Well now, *that* just begged for a response.

"Well now, *that*—"

Alex bent his head and kissed her. Whether it was to silence her, or simply because he wanted to, she didn't know. Nor did she care, because *this* was her first real kiss.

And it was amazing. It wasn't the gentle pressing of lips she had always imagined kissing to be, and to be honest, she had done a good deal of imagining. No, this kiss was forceful, wild, incredible. His arms wrapped around her and pulled her against him, molding her form against his length. Sophie lost all sense of reason, all sense of time and place, lost everything but the ability to feel.

Her hands found his chest, his neck, his face. Her fingers speared into his hair, brushing through that endearing lock in front that she'd wanted to touch for days now, and tangling in the back as she struggled to bring him closer. She could never be close enough for this, close enough to him. He groaned and nipped her bottom lip. Something hot settled in her chest and spread down to her toes.

Alex abandoned her mouth to trail his lips down the side of her throat. She tasted like every sweet thing he had ever craved. His hand stole up and lightly brushed against her breast, teasing the both of them. She gasped and the soft sound sent a fierce wave of desire through him. "My God, Sophie."

Sophie . . . Sophie Everton.

The name sent off bells in his head. They weren't loud enough to stop him from kissing her again, but they were persistent. Little chimes that snuck past the lust.

Miss Sophie Everton, the woman he had been sent to watch. The woman whose cousin was a suspected traitor. The woman who had *him*, the Duke of Rockeforte, scouring ballrooms, jumping off balconies, and acting like an overbearing, possessive . . . orangutan.

Alex broke away and used his last remnants of willpower to grab Sophie's shoulders and set her at arm's length.

Sophie stumbled a bit before regaining her balance. If the kiss had been unexpected, its conclusion was a complete shock. She wasn't an expert on these matters, far from it, but . . . shouldn't they have wound down a bit first? It all seemed rather abrupt. Her heart and mind were still whirling away, still lost in the kiss. And she realized—she wasn't quite ready for it to end.

Alex, on the other hand, looked done in. He was bent over at the waist with his hands braced against his knees. She couldn't see his face, but his shoulders were shaking like . . . like he was laughing.

"Are you *laughing?*" she demanded, wishing the words had come out as something more than a horrified whisper.

Alex took a deep breath and straightened. "Sophie—"

"You *are* laughing!" *Good. God.*

"No! Well, yes I am, but—"

"You heartless . . . foul . . ." Oh, how she wished her best curse words were in a language he'd understand. "I cannot believe—no wait, yes I can. Yes, I can! You're despicable. You're . . . you're . . ." *Argh!*

"Sophie, please, if you would just—"

"No! Don't! Don't touch me," she hissed, seeing red. Absolute fire and brimstone crimson red. "Don't ever touch me again. Don't even come near me, or so help me God, I will *geld* you. Now, do I make myself clear?" She didn't wait for an answer, just turned on her heel and left.

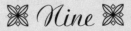

❋ Nine ❋

*Y*ou laughed at her?" Whit's forkful of eggs was halfway to his mouth when Alex finished the retelling of last night's events.

"I did not laugh at *her*," Alex growled. "I laughed at the situation." The excuse sounded even lamer spoken aloud than it had in his head.

Whit eyed him dubiously. "I'm sure Miss Everton was delighted to hear that."

Alex cringed visibly. Sophie's reaction could not, by any stretch of the imagination, have been described as one of delight.

Whit made a noise somewhere between a snort and a laugh and then finished cramming the eggs into his mouth.

Alex eyed his own plate with disinterest. He really wasn't hungry anymore. He had woken Whit at the ungodly hour of eight this morning and bribed him into coming to White's with the promise of a free breakfast and the loan of his matched grays. Whit was his oldest and most loyal friend, and would probably have agreed to accompany Alex without the extra incentives, but Alex had been unwilling to take the chance. He was that desperate for advice. Now, watching his friend alternately chuckling and wolfing down his breakfast, Alex was left to wonder why he had taken the time to bother.

Clearly, Whit was not going to be of any help.

"Whatever made you do it?" Whit asked, stabbing a piece of ham.

"I've been asking myself that for the last eight hours." Actually, he had asked himself that very question three times a minute, every minute, for the last eight hours.

"And?" Whit prompted, popping the ham into his mouth.

Alex groaned and set down his fork in disgust. "And I do believe I've come unhinged."

Whit bobbed his head agreeably and kept on eating.

Alex really wished he hadn't offered his grays. "I can only hope it's not a lasting affliction," he grumbled.

"Or catching," Whit added, then shrugged. He swallowed and said, "Flowers, candy, and an explanation would be a damned sight better than, 'it was the situation.' Also, I'd advise you to seriously consider groveling. The sooner the better."

"I'm certain you would."

"Why don't you call on Sophie this afternoon? No use letting the problem fester. I'll come along, for moral support, of course." Whit grabbed a scone and then by some means unholy, managed a truly evil smirk with a mouthful of food.

Alex briefly entertained the idea of pummeling his friend, but the man had just inhaled an entire plate of eggs and ham. The resulting mess wouldn't be worth the satisfaction.

"I'll see you tomorrow," Alex snapped. He dropped his napkin on the table and stood. "Not one minute sooner."

Whit gave him a jaunty one-fork salute and kept chewing. Alex glared, reconsidered the pummeling, then settled for a single vulgar epitaph and left.

Sophie watched the passing scenery from inside her carriage without interest. She really didn't feel like shopping, but she had made the commitment to Kate and Mirabelle yesterday. They were delightful girls and on any other day Sophie would be eager for their company. But not today. Today she wanted nothing more than to lie in bed and indulge in a hearty wallow of self-pity and self-recrimination.

He should never have kissed her. That was all she could think about. And she should never have kissed him *back*. But he had, then she had, and there was no undoing it. If she were to be completely honest with herself she'd have to admit she didn't really want to undo it. She did, however, fervently wish that the interlude had ended with something other than Alex laughing at her.

It had been a wonderful kiss, at least from her inexperienced standpoint. Sophie frowned and slumped back against the seat cushions. Apparently, Alex viewed the interlude from an entirely different perspective. Specifically, from that of a rake. Probably, he had kissed scores of women, *legions,* and undoubtedly most of them were a great deal more versed in the art of kissing than she, but really, it had been unforgivable of him to be so cruel as to laugh at her lack of skill.

It had been humiliating. And it hurt, even more than she would have expected. She had truly begun to like Alex, and for one glorious moment, when he had wrapped his arms around her and pressed his lips against her own, she had felt beautiful, cherished, and desired.

And then he had laughed. And she had run home, feeling every bit the gullible country girl, and cried.

Sophie was saved having to relive that painful memory, yet again, by the sound of the carriage door opening. She blinked twice at the footman, before realizing they had reached the Cole town house. She allowed herself to be handed down and then took a moment on the front steps to square her shoulders and clear her thoughts.

Rockeforte was a cad, a rake, a bounder and . . . several other atrocities that didn't come to her at the moment. He was not worth the effort it required to be angry and definitely not worthy of her tears. In the future she would, quite simply, have absolutely nothing to do with the man.

"Sophie! Whatever are you doing standing on the steps?"

It took a moment for Sophie to realize the voice was coming from Kate, who was leaning out an upper-story window. Sophie remembered the young woman's propensity for clumsiness and cringed.

Kate seemed not to notice the precariousness of her position. "Do come in. Mira and I are most eager to be off. Oh wait!" Kate disappeared for a moment and then returned to the window, dangling half her body over the window sill. Sophie was relieved to see a hand dart out and latch firmly on to the back of her dress. "Don't bother, Sophie," Kate called cheerily. "We'll be right down."

In good time, Mirabelle, Kate, two maids, and two footmen were arranged in, on, and around the moving carriage.

It was hard to retain a bad mood in the company of Kate and Mirabelle. Kate's natural buoyancy and Mirabelle's quick wit had Sophie smiling, then grinning, then laughing before they reached the fashionable shopping district of Bond Street.

And then of course, there were the shops themselves. Sophie's previous London shopping excursion had been rushed and purposeful, really much more of a chore. Ambling from store to store without lists or agenda was a world removed from trying to obtain an entire wardrobe in under a week.

The girls were a lively pair, far more interested in having a pleasant time than searching for that perfect bonnet or the newest muslin. By Sophie's calculation, they had visited a dozen shops in under two hours and had, among the three of them, purchased two new ribbons and a quill.

The whole morning had been really quite wonderful, marred only slightly when Kate had tripped over what Sophie could only assume was her own feet and collided with a portly gentleman coming out of a bookstore. He didn't seem the least put out by the incident. Kate had looked adorably sheepish during her apology and in the end, the man had somehow contrived to take the blame for the incident and walked off with a rather foolish sort of smile on his face. Mirabelle had looked like she very much wanted to roll her eyes, and Sophie barely contained her laughter until the hapless victim was out of earshot.

By the time they stopped for ices at a confectionary shop, Sophie was feeling remarkably better.

"Oh! Look, look it's him," Kate cried, nearly toppling over her chair and half the table in an effort to obtain a better view of a young man walking slowly down the far side of the street. Mirabelle steadied her friend's chair with a practiced ease.

"Him who?" Sophie asked.

"Lord Martin," Kate whispered reverently.

"She has a *tendre* for him," Mirabelle explained.

Sophie moved an ice before Kate could knock it over as she leaned out even farther. "You don't say," Sophie replied dryly.

Turning her attention to the window, she eyed the young man with academic interest. She estimated Lord Martin near her own age, perhaps a year or two older. Tall and blond, with wide shoulders and narrow hips and waist, he was impeccably turned out in a green coat of fashionable cut, fawn breeches, and the requisite Hessians. He was also too far away for an accurate assessment of his facial features, but even from a distance she could tell he was handsome. Sophie could certainly understand Kate's interest. Lord Martin seemed to embody every current standard of masculine beauty. Almost too well. She squinted. Then cocked her head.

"He pads," Mirabelle supplied.

"What's that?" Sophie asked.

"Mira!" Kate exclaimed at the same time.

Mirabelle turned to answer Sophie first. "The use of padding to enhance the shoulders or thighs is a fairly common practice among gentlemen these days," she explained before turning to Kate. "So, I am not disparaging your Lord Martin. I was merely stating a fact."

Kate gave a disbelieving snort before returning her attention to the view. "With what I wear to transform my natural shape, I would be the proverbial pot calling the kettle black to judge Lord Martin." She watched the man until he disappeared around a corner, then settled back in her seat with a sigh and gave Mirabelle a small smile. "I don't doubt your sincerity, Mira," she said sweetly. "Only your accuracy."

Mirabelle shrugged. "To be honest, his legs may very well be . . . well *his,* but his shoulders are not. I noticed it when we waltzed. They're not squishy exactly, but—"

"You *waltzed* with him?" Kate demanded. "I cannot believe you didn't tell me that you *waltzed* with him!"

Mirabelle's eyebrows shot up. "Don't be silly, of course I told you. You insist upon hearing every detail of every occasion at which both his lordship and I have been in attendance. I tell you when we've danced together, or talked together, or even walked in the same room together."

"Danced together, yes," countered Kate. "*Waltzed* together, no."

"Waltzing *is* dancing," Mirabelle rejoined.

"A quadrille is a dance, a waltz is . . . is. . . ."

"A serious of established steps set to music, therefore, a dance," Mirabelle finished for her. "Like any other."

"Except," Sophie remarked, "that it's possible to employ the word as both a noun and a verb."

Kate and Mirabelle looked blank.

"It does seem notable that one may waltz," Sophie continued, "as well as dance *a* waltz."

Kate thought about that for a moment. "I waltz, you waltz, he, she, it waltzes . . . you're quite right, Sophie." She turned her attention back to Mirabelle. "It's not as if one may say 'I was quadrilling with Mr. so-and-so,' or 'Thank you, Lord Whomever, I enjoyed reeling with you.' Not without sounding foolish anyway."

"Oh very well," Mirabelle conceded with a chuckle. "I'm not entirely certain it's incorrect to refer to oneself as having been quadrilling, but I will grant that it's highly undesirable."

"And alter your future reports accordingly?" Kate inquired.

"If you insist," Mirabelle sighed.

"Oh, I do."

Mirabelle turned to Sophie with a rueful smile. "Kate's been madly in love with Lord Martin since the tender age of eight," she explained.

"I'll not deny it," Kate responded pertly. "And thank you, Sophie, for your assistance, it was very cleverly done. I so rarely win these arguments with Mirabelle and find I quite enjoy the sensation."

"It's not for lack of trying," Mirabelle replied. "You would argue with a brick wall."

Sophie laughed. "Perhaps you'd have fewer losses if you chose your battles more carefully."

Kate snorted. "Where's the fun in that?"

They finished their luncheon immersed in the same light sort of conversation. Sophie enjoyed every minute. She enjoyed the laughter, the closeness, the good-natured banter that never slipped anywhere close to the boundary of cruel. She enjoyed having friends. Yesterday she had enjoyed their company, but today she was enjoying their friendship.

She had real, honest-to-God friends.

The joyful headiness that accompanied that revelation was nearly overwhelming. Sophie had never had friends before. Not since her sister had died. These were young women her own age whose company she wanted to be in and who, in return, wanted her own. They included her in their jokes and tales, their secrets and dreams without awkwardness or artifice, and she felt accepted.

"Good Heavens," Mirabelle cried, startling Sophie out of her reverie. "Look at the time!" She reached into her reticule and drew out a few coins which she placed on the table. "I'll see you at your home, Kate. That should cover my share."

Kate looked at the coins and sighed. "Won't you let me——?"

She stopped at the sight of Mirabelle's glare.

"Very well," Kate muttered.

Sophie reached for her own bag. "Are you not returning with us, Mirabelle?"

Mirabelle shook her head. "No, I have another errand to run, but I won't have you two late on my account. I'll take a hackney back. And stop looking at me like that, Kate, I'll take one of the footmen along with one of the maids, and your mother need never know."

"I don't mind waiting if you'd like," Sophie offered.

"That's kind of you, but I insist you return to your Mrs. Summers. She sounds a veritable hawk."

"Usually," Sophie said. "But she's been remarkably lax of late."

Mirabelle pressed a kiss on Kate's cheek and then turned and did the same to Sophie. "I'll see you tomorrow at tea then," she said, and left.

It hadn't been a request, but an open invitation. Sophie only barely managed to conceal the huge smile that would have reached from ear to ear and no doubt served to make her look half mad. She had friends.

Kate and Sophie settled their bills and headed out into the street to await their carriage. It really was a lovely day, sunny but with enough chill in the air that Sophie did not feel overheated in her layers of clothing.

"Our driver should be around any minute," Kate remarked conversationally. "One of the . . . I say, whatever is that girl doing?"

Attempting to figure that out for herself, Sophie didn't immediately answer. A young girl, or perhaps a woman—she was too swathed in rags for Sophie to make a reasonable determination of age—had skirted out to the very center of the street and crouched over the cobblestones. Her back was turned to the girls but even so, Sophie could see that she was digging at a gap between two stones with her fingers.

"Do you suppose she's lost something?" Kate asked hopefully.

"I think she has, but I sincerely doubt it's anything tangible,"

Sophie replied sadly. The woman was quite obviously mad. It was a common enough affliction, and there was precious little that could be done, or would be done, for women like the one in the street. She might be locked up in a third-rate asylum, which, considering how horrific first-rate asylums were rumored to be, would likely do more harm than good. Or perhaps she would just be run off and left to starve. Sophie wondered if she could approach the girl with the offer of assistance. At the very least, she could offer her enough money for a proper meal and a place to sleep.

She had no experience dealing with a madwoman, however, and wasn't quite sure how to go about it. What if she were violent?

"This street is usually quite busy," Kate murmured. "This can't be safe."

Kate was right. Bond Street was a favorite haunt for young unmarried ladies, and therefore, an ideal hunting ground for young gentlemen. Sophie had seen them parade up and down the street all morning, showing off their new mounts, their fancy carriages, their fast phaetons . . . like the one now careening around the corner.

Both the girls started and gasped at the sight.

"Look out!" Sophie yelled waving wildly at the oncoming phaeton.

"Get up, girl!" Kate cried at the crouching figure.

Neither took notice of the screeching girls on the sidewalk. The young man behind the reins was too busy craning his neck to see who might be watching his daring little drive, and the girl, well, there was simply no telling what she was doing.

"Get up!" Sophie yelled again and amazingly enough, the girl did. She turned to face the phaeton, and made absolutely no move to get out of its path.

"Dear God," Kate whispered in horror.

Sophie didn't hear her. She was already moving forward.

❃ Ten ❃

It would have been a spectacular display of heroics.

It would have been hailed as bravery personified.

It *would* have been, had not the girl decided to jump to safety of her own accord at the last possible second, leaving Sophie running full tilt and off balance.

She had thrown herself forward in an attempt to grab the girl and hurl them both to safety by means of brute force. Now she was hurtling quite alone with her feet moving too fast to stop and too slow to catch up with the top half of her body. She felt a burst of air as the phaeton raced past, missing her by inches. She should really just fall. She knew she should. Eventually, she would have to. There was no pulling out of it now, and if she didn't fall, the only other way she could possibly stop would be to—

Sophie caught a glimpse of the carriage door before she hit it. Then everything went black. Her legs gave out from under her. She anticipated the hard impact of the cobblestone on her knees and had a brief hope it would distract her from the blinding pain of her forehead. It never came. Instead she landed on something soft, warm and . . .

Oh no. Please no, please no, please!

When the smell hit, Sophie realized no amount of begging was going to save her.

She felt Kate tug her arm. "Get up, Sophie, you're kneeling in horse—"

"I know!"

Sophie ignored the snickers and outright laughs of the crowd beginning to circle, and allowed Kate to help her to her feet and assist her to the sidewalk. She forced her eyes open.

"Are you hurt?" Kate asked with quite the most sympathetic expression Sophie had ever seen.

"No," Sophie replied miserably. *And why the devil not?* Surely, if one were going to throw oneself headfirst into the side of a carriage, one should expect to be rendered unconscious.

Preferably for several days.

"Are you sure?" Kate continued staring at her forehead. "You took a rather nasty blow to the head and were babbling something awful there for a moment."

"I was swearing."

"Really? In what language?"

"Mandarin, I think."

"Oh."

"Do stop staring at my forehead, Kate, I'm quite all right. I just want to leave."

"Oh, I believe you, that you're all right that is. It's . . . it's just that you seem to have struck the earl's coat of arms on the carriage door and you now have the most astonishing imprint of a fleur-de-lis"—Kate pointed to Sophie's forehead, slightly left of center—"right there."

Sophie touched the offending spot gingerly and groaned. Really, could things get any worse?

Kate titled her head objectively. "I wonder if it will bruise like—oh, look, here comes Alex."

Oh. Dear. God.

Sophie felt her fingers fall from her forehead. She didn't suppose there was any real chance he had failed to witness her humiliating episode. He was coming from a shop on the corner that, naturally, had two large windows facing both streets.

"Let's just wave and go," Sophie whispered in a panic.

"We'll do no such thing," Kate sniffed. "It's cowardly."

Sophie looked down at her manure-smeared gown and made a decision.

"I can reconcile myself to that."

"Pfft, you'd only regret it later," Kate stated firmly. "Besides, at least a dozen members of the *ton* are here, several of them notorious gossips, and *all* of them will now witness the Duke of Rockeforte coming to see to your welfare. It will go a long way to repair any damage done to your reputation by your little mishap. Now chin up and smile." Kate's speech had come out low and rushed in an attempt to finish before Alex arrived.

"Are you hurt, Sophie?" Alex looked concerned rather than amused. Sophie wasn't sure if that fact made her more embarrassed or less.

"No, I'm quite well," she mumbled.

"What is your full name?"

"I beg your pardon?"

"Your full name," Alex repeated. "What is it?"

"You can't be serious," she scoffed.

He took her face in both his hands and leaned down closely, too closely. Really, they were in a crowd of people. Most of them were beginning to disperse, but all the same what could he be thinking? She saw his eyes catch on her forehead for a moment before his gaze met her own.

"Your full Christian name, Sophie," he prompted.

"Oh for the love of—Sophia Marie Rose Everton, Countess of Pealmont, if you want to be fastidious about it. Are you quite satisfied?"

She saw his eyebrows raise and he straightened up an inch. "Countess?"

"She was speaking in a foreign language earlier," Kate supplied in a low whisper.

"I'm perfectly lucid," Sophie insisted. "And I do happen to be a countess. I received the honorary title as a child for fishing King George out of my father's pond, but it was so silly, and he'd only fallen in because I'd . . . never mind, may we leave now?"

She placed the question to Kate, but it was Alex who answered.

"We'll take my carriage. Fetch your abigail, Kate."

Sophie almost argued, but the last thing she wanted to do was continue standing on the crowded sidewalk covered in horse dung. She could suffer through one carriage ride with the high-handed Duke of Rockeforte to get away from the scene of her embarrassment, even if it was the *second*-to-last thing she wanted to do.

Once in the carriage, Kate seemed to sense that something was amiss between her two friends. After her few attempts at friendly conversation were greeted with monosyllabic answers, she gave up and took to studying her companions as they tried very hard not to look at each other. She must have come to some sort of conclusion, because when she alighted from the carriage with her maid at her mother's home she turned and gave Sophie a kiss on the cheek and a reassuring smile. "I'll send your driver behind you." Alex, on the other hand, received a suspicious glare for a farewell.

Alex watched Kate go into the house. Apparently, he had moved down the pecking order of Kate's friends.

"You told her," he said to Sophie, knocking on the roof to start the carriage.

"Oh, *yes*," Sophie drawled, keeping her eyes firmly trained on the passing scenery. "I can think of nothing more sensible than regaling Kate, whom I've only very recently gotten to know, with tales of my humiliation at the hands of one of her oldest and most beloved friends. A cunning plan indeed."

Alex grimaced. It had been a ridiculous assumption. "My apologies," he mumbled.

Sophie's head snapped around. "For what, exactly? Treating me like a common doxy? Laughing at me? Insulting me now? You'll need to be a bit more specific, I'm afraid."

"If you'll grant it to me," he began in what he very much hoped was a properly conciliatory tone, "I should very much like the chance to apologize for all of it."

Sophie made a scoffing noise in the back of her throat. "You'd need more contrition than you could fit into the duration of this carriage ride, Your Grace. In fact, we could go straight through to Dover—"

"Sophie."

"It is Miss Everton," she said peevishly.

"I thought it was Lady Pealmont."

"As I've no interest in speaking with you, I can't see how it matters."

Alex took a deep breath and decided to ignore that. "I am sorry," he said clearly. "I am well and truly sorry. I behaved terribly last night, but I had no intention of insulting you in any manner."

"Then why did you?" she cried.

"I didn't!" Alex bit off before he could stop himself. He took another deep breath. "Insult you on purpose, that is. My behavior last night was, without doubt, offensive, but not intended as an insult."

"Well, you did a remarkable job disguising that rather pertinent fact," she grumbled.

"You should have given me the chance to explain," he snapped.

"You shouldn't have behaved in a manner that required explanation," she rejoined.

"I am aware of that. But as much as I might like to, and I *very much* would, I cannot undo the past."

"Would you really?" she asked quietly.

"I . . . really what?"

"Undo the past, if you could? At least this one part of it?"

"Only part of the one part of it." Good Lord, had he really just said that?

"Oh." Sophie seemed to consider this for a moment. "Which part?"

"You know very well which part."

"No," Sophie stated clearly. "I don't know. At least not 'very well.' I could assume from our conversation that you are referring to your laughing, but since you *did* laugh, and I certainly hadn't seen *that* coming, I think it best I assume nothing where you're concerned."

"Then don't assume my guilt."

"You *did* laugh. I was there, remember?"

"Yes," Alex growled, "I did laugh. It was very, very badly done of me. Yes, I would take it back if I could. But truly, there are only so many ways I can tell you I had no intentions of insulting you, and only so many times I can apologize for having done so, before I—"

"So you wouldn't take back the kiss?"

"What?"

"I believe you heard me."

Alex had no idea when he had lost control of the conversation, although he thought it a fair bet to place that event somewhere in the vicinity of when Sophie had first opened her mouth. He certainly had no clue as to when he had lost all comprehension of *what* was being discussed, because he had *thought* they were speaking of his having laughed, and here she was asking about the kiss. He did know, however, that he was very, very uncomfortable with this unfamiliar feeling of bewilderment, and it was on the tip of his tongue to say something flip, to knock the scales in his favor. But something in the way she was looking at him gave him pause.

She didn't appear angry, nor was she pouting or crying or anything else one might expect under the circumstances. She was sitting straight-backed as usual, but her eyes were downcast and her hands were working knots into the front of her dress again.

Would he take back the kiss? Hell no. He wanted to say just that, *hell no.* But he knew, somehow he knew with his whole being, right down to his toes, that her question was more important to her than everything else that had been said between them. Somehow his answer had to reflect that, not just in what he said, but how he said it. He had one chance to make all of this right, one chance to gain back her trust. It amazed him just how much he wanted that.

Gently, Alex reached out and took her chin in his hand, turning her so she had to look him in the eyes. "I would not," he said slowly and carefully, "trade that kiss for all the world and everything in it. It was perfect."

Sophie's eyes grew alarmingly wide. He took that as an encouraging sign. "I would," he continued, "gladly give up all I have to take back what happened after. Truly, Sophie, I am sorry." He paused a moment to let his words sink in. "Will you forgive me?"

She looked at him with such intensity and held herself so very still that for one terrifying moment Alex thought she might say no. But then she blinked, pursed those remarkably eloquent lips, and nodded as if she had just read through his thoughts and found them satisfactory.

"Yes," she said quietly, but distinctly. "I forgive you."

And then she smiled. It was really more of a wisp of a smile, but it was enough. Alex leaned forward, took her face in his hands, and kissed her with an intensity that surprised him.

He wanted to show her something. Tell her something. Convince her of something important. Only, he had no idea what that something was. That she wouldn't regret having forgiven him? That he desired her more than any woman he had ever known? That—

And then all thought was lost in a heartbeat, because she was kissing him back. Still adorably unpolished, still stirringly eager. She let out a tiny feminine moan, and he was lost, uncaring that she was an innocent, that he had an assignment. He would have her. He *had* to have her. His arms went around her shoulders and waist, pressing her body tightly against his. He wanted to wrap himself around her. To feel every inch of her. To taste her. Devour her. His lips left her mouth to trail down her neck. She moaned again. The carriage hit a rut.

The carriage. They were in a carriage. On the way to her town house. He would need more time. As a gentleman, he should have been disgusted with the idea of making love to a lady in a carriage. At the moment, however, his thoughts were focused not on where they were, but on where he wanted her to be—namely naked and under him.

More time. He needed more time. He needed to tell the driver to take the long way about. He let his lips trail down to the hollow of her collarbone, then took a deep breath to clear his head.

And gagged.

Sophie's eyes flew open at the sound.

". . . Alex?"

For a moment he neither spoke nor moved. Then, slowly, ever so slowly, he raised his head to look at her. Sophie had never seen that particular expression on anyone's face before. He looked sheepish, a little green around the edges, and something else she just couldn't identify.

"I am so sorry, Sophie," he groaned in what Sophie thought might be the most fatalistic manner she had ever heard.

"Did you just . . . ?"

"It's the dress."

"The dress? What's wrong with—oh, no. I'd forgotten . . . how mortifying."

Alex grunted. "You're not the one who just gagged."

"Yes, that's true. Well, it could have been worse. You didn't actually retch." She glanced down at her dress. "Did you? I'm not certain I'd be able to tell. . . ."

"No," he stated emphatically. "I managed to spare us both the indignity of becoming sick on your dress." He dragged a hand over his face and let out a frustrated groan.

Sophie wasn't sure how to respond to that, so she just gave him an encouraging little half smile. The effort started some sort of bizarre chain reaction. The corners of her mouth began to twitch uncomfortably, her chest tightened, her shoulders shook, and her breath kept escaping in erratic gasps. She kept her lips pressed firmly shut and tried breathing through her nose, but it didn't help.

"Go ahead and laugh, Sophie," Alex groused. "You're likely to injure yourself otherwise."

She took him at his word and laughed. Hard.

"I'm sorry. Really. It's just . . . all so absurd . . . and *unbelievably* embarrassing . . . It was either laugh or cry and . . . And I. . . ."

"You don't need to make excuses. God knows I'd rather see you laughing, and if any situation warranted it. . . ."

She heard him break into an easy laughter himself. When she finally managed to regain some control, she realized she felt much as if she had been crying. Her sides hurt, her eyes and nose felt puffy, and she was tired. But she was smiling, and thankfully, so was he.

"That felt good," she murmured, suddenly feeling awkward.

"So it did."

The carriage rolled to a halt. Sophie reached for the door, but was stopped by Alex's grip on her wrist. She turned back to find him suddenly very serious. His other hand reached up to gently caress the side of her face.

"Someday, Sophie," he said quietly, "I'm going to do this right with you."

He let his hand fall from her face, but his other moved from her wrist to her hand. He brought it to his lips and pressed a tender kiss on her palm.

"Soon," he whispered.

She wasn't sure if he meant it as a promise or a threat. She wasn't sure which one she wanted it to be. Checking first to make certain no one was about to see her exiting the Duke of Rockeforte's carriage, she all but bolted the short distance to the house. She had one foot inside the door when she heard Alex call out behind her.

"Sophie, about that other person who kissed you . . ."

"Mrs. Summers," she explained with a wide grin. "Just a peck on the cheek for luck."

"She's innocent."

William Fletcher looked up from his work to scowl at Alex, who had just burst into his office unannounced. A moment later a rather harassed-looking young man stumbled through the door, breathing hard and flushing to the roots of his pale blond hair. "I'm sorry, sir, I tried to—"

"It's all right, Sallings, no harm done." William dismissed the boy with a wave of his hand.

Alex watched him go. "New secretary?"

"Yes. Don't you knock these days?"

"Mostly. What happened to Kipp?"

"He was reassigned."

Alex took a seat in front of the desk and stretched out his legs in complete ease, looking for all the world as if he hadn't just bullied his way into the office without so much as a "good morning." "Where to?" he inquired offhandedly.

William stuck his quill in the inkstand. This was going to take a while. "To the continent. Why?"

"He owes Whit money. An extended reassignment, I hope?"

William fought the urge to reach for his brandy. It wasn't even noon yet. "Is there a particular reason you came barging in here, Rockeforte?"

Alex's grin faded, and for the first time William noticed that the man's right hand was closing and unclosing on the chair's arm. He was agitated, and trying not to show it.

"I apologize for the rude entry, but I sent a note. You didn't answer."

"Perhaps I was busy."

"This is important."

William stifled a sigh. "Very well, you're here now. I believe your greeting this morning was 'she's innocent'? I assume you were referring to Miss Everton."

"Yes." Alex punctuated the statement with a sharp nod. "If Loudor is up to something, she doesn't know anything about it. She isn't involved."

"You're sure of this?"

"I've been chasing her around for the last ten days. I've attended two balls, a dinner party, and escorted her to the opera. I've gotten drunk with Loudor twice, and you've had men trailing both of them, without, I understand from Whit, any success. Loudor might have something to hide, but Miss Everton does not."

"Ten days is hardly—"

"We've assigned or cleared individuals of guilt in fewer than ten days before. I've spent a good deal of time with her, William, gotten to know her as you asked. Now I'm telling you, she's innocent."

William leveled a hard stare across his desk. "Your assignment was to use Miss Everton's connection with Loudor regardless of her own role—"

"I've already worked my way on to Loudor's guest list. We don't need her."

"Either you keep an eye on her or—"

"Leave her alone, William."

"I really wish you would stop interrupting me. It's irritating."

"And I'd like for you to trust me on this."

"I do. If you would let me finish—either you keep an eye on her, or I'll see that someone else does." William put his hand up to forestall any possibility of an argument. "I want her protected. I trust your assessment of the situation, but if Loudor is a traitor, she may be in danger by virtue of mere proximity."

Alex nodded and leaned back in his chair, some of the fight seeming to drain out of him. "You're right. Of course, you're right. I'll watch her, but I want your men called off."

"You can't watch her twenty-four hours a day, Rockeforte."

Alex swore under his breath. "They can watch the house when I'm not there, and trail her when she leaves, but that is all."

"Agreed."

Alex narrowed his eyes. "I mean it, William. No rooting through her room, no—"

"You have my word," William interrupted, more than a little pleased to have had the chance. "Miss Everton seems to have made quite an impression on you."

"She's an impressive young woman."

"I've no doubt she is. It's not like you to—"

"Don't say it, William."

Alex sent his carriage back without him. It was only a couple of miles to his town house, and he needed to think—something he had failed to do this morning. Bloody hell, he had all but barreled his way into William's office. No, scratch that, he *had* barreled his way into William's office.

It had seemed like a perfectly sensible thing to do at the time, which, he thought, was a clear indicator of just how little thought he'd given the idea.

Except he had been thinking. Of her. And only her. Miss Sophie Everton. She had occupied his every thought since the moment he had picked her small unconscious form off the street almost two weeks ago. Usually, if he wasn't reminiscing about some amusing little comment she had made, then he was daydreaming about what she would look like in his bed and how he might arrange matters to get her there. All that rich sable hair spread out across his pillow, all that soft skin flushed pink with desire. And those lips, those marvelous lips, parting—for him. The image had given him more than a couple of sleepless nights.

And every moment he wasn't in her company, he found his mind repeating the same questions over and over again. Where was she right now? Was she safe? Happy? What was she doing? And who was she with? This last part really irked him.

Finally, it occurred to him that for all his apparent fascination with the girl, not once in the last week had he wondered what she might be hiding. In fact, to Alex, the notion that she might be a spy for France seemed not only absurd but uncomfortably disloyal.

Hence the note he had sent to William (he hadn't actually bothered waiting for a reply) and ensuing carriage ride. By the time he had gotten halfway there, Alex had started feeling rather guilty for agreeing to spy on Sophie.

By the time he was two-thirds of the way there, he had successfully manipulated matters in his mind to the extent that he was certain Sophie had been grossly insulted by the suspicions leveled against her. And it was all William's fault. No mean feat in less than two miles, but then Alex had never been particularly fond of feeling guilty.

He was more than happy, however, to play knight-errant. And by the time he had actually arrived at the office he was feeling righteously indignant on his fair maiden's behalf and determined to clear her name. In short, he had worked himself into an embarrassing lather.

Only once he'd actually gotten inside and settled himself firmly into a seat—the familiarity of which reminded him that he was the Duke of Rockeforte, damn it, not a green boy demanding satisfaction for some imagined slight—had he been able to calm down enough to, at the very least, *appear* sane.

The meeting had been a success, of sorts. Sophie's good character had been assured. But the larger issue, namely his ridiculous fixation on the girl, still remained.

He needed to step back for a few days, regain some perspective, and more importantly, some of his common sense. He needed to remember who he was. A peer of the realm. A battle-hardened soldier. An agent of the Crown. He was a man, by God, not some lovesick swain who let every pretty thing in skirts tie his mind and body into knots. He needed to—

Alex paused at the corner of Sophie's street. If he took the long way home, it would be simple enough to . . . He swore and turned away, quickening his steps as he made his retreat.

He needed to do *something*. This wasn't healthy.

"Sophie dear, a note was delivered for you from Miss Browning."

She'd had to change her clothes and run an important errand. Now Sophie handed her gloves and bonnet to a waiting maid and took the proffered note from Mrs. Summers. Her former governess had been sitting in the front parlor with the door open, obviously waiting for her return and wanting to have a few words with her charge. She'd nearly bounded out of her chair when Sophie had walked through the door.

Now it seemed she was unable to decide what, exactly, was more important to discuss; the note or that Sophie had been out without a proper escort.

Sophie sincerely hoped it would be the note. She had just been to the solicitor's office, dropping off her own note detailing just how little she had discovered at the Pattons' ball. It had been a depressing errand.

Mrs. Summers lifted her pointed chin to better look down her long nose. "It simply will not do for you to be traipsing about London by yourself, Sophie."

Ah, she should have known. Good manners always came first with Mrs. Summers.

"I know," Sophie responded, "but I thought it best to let you rest, since you haven't been feeling well, and I did take a footman."

"I am perfectly recovered. You should have waited for me or your cousin."

"I might've died of old age waiting for that man. Have you noticed how little he's been about? He's supposed to meet with me today, but. . . ."

"That is not the point."

"Oh, please, Mrs. Summers, let's not argue. I promise to be

more conscientious in the future. Don't you want to know what Miss Browning's note says?"

Mrs. Summers must have realized she wasn't going to get a better concession than the one offered, because she threw up her hands in exasperated defeat—an unladylike and therefore very un-Mrs. Summers-like gesture that surprised Sophie.

London must be good for her, Sophie thought. This new Mrs. Summers was certainly good for Sophie. The woman had been a wonderfully inattentive chaperone at the ball. She hadn't even noticed that her charge had gone missing for over an hour.

"Are you going to open that letter or stare at me all day, which, by the by, is very rude."

"Oh. Right. Sorry. It's just . . . are you sure you're quite well, Mrs. Summers? I mean, you haven't been overtaxing yourself after that head cold, have you?"

"It's very sweet of you to ask, dear, but I assure you, I am fine. Now the letter, please."

Sophie dug a finger under the flap and tore the envelope open.

"You really should use a letter opener, Sophie."

"Probably," she said smiling, "but you seemed in something of a rush. In case you haven't noticed, we're still standing in the foyer."

"Yes, well, as it happens, I am in a bit of a hurry. I'm on my way out. Penny has gone to fetch my cloak and—"

"Out?"

Mrs. Summers never went out. Not alone. Not ever. Now she was going out alone nearly every day.

"Yes, out. I'm going to visit some old friends for the afternoon."

"You have an astounding number of old friends, you know. It's a wonder you haven't beggared yourself with postage. How did you find the time to write so many—?"

"The letter, Sophie."

Sophie gave her companion one more baffled glance before pulling out the note and scanning its contents.

"What does it say, dear?"

"It's a reminder that I am invited for tea."

"Well, that was worth the wait."

Sophie blinked. "Was that sarcasm?"

"Oh look, here's Penny. Would you care to join me, dear? I'm sure the ladies won't mind."

Sophie shook her head mutely. She was feeling a little disoriented.

"Right then." Mrs. Summers looked out the door. "You'll have to use the second carriage since the other is already out front. You don't mind, do you?"

"No."

"Good. Give my regards to Lord Loudor. And bring at least two footmen if you decide to join your friends."

"All right."

"Excellent." Mrs. Summers gave her a quick buss on the cheek, then swung out the door. A moment later it swung back open. "And no stopping for sightseeing, shopping, or errands. You are to go straight to the Thurstons' and come straight back, do you understand?"

Sophie breathed a small sigh of relief. This was the Mrs. Summers she knew. "I understand."

"Good."

Sophie walked into the front parlor and watched from the window as the carriage pulled away. She sighed as it turned a corner and pulled out of sight. She was happy to see Mrs. Summers enjoying herself, but she couldn't help feeling a twinge of disappointment. It was going to be a long, lonely wait for her cousin. He was sure to be late. If he showed at all.

For almost a full two hours, Sophie managed to resist the temptation to rifle through his desk. Considering that he hadn't even bothered to send a note explaining his absence from their scheduled meeting, she felt her restraint was commendable.

She had been waiting patiently in the study since noon, eating, drinking, making mental lists of questions she meant to ask, and finally walking aimlessly about the room. Well, perhaps not entirely aimlessly, her path had taken her around the back side of the desk with a regularity that perhaps exceeded coincidence.

Twice she had even stopped to finger a small cast-iron paperweight. On her fourth pass, when she realized she was inspecting the object to such extent as to move it completely off the pile of papers it was meant to anchor, and was even now letting her eyes scan those papers, she gave up all pretense at casual interest and begin digging through the desk in earnest.

Her search brought up nothing more enlightening than a rather disturbing personal correspondence that Sophie could only imagine was from his mistress, and two locked desk drawers which were, by their very nature, very interesting indeed.

❋ *Eleven* ❋

"*W*hat. Is. This?"

Sophie had never been known for her consistent temperament, but she was quite sure she had never been so angry in her entire life. She was equally certain that her cousin was contemplating that possibility. He was standing in the doorway with his mouth agape, his eyes alternately darting between the papers she was holding and her furious expression.

He started to stutter, then sweat, then swear.

Sophie shot up from her seat behind the desk. "Answer me!" Her fist came down hard on the desk and a nervous footman appeared at the door.

"Er, begging your pardon. Is everything—?"

Loudor seemed to take strength from the appearance of an underling. "Quite all right, man, quite all right." He waved dismissively, but the footman waited for a nod from Sophie before leaving.

Having regained some of his composure, Loudor turned a patronizing expression on his cousin. "Now, Sophie, dear, calm yourself. I can explain everything and you're creating an embarrassing scene."

Sophie resisted the urge to find the heaviest object in reach—the cast-iron paperweight looked like it might do— and toss it squarely at his head. Reminding herself that it might prove difficult to obtain answers from an unconscious man, she drew a deep breath and sat down with rigid composure.

Loudor looked relieved. "That's better, isn't it? No good working yourself up, you'll only make yourself ill."

Of course if she aimed for his knees . . .

"I'm hale and hearty," Sophie bit off, hoping conversation would distract her from her more violent inclinations. "As is my father. So explain to me why I am holding a document that claims otherwise."

Loudor cleared his throat. "I was only doing what I felt was best—"

"For whom?" Sophie demanded. "Not for me, and certainly not for my father! You've stolen from us! How could you? You're family!"

"Now, Sophie—"

"Do *not* patronize me. You've been taking bits and pieces of my father's estate for years. Whittling away our lands and funds with *these*." Sophie waved the handful of paper in the air. "There are eight of them! *Eight!* Eight times you've de-filed my father's character! 'Unstable,'" she cried, slamming one of the papers against the desktop. "'Infirm'!" Another piece followed. "'Unbalanced'!" And another. "'Unsound'!" She threw the rest in his direction with disgust and grabbed another paper from the desk. "And this! A legal marriage to a gentleman of good character by my twenty-fifth birthday or you receive the deed to Whitefield? You're nothing but a common thief!"

Loudor's expression turned dark. If Sophie hadn't been so angry, she might have been frightened, but her vision was significantly skewed by fury.

"Now see here, cousin," Loudor sneered, jabbing his finger in her general direction. "You may call me any name you please, but those transfers are legal and binding. The courts granted me full control over your father's income."

"Through deceit, which I intend to bring to light!"

Loudor snorted and dropped his finger. "You may try, but those documents will hold up in any court of law. They're signed by some of the most respected men of—"

"Who have not laid eyes on my father in over a decade, if they've ever met him at all! They're false witnesses, they have no proof—"

"Ah."

Something about the patently false smile on Loudor's face gave Sophie pause.

"Ah *what?*"

"Proof, my dear girl, proof." Loudor strode over to a brown overstuffed chair and sprawled out comfortably. " 'Fraid I have it. The letters, you see. . . ."

"What letters?" she ground out.

"The letters from the good viscount, your father, of course. Most incoherent, very troubling to his friends and family."

There was thick silence before Sophie realized what Loudor was saying. "You forged letters from my father," she whispered in horrified disbelief.

"Not personally, no. I haven't the talent."

Sophie shook her head. "It doesn't signify," she stated, mostly for her own benefit. "Once my father arrives, they'll only serve as one more piece of evidence of your guilt."

"Do you think so?" He asked in such a pleasant tone that

Sophie found her fingers crawling toward the paperweight of their own volition. His next words, however, stopped her cold. "Awful detailed things, those letters. All kinds of interesting bits about you and your father's daily life in any number of distant lands. Once you work through the nonsensical babble of course. Seems rather unlikely just anyone could have written them. One had to have been there. And it would seem very unlikely that one would forget having written them, unless of course one was a bit touched, don't you think?"

The knot in Sophie's stomach started to burn. "*I* told you about our lives," she whispered, or said, or maybe shouted. She really didn't know because the burning sensation had traveled up to her chest, then throat.

"You were a most dedicated correspondent."

It reached her face, her ears. "You're beyond despicable."

"Thought I made myself clear about the name-calling. Better learn to bite your tongue now, m'dear, unless you'd like to find yourself on the street and your father with you," Loudor said with a nasty smile. "Or he would be, if he weren't half a world away."

In one swift motion Sophie moved around the desk and came to stop before her cousin. Hands clenched at her sides in fists and jaw tensed so tightly she feared cracking a tooth, she managed one word.

"Out."

Loudor's eyebrows rose, but he made no attempt to speak or move.

Sophie raised a shaking finger and pointed clearly at the study doors. "Get. Out."

Still no movement. Taking a step back to keep herself from using her still clenched fist to knock him into action, she took a deep breath and started talking. Slowly and clearly. "Whitefield *still* belongs to my father, and this house will *always* belong to me. It has never been my father's for you to steal. And *you* are no longer welcome here. So stand up and get out."

Loudor looked like he might argue, but Sophie cut him off

before he could start. "If you do not remove yourself from my presence and my house this instant, I will see you thrown out in the street like the very trash you are."

Sophie turned to move toward the bell pull to make good on her threat. Loudor was on his feet and had her wrist in a painful grasp with a speed that surprised her.

She reacted purely on instinct. Grabbing her skirts with her free hand, she pulled them up far enough to allow her right leg to strike out and connect powerfully with Loudor's knee.

He howled and released her arm, collapsing to the floor in an undignified heap. Swiftly stepping back to the desk, Sophie snatched up a letter opener. Keeping the sharp end of her makeshift weapon directed at Loudor, she edged around the room toward the bell pull, taking care to stay out of his reach. For a moment she regretted not having strapped her knives to their usual place above her ankle, but she never imagined she might need to take such precautions in her own home.

She was more than halfway around the room when Loudor raised his eyes to hers and made a move to stand. "You little—"

Sophie tossed the letter opener up and caught it deftly by its tip. Perfect for throwing at his nasty little head. She smiled at the thought and said, "Make no mistake, cousin dear, I can and will use this. Unlike you, I am just full of hidden talents."

Loudor paled and remained seated. She reached the bell cord and yanked. Hard. Two footmen and the butler arrived on the scene so quickly that there was no question that they had been hovering outside the door. She could have just yelled for assistance, Sophie realized, but then she would have forgone the pleasure of kicking Loudor.

"Miss?" All three servants addressed her at once. Sophie's tension eased greatly at the arrival of the men, who, she could not help noticing, had looked to her for direction and completely ignored the felled Loudor.

"I want Lord Loudor, and whatever of his personal possessions he can pack in fifteen minutes, out of this house. He can pay to have the rest sent on. If he gives you any trouble, call a constable."

"Very good, miss."

Sophie gave herself exactly one hour to come up with a viable solution to her problem. The first half hour was spent pacing her bedroom floor, listening to the distant chaos of Loudor being relieved of his residence, and alternating between bouts of sheer fury and utter panic. She was going to lose Whitefield whether she accomplished her mission or not. She was going to lose everything.

Damn. Damn. *Damn* him.

A shout and a large thump interrupted her mental tirade. She stormed to the door, swung it open, and yelled at the top of her lungs, "He's had twenty minutes! Call the constable!" Then she slammed it shut.

Five minutes later the house was silent. Sophie guessed the constable hadn't been necessary after all, since no one came looking for her. Feeling better at just the thought of her cousin's departure, Sophie threw herself into a cushioned chair and began to review her options.

She couldn't let Whitefield go. Not only was it the beloved ancestral home of her childhood, it was the only reliable source of income for her and her father. The work they did overseas with antiquities was a labor of love. They had never managed to turn a profit, and she rather doubted they could. Probably, they could live off the money offered by the Crown if she managed to accomplish her mission, but that was a fairly significant "if." Particularly in light of her recent failures to acquire any useful information from the homes of Patton and Calmaton.

She might take what few funds her family had left—and any money she might earn—and invest it, but neither she nor her father knew anything about business ventures.

Maybe she should use their money to hire a solicitor to stall the transfer of ownership in the courts long enough for her father to make the trip from China.

She groaned and dropped her head to her hands. It would never work. She'd have to get a letter to him first, and then there were the usual arrangements to make—it would take months for him to arrive. She didn't have the funds to hire a decent solicitor for that long. And if it failed, she'd lose what little money they had left.

She sat up and scowled. This was, obviously, a very unfortunate business. Surely something brilliant would turn up to balance things out. But what? And more importantly, when? She couldn't very well sit about and wait for that something to happen. She needed to do something.

She needed . . .

Twenty minutes later she was traveling across town. She'd left a note to Mrs. Summers in Penny's care briefly explaining Loudor's new living arrangements.

She had a plan.

"Sophie, you came!"

Sophie returned Kate's bright smile and followed her into a smaller parlor in the back of the Cole town house.

"Mirabelle and I have decided not to be at home to other visitors today," she explained. "Rather hard to do when all the world can see you through the front windows."

"I would imagine so," Sophie murmured, only half listening. "I apologize for not sending a note in advance—"

"Nonsense," came Mirabelle's voice as she stepped into the room and plopped down on a settee. "You were invited."

Sophie smiled her thanks and took her own seat uneasily. She felt awkward all of a sudden, and nervous. She had never asked for help from anyone before, at least not since she was old enough to dress and feed herself, and certainly never from someone she had known for less than a fortnight. Exactly how long was one supposed to wait before partaking of the full advantages of friendship? And what exactly *were* the full advantages? Asking for money wasn't appropriate, she knew that much at least. And even if it were, Sophie could never bring herself to make such a request. But if one were only seeking advice, of a sort, surely that would be acceptable, wouldn't it? Maybe even appreciated?

"You look distracted, Sophie," Mirabelle commented.

Sophie looked up to find both girls staring at her expectantly. Kate was holding out a cup of tea. Good Lord, someone had already come and gone with the tea service and she hadn't even noticed. She *was* distracted. No, she was more than distracted, she was going mad under the strain. The thought frightened her, enough so that her brain seemed to shut down completely, and without further ado she announced, "I evicted my cousin."

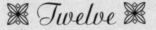

❈ Twelve ❈

Kate dropped the teacup. Which turned out to be a good thing for Sophie. She was too busy righting the mess at her feet to heed the little voice in her head that demanded she kick herself in the shin for her outburst. She handed the empty and somewhat sticky cup back to Kate, who took it without looking. Kate's mouth and eyes were wide open in shock. Mirabelle looked much the same.

"Oh, do say something, please. I—" Sophie started.

"Can you do that?" Mirabelle asked in an awed whisper.

"I can, and I did," Sophie stated resolutely. "And with good reason, I assure you."

"I'm sure," Mirabelle offered sincerely, "but what I meant was, can you evict someone from their own—"

"The town house belongs to me," Sophie interrupted. "It always has."

Mirabelle considered that. "Oh," she finally said, still looking a little dazed. Then she added, "Close your mouth, Kate. You'll catch flies."

Kate's jaw shut with an audible *clack* that made Sophie wince.

"It's a very long story," Sophie explained. "But the long and short of it is, Lord Loudor has been stealing from my father in a positively reprehensible and revoltingly legal manner."

"Well," Mirabelle replied, clearly searching for something, anything, to say. "Well."

As there was nothing intelligent she could add to that, Sophie turned to Kate. "Are you upset with me, Kate?"

Kate shook her head mutely but emphatically.

"Well," Mirabelle said again. "Perhaps it would help if you told us the whole story."

Sophie did just that. Well, not everything, precisely. Prudence dictated she keep the bit about spying for the Prince Regent to herself. But she told them everything else. There didn't seem any reason not to. In fact, it would probably have been wrong to hold back, since she was going to ask for their help. And it felt so very good, as if she were easing a little of the burden onto someone else's shoulders.

"I've gone over all my options," she said, after reciting the day's events, "and I think . . . I know, that the only solution is to marry, and marry quickly. By the terms, the *ridiculous* terms, set out by the courts, if I find a husband before the age of five-and-twenty, Whitefield falls to me."

Mirabelle gave a thoughtful nod of agreement.

Kate, whose stunned expression hadn't changed since she closed her mouth, let out an audible whoosh of air, blinked once, then said, "Well," giving Sophie the impression that the poor girl was several steps behind in the conversation.

"Are you sure you're not cross with me, Kate?"

"Oh, quite," Kate replied earnestly. "I was just a bit stunned that's all. But I'm fine now, really." To prove her point, Kate reached for a clean cup and saucer and poured Sophie another cup of tea. "How can Mira and I help?"

Sophie felt like crying with relief and gratitude. There wasn't so much as a whisper of uncertainty in Kate's voice. She hadn't hesitated a moment before offering assistance. She hadn't even waited for Sophie to ask. And by Mirabelle's expression, Sophie guessed her to be every bit as determined as Kate.

"I know," Kate said, not waiting for Sophie to reply. "We can apply to my mother. She knows everyone, and this is just the sort of project she delights in, matchmaking that is. She'd find you a husband in a trice."

"Perhaps," Sophie mumbled evasively. Lady Thurston was a lovely woman, but Sophie wasn't entirely comfortable involving Kate's mother in her tangle of problems. "I had hoped the two of you might know of some suitable gentlemen."

Mirabelle nodded and stood. "We'll need to make a list," she stated, crossing over to a small writing desk to retrieve paper, ink, and quill. "Best to keep your mother out of this for now, Kate," she said handing the supplies to Sophie and resuming her seat. "I love her dearly, but the woman is a prodigious gossip."

"That's true," Kate admitted. "Very well, whom do we know, or rather whom do you know, Mirabelle? As I'm not out yet and by all rights shouldn't know any gentlemen."

"Thanks to your mother, however, you know of every gentleman within a hundred-mile radius," Mirabelle replied.

"Yes, but I learn the best bits from you and Evie."

"Er, before we start," Sophie began, hoping they were going to start sometime soon, "I think I should mention a few . . . requirements."

Kate and Sophie looked at her expectantly.

"I know beggars can't be choosers, but . . ."

Kate cut her off with a dismissive wave of her hand. "A girl needs to have some standards, of course. What are yours?"

Sophie stalled by clearing her throat. She only had one standard, but it was both demanding and nonnegotiable. "I intend to return to my father at the end of the season, next spring at the very latest. I need a husband who is willing to let me go." She braced herself for their response.

"Oh," Mirabelle replied quietly. Kate said nothing but shot a quick look to Mirabelle.

"I know it's a lot to ask of a new husband," Sophie continued, "but I have the town house and Whitehall as a dowry, and I am the daughter of a viscount."

"It's not that, Sophie," Kate explained. "It's just . . . we had so been looking forward to having you around."

Sophie felt inordinately pleased. "That," she said, "is quite the nicest thing anyone has said to me in a very long time. Thank you."

Kate blushed adorably. "Well," she said affecting a nonchalant air, "I am a very nice person."

Mirabelle snorted. "You spend too much time in Evie's company to be a truly nice person. Now, as much as I'll hate to see you go, Sophie, I'd hate it even more to see you go and Lord Loudor stay in your house. We should start that list."

Kate and Sophie both nodded, but after several minutes of considering, then rejecting, various gentlemen as possible husbands, Sophie began to grow nervous again. Apparently, there weren't many men in a position that would allow their new wife to live on the other side of the world.

"We're going about this all wrong," Mirabelle finally declared. She tapped her finger to her chin in a contemplative gesture. "I think," she said thoughtfully, "that we should limit the list to widowers."

Kate looked delighted. "Oh! That's very clever. But not just any widowers."

"Of course not," Mirabelle returned.

"Only widowers with an heir," Kate clarified.

Mirabelle nodded. "And preferably a spare."

"Naturally."

Sophie help up her hand. "Why would I want . . . ooh, that *is* clever."

A widower already blessed with two sons was far more likely to accept her offer of a marriage in name only. To Sophie's understanding, most *ton* marriages were continued only on paper after the production of heirs. She needed a husband willing to forgo the preliminaries.

"Won't that just further limit the number of suitable candidates?" Sophie asked.

"Actually," Kate said brightly, "I rather think there are more gentlemen with whom one might be willing to marry, provided they stay several thousand miles away, than there are gentlemen whose presence one could tolerate on a daily basis."

Sophie thought so too. "Right. Shall we begin anew then?"

The task proved considerably more challenging than anticipated. After two hours, two pots of tea, and too many biscuits, Sophie's list of eligible bachelors remained depressingly short. She was tired, frustrated, and beginning to entertain the rather unkind notion that England needed more dead wives.

Her guilt was somewhat assuaged when Mirabelle sighed and said, "There aren't enough widowers." Which was really just a more tactful way to say the same thing.

"I wish Evie were here," Kate said.

"Evie?" Sophie inquired. She had heard the name a few times but had always been too interested in the conversation at hand to request an explanation. Now, however, seemed a very good time to ask about a perfect stranger. Anything for a few moments' respite from the topics of traitorous family members and an eventual loveless marriage.

"My cousin," Kate explained. "She lives at Haldon Hall and usually comes to London with us, but she insisted on staying on in the country this year."

"Why? Is she unwell?"

"Well, she's mad to hear my mother tell it, but no," Kate replied, "she's perfectly well. Evie's had four seasons already, and she insists she's not going to marry anyway, so what does one season at Haldon matter?"

"Evie's painfully shy with people she doesn't know well," Mirabelle explained, "and a radical around those she does. She also has a couple of . . . physical reminders of a childhood accident that I suspect she's rather sensitive about. All in all, not a matrimonial prize in the narrow view of society."

"I see," Sophie replied, because she couldn't think of anything else to say.

"But she's very good at this sort of thing," Kate added.

"What sort of thing?"

"Scheming," Kate replied, and with such fondness that Sophie could only assume it was meant as the highest of compliments.

"Oh!" Mirabelle cried suddenly, sitting up straighter in her chair. "That reminds me of something Evie said. Write down Sir Frederick Adams and Mr. Weaver."

Kate looked confused. "Sir Frederick? But he's not a widower."

Mirabelle waved her hand dismissively. "He's perfect, trust me. Put him on the list, Sophie."

Sophie lifted the quill but hesitated. She looked at Kate, then Mirabelle, then back again. It wasn't that she didn't trust Mirabelle, she just didn't know her as well as Kate did. And Kate was looking at Mirabelle as if she'd lost her mind. It would probably be best to err on the side of caution. Sophie was willing to take a few leaps of faith where her new friends were concerned, but they were discussing a potential husband for her, not a new bonnet.

She turned back to Mirabelle. "Why?" she asked, still holding the quill suspended over the paper.

"Why is he perfect, why should you put him on the list, or why should you trust me?"

"The first two."

Mirabelle took a deep breath, carefully considering her

next words. "Sir Frederick," she began slowly, "is the type of man who . . . who eschews the company of women."

"Ohh," Sophie replied in sudden understanding, her eyebrows rising, and her lips retaining the 'oh' position long after the sound was gone.

Kate's lips did the same thing, but her eyebrows went down in befuddlement instead of up. "How's that?" she asked.

Mirabelle and Sophie both shifted a little uncomfortably in their seats. Kate looked to Sophie, who quickly busied herself adding the names to the list. She didn't know Kate all that well either, she reasoned. Surely this sort of enlightenment was best left to an old friend.

Mirabelle grimaced and mumbled something about "Lady Thurston" and "certain banishment" before clearing her throat and forging ahead.

"You see, Kate, some men—and, to my understanding, some women—prefer the company of their own sex."

"I prefer the company of my own sex," Kate argued reasonably. "Quite a lot, actually."

"Yes, but not nearly so much as Sir Frederick," Mirabelle said pointedly.

"And not in an illegal sort of way," Sophie added, thinking that they would be here all day the way Mirabelle kept dancing around the issue, and then finding herself unable to come to the crux of the matter herself.

"Illegal," Kate repeated.

"*Intimately* illegal," Mirabelle hinted.

It took a moment, but eventually the light of realization dawned on Kate's pretty face.

"Ooh." This time her eyebrows went up. "Really?"

Sophie and Kate both nodded.

"And Mr. Weaver?"

"Is Sir Frederick's . . . good friend," Mirabelle answered.

"Well, that's . . . well, I don't know what that is. Interesting I suppose, but what has it to do with Sophie's list?"

"It's simple," Mirabelle replied. "Men like Sir Frederick and Mr. Weaver need to marry to protect their reputations, but like Sophie they need a partner willing to have a marriage in name only."

"That does seem perfect," Kate murmured.

"Doubly so, because they can be blackmailed if they prove unaccommodating," Mirabelle offered with a grin just wicked enough to betray her jest.

"Well, that gives us five names," Sophie remarked looking down at the list. "I don't suppose Evie happened to have mentioned anyone else?"

"No, sorry. But we can ask her at the Cole house party in a few weeks," Mirabelle said. "You'll receive an invitation in the next day or two, I imagine, and this is not such a poor beginning, five names."

"I suppose not," Sophie conceded.

"Now for the rest," Kate stated resolutely.

"The rest of what?" Sophie asked, sincerely confused.

"The rest of the preparations, of course. You'll need to change some of your gowns—"

"I just purchased some new gowns," Sophie replied a little defensively.

"And they're lovely. They really are. Even my mother remarked on them, and she's fanatical about that sort of thing."

Well, that was a little mollifying, Sophie supposed.

"It's true," Mirabelle remarked. "She refers to my wardrobe as the bane of her existence."

"But if you want to bring a man up to scratch in under two months, you're going to need to be a bit more forward," Kate announced.

"I'm not sure—"

"Not scandalously forward," Kate clarified. "You're looking for a husband, not a protector. Just a little more . . . tempting. A few alterations will do."

Sophie turned to Mirabelle for reassurance.

It wasn't forthcoming. "Don't look to me," Mirabelle

replied, sweeping her hand down her decidedly drab gown. "This is Kate's forte."

With all the fittings, the next four days were a bizarre repetition of Sophie's first days in London. With the notable exception of Mrs. Summers' absence. After considerable internal debate, Sophie had decided not to inform her companion of the full extent of Loudor's treachery. Since arriving in London, Mrs. Summers had smiled more, laughed more than Sophie had seen in some time. If Mrs. Summers' gaunt form and rigid posture had been capable of it, there might have been a bounce in her step. Sophie hadn't the heart to dim the light in the woman's eyes any more than was strictly necessary. Added to the desire to see her friend happy was the fear that Mrs. Summers might take it into her head that she was a burden on the family and seek employment elsewhere.

With that terrifying thought in mind, Sophie glossed over the worst of their predicament. She explained that Lord Loudor had been stealing from the estate—not significantly enough to cause immediate worry, but Sophie was now willing to consider the wisdom of making an advantageous match to shore up the family estate. Her companion had taken the news with surprisingly good cheer. Particularly after hearing of her charge's sudden interest in finding a husband. She had even gone so far as to allow Sophie to progress with the matter of altering gowns and whatever else was needed, as she saw fit.

Provided, of course, that Sophie promised to take along her maid and at least two footmen, and remain in the company of Miss Browning and Lady Kate (whose mother was, naturally, an old friend of Mrs. Summers), at all times.

Between shopping excursions, social calls, and brief but intense lessons from Kate in the art of flirting, Sophie barely had time to sleep, let alone dwell on the odd behavior of her chaperone.

Nothing, however, seemed capable of distracting her from thoughts of Alex. Everything seemed to remind her of him, and of the fact that he had neither called on her nor sent word in the five days since they had kissed in the carriage.

After her visit with Mirabelle and Kate, she had wanted to run straight to Alex. Wanted to tell him everything, so he could . . . what? What would he do? Offer her the role of mistress, and the protection that came with it? Admittedly, the idea held some appeal, but it wouldn't guarantee the safety of Whitefield. Moreover, it would break the hearts of the people she loved.

Perhaps he'd offer to help her secure a husband—which would, no matter how irrational she knew it to be, break her own heart.

Perhaps he'd tell all and sundry there was a rift in the family. Really, how well could you know a person after so short a time?

Perhaps he'd mention to Loudor how desperate she'd become. Or perhaps. . . .

Perhaps she needed to keep her mouth closed and forget him entirely.

A round-nosed man in a gray coat and a tall, thin woman in a blue dress sat on a bench in Hyde Park.

They watched as the birds flitted from tree to tree and the occasional squirrel chattered its annoyance at the intrusion. To any passerby, they were an unremarkable couple enjoying the rare appearance of the English sun.

"How are things progressing?" he inquired, lifting his face into the wind, enjoying the way it brushed lightly across his skin.

"I'm not certain," she replied. "They haven't met for several days, as far as I know."

"Hmm."

"Could you be mistaken about him?" she asked.

"I don't think so."

She nodded thoughtfully and turned her attention to her toes. They were covered in the not-quite-yet-soft leather of new boots and peeking out from under the hem of her dress. It had been a long time since she had bought new shoes.

"And you?" he asked, watching her watch her toes.

She looked up. "I don't even know him."

"I meant her," he replied with a small smile.

"Oh." She resumed the inspection of her footwear. "No, she is perfectly suited. I suppose things shall come about. We need only be patient."

"I am not a patient man."

"No, you are not," she chuckled. "If it's any conciliation, there is the most intriguing rumor being circulated."

"And that rumor would be?"

She raised her head to meet his eyes. "It's being said that she is looking for a husband."

By the night of the Forents' ball, Alex was very nearly climbing the walls of his London home. His self-imposed exile had proved a spectacular failure. He'd spent the last few days alternately anxious, bored, and intolerably frustrated. His usual pursuits had done nothing to relieve his mind, and subsequently his body, from thoughts of Sophie.

He had worked on estate business, taken a quick trip to Rockeforte for some fishing, read two books on the history of China (for self-improvement and his own edification, of course), gotten drunk once with Whit and Lord Loudor, once with just Whit, and once entirely by himself.

The first bout of drinking had been all business, with Alex steering the conversation toward the unpopular Prince Regent, the war with Napoleon, and what Loudor made of the whole messy affair. But then Loudor's change of residence had come up. Sophie's cousin had given the excuse of needing more privacy. Alex thought it a weak explanation at best, and so he invited Whit over for a few drinks the next night to discuss the matter. That bout of drinking had resulted in nothing more productive than an endless demonstration of Whit's clever—and vastly amusing to Whit—insights on

Alex's interest in Sophie. This had prompted the final, solitary bout of drinking which, sad to say, had coincided with his perusal of the second book, leaving Alex with the muddled idea that China had somehow once belonged to the French.

He was tired, hung over, and annoyed by the certain knowledge that he would have to reread that book before attempting any sort of conversation on the topic with Sophie.

And he had every intention of speaking with her tonight. And the night after that. And every night thereafter until he was finally sick of her.

He had to have her. There was nothing else for it. He wasn't sure in what capacity he wanted, no *had,* definitely *had* to have her, although in his bed was a certainty. And if it became necessary—and with this thought he gave a long-suffering sigh that some small part of his brain recognized as an affectation—he would marry her.

The idea had some merit, really. He needed to marry sometime, didn't he? He needed to produce an heir. She seemed as likely a candidate for a bride as any. He might even go so far as to say better than most since he truly liked Sophie.

Liked? Hell, he was obsessed with her. Every part of her. Her broad smile, her quick mind, her adorable struggle to reconcile the proper British lady with the world traveler, her complete indifference to his wealth and rank. Of all Sophie's fine qualities, this last was one of his favorites. She made no effort to butter up the Duke of Rockeforte, preferring to match wits with the man rather than the title.

She'd make an excellent duchess, he decided. She was strong, intelligent, and fortunately—because she was going to be *his* duchess—highly desirable.

No simpering, flirting miss, his Sophie.

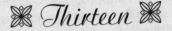

❈ Thirteen ❈

*S*he was simpering and flirting.

From across Lord Forent's ballroom, Alex watched in absolute shock. Sophie was smiling demurely, fluttering her fan seductively, and—dear God, this was the most disturbing part—batting her eyelashes like a well-trained debutante fresh out of the schoolroom.

Worse, she was good at it. There wasn't a man under the age of seventy not taken by her charms.

Not that he could blame them. A good deal of her charms were on display at the moment. Sophie was wearing a concoction of ivory silk designed to attract a man's attention. It turned her thick hair the color of the most decadent of dark chocolates, her eyes the clearest of sapphires, and her skin the richest of creams.

Like her previous gowns, it was relatively unadorned, with only a simple gold ribbon trimming the puff sleeves and hem. Unlike her other gowns, however, it hadn't been cut with an eye for modesty. Oh, it was still well within the bounds of propriety—she hadn't dampened her skirt to make it cling to her legs, or raised the hemline. But the material hugged every curve of her body, and there was an unmistakable extra inch or two of bosom showing. Alex could make out the swell of her breasts and a tantalizing line of cleavage.

He scowled. What he could see, everyone could see. And by the looks of the veritable swarm of eager young men attending upon Sophie, they all liked what they saw.

"You're looking very fierce."

Alex barely turned his head to acknowledge the arrival of a chuckling Whit. How hard could it be to scatter the fops? Surely not that difficult. He could easily manage at least two and probably that would prove sufficient incentive for the rest to flee. His mood lightened considerably.

Of course, there was the slight chance they'd have the sense to join forces. He doubted it, but one never knew for certain, and then what would he do? Alex smiled and turned to Whit. *That,* he figured, was why one had friends.

"Absolutely not," Whit said.

"Do you even know what you're refusing?"

"I haven't the foggiest notion. I know only that you were glaring at them," he indicated the offending group of men, "and then grinning at me." He shook his head. "And it was enough to surmise that no good would come of it. Particularly not for me."

"And that's all that really matters?"

"Yes," Whit responded with good humor.

Alex turned back toward Sophie just as some libertine escorted her to the dance floor.

"Again. Fierce," Whit said.

"Hmph."

"I spoke with her earlier this evening."

"Did you?" Alex snapped his head back toward his friend.

"Easy, good lord, I only wanted to take her measure."

"And?"

"And she reminds me of my sister."

Alex was surprised to hear Whit's assessment in such an ominous tone of voice. "You like Kate," he pointed out.

"I adore the chit. I'd walk over hot coals for her, stand still on them if she asked me to, but she's a hellion and well you know it. She'll be nineteen this winter," Whit continued. "Mother's decided to postpone her debut so Kate can have a year of intensive deportment lessons."

"Does she really think that will help?"

"She must, or she wouldn't be doing it. Mother's just itching to get the lot of us married off. She was bad enough when I came of age, but I'm a son. Poor Kate, Mother's preparing for her first season like they're going into battle. It's quite disturbing, actually."

"Yes, well for Kate's sake, I hope your mother's efforts are met with success."

"I intend to see that they are," Whit said with unusual fervor. "I won't have Kate trampled by the nastier members of society. I won't have her stepped on by anyone, come to that, and I expect your assistance."

"You should expect it. For all that we are not blood relations, you know I still consider Kate a sister."

"And accept the responsibilities that come with such a connection?"

"Of course."

"Good, then we shall be miserable together."

"Splendid."

Alex practically snapped that last word. His irritation with Sophie's admirers was growing by leaps and bounds. He wasn't a jealous man by nature; possessive, yes, but not jealous. If asked what the difference was a month ago, Alex likely wouldn't have been able to answer with any degree of eloquence. That had changed, however, the moment Sophie had teased him about meeting someone else in the Pattons' garden. And she had been teasing, he decided firmly. Not just because Sophie was not the type of girl to make a midnight assignation at a stranger's ball, but because the alternative—that she was *exactly* that kind of girl—was too disturbing to consider.

And that was the difference between feeling possessive and feeling jealous. Fear.

Fear that she might be playing him for a fool. Fear that she would seek the arms of someone unworthy of her. Fear that she might find him lacking. Fear and all the uncomfortable side effects that came with it—anger, suspicion, insecurity.

Alex focused on the anger. He waited until he caught the eye of one unfortunate young man in Sophie's entourage, then gave one very menacing, very ducal shake of his head and began to move in the group's direction.

As he anticipated, the first young man whispered to the not-so-young man next to him and then left. The not-so-young man repeated the procedure with the positively elderly man at his side. By the time Alex crossed the room, only three dawdlers remained. Either they were very brave or very stupid. Alex managed to dispatch them in quick order with a glare, a scowl, and for one stupidly brave lieutenant, an actual growl.

Alex watched him flee with no small amount of satisfaction before turning his attention to Sophie. It was on the tip of his tongue to demand just what in hell she meant by wearing that dress. But upon further consideration, he felt it might be best to ease into that line of questioning. Sophie already looked a little put out with him. And he was interviewing for the role of husband, not chaperone. Speaking of which . . .

"Where is your Mrs. Summers?" he demanded, his voice sounding harsher than he intended.

She scowled at him. No sickly sweet smiles for him, he noticed. Alex wasn't sure if he was pleased by that or not.

"Why did you do that?" she snapped crossly, ignoring his question.

"Do what?"

"Charge over here and chase off my new friends like some great snarling—"

"Orangutan?" he offered.

"Bear," she concluded.

"What a menagerie you seem to think me."

"It's not my fault you behave like an animal every time I see you."

Alex stifled a groan. He'd like to be able to behave like an animal every time he saw her. He caught sight of a young man who looked to be headed in Sophie's direction, and glowered.

The youth veered off toward the refreshment table.

"Stop *doing* that," Sophie hissed.

"I wouldn't have to if your chaperone was where she was supposed to be," he snapped, growing irritated.

"Mrs. Summers is with all the other chaperones, if you're so desperate to find her. Their chaperoning duties being somewhat diminished as their charges are all in clear view of half the *ton*. Besides," she caught sight of the elderly Lord Buckland and gave him an encouraging little smile and wave before continuing, "I'm not doing anything that requires censorship."

Alex followed her line of vision.

"That's it." Taking her by the elbow, he half escorted, half dragged her to the terrace doors.

Sophie resisted only briefly before apparently deciding it wasn't worth the attention it would draw. She smiled pleasantly at the people they passed, but Alex heard her mumble something about chaperones not being forced upon the right people.

Finally they reached the relative privacy of the stone terrace. She dropped her smile at once.

"What do you think you're doing?" she hissed angrily.

"I could ask the same of you," Alex bit off. "This isn't like you, Sophie."

She jerked her arm from his grasp and took a step back. "How would you know? You've known me for less than a month. That hardly makes you a qualified judge of my character."

There was simply no rational argument against that observation. Alex felt in his gut that he did know Sophie, that he understood her—and he made it a point to always trust his gut. But somehow the phrase, *I just know,* no matter how sincerely spoken, seemed unreasonably juvenile. He chose to ignore her words instead. It seemed the next best thing to logic.

"Why are you encouraging those men?" he demanded.

Sophie lifted her eyes heavenward and blew out a long breath. "Because it was enjoyable, Alex," she said as if explaining something to a small child, one who had long, long ago exhausted her patience. "Because it was fun. I was having fun. And now," she said pointedly, "I am not."

Alex forced himself to relax, reminding himself again that he was trying to woo this girl.

"We can fix that easily enough, I imagine." He leaned back against the side of the house and crossed his arms. "What would you like to do?"

"I beg your pardon?"

"What would you like to do?" he repeated. "You expressed a desire to have fun. I am at your disposal. We can dance, if you like."

"My card is full."

"I could fetch you some champagne."

"I'm not thirsty."

"We could sneak into the garden."

"Nor am I stupid."

"That last bit is what I would like to do. In case you were interested."

"I wasn't."

"So make a suggestion, Sophie. Help me along here."

"What I would like," she said, "is to return to my friends."

"Not an option."

"Perhaps you're not clear on the concept of being disposable."

"You'll have more fun with me."

She gaped at him in astonishment. "Do you *realize* how pompous that sounds?" she asked, sounding more amazed than offended.

He merely shrugged. "I've only the vaguest of notions, actually. It's part of being a duke."

"You are really quite unbelievable."

"Thank you."

"That wasn't intended as a compliment."

"A small oversight on your part, I'm sure."

She looked at him curiously. "Do you know, there's a very good chance if your head grows any bigger, there won't be enough room for both of us on the terrace." As the terrace extended the entire length of the house, this was saying something. "I'm a little frightened for you."

"I'm touched. Does this mean you've decided to remain out here with me?"

She shot him a scathing glance and walked over to lean against the far railing. "I believe *you* decided I'd be staying."

"Fortunately, that amounts to the same thing."

"*I'm* deciding how best to go about detaching your enormous head from your body."

Alex smiled and followed her to the rail. "You may try if you like, but by your own account it's too big for you to get your hands around. You'd never be able to get a proper grip."

She struggled to hide a smile. "How bloodthirsty you must think me—"

"Well, if your choice of entertainment is decapitation—"

"—ripping your head off with my bare hands," she continued.

"—I think the description is justified," he finished.

"—and Lord Heransly right inside with a perfectly good saber."

"Sophie."

"I'm sure he wouldn't mind my borrowing it for a few minutes. He was most attentive before you scared him off. Perhaps I'll just pop back inside and see if I can find him."

Alex's amusement had faded, then faded further, then disappeared all together.

"You're not to have anything to do with Heransly."

"And why is that?" she murmured thoughtfully.

"Because I forbid it."

"Hmm," she mumbled, tilting her head assessingly to one side. "Perhaps the swelling process is a delayed one. . . ."

Alex took her chin in his hand and forced her to meet his

eyes. "Listen to me, Sophie. This is not a game. Lord Heransly is not a man to be trifled with. You may have your fun with your new admirers." He nearly choked on the lie. "But keep clear of Heransly. He's a bounder, a rake, and—"

"So are you," she said breathlessly.

"And he's a personal friend of your cousin."

She blinked at that, a shadow fell over her face for a split second before she righted her features into a mask of nonchalance. She reached up and pushed his hand away.

"Why should that matter?" she asked with assumed indifference. "You're a friend of his as well."

"I'm an acquaintance. And you tell me why it should matter. What happened between you and Loudor?"

"Surely you've heard. It's nothing remarkable. He's lived alone for years now and wasn't comfortable with all the commotion caused by two women." She said the words calmly, but failed to meet his gaze.

"One could argue that as your nearest male relative, his comfort should not have taken priority over your safety."

"Oh, Mrs. Summers and I are perfectly safe. We've two dozen servants at least, some of them quite burly."

She *was* safer, Alex thought, with Loudor out of the house, but there was more to it all than a man desiring his space.

"Sophie," he said quietly. "Sophie, look at me."

She looked up a little reluctantly. Alex knew she was hiding something. She seemed nervous, maybe even a little afraid. He wanted to pull her into his arms. He wanted to kiss her lips, her ear, her neck, until the little furrows in her brow eased away. But most of all, he wanted her to trust him.

He reached up and gently grasped a lock of hair that had been strategically left loose to curl seductively down the side of her face. He rubbed the strands between his thumb and forefinger, marveling in the softness, before tucking it behind her ear as if to keep it safe. He pulled his hand back slowly and caressed her cheek and jaw with his thumb.

"I want you to know you can come to me for anything,

Sophie," he whispered. "Anything at all. There is nothing I would deny you."

"I . . ."

"Nothing I would not do for you."

Bewildered, it was Sophie's first instinct to say something coy, something sarcastic. Something that would shore up the wall she had spent the last week building to protect herself against the charming Alex. A wall that had been shaky at best, and now that she stood next to him, felt the heat of his caress, the warmth of his words, crumbled completely.

She had been angry with him for chasing off her suitors tonight, but she had been angrier at herself. She'd been so happy to see him, so relieved to be rid of the company of men who valued a well-practiced giggle over a well-read mind. The charade had grown increasingly depressing with each passing minute. She hated pretending to be something she was not, hated catering to the whims of men she couldn't respect, hated the knowledge that by binding herself to one of them in marriage, she would be giving up the chance of love forever. It was likely she would never know the joys of mutual respect, affection, and desire with her husband.

But perhaps she could know them tonight.

"Walk with me," she whispered.

It was a terrible idea. A dangerous idea. She had a husband to find and Whitefield to save. She needed to make her way into Lord Forent's study, find proof of treason. But she couldn't bring herself to see to those tasks just now.

Whatever it took, she would secure her family's survival. She'd traveled the world, seen more places in a decade than most people would see in their lives. Only one place was home. Only one held memories of a mother and sister she'd adored and lost.

She would give her future to Whitefield. This moment, this small sliver of tonight, would be hers.

Alex took a cursory glance across the interior of the ballroom to make sure they wouldn't be seen. Then he was leading her quickly down the stone steps and into a maze of well-lit paths past rosebushes, and fountains, and hedges, and more rosebushes, until she was completely lost.

Alex brought her to a small gazebo, pulled her behind one vine-covered wall and then into his arms.

For a moment, he simply rested his forehead against hers and held on. Nothing had ever felt so good, so right, as holding Sophie. In the past, holding a woman was merely one of the steps to lovemaking, a sensual act that added pleasure to the occasion.

It was different with Sophie. Her soft form molded against his was much more than a formality to seduction, much more than one step in a sequence of steps needed to reach that ultimate goal. Having Sophie Everton in his arms was an end in itself.

He could feel her every curve, every angle through the fabric of their clothes. He could hear her heart pounding, feel her breath against his neck. He felt the way she relaxed against him and it sent a surge of pride and possessiveness through him.

She was his.

And suddenly it wasn't enough just to hold her. He needed to taste her, to mark her as his own. To leave no question of to whom she belonged.

His lips danced over hers lightly until he felt her yield. Then he slanted his mouth over hers hungrily, teasing her jaw open with his thumb until her lips parted enough to allow his tongue to slip between them. She gasped into his mouth at the new intrusion and his muscles tightened in response.

"So good," he groaned, leaving her mouth to taste her ear, then the side of her neck. He lingered in the tender spot where the base of her neck met her smooth shoulders.

She gasped again and Alex knew that if one of them did not call this to a halt soon, it would go too far. As a gentleman, he should do it. He should set her away from him.

His arms tightened around her instinctively at the thought. A few more minutes he decided, just a few more minutes.

He returned his attention to her mouth, delighting in the little sounds she made, the tentative movements of her tongue against his, the shy exploration of her hands against his back.

Without conscious thought, one hand stole up from her waist to settle lightly against her beautifully displayed breast. Perhaps her new dress had benefits after all. He felt her tense and he expected her to pull away. When she leaned against his hand instead, he knew he had to end it now or it would be too late.

He pulled back from her, a little surprised at how wrong the movement felt. It took every ounce of his willpower not to snatch her back up again. He took a step back just to be safe.

She blinked up at him. "Why did you stop?"

"One of us had to," he said in an equally strained voice.

"Oh," she responded, a bit stupidly she imagined. It took a moment for her to grasp the meaning of his words.

"Oh," she finally said with a great deal more feeling. "Oh, no. How long have we been out here?"

"Not nearly long enough," Alex muttered under his breath.

"Mrs. Summers is sure to be looking for me."

"She shouldn't have let you come out here in the first place," he pointed out. And without the slightest trace of rancor, she noticed.

"She could show up at any minute," Sophie replied, mostly because she felt she owed it to Mrs. Summers.

He caressed the side of her face with one finger. "No doubt you are right. Back to the ball with you then." He wanted to press her about Loudor, but he'd kept her out too long already.

"And you?"

"I shall wait an appropriate amount of time before returning in case someone noticed our absence."

"And then?" Sophie rather hoped he would ask her to dance.

"And then I shall take my leave. A duke is never first to arrive nor last to leave," he explained with a touch of self-mockery. He also needed to put some distance between them before he did something they would both regret. Like tossing her over his shoulder in front of two hundred guests and hauling her into the nearest room with a door.

"I see," she laughed. "Well then. Good-bye."

And with that she leaned up on her tiptoes, gave him a parting peck, and took off for the house at a dead run.

Alex almost called out for her, but swallowed the shout lest they be discovered. He hadn't expected to end things quite like that. He thought a few whispered compliments, maybe an endearment or two were in order. Apparently, Sophie was not the sort of woman who put much stock in sweet words. That was a good thing to know.

He hoped she was a fairly decent liar as well. She hadn't given him time to recommend she straighten her appearance a bit.

She had run off looking thoroughly, adorably rumpled.

Sophie used the terrace doors leading into a small parlor rather than the ones leading to the ballroom, and made her way quickly to the ladies' retiring room. Breathing a sigh of relief at finding the room empty, she sat down heavily on a cushioned stool facing a small mirror.

"Good Lord." She was a mess. She'd avoided the crush in the ballroom because she felt disoriented, flushed, giddy. She thought she'd need only a moment or two to straighten out her thoughts. By the looks of her, she'd need a quarter hour to straighten out everything else.

A blush rose up her neck and spread out to her cheeks as she tidied her hair and thought, in detail, of how it had gotten so out of place.

Alex's hands.

Everywhere. And still somehow not exactly where she needed them.

Alex's strong arms around her, his broad chest against hers, his soft lips moving over her own, his tongue . . .

"No." She glared at image in the mirror. Later. Later she could, and would, revisit that memory. But now she needed to concentrate on finding proof of treason and returning to her chaperon before someone sent out a search party.

She took a fortifying breath and slipped out of the room.

Earlier that night, she'd discovered the study unlocked and slightly ajar, and she'd been sorely tempted to slip inside and be finished with that particular business for the night. But it hadn't taken her long to change her mind. She had no desire to spend the whole of the evening hiding incriminating evidence on her person.

That she would find something incriminating, she was certain. Her last two endeavors had been alternately questionably successful and completely useless. She was due for a change of luck.

She was halfway to the door before realizing the study was occupied. Masculine laughter and the smell of cigars drifted down the hall.

Damn. Damn. Damn.

She'd missed her chance. Scowling, she continued on to the ladies' retiring room for the sake of appearances. She'd just have to wait for another opportunity. And if that didn't happen fast enough, she'd make her own.

❋ *Fourteen* ❋

*T*he next morning, the front hall of Sophie's house was filled with flowers from her admirers.

None of them came from Alex. Sophie told herself it was for the best and settled down to the task of writing thank-you notes, which seemed a pointless endeavor as most of them would be by in person in the next day or two. Even Sir

Frederick had sent along a delightful mixture of tulips and roses.

Sophie laughed softly to herself at the memory of the pained expression on Sir Frederick's face when he'd been forced to play the ardent admirer to keep up appearances. Of all the men on the list, Sir Frederick was her first choice. He'd seemed as annoyed with her silly debutante imitation as she'd been. He'd even tried to engage her in intelligent conversation once or twice. She would have jumped at the chance, but the rest of the men, including Mr. Weaver she couldn't help noticing, had looked at Sir Frederick as if he'd lost his mind. So she'd taken their cue and continued playing the adorable dimwit. She wasn't quite ready to give up her chances with all of them just to impress one. If Sir Frederick didn't come to call in the next few days, she'd simply have to seek him out. If they had an opportunity to form a better acquaintance, she reasoned, it was very possible they could become friends.

Determined to redeem herself in Sir Frederick's eyes, she sent her thank-you note to him first, careful to fill it with what she hoped was some semblance of intelligence and humor. No doubt he viewed his task of courting young ladies in much the same way as did the gentlemen who danced with wallflowers. If it had to be done, best to do so in the least painful manner possible.

Sophie thought over the remainder of candidates on the list. Lord Verant hadn't been in attendance last night, and Mr. Holcomb had danced with her once, then promptly ignored her in favor of an attractive woman closer to his own age. Sophie had briefly considered trying to entice him away, but found she couldn't bring herself to do it. One look at the adoring glance the woman had sent Mr. Holcomb's way, and Sophie had felt disgusted with herself for even contemplating coming between the two of them.

She had panicked a bit at the thought of further shortening her already meager list, but then she'd been introduced to one middle-aged man and one perfectly ancient man who had recently returned from America and the continent respectively. The first had lost his wife several years ago at the birth of his only son. The second was a childless widower, but Sophie figured his age precluded any chance he might expect a wife to give him an heir.

She hadn't any preference for any one of her remaining candidates, although she was disinclined to like Mr. Johnson on the basis that he had spent the majority of his time speaking to her chest. She had the sneaking suspicion he wouldn't be amenable to the idea of her leaving for China. Not alone anyway.

Well she couldn't afford not to give him another chance, she decided resolutely, but she sent his note out last.

England was a beautiful country, Alex decided as he headed on foot toward Sophie's house in the rain. And London was a beautiful town, he thought, sidestepping a suspicious pile on the sidewalk. Mayfield in particular was very nice, he mused, passing the fourth red brick house on that block. In fact, the world in general was a rather fine place, and Alex felt rather fine in it.

All because he had finally kissed Sophie Everton properly.

No laughing this time around, no gagging, no humiliating either of them. It had been damn good. *He* had been damn good, he reflected with purely masculine pride. He'd had her moaning and purring. And sweeter sounds coming from sweeter lips he could not imagine. Of course if memory served, she'd had him gasping and groaning, which meant she'd been damn good too.

They were good together. And that knowledge put an extra spring in his soggy step and had him grinning like an idiot.

Until he saw the carriage.

A black shiny carriage parked outside Sophie's house. A black shiny carriage he knew didn't belong to Sophie.

"Damn."

He took the front steps two at a time and wondered which

one of her admirers he was going to have to frighten off. Scowling, he pounded on the front door. It seemed to take forever to open and when it did he had to fist his hands to keep from shoving aside the elderly butler, charging into the sitting room, and forcefully dragging out whichever swain was in there with Sophie.

He could hear her laughing. Not the nauseating tittering she'd been doing last night, but that genuine soft melodic laughter that made his heart go warm. Or did, when she was laughing with him.

"The Duke of Rockeforte," the butler announced grandly.

Behind him, Alex rolled his eyes. He hated being announced like that. He didn't care for being announced at all, but it was particularly irritating to have one's presence trumpeted to *two* people sitting in a drawing room in the middle of the afternoon.

Remembering there were indeed two people in said drawing room, instead of just the one there ought to be, Alex girded himself for battle, stepped around the butler . . . and stopped.

"Sir Frederick?"

"Rockeforte, good to see you."

Sir Frederick?

Feeling a little disoriented, Alex shook the man's proffered hand.

What the devil was Sir Frederick doing here?

Alex gave himself a sound mental shake. What the devil did he care? The man was no threat. He would even go so far as to say he liked Sir Frederick. He didn't understand him necessarily, but that was beside the point.

He crossed the little parlor and took a seat, a little disappointed at a lost opportunity to thrash a potential rival. Although, in retrospect, that was probably for the best. He doubted that kind of behavior would go over well with Sophie. He glanced at her. She beamed at him.

Ah yes, the world was a fine place indeed.

"Sir Frederick was just telling me about Carleton House,"

Sophie explained, passing Alex a cup of tea. He wasn't thirsty, but she had never served tea for him before, and he found the feminine act oddly pleasant. He took the cup and looked to Sir Frederick.

"I take it you've been?"

Sir Frederick nodded grimly. "Only once, but once was quite enough."

"Is it as bad as all that?" Sophie inquired.

Alex shrugged. "It certainly is . . . elaborate."

"And ever changing," Sir Frederick added. "Prinny has commissioned more alterations than most men demand of their tailors."

"Part of the reason the man is so in debt," Alex said. "And his enormous parties can't help matters."

"Elaborate as well?" Sophie asked.

"The dinner party I attended featured a scantily clad young woman as the table centerpiece," Sir Frederick said by way of answer.

Sophie's eyes grew round. "Why ever would he do that?"

Alex chuckled. "There is little hope in grasping the complexities of Prinny's mind. I suggest you not attempt it."

"Oh." Sophie stifled a nervous laugh. "It's not funny, of course. . . ."

"Of course," Alex agreed, not bothering to hide his own amusement.

"And he is our Prince Regent," Sophie continued.

"God help us," Sir Frederick offered.

"But, and I hope you don't think this terribly unpatriotic of me, but could he . . . that is . . . do you suppose he might take after his father?"

The men laughed outright at that.

She smiled and tried not to squirm in her chair. King George was as mad as a hatter. A sad fact in and of itself, but the idea that the man who promised to pay her a fortune for spying on prominent citizens of London might be unhinged as well was truly disturbing.

"Don't look so frightened, Sophie," Alex chuckled. "We promise not to denounce you for treason."

Sophie shot him a quelling glance for using her given name in front of Sir Frederick. He smiled innocently.

"I don't think Prinny's mad," Sir Frederick said, seemingly oblivious to the silent communication. "Just very, very eccentric and probably not overly bright."

"Actually, he's fairly clever," Alex commented. "But he has an alarming propensity for drowning his best attributes with spirits and laudanum."

Sir Frederick nodded and finished off his tea before standing. "It's time I was going. Thank you for a lovely afternoon, Miss Everton. I hope I may call on you again? Excellent. Rockeforte, pleasure seeing you again."

"Sir Frederick."

Alex waited for him to leave before turning his attention to Sophie. "You look pleased with yourself."

Sophie gave a small smile. She was pleased with herself. Things had gone very well with Sir Frederick.

"Care to tell me why?" Alex inquired casually.

"Not really."

"I expected as much. Come for a walk with me."

"A walk?" She looked out the windows as if confirming something. "It's raining."

"A light misting," he countered.

"It could downpour at any minute."

"Surely not. It's been fairly consistent all day."

"I don't think that's a reliable means of predicting the weather."

"Have you never taken a walk in the rain, Sophie?"

"Yes, I have but. . . ."

"But?"

"But not since I was a child. Not intentionally anyway. Mrs. Summers wouldn't approve."

"Ah, the elusive Mrs. Summers. Where is that extraordinarily lax guardian of your virtue anyway?"

"Out visiting old friends, and mind your tone when you speak of her. I won't tolerate insults."

"You misunderstand, sweetheart."

She blushed at the term of endearment.

"I wouldn't dream of speaking ill against the woman," he continued, rising from his chair. "I adore her negligence. In fact, I'm counting on it."

"What are you doing?"

"Moving closer to you."

"Why?"

"I should think that would be obvious."

"Well, don't."

Alex settled himself next to her and then, before she even realized what he was about, he'd scooped her up onto his lap.

"Alex!" She struggled to get up, but it was a futile effort at best, at worst an embarrassing one. His arms were like bands of rope.

"See now, isn't this better?" Alex wasn't entirely sure it was better. There was something hard poking into his back, and his seat felt as if it were sitting on a pile of rocks.

"Good Lord, what is wrong with this thing?"

"It's old," she snapped. "Go back over there." She stopped trying to push herself up and pointed at his abandoned seat.

"An excellent notion," he replied, sliding an arm beneath her knees.

"By yourself," she clarified.

"And leave you to the mercy of that lumpy old thing? Nonsense. Stop squirming, sweet. I'd hate to drop you. I have my pride, you know."

"I hope you strain your back," she grumbled.

He didn't dignify that with an answer. Instead he sat down with a contented sigh and settled her more comfortably in his lap. "Ah, now this is better. Why haven't you gotten rid of that?" He jerked his chin toward the offending settee.

Because she couldn't afford it. The accounts in her name did not extend to home furnishings.

"Because I like it," she lied, trying to ignore the way one of his hands was playing with her foot. "I believe it belonged to my grandmother."

She believed it *might* have belonged to her grandmother, which was very nearly the same thing.

Alex eyed it dubiously. "Your great-great-grandmother at the very least. And as she would be very, very dead by now, I believe you could dispose of it without injuring her feelings." His hand slipped up to her ankle.

"Alex—"

"I see that you changed the curtains. Very wise." His hand moved up to caress her calf.

She'd found the lighter, considerably less musty set in the attic. "Thank you," she said automatically. "Now please let me go. Someone could walk in."

"They could, but they won't. Not if your butler has anything to say about it. I think he was rather taken with me." His hand slid up just a little.

"He was taken with your title."

"I knew it would come in handy someday," he murmured.

"Mrs. Summers may return."

"You are always saying that, and she never does. I'm beginning to wonder if the woman is a figment of my imagination."

He leaned down to kiss her, but she jerked her head to the side and his lips brushed her cheek instead. He gave a weary sigh. "What is it, Sophie? Last night—"

"We were in a well-concealed gazebo with little chance of being seen."

"Yes, but now—"

"Now we are in my front drawing room where anyone might walk in."

"Perhaps, but it—"

"Will not be repeated, Alex," she said resolutely. "I don't regret last night, not one second of it, but it can't happen again."

"Why the hell not?" he demanded, his hand stilling on her knee.

"Because I said so."

"That is the single most infantile excuse I have ever heard."

"That may be, but if you are a gentleman you will respect my right to use it."

Alex opened his mouth to reply but was cut off by a knock at the front door. With all the interruptions, he was beginning to understand how William had felt that day in the office. He didn't like it one bit.

"Alex, *please.*"

He swore under his breath, but let her slip off his lap. She was across the room and sitting primly on the settee by the time her guest arrived.

As was the habit of all gentlemen, Alex stood whenever a guest entered the room. He didn't actually own the room, but he was feeling rather possessive of the woman who did, and he liked the idea of him and Sophie standing together against a common intruder. He immediately wished he had kept his seat. Lord Heransly didn't warrant common courtesy, even when he wasn't trespassing on Sophie's presence. The man was a vile reprobate—even his parents despaired of him. Rumor had it his father had drastically cut his son's allowance in order to support the young man's growing legion of bastards, and Heransly had complained bitterly over the expense. One night at White's Alex had heard him whisper, "That is why we have poorhouses."

"Lord Heransly." Sophie's tone was pleasant enough, but Alex could detect a hint of dismay in her features. She wasn't too pleased to see the man either. Good.

"Your Grace." Lord Heransly gave a low bow.

Alex barely inclined his head. "I believe Miss Everton greeted you."

Heransly looked taken aback at the rebuke. "Er . . . yes, of course. My apologies, Miss Everton." He bowed again, this time to Sophie. "It is a pleasure to see you, as always."

Alex was sorely tempted to jerk his knee up into Heransly's face. He could always claim an unfortunate tic, the result of an old battle wound, perhaps. He forced himself to relax. This man was a close friend of Loudor's. Alex couldn't afford to beat him senseless.

"What brings you here, Heransly?" Alex strove for, and to his own amazement managed, a friendly sort of tone. He knew exactly what Heransly was after, and he didn't like it.

"I suspect the same thing that brought you here." Heransly gave him a conspiratorial wink that made Alex want to reach out and tear an eyelid off. It was a shame he couldn't blame that on a muscle spasm.

"I'm afraid I've already engaged Miss Everton for—"

"A drive," Sophie said quickly.

Alex shot her an amused glance. "A drive," he allowed.

"In this weather?" Heransly inquired, glancing around Alex to peer at the windows.

Sophie nodded. "Seems silly to wait about for a sunny day," she explained. "Especially in England. I expect Mrs. Summers will be here any minute to chaperone."

"I suppose," Heransly said skeptically.

"I'll just have the carriage brought around." She skirted both men and furniture alike, and went in search of James, the butler. Something about Lord Heransly made her a little edgy, and the way Alex's jaw kept clenching and unclenching made her downright nervous.

Heransly watched her go, looking increasingly confused. "You didn't bring your own carriage, Rockeforte?"

"The drive was a last-minute decision," Alex explained easily. "Won't you have a seat?" Alex relished the chance to play host in Sophie's house. It was almost as effective as an outright crowing of his territorial rights. Sophie and every-thing that came with her was his. The house was his, not that he needed another one; it was the principle of the matter. The chairs were his. Even the dainty little tea set was his. The

ooner Heransly . . . no, the sooner *everyone* understood that,
he better.

It appeared Heransly was already getting the hint. "No,
hank you. If you've engaged Miss Everton for the afternoon,
 suppose I ought to be off."

Alex walked him to the front door.

"It occurs to me that I hold some vowels of yours," Alex
aid as Heransly pulled on his coat and gloves.

"Er . . . yes. Yes, you do."

"I won them from you the very day I first made Miss Ever-
on's acquaintance. Did you know that?"

Heransly tugged at his cravat. "No, I didn't."

"I hadn't given them much thought at all until today. I be-
ieve seeing you here in Miss Everton's company reminded
me of them."

"I see."

"Do you? I suspect that the moment the two of you part
company I shall forget them all over again. It's the oddest
hing. In fact, I'd wager good money I could go months, years
even, without thinking about them, but should I so much as
hear your names spoken in the same sentence . . ." Alex
shrugged and let the sentence finish itself. If Heransly wasn't
clever enough to get the hint, he'd just break the man's nose
and the War Department be damned.

Fortunately, it didn't come to that.

"Fair enough, Rockeforte, fair enough," Heransly chuckled, finishing the last buttons on his coat. "Nothing I don't
deserve. Loudor did try to warn me after all."

"Warn you about what?"

"That you'd staked your claim. Shouldn't have trespassed
on your grounds, but I only half believed the man. Not the
sharpest of tools, now is he?" He gave another wink, and
Alex, though it chafed him badly to do so, smiled.

Perhaps he had just found Loudor's weak link. A confidante
more impressed with a dukedom than loyalty. Alex's title had

come in handy twice today. For once, he was grateful for the *ton* tradition of bootlicking.

"I suspect his mind hasn't encountered a whetstone since he left the schoolroom," he commented. It was a decidedly lame joke, purposefully so. He wanted to test his toad-eating theory. Heransly laughed uproariously.

Perfect.

"Speaking of Miss Everton's cousin, I'd plans to call on him for a drink at White's tonight," Alex lied casually. "But I think I'd prefer the company of a man who shares my taste for beautiful women and fine wit. Interested?"

Alex thought the man might swoon. "I'd be delighted, Your Grace. And about . . . about my vowels . . ."

"Forgotten," Alex said with a dismissive wave of his hand. "Can't blame a man for trying, can I?" Alex punctuated this last remark with two hardy slaps on Heransly's back. And if they were a bit too hardy, well that couldn't be helped.

"Lord Heransly?"

The two men turned at the sound of Sophie's voice.

"Are you leaving so soon?"

Alex hid his smile over that polite inquiry. She didn't appear the least sorry at the idea of him leaving.

"I'm afraid I must," Heransly answered smoothly. He gave her a parting bow, then Alex. "A pleasure, Miss Everton. Your Grace."

Sophie watched him go. "He seems awfully cheerful."

"Did he? I hadn't noticed. Is the carriage coming round then?"

"Hmm? Oh, yes." She heaved a sigh and began pulling on a bonnet. "I suppose I must go now."

"You needn't sound as if you were about to be martyred."

She shot him a glance that said his words weren't far off the mark.

"What did the two of you talk about while I was gone?" Sophie inquired once they were comfortably ensconced inside the carriage.

"Just this and that. Where are we off to?"

She looked at him blankly. "I have no idea."

"You'll have to think of something. This was your idea, re-member? I wanted to go for a walk."

"Well, where were we going to walk to?"

Alex had no idea. "Just around the block."

"That's it?"

"Well, it is raining."

Sophie let her head fall back against the swabs and let out an irritated groan.

Alex took pity on her. "Have you been sightseeing yet?"

She lifted her head. "No actually, I haven't."

Alex grinned and stuck his head out to holler at the driver. And they were off.

❈ *Fifteen* ❈

To keep her reputation intact, Alex took her to places rarely frequented by good society, and a few places they avoided alto-gether. Sophie enjoyed the sights and sounds, and occasionally even the smells, of London, but it was her guide that truly held her enthralled. Alex had a story for every site they vis-ited, his anecdotes so entertaining she frequently forgot to pay attention to the very surroundings in which they were staged.

Over there was the first tavern he and Whit had ever vis-ited. At the ripe age of fifteen, they had managed to become entirely foxed before the hour struck eight, necessitating their removal from the establishment over the backs of two sturdy footmen.

And there was the corner at which a ten-year-old Alex had

accidentally knocked over a fruit vendor's cart in his panic to outrun Lady Willard's nasty little dachshund. That misadventure had ruined his first pair of breeches—of which he'd been exceedingly proud—and had required him to purchase six bags of mashed apples and fourteen lemons.

Sophie listened to the inflections of his voice, the gravelly pitch, the cadence, the ups and downs that were uniquely his. She watched the way he frequently cocked his left eyebrow but never the right. She noticed he tapped one finger on his knee whenever lost in thought, and when he laughed he tilted his chin up. She saw the way hard muscle moved beneath the fabric of his clothes, and how the mere brushing of his arm against hers started a slow traveling burn along her skin. She noticed that his eyes seemed to dart to her mouth every time it happened. She observed every detail about him, and it unnerved her.

She couldn't afford to lose her heart to the Duke of Rockeforte. Never mind that he appeared to be in the habit of seducing women, and that he had never professed any feelings for her beyond simple physical desire. She couldn't risk having her heart distracting her from the necessity of marriage to a suitable gentleman. The task was quite difficult enough without the added complication of unrequited love.

Over the next hour, she made a near heroic effort to emotionally distance herself from the man sitting across from her. And failed miserably. Only she wasn't miserable. She laughed and teased, talked and debated. She felt more relaxed and happier than she'd been in a very long while. Since that seemed unlikely to change during the course of the afternoon, she decided to let be the matter of safe distances and simply enjoy herself.

"Are you hungry?" Alex asked.

"A bit."

"Excellent. I know just the place."

Just the place turned out to be a ramshackle inn and tavern near the docks.

"Are you sure no one who knows us will be here?"

"Absolutely," he replied. "This place is far outside the bounds of the fashionable."

She had no trouble believing that. The large room was crowded with boisterous patrons in serviceable work clothes who spoke loudly and laughed even louder. Several small children darted from table to table with such gleeful abandon that it was impossible to determine which child belonged to which parents. A steady stream of friendly barmaids poured in and out the kitchen doors. To the *ton,* the room would be a study in the uncouth. To Sophie, it was a clean establishment where the majority of the diners were happy, well-fed families. She could think of vastly more respectable dining rooms where the miserable occupants were fed third-rate food prepared by an overpaid, fifth-rate chef.

"You've obviously been here before," she said once they'd taken a table.

"Mr. McLeod was a groom of my father's," Alex explained. "Once, when I was a small boy, I toddled away from my nurse and fell into a fishpond. It was Mr. McLeod who found and pulled me out."

Unnerved, Sophie took a swallow from the mug of ale a server had brought. "He saved your life."

"He did. When my father died, he settled a small sum on the McLeods, and they used it to open this tavern. His wife and daughters have always been gifted cooks."

"Your father must have been a very kind man," Sophie remarked softly.

"And determined," Alex agreed with a fond smile. "He tried rewarding McLeod for his good deed in life, but the man stubbornly refused every offer. Said he hoped someone would do the same for one of his children if need be, even if he couldn't afford a reward. So in his will, my father claimed it was his dying wish—one of many it turned out—to see the McLeods comfortably settled. He was quite poetic about it. I could almost hear him laughing as he wrote it. He was a bit of a trickster, and he knew McLeod could never deny a man his final request."

Sophie started to ask him more about his father, but stopped when a young woman brought a large platter full of a food she had never seen before.

"What are those?"

"Jellied eels," he supplied.

If she had been looking at his face rather than the platter she might have noticed the mischievous glint in his eyes, and hesitated before saying "Oh!" and immediately reaching for one.

Alex couldn't hide his startle. "You like them?"

"I've no idea," she answered truthfully. "I've never had one before."

Alex viewed her enthusiasm with a sense of wonder. It was refreshing to see someone so overtly intent on enjoying life rather than affecting a more fashionable ennui. The world was full of new things to discover, one simply had to look beyond the front door to find them. Sophie, it seemed, understood that.

His thoughtful smile spread to a full-fledged grin as he watched her pop an eel into her mouth, chew for half a second, then blanch. Her chin dropped without her lips separating and Alex got the distinct impression she was attempting to keep the food from coming into contact with as little of her mouth as possible. That, or she was gagging with her mouth closed.

"Here." He reached into his pocket and retrieved a handkerchief, but she shook her head. Then, to his utter astonishment, she squeezed her eyes shut, gripped the edge of the table with her hands and chewed—very, very quickly.

It was the most adorable thing he had ever seen.

She swallowed, gasped, and reached for her mug of ale, downing half the contents before speaking. "That was horrible. Truly horrible," she laughed. "I can't imagine why Mr. Wang carried on so about them during the trip over." Her brow furrowed a bit, and she twisted her lips. "I think he might have been having me on."

"Perhaps," Alex conceded, still chuckling. "Or perhaps he likes them. A great many people do, you know."

She made a disgusted face. "Do you?" she asked with clear disbelief.

"Good Lord, no, they're awful. I just thought you might like to try something new."

"Oh," she said, a little taken back at his thoughtfulness. "I did. I mean, I do. I never pass up the chance to try a new dish." She reached for some bread. She couldn't quite get the taste of eel out of her mouth. She had the bread halfway to her lips before she stopped and added, "Unless it's made with brains. I realize calf brains are a delicacy, but I don't much care for the idea of eating an animal's head."

"Perfectly understandable," he assured her. "Would you care to try something else? Mrs. McLeod would be delighted to introduce you to a few Scottish dishes, I imagine. Ever had haggis?"

After several of said dishes, Sophie commented that such food might be the reason the Scottish were so renowned for their strong builds. Alex looked at the array of dishes still on the table with a dubious eye. "It's sturdy fare, I'll grant."

"More to the point, a person would have to be sturdy to eat this sort of fare on a regular basis and survive."

"I hadn't thought of that. An unusual means of culling the herd, but effective, I warrant."

"Hmm. Pass the bread, would you?"

Alex handed her his share. "You'd be one of the first to go."

"I'm afraid so. I haven't a drop of Scottish blood in me."

"Pity," Alex decided. "They say Scottish lasses are a delightfully fiery lot."

He gave a meaningful glance toward the kitchen where the laughter of the McLeod daughters could be heard over the sound of clinking pots and pans.

Sophie rolled her eyes. She'd met the McLeod women earlier. They were friendly, congenial, and decidedly sturdy.

"Tell me more about your father," she prompted.

Alex looked at her with surprise.

"I'm sorry," she said. "I didn't mean to upset you. If you prefer—"

"Not at all. I'm not upset in the least, and I don't mind speaking of my father. I'll never understand this odd habit people have of pretending the dead never existed."

Sophie nodded in agreement. "It can be difficult, but in some ways it's insulting to their memory not to at least try."

"Your mother and sister were killed in a carriage accident before you left England, weren't they? Is it difficult for you to speak of them?"

She looked up in surprise. "I hadn't realized you knew about my sister."

"I believe Lady Thurston told me," Alex replied smoothly while calling himself a dozen kinds of cad for the lie. "She's an old friend of your Mrs. Summers."

Sophie nodded. "Yes, of course, Mrs. Summers mentioned that."

"Will you tell me of her, and your mother?"

Sophie found that with Alex she could speak of her lost loved ones without feeling overwhelmed. She told him some of her and her twin sister Elizabeth's more ridiculous antics and how they'd tried once, at age eight, to switch identities. They spent an entire day believing they had fooled everyone until one of the upstairs maids pointed out that they had two very different haircuts.

She spoke of the way her mother used to visit the nursery every day to take tea with them and how at night she would crawl into the giant bed Sophie and Elizabeth shared, sit between them, and read stories aloud. When they had outgrown children's books, she brought novels instead, refusing to give up the tradition, and read a chapter each night.

"I miss her terribly," Sophie mused quietly. "But I miss Lizzie more. Do you think that's awful?"

She had never admitted that to anyone. It had always seemed so heartless to grieve for the loss of one family member more than another. But it didn't feel heartless, sitting there with Alex. It felt like the truth.

"I don't think it's awful at all. I think it's perfectly understandable. We expect our parents to pass on before we do, it's the way of nature. But a sibling, and even more so a child, we expect to live as long or longer than ourselves. And then there is the fact that she was your twin. . . ."

Sophie nodded thoughtfully. "With my mother, I lost her laughter and her love. With Lizzie, I feel I lost half of myself."

"I cannot imagine what that must be like," Alex said softly.

Sophie gave him a wry smile. "I think this is why people avoid speaking of the dead. We're becoming maudlin."

"And on such a lovely afternoon too. Did you notice that the sun has come out?"

She had. A beam of light was coming through a nearby window, occasionally catching him in the eye and bringing out shards of gold in the green she hadn't noticed were there before.

"Tell me more about your childhood," Alex prompted.

They spent the remainder of the afternoon speaking of their families, their friends. They spoke of their past and shared their dreams of the future. They drifted idly from topic to topic, by no means consigning themselves to the distressing themes of death and loss. They laughed a great deal and argued good-naturedly a little, and when Sophie took the time to stop and think about it, she realized she was, in that particular moment, truly happy.

The sun was beginning to set by the time one of the McLeod women cleared away the last of their plates. Sophie would have liked to remain there well into the night, sipping her ale and enjoying Alex's company, but she knew she could not. Mrs. Summers was sure to be near to the vapors by now, and Sophie had no idea how well lit the streets in that part of London might be or if the moon would be out. She wanted to be home before the city became well and truly dark.

Alex sent someone round for their carriage, paid for their meal, and escorted her to the door.

"Your Grace!"

They turned to find Mr. McLeod calling to Alex from the kitchen door. "Your Grace, a moment. If you don't mind overmuch, Molly's made a fresh batch of biscuits for you and the lass to be taking with you."

"Molly is his wife," Alex explained with a barely concealed smile. He'd felt Sophie tense at his side at the woman's name. He was a small man for it, but that sign of jealousy made him feel like crowing. He liked that she felt territorial.

"I'll wait in the carriage," Sophie said, clearly relieved. "Go say your good-byes, and do give the McLeods my thanks and compliments. Everything was wonderful."

Alex took a quick look out the front door to assure himself the carriage was already across the street, then followed Mr. McLeod into the kitchens.

Sophie made it halfway across the street before she felt the hand come down on her shoulder. Whirling around, she found herself facing a thickset man with a barrel chest and squashed face, and a considerably weedier man with black hair that fell in greasy lengths around his pinched face. Both looked strong, smelled foul, and were obviously drunk. The larger man's hand slid from her shoulder to grip her upper arm.

"Ey now, li'l bird. Where you flyin' off to so fast?"

His accomplice tottered out from behind him to loom over her like a vulture. Sophie had to keep from screwing up her face at the overpowering odor of unwashed body and cheap gin. She'd come across men like this before in her travels. Any reaction beyond cool disdain was an open invitation for trouble.

She looked dispassionately at the foreign hand on her arm, then let her eyes travel up to fix the man with a cool stare.

"Release me."

The men both guffawed with such similarity one could only assume they were related.

"Unhand her!"

All three turned to see her driver hop down from his box with whip in hand.

Her assailants were surprisingly agile for drunk men. Before Sophie could react, the larger man pulled her arm behind her back and covered her mouth with his free hand. The thinner man raised his arm to ward off the whiplash. After the first strike he caught the weapon in his hand and wrenched it free from the driver, then reared back and plowed his fist into the man's face.

Sophie could only assume her driver had gone down. Her attacker was forcibly dragging her into a deserted alleyway, and as he pulled her into a shadowed recess, she lost sight of her would-be rescuer.

The big man released her arm and spun her around to pin her back against the wall. Sophie immediately used the opening to lash out with her fists, catching him in the nose. He emitted a staccato yelp of pain, but didn't let her go, just shoved her harder against the brick and began pawing at her skirts. She struck out again and again, using every trick she knew, pummeling him with her fists and feet. For a moment she thought she might gain her freedom, or at least enough of it to retrieve the knife strapped to her leg, but then a second pair of hands was there, holding her arms at her sides.

"Bitch is feisty, eh?"

"Shu'up and 'old 'er then."

Sophie filled her lungs with air, intending to let out an ear-piercing scream, but the sound of a furious bellow from behind the men cut her off. In a heartbeat both men were gone from her, leaving her to lean breathless and shaking against the wall.

Alex felled the thinner man with a single blow to the head. The second man circled him warily. Having sized up his opponent and finding himself lacking, the drunk tried soothing Alex with an explanation. "Just a bit o' fun, what guv? Didn't know the bird was spoke for, out all alone as she were."

Alex didn't look ready to be soothed. He looked ready to kill. In one quick lunge he brought the man to the ground and straddled him, savagely driving his fists into his face and chest.

Sophie wasn't a forgiving enough soul to feel the least bit sorry that Alex had hurt the two men. She'd have done the same, if she'd been able. But she couldn't let him beat the man to death. If for no other reason than she didn't want to be responsible for the taking of a life.

"Alex! Alex, stop! You'll kill him!"

He paused midpunch to look at her. Had she not already been standing against a wall, she would have taken a step back. He looked half wild. His breath was coming in pants, his mouth set in a snarl, and his eyes had narrowed to angry green slits. Sophie looked to the opening of the alleyway and noticed a small group of people had gathered there.

"Fetch McLeod," she instructed before turning her attention back to Alex. "Alex—"

"He shouldn't have touched you!" he roared, and she pressed her back tighter against the wall.

"No, he shouldn't have," she said in her most placating voice, "but—"

He punched the man again.

"Alex! Please, you're frightening me."

"Get in the carriage!"

"No."

"Now!"

"No!" she yelled, amazed at her own courage. "Not without you."

He glared at her but didn't loosen his hold on the man's collar. She tried a different tactic. "Alex, please. I want to go home."

He looked down at the prostrate man and then back to her

again, uncertain. Sophie opened her mouth to speak, but stopped when Mrs. McLeod stepped forward and rested her hand lightly on Alex's shoulder. "You've done well, Your Grace. It's time to see to the lass."

Alex stared at the hand on his shoulder, then followed the arm with his gaze until it reached the woman's face. Sophie didn't know what he saw there, but whatever it was, she would be eternally grateful for it. Alex seemed to come back to himself. He stood, dropping the man's head to the pavement with a gruesome thud.

"McLeod!"

"Right here, Your Grace."

"See to this trash."

"Aye. Move aside now, Molly, and let His Grace stand up. You there . . . !"

As quickly as the crowd had formed, it dispersed. Someone grabbed the unconscious men and began to drag them off. To where, Sophie didn't care. Her attention was riveted on Alex.

❈ *Sixteen* ❈

*A*lex didn't say a word, just took Sophie's elbow in a firm grip and led her toward the waiting carriage. She sneaked a sideways glance at his profile. He looked furious.

He assisted her in, then exchanged a few curt words with the bruised, but otherwise uninjured, driver before climbing in after her.

Did he blame her for what happened? The thought felt like a knife to her chest.

Alex raised one fist to pound sharply on the ceiling to start the carriage rolling. The sound made her flinch. And then snap.

"I didn't do anything wrong!" she exclaimed in shaky voice. And then, to her shock, and absolute mortification, she began to cry. She wasn't a weeper, as a general rule. And she'd certainly been through more traumatic experiences in the past than what had just occurred. Nonetheless, she could feel the tears begin to leak from the corner of her eyes and couldn't hide the catch in her breath.

Alex reached for her at the sound. Before she knew it, she was settled on his lap, her head tucked neatly against his shoulder and his arms wound tightly around her.

"Hush, sweetheart. Hush. This wasn't your fault."

"You're angry," she accused between sniffles.

He tightened his arms around her. "Not at you, Sophie."

"You're mad at something," she pointed out.

"I'm furious with those men."

"Yes, but they're not in this carriage and—"

"And I'm mad at myself," he finally acknowledged.

Sophie tried to sit up to see his face, but he gently pressed her head back. "Just relax now. You've had a scare."

"I'm much better, really," she insisted but leaned against him all the same. "Why are you mad at yourself?"

Alex hesitated before he answered, and when he finally spoke his voice was rough with emotion. "I should never have let this happen."

"It wasn't your fault either, Alex."

"I should have walked you safely to the carriage."

"That's absurd," she declared. "It was only across the street."

She felt him shake his head, his chin rubbing a scratchy trail across her forehead. "It doesn't matter how close it was, it was my duty to see you safely there. I failed in that."

A long silence followed in which Sophie gave thought to what he had said and what she might say to make things right again. Finally, she decided on, "Hmm."

Alex pulled her up by the shoulders to look at her. "What does that mean, 'hmm'?"

"Oh, nothing," she responded offhandedly. "I just realized this is one of those silly masculine things."

Alex rewarded her impertinence with a small smile. "I don't think you're allowed to use the words 'silly' and 'masculine' in the same sentence."

"Really? How odd I've only just now heard of this rule."

"Well, you have been out of the country for a while."

"Hmm."

Alex moved to settle her back against him.

"Alex, I'm much recovered, please let me go."

"Not quite yet."

"Now," she insisted.

He only partially relented, allowing her to remain sitting upright but refusing to let her off his lap. "I can't understand this sudden aversion you have—"

"It's not an aversion," she interrupted. "It's a matter of employing a little common sense and good judgment."

"Fine, stop wiggling, sweetheart. I can't understand this sudden interest in proper decorum. You were perfectly willing to forgo such nuances last night."

"That was last night."

"I am trying to understand what has changed between last night and this evening. Have I done something to upset you?"

"No! No, it isn't that. Truly, I just . . . We can't . . ." She heaved a frustrated sigh and gave up. "We just can't."

"Again, I don't understand."

"And I can't explain it to you. I just need you to respect my wishes in this."

Alex picked her up and reluctantly placed her on the seat across from him. "If this is a game you're playing, Sophie," he whispered, "I'm warning you now, you won't like it when I win."

Sophie scowled at him. "I'm not playing a game with you. You needn't become insulting."

"Isn't that what you're doing with all your suitors—Sir Frederick, Lord Verant, and their ilk—playing them for fools?" he asked with a trace of venom.

"I most certainly am not!" She knew he was annoyed by her rejection and was lashing out in reaction, but that didn't make his remarks any less cutting.

She wasn't playing with those gentlemen; she had very specific plans where they were concerned. Perhaps plotting and scheming were no more honorable than indulging in a game, but the final results were certainly different. She wasn't trying to break their hearts or bilk them out of a fortune. She intended to make one of them into a respectable husband. It was a time-honored pursuit amongst unmarried women, and she refused to feel guilty about it. Or, at least, she refused to let Alex make her feel worse about it than she already did. He was wealthy, titled, and a man. The entire world was at his fingertips. He was in no position to judge what she did to survive.

She crossed her arms and stared out the window, pointedly ignoring him.

She heard him grumble to himself. Then shift in his seat. Then grumble some more. "I apologize if you felt insulted."

"But you're not sorry for the actual insulting," she scoffed, turning her head to glare at him.

His forehead furrowed in a combination of frustration and confusion. "I fail to see the difference."

"You just apologized to me for the way I felt, not for what you said. There is a world of difference, I assure you. Your version of an apology implies that you are in no way responsible for my feelings."

"I am not interested in arguing semantics with you, Sophie."

"That's another evasion. And should you be interested, wars are fought over semantics."

"I am not at war with you. This is a disagreement, not a battle. *And* I apologize for insulting you."

He looked like he wanted to add a sarcastic little "happy

now?" to the end of that apology, but to his credit, he held his tongue.

"Thank you," she replied sincerely, albeit a little primly. "Forgiven."

"And forgotten?"

"Not yet. I'm not sure I've milked it for all it's worth," she said with a small teasing smile.

Alex accepted her overture of reconciliation with a smile of his own.

They rode a while in thoughtful silence. Sophie thought of all the ways she could shore up that wall she envisioned earlier between her and Alex.

Alex thought of all the ways he could bring down that wall Sophie seemed so intent on erecting between them.

They were nearly to her house when he suddenly transferred to the seat beside her and took her hand in his. "I will respect your wishes as you asked, Sophie. However, I ask that you respect mine as well."

She narrowed her eyes suspiciously. "And what might those be?"

"You retain the right to rebuff my advances as you see fit, and I retain the right to make them whenever I can."

She made a face of patent disbelief. "The two are hardly compatible."

"But doubtless the combination will prove entertaining."

"I don't think—"

"You needn't worry. I'll not embarrass either of us by acting like one of your lovesick swains . . . hauling cartloads of flowers to your door and the like. I merely wish for us to spend some time together—go driving in the park, dance at the balls, visit some museums, that sort of thing."

"I'm still not sure . . ."

"You needn't worry I'll scare off your beaux, either," he stated impatiently. "The attentions of a duke will only increase your appeal, not diminish it."

She hadn't thought of that. A little healthy competition

might be just the thing to speed things along. Unfortunately, there was the small problem of Alex's possessive tendencies.

"That might be true in the case of some dukes. You, however, tend to behave rather, shall we say, territorially?"

Alex grimaced, then sighed in the manner of one much put upon. "I hereby vow not to frighten off any young gentlemen—"

"Or old."

He shot her a look of annoyance. ". . . not to frighten off *any* gentlemen who should choose to further their acquaintance with you, unless specifically asked to do so by yourself, or in the event that you are in immediate danger of harm."

"Physical harm," she amended. "I wouldn't care for you to use that particular loophole every time I look like I might possibly be a little exasperated."

"Good Lord, you are a natural-born barrister."

"Yes, becoming a barrister was my second choice after ambassador. Sadly, both professions remain elusive to me. Now, finish the promise, if you please."

Alex groaned but capitulated. "I promise not to frighten off any gentlemen who should choose to further their acquaintance with you unless specifically asked to do so by yourself, or in the event that you are in immediate danger of physical harm," he recited dutifully.

She nodded along, then added, "Or serious social harm. I suppose that would be all right as well."

"I'm not repeating that ridiculous promise again."

"Of course not, it's not as if you won't be finding every possible excuse to get around it already. I simply meant that, should you choose to save me from social ruin, I won't hold it against you."

"How thoughtful," he drawled. "You are a veritable fount of generosity," he said wryly. In reality, he was already plotting ways around his impromptu vow. He still thought the old battle-wound tic had merit.

"I certainly try," she returned pertly.

"Are we agreed then? Shall we respect each other's wishes in this matter?"

"I'll agree to spend some time with you, Alex. It's not exactly a chore, is it? But I don't promise to spend all my time with you."

"Of course not," he replied, mentally scratching the idea of working around his promise by keeping her too busy for it to become an issue.

"Then I agree to the arrangement."

"Excellent. I suggest we seal the pact with—"

"A handshake?" she offered helpfully.

His gaze tracked down to her lips. "I was thinking of something a bit more binding."

"A handshake is customary, I believe."

"But hardly in the spirit of our little contract."

"I think this argument might be in the spirit of our little contract," she grumbled.

He couldn't argue with that, so he ignored it. "I was thinking more along the lines of—"

"A blood oath?" she tried.

"What? No, a kiss. Where do you get these ideas?" he asked in bemusement.

"I believe I am allowed to rebuff your advances as I see fit."

"You'd prefer a bloodletting over kissing me?"

"Well, it needn't be a large cut," she pointed out reasonably. "A minor pinprick would suffice. I have a hat pin in my reticule that will do nicely."

Sophie reached into her bag and retrieved an implement that looked, to Alex at any rate, more like a lethal weapon than a clothing accessory. She waved it in front of him with a flourish.

"Here we are."

He dropped her hand. "You have succeeded in ruining the moment."

"What a pity."

"Round one goes to you," he said without rancor.

"I thought you said we weren't battling."

"As you're brandishing a dagger, I'll own myself wrong."

"Well if we're to spend any time together, you'll have to get used to it."

"The hat pin?"

"No, being wrong, as you will invariably be whenever we argue."

"I am duly warned. Put the pin away, Sophie."

She eyed him assessingly. "I'm not certain that's a good idea just yet."

"Perhaps not, but we're about to arrive at your front door."

"Oh!" She replaced the hat pin in her reticule and began making futile attempts to straighten her disheveled appearance. "Thank you for everything, Alex," she said sincerely, if a bit distractedly.

"It was my pleasure. Shall I see you tomorrow then?"

"I don't know," she replied, slapping at the dirt on her skirts. "I may have other plans."

"What a flatterer you are."

She crammed her mostly crushed bonnet atop her head and tied the ribbons in a limp bow beneath her chin. "How do I look?"

Bedraggled, wrinkled, dirty, mussed and heart-wrenchingly beautiful.

Alex took her face in his hands and kissed her. He didn't have time for anything more than a brief but passionate pressing of his lips to hers. But it was enough to heat his blood and render her breathless. He nipped her bottom lip playfully, then kissed her gently on the brow.

"I thought you said I had ruined the moment," she whispered.

"You had," he replied, "but only for a moment."

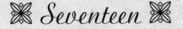

❋ Seventeen ❋

$\mathcal{S}$ophie sighed and stared listlessly out the parlor window. For the last week she had attended every dinner, soiree, picnic, ball, and musicale that had promised even the smallest chance of interaction with one of her "Listed Gentlemen," as Kate and Mirabelle had taken to calling her matrimonial candidates. To the delight of her suitors, she had diligently played the role of adorable twit at each event. And at each event she grew increasingly tired and disheartened by the charade.

Prior to coming to London, Sophie had participated in less than a dozen social occasions in her life, and she had been excited by the prospect of everything a season in London had to offer. But not like this.

She had never wanted to be an actual debutante. She just wanted to *see* them.

Now that she'd had the opportunity to do both, she was more than ready to move on to more pleasant endeavors. Thanks to her cousin, however, moving on wasn't an option. She had to continue to act the insipid miss and catch a suitable husband. The trouble was, the more ardent her suitors became, the less confident she felt about her plan to marry one of them.

She didn't want to be the wife of a man who thought all women were just pretty keepsakes to be bought or won. She felt guilty for deceiving them about who she really was, saddened by the realization that she would forever lose any chance of having a real husband and family. And she was overwhelmingly depressed by the certainty that she would never, ever, even if she lived to be a widow, feel as happy and free in the company of a man as she did in Alex's.

Of course, she'd had precious little opportunity to challenge that certainty. She'd caught only glimpses of him since they'd struck their odd little deal in her carriage last week. A peek from across a ballroom before he'd disappeared with her cousin into the card room, a distant view of him in Hyde Park riding alongside Lord Thurston and Lord Calmaton.

She'd have thought he'd forgotten her entirely, a notion that brought both relief and terror, but two nights ago she'd settled into a seat at the opera, trying very hard not to think of the last time she had been there, with Alex, when she'd felt the hair on the nape of her neck stand on end. She turned her head and there he was, ignoring the small crowd of people in his box and just . . . looking at her. She'd felt herself blush and he'd sent her a smile that was no smile at all. It was a long, slow, wicked grin. And it sent her blood racing. She wanted his arms around her again, his lips against her mouth, at her throat, his hands roaming, taking. She wanted the feel of him, the smell of him, the taste of him.

She ached, quite simply ached, with wanting him.

And it wouldn't do.

"Why the long face, miss?"

Licking dry lips, Sophie glanced up to see Penny setting a tray of refreshments on a side table. The young girl had been exceedingly helpful since Sophie took over the town house. Penny knew everything about the staff. Who did what, who worked best with whom, who should never be in the same room with whom. She'd even found James, the butler, after the first butler had opted to leave with Lord Loudor. She'd make an excellent housekeeper one day. If Sophie had the resources, she would have given the maid a well-earned raise by now.

"It's nothing, Penny. I'm just not used to all this rain, I suppose."

"It is dreary, isn't it?" Penny remarked, taking a quick glance out the window. "I find it helps to spend some time in the garden now and again, to remind me of all the good rain does. Think of the lovely blooms you'll have, miss."

"You're right, Penny. The flowers will be lovely. Thank you for cheering me up." The thought of a colorful garden wasn't really sufficient to improve Sophie's mood, but it seemed unkind to say so.

"Why did you need cheering?" asked a male voice from the doorway. Sophie jumped, hoped fervently her reaction hadn't been noticed, and turned in time to see Alex enter the room and claim a seat. He was immediately followed by Sophie's butler, looking harried but determined.

"The Duke of Rockeforte!" James announced breathlessly.

"Yes, thank you, James."

"I wish he'd stop doing that," Alex grumbled as the man took his bow and left.

In an effort to appear mildly amused rather than suprised and imprudently delighted at his sudden appearance, she pasted on a smirk. "You tried to outrun him, didn't you?"

"Yes, and an undignified spectacle it was too, racing past your manservant like a twelve-year-old boy."

"I could have told you it wouldn't work," Sophie informed him. "I specifically instructed him to announce your arrival regardless of the fuss you might make. I've noticed how much you enjoy extra attention."

Alex just snorted.

Penny did an admirable job of smothering a giggle. "Will you be needing anything else, miss?"

"Thank you, no. You may take the rest of the day for yourself if you like, I won't be going out tonight."

"Thank you, miss."

Sophie watched her maid depart, then turned a critical eye to her guest. True to his word, Alex hadn't brought flowers, candy, or poetry. Sick to death of the vapid conversation she'd been forced to endure with other gentlemen, Sophie was forced to admit she would have welcomed Alex today with open arms if he had come bearing a basket full of poisonous asps. She was that desperate for a respite from her exhausting charade, and Alex provided the first chance she'd had for one in days.

Kate had left for Haldon Hall, her family's country estate, to assist her mother with the final preparations before their house party, and Mirabelle had reluctantly gone to her uncle's for a short visit. Sir Frederick's company had allowed for some measure of relief, but he seemed rather preoccupied with personal matters of his own and made only sporadic appearances at events. It seemed terribly unfair that the one gentleman on the list she actually liked was the one she saw the least.

"You're woolgathering, Sophie."

"Hmm? Oh, so I was."

"You haven't answered my earlier question. Why did you require cheering?"

He asked the question lightly, but she noticed the careful way he studied her face. She kept her voice and expression shuttered.

"Just the weather," she remarked with a dismissive wave of her hand.

"You're lying."

She looked at him in surprise. "Why would you say that?"

"If I told you how I know, you'd take more care in the future and I'd lose that particular advantage, wouldn't I?"

"I believe I was inquiring as to *why* you thought you knew I was lying, not *how* you knew I was lying, which would imply that I actually *was* lying." And if that tangled mess of words didn't distract him from his original query, she rather thought nothing would.

"I've no interest in deciphering that, let alone responding to it. Just answer the original question, if you please. Why did you require cheering?"

Damn. She should have known that tactic wouldn't work

on him. She tried not saying anything at all, but Alex quickly filled the silence.

"You're not going out tonight," Alex murmured thoughtfully. "You're not ill, are you?"

"No, I'm not ill. I'm just tired. Am I not allowed to have a bad day?"

"Of course you are. I'm just curious as to why today receives that particular distinction."

Sophie slumped in her chair. She simply could not think of a way to answer him without lying.

"Did something happen this morning?" he asked. "I ran into your Mrs. Summers in the park this morning. She mentioned you had a pleasant time last night . . . said you looked happy."

She hadn't been happy last night. She just hadn't been miserable, at least not until the very end. She'd attended a large dinner party at Mr. and Mrs. Granville's Mayfield home. The only affair of the week that had not claimed a single one of her suitors as a guest. That alone had made the dinner more pleasant than most.

She'd accepted the invitation because Mr. Granville was on her *other* list—the one of possible traitors given her by Mr. Smith. She'd enjoyed an evening of good food, and surprisingly good company considering the host was a possible Napoleon sympathizer. And, once again, she had done her duty by sneaking about his house and slipping into his study while the ladies went to the drawing room and the gentlemen stayed in the dining room to enjoy their port. And once again, she had come up empty-handed.

To make matters worse, she'd returned to an animated discussion about the Duke of Rockeforte and Lord Thurston. Both of whom, it seemed, had been recently heard at White's making a solemn pledge to remain unmarried until the age of forty. Lord Loudor had acted as witness.

The evening had lost a good deal of its charm after that.

No matter that she'd known all along that Alex wasn't wooing her as one does a wife, to hear his intentions so plainly spelled out pinched at her heart. She could have done with the illusion that the idea of marriage to her had at least crossed his mind.

In the parlor, Alex continued to speak in spite of her obvious reticence. "Last night aside, I haven't personally seen you truly enjoying yourself at a single event you've attended."

"Not every event I've attended included you."

"True," he replied. But most of them had; she simply wasn't aware of it. He'd wanted to give her some degree of space. A chance to come to him for help with whatever was eating at her. And, he could acknowledge to himself, a chance to miss him, just a little. "But I've been present at a few, and at every one you made certain to surround yourself with the same group of men with whom you have nothing in common. I'm willing to wager that has something to do with your current dissatisfaction."

"Alex, we've been over this."

"But I've yet to receive a satisfactory explanation for your behavior. You evade, you equivocate, and you lie. I want to know why." He leaned forward in his chair and leveled a hard look at her. "Why are you so determined to encourage the attentions of men you don't care for?"

"They're only white lies," she grumbled. "And I only make them when you press me for information I'm not ready to give." She didn't bother denying his correct assessment of her feelings toward the Listed Gentlemen, not when he could so easily tell when she was lying. She studied his face a moment, and in her mind's eye she saw herself confiding in him, heard him offer his help . . . as a protector, or worse, as a matchmaker. Her stomach rolled at the thought, and she sat up straighter, lifted her chin.

"That's an evasion," Alex pointed out.

"It happens to be the truth. I'm not discussing this with you,

Alex. You can either accept that and we can move on to far more agreeable topics, or you can leave, but I've no intention of squandering the rest of my afternoon arguing with you."

Alex deliberately took his time deciding, and Sophie barely refrained from squirming in her seat, or worse, admitting to her bluff. Even fighting with Alex was preferable to sitting alone in the house with no distraction from her troubles.

Alex stared at her a moment longer, then relaxed once again. "Very well."

"Very well, you will abide by my wishes and stay, or very well, you will abide by my wishes and leave?"

Alex smiled at her little jab. "The former. So come, you offered agreeable conversation. Let's have it then."

Sophie nearly closed her eyes in relief. Now she could spend the rest of the day sitting here with Alex discussing everything from politics to fashion. He wouldn't speak down to her or temper the choice of topics. He'd ask her opinion, listen carefully to what she said, and almost certainly disagree with her. But rather than give her a patronizing pat on the hand and an equally patronizing smile, he'd debate the subject with her as an equal. She adored their verbal sparring, even when she suspected he was being difficult on purpose. Alex might see her as a pretty keepsake to be won, but at least he regarded her as a pretty keepsake with an active mind.

They were in the midst of a perfectly enjoyable debate regarding the likelihood of a war with the Americans when he stood and said, "We'll have to continue this another day. I must be going."

"What? But you just got here." Good Lord, she hoped that didn't sound quite as pathetic as she thought it did.

"It's coming on five," Alex said checking the wall clock. "I've been here near two and a half hours."

"But I thought . . ."

"What did you think?" he asked sincerely, smoothing his coat and straightening his cravat.

That he would stay for dinner, she thought. That he would convince her to go out tonight after all, just the two of them, unless a proper chaperone was required.

"That you would stay longer," she said instead, hoping to salvage what little pride her overeager mouth had left her.

"Why, Miss Everton, will you miss me?"

Sophie snorted by way of answer.

"I don't suppose that translates to 'yes, dreadfully,' in any of those languages you know?"

"I'm afraid not."

"Pity." He walked over to give her a chaste peck on the forehead. "If you were willing to beg, I might be willing to stay. Now, I shall have to keep my other appointment."

"With my cousin?"

Alex appeared not to hear the censure in her voice. "No actually, I have business with his friend Lord Heransly."

The earl's son? The one he had warned her about?

"I'll see you at Haldon," he said.

"Not before?" So much for her pride, but the house party was still several days away, and—

"Certain you aren't willing to beg?"

She gave him a sarcastic little sneer, then added, "That was in English as well, in case you were wondering."

Alex just laughed, took two quick strides, and kissed her hard and fast before she could argue. He pulled back and stared at her for a moment, brushed a thumb along her bottom lip. "Lord, I love your mouth."

By the time Sophie had gathered wit enough for a response, he was gone.

The next day, she received a note from Alex.

Dear Sophie,
Should you find yourself in need of my assistance on some matter, please do not hesitate to send immediate word to my country estate. The address can be found below.

Yours,
Alex
P.S. *I promise not to make you beg.*

She kept it on her nightstand.

A stocky, middle-aged man sat, brandy in hand, in one of London's quieter taverns. Across from him sat a much shorter gentleman whose exotic features, and tastes in spirits, marked him as a foreigner.

"This is quite an undertaking," the shorter man commented. "Are you sure it will work?"

"As sure as anyone could be, I suppose. It's been given a great deal of forethought and planning."

"We are still relying heavily on luck."

"It was my understanding the girl has an abundance of luck," the stocky man replied.

"Both good and bad, same as the rest of us."

"Perhaps, but some of the situations she has found herself in—"

"Have been primarily of her own making. The girl is headstrong and rash."

The stocky man smiled and tapped his over-large nose. "Which makes her perfect for the job."

"Yes, but we've still to see if she'll accept it."

"I believe she will. By all accounts she's enjoying herself immensely."

"That she is, the little hoyden." The shorter man smiled and stood. "I'll be leaving for Wales for a few days. She'll be attending the Coles' house party, and I suspect she'll be safe enough there without my following her."

"She's safe enough anywhere."

The shorter man shook his head and tossed a few coins on the table. "As I said—headstrong and rash. The girl needs watching."

❊ Eighteen ❊

The Cole house party was considered by many to be the high point of the season. The widowed Lady Thurston, or her son rather, spared no expense on the affair. Every year, the enormous house was packed to the rafters with people eager to enjoy the entertainments Haldon Hall offered—two weeks of the finest meals, some of the best hunting grounds in England, and opening, mid, and closing balls.

Lady Thurston had confided to Sophie that as much as she enjoyed entertaining, she would rather have a usual house party, with fewer guests and just one ball. But her husband had started the tradition years ago, and now she felt obligated to keep it.

Haldon Hall was a massive manor that seemed to ramble for miles. The original structure was built when the first Cole was granted the title of baronet some three hundred years ago. From the looks of the house, Sophie guessed that every ensuing generation had made an addition to the home, and it was clear they varied wildly in their tastes. The effect was disorienting.

She got lost in the maze of corridors twice before making it to dinner the first night. An unsettling notion for a girl who prided herself on her sense of direction (a skill she'd honed in the jungle). When she finally managed to locate the front staircase, it was only to find Alex waiting for her at the bottom of the steps wearing a knowing smile.

"You'll get used to it," he guessed.

"I beg your pardon?" she asked innocently. She wasn't

comfortable with the idea that he knew her well enough to know she'd gotten lost. So her room was nowhere near this particular staircase. How did he know she hadn't just been exploring? She was even less comfortable with the almost overwhelming desire to just . . . touch him. Everywhere. Lord, he was handsome, and she hadn't seen him for days.

"You needn't beg mine," he returned smoothly. "Lady Thurston, however, has been in quite a dither about her lost guest. You're twenty minutes late for dinner."

"Damn." Sophie picked up her skirts and hurried down the stairs, deciding now wasn't the time to worry about wiping that smug smile from Alex's face.

Alex took her hand and tucked it into the crook of his arm. "I'll give you a tour after dinner if you like."

"That won't be necessary, thank you."

"I could show you all my favorite spots," he argued pleasantly.

"All of them dimly lit and well concealed, I imagine."

"I'll do my best to make them your favorites too," he whispered as they entered the dining room.

"Also unnecessary," she whispered back, before taking her seat.

Lady Thurston wasn't the least put out by Sophie's tardiness. She was too busy sending servants to search for the six other missing guests. Apparently, getting lost in Haldon Hall was also something of a tradition.

The dinner was an elaborate affair, with dish after dish of foods Sophie had never tried before . . . lobster, oysters, escargot. Unfortunately, she was unable to enjoy much of it. Lady Thurston had seated her between Lord Verant and Mr. Johnson, both "Listed Gentlemen" and both exceedingly dull dinner companions. It took all her energy to maintain a conversation and appear suitably silly in the process.

Farther up the table, Alex viewed his plate dispassionately. He loved oysters, but watching Sophie flirt shamelessly with her two companions turned his stomach.

Enough was enough, he decided. He'd shown the patience of Job these last few weeks, stifling every instinct that screamed at him to set himself between Sophie and her admirers and yell, "Mine!" Maybe even thumping his chest once or twice. Certainly, he'd wanted to thump their chests a few times, and what he ached to do with her chest didn't bear pondering in public.

And all for what? A few stolen kisses. As lovely as those had been, Alex wanted more. He wanted all of her. Her time and attention. Her affection. And he didn't want to share.

He watched her giggle at something Lord Verant said. Oh, he'd been patient all right. He deserved a bloody sainthood.

"Do stop glowering, Alex dear. People will think there's something wrong with the food."

Alex gave his hostess an apologetic smile. "The food is wonderful. I'm afraid I was lost in thought."

"Yes," Lady Thurston replied nonchalantly. "She is a lovely girl. And such an eye for fashion."

Alex prudently kept his mouth shut and found a renewed interest in shellfish.

Something had to be done.

The next night featured the opening ball that signaled the official start of the party. Sophie stood with Mirabelle and the newly introduced Evie Cole a little way from the dance floor. Poor Kate had been left behind in her room. Not yet officially out, she would have to settle for a detailed account of the ball from her friends.

Sophie found Evie fascinating. She was shorter and a good deal more curvaceous than the other two girls, with light brown hair and a face that Sophie thought was rather pretty despite the thin scar that ran from her temple to her jaw.

There was a shy wariness about her at first, and she was given to the occasional stutter. But after a time, Evie began to relax. And as Mirabelle related the story of how Sophie had tossed out her own cousin, Evie grew more and more animated, revealing a woman of clever mind and sharp tongue. It was, to Sophie's mind, a considerable transformation of appearances.

Their conversation lulled as Alex and Whit approached. As always, Alex was splendidly turned out in his formal attire, opting for black when some of the young gentlemen were sporting waistcoat colors that bordered on outrageous, putting Sophie to mind of overgrown flightless parrots.

The usual round of greetings followed, strictly adhering to tradition and the rules of etiquette, until Whit turned to Mirabelle and, in a surprisingly cool tone, said, "Imp."

Sophie watched as Mirabelle's normally luminous eyes slowly narrowed into angry little slits before she dropped a quick and careless curtsy.

"Cretin." There was a wealth of feeling in Mirabelle's greeting, and none of it pleasant.

Whit returned her glare with a cocky grin. "Suppose I shouldn't be surprised to find you here. Lord knows you're never anywhere else."

Mirabelle pasted on a coy smile and opened her eyes wide in mock distress. "Oh dear, you're displeased with my attendance tonight, aren't you? Well, this *is* your home so if you'll excuse me, I'll just say my good-byes to your mother and be on my way."

"Mirabelle," Whit growled.

"She did issue the invitation after all and I would be remiss in not giving her a full and detailed explanation for my early departure. What would you like me to tell her, Whit? Shall I just mention that you asked me to leave?"

"Don't you dare."

"No? Well, that you turned me out then? Sent me packing?"

"Mirabelle—"

"Really, you are entirely too difficult to please. Tossed me out on my ear, strenuously encouraged my immediate absence?"

"If you even *think*—"

"Booted, exiled, or otherwise uninvited me? Come now, Whit, don't look so frightened, it's most unmasculine of you. Surely your mother will acquiesce to your wishes. You *are* the man of the house are you not?"

"*That* is enough."

"Yes. I rather think it will do," she replied jauntily. "Now, if you'll excuse me, it's far past time for me to pay my respects to the hostess." Mirabelle left with what could really only be called a smirk and a swagger.

Sophie rather felt Mirabelle deserved her victory. Whit had been decidedly rude. At the moment he was watching Mirabelle with some trepidation. "She wouldn't."

Alex barely managed to speak through his stifled laughter. "She does seem to be headed in that direction."

They all watched Mirabelle make her way efficiently through the crowd. When she reached Lady Thurston, a strangled sound issued from Whit's throat and he set off toward the two women without a backward glance.

Alex laughed at the sight.

"Mirabelle won't really—" Sophie began.

"No, she won't," Evie replied. "She loves Lady Thurston like a mother and wouldn't upset her for the world, certainly not just to spite Whit. She just wanted to make him squirm."

"I'd say she succeeded rather nicely," Sophie commented.

"Yes, she did," Evie agreed. "She manages to best Whit on a fairly regular basis. It bothers him no end, and amuses the rest of us even further. If you'll excuse me, I had better make certain they stay clear of each other for a while."

Sophie waited until Evie left, then turned to Alex. "Is there a particular reason those two are so angry with each other to-night?"

"Not just tonight, Sophie, *every* night, and every day between those nights. They've never gotten along."

"Really? Why ever not? She's best friends with his sister

and cousin, and his mother likes her. *I* like her. What's not to like about her?"

"Don't work yourself into a snit. I like her too. Just don't ask Whit for a list of her faults, it's bound to prove extensive."

"And imagined," Sophie scoffed.

"Now, to be fair, Mirabelle gives as good as she gets."

"Perhaps," she allowed. "It seems odd, though, that they shouldn't get on together."

"Not so unbelievable if you know the story behind it."

"Do you know the story behind it?" she asked.

"Of course, everyone does. It's no secret."

Sophie thought about that for a moment. "Well, then we wouldn't *really* be gossiping about our friends if you told me, would we?"

Alex gave her a winning smile and Sophie's heart lurched in reaction. She really, really needed to get a hold of herself. Or at least learn to keep her eyes trained on the floor.

Alex chuckled. "You really are an original, and a higher compliment I cannot think to pay."

"Oh, well . . . thank you then," Sophie mumbled, feeling awkward and a little letdown. She could certainly think of a few compliments she'd rather hear from him.

Alex took her arm gently. "You're quite welcome. Come, are you thirsty? I'll procure us some champagne, we'll have a seat out on the terrace, and I'll regale you with all the sordid details of Whit and Mirabelle's story. How does that sound?"

"If you're sure they wouldn't be upset."

Alex led them to the refreshment table and handed her a flute. "I promise you they won't mind at all. In fact, both would be more than happy to relate, at length, every nuance of that fateful afternoon, but their views are decidedly skewed. You require an objective narrator."

"You."

"Oh, yes. I was *there*, you see."

"I feel as if we're about to discuss the details of some horrid crime to which you were witness," she said as he took her arm and led her outside.

"The players in this particular drama would probably agree with that description, but really it was not so very bad. They're just too stubborn to admit it. Ah, this should do."

The terrace was large and well lit with a few people sitting or walking about. He led her to a relatively secluded bench at the far end that afforded them a degree of privacy.

He took a drink of champagne and cleared his throat dramatically.

"The theatrics are unnecessary," she laughed.

"Yes, most pleasures are. Now behave, I'm trying to begin an epic tale here. It requires a certain degree of concentration."

"Yes, of course, terribly sorry."

"Quite all right. . . . Where was I?"

"You hadn't yet begun."

"Ah, yes. It was the summer of . . . well, I don't remember what year it was, but Whit and I were seventeen and here at Haldon Hall on holiday from Eton."

"That would be 1798."

"Beg your pardon?"

"You were seventeen then, and you're one-and-thirty now, so the year was 1798."

"Right. Yes, 1798 it is, or was, rather. Whit and I were home on holiday and Lady Thurston was having a house party. Quite a few people attended, including a very lovely young woman by the name of Sarah Wilheim. She was about our age, perhaps a year or two younger and an absolute angel to behold. Glorious locks of golden spun hair, eyes the color of the sky, and a bosom a man could—"

"I quite understand, Alex. She was attractive." She scowled at him.

He winked.

Her heart lurched again.

"She was a vision," Alex continued. "And Whit fell for her like a rock. As it happens, Mirabelle's guardian, her uncle,

lives but two miles from Haldon Hall and she was more often here than not, as is still the case. That summer she was
just a tiny mite of a girl—couldn't have been more than
eleven."

"Ten, and Kate would have been seven."

"Excellent. May I continue?"

"Please do."

"The girls were ten and seven, and forever following us
about the estate."

"How sweet."

"The sweetness was lost on us at the time. We were seventeen if you recall and quite puffed up with self-importance as
only boys on the verge of manhood can be."

Sophie took mental exception to the use of "only" in that
statement, but wisely held her tongue.

"One fine afternoon, a small group of us decided to picnic
down by the lake. It had been an unusually hot spring and the
water had turned rather green and murky, but Whit insisted
on securing the lovely Miss Wilheim for a row on the water.
And she did indeed look lovely, all peaches and cream in a
fetching little ensemble with matching bonnet and—"

"Alex."

"Right. Well, Kate and Mirabelle took it to mind to go out
on the lake as well. They stole off with the only other boat—"

"Borrowed."

"Fine. They *borrowed* the remaining boat and in less than
five minutes managed to ram the vessel straight into the unsuspecting Whit and lovely Miss Wilheim."

"Oh, dear."

"Quite. A tremendous to-do followed. Whit, besotted fool
that he was, had been so occupied gazing at his future bride
that he hadn't noticed the girls' approach, nor had he the prudence to keep a firm grip on the oars. He lost them both in
the collision. And while I'm sure he would have been perfectly
happy to spend the rest of the day, and certainly the night,
trapped with Miss Wilheim in a small boat, he was sensible

enough to realize that the young lady would undoubtedly feel differently about the matter. So, in an attempt to take control of the situation, he demanded that the girls turn over their oars, so that he might row his guest to shore and then return to collect the children."

"Seems reasonable."

"Not to a pair of frightened little girls. They were utterly terrified of Whit's wrath, and he was visibly upset at the time. They were certain he would abandon them in the lake as revenge for the accident. They refused to turn over the oars."

"That can't have soothed his temper."

"Indeed it did not. He started in on Kate immediately, berating her for her already legendary clumsiness. It was terribly unfair of him, as each girl had an oar and was equally responsible, but that fact was lost on him at the time, and he chastised her until the poor chit started crying. Mirabelle has always been uncommonly protective of Kate and she simply would not abide Whit's behavior. She stood up, oar in hand, and positively roasted Whit. The girl's always had a tongue like a rapier, for all that she generally keeps it in check. By the time she was through, Whit's ears were exceedingly red at the tips."

Alex chuckled at the memory. "Poor Whit. Reduced to shamefaced silence by a mere slip of a girl. He was mortified, furious, and he acted on instinct, reaching over and grabbing Mirabelle's oar."

"Oh, no."

"Precisely what Mirabelle said with an added 'you don't' at the end. She had an impressive grip for a ten-year-old, and she pulled that oar back with every shred of strength she owned. Whit came right along with it."

"Oh, heavens," Sophie laughed.

"It gets better. He wasn't fully standing, and as he went over his knees caught on the side of the boat." Alex demonstrated Whit's unfortunate predicament with a brief pantomime of his hands. "The girls screamed. Miss Wilheim screamed. Hell, Whit may very well have screamed, but he was already half submerged, so we'll never know."

"Oh, dear Lord!" Sophie was laughing hard enough to draw attention to herself, but she didn't care.

"And *that* is precisely what the lovely Miss Wilheim screamed. Right before she was tossed headfirst into the water."

"How awful." She was barely able to get the words out between fits of giggles.

"I found it rather amusing from my standpoint on shore."

"I'm certain you did. Whatever happened?"

"Well, the girls beat a hasty retreat to the far shore and disappeared into the house. Whit was forced to assist the now considerably less lovely Miss Wilheim to shore. Fortunately, the water only came up to her chin so she was never in any real danger. But they did look a sight, covered in green. And she rather like a disembodied head, complete with bonnet of course, bobbing in the water like a cork."

Sophie felt tears of mirth on her cheeks. "The poor thing. Was she very angry?"

"She and her mother packed up and left that very afternoon."

"Really? That's a bit unforgiving. I suppose Whit blames Mirabelle for the loss of his one true love."

"He did, for a few months, until it finally reached his ears that the girl was a vain and spiteful little thing. But there was still the matter of his damaged pride, and by the time the two hotheads calmed down enough to realize the absurdity of the situation, more than enough cruel words had passed between them to render the rift unbreachable. They've continued on in the same fashion ever since, tolerating each other's company, and barely that, for the sake of mutual loved ones."

"Hmm," Sophie murmured. "Seems to me Whit should have thanked Mirabelle for saving him from a disastrous union."

"He might someday, if she ever gets around to apologizing for tossing him into the lake."

"She never did?"

"No, she insists it was nothing more than he deserved for behaving so poorly to Kate."

"I see. It's a shame they're both so stubborn."

"Stubborn, I believe, is far too tame a word for the pair. Unfathomably mule-headed suits better, I think."

"That's more than one word."

"In this particular case, more than one is required. I stand by them."

Sophie frowned in thought. "It's odd," she mused, "that I've never heard so much as a hint of this before."

Alex shrugged. "It's a rather long tale."

She shook her head. "I meant their general feelings toward each other. I've spent a good deal of time in Kate and Mirabelle's company since coming to London. Naturally, Whit has been a topic of conversation on more than one occasion, and I've never heard Mirabelle say anything un-kind or—"

"Just Whit?" Alex asked.

"I'm sorry?"

"Is Whit the only *natural* topic of conversation?"

"Don't be absurd, we discuss a great many things."

Alex's eyebrows went up expectantly.

"Including you," Sophie finally admitted with a roll of her eyes. "But we are not discussing you right now—"

"Oh, but we should. I'm a great deal more interesting."

"You're a great deal more *something*," Sophie replied.

"Handsome?" he offered with a grin. "Dangerous?" he guessed, leaning toward her. "Irresistible?" he very nearly purred.

Sophie leaned away from him, her eyes darting frantically about the terrace. "Alex—"

"Don't worry," he whispered. "They've all gone in."

And with that rather unromantic, but nonetheless thought-ful reassurance, he took her chin in his hand and kissed her softly, his lips gentle and undemanding. Sophie felt his free hand snake around her waist to press the lightest of touches on the small of her back. She melted into him, the world around her disappearing.

There was only Alex. She felt only his hands, heard only his whispered breath, tasted only his mouth upon her own.

Too soon he pulled back, and she felt her body involuntarily follow his retreating form. She wanted more, so much more. He chuckled softly against her lips and she opened her eyes. Good Lord, she had gone from leaning a considerable ways back to practically sitting in his lap. She sat back and gave him an embarrassed smile.

"I should go," she said, mostly to fill the silence.

"Come with me," he urged.

"Where?"

"Someplace more private."

Sophie pulled away, the haze in her mind instantly clearing. If he needed someplace more private than a spot suitable for heated kissing, then he wanted to do more than just kiss.

"We've been out here too long already," she told him. "And I promised Lord Verant the first waltz."

Alex's visage darkened immediately. "What are you hiding from me?"

Sophie stood to leave. She couldn't deny his accusation, nor was she ready yet to explain her behavior.

Alex grabbed her wrist before she could make a single step toward the door. He stood and yanked her closer to him in a single fluid movement.

"Enough," he growled. "You're mine, Sophie, not Mr. Johnson's, not Lord Verant's, and God knows not Sir Frederick's. I have allowed you your fun, but no more. No more games, Sophie, and no more secrets. Do you understand?"

"It is not a game," she whispered through dry lips.

"Then tell me what it is," he snapped.

She wanted to. She wanted to tell him everything and then cry in his arms. She no longer feared his betrayal, but . . .

What if he tried to talk her out of it? Her determination

was unreliable at best these days. If he convinced her to forgo her plan in favor of a liaison with him, she'd likely be ruined—along with her father, Mrs. Summers, and Mr. Wang.

And what if his intentions were honorable? Certainly he hadn't been courting her in the traditional sense of the word, but he'd always taken pains to see that her reputation remained intact. What if he offered to marry her? She didn't think it particularly likely, but her heart did a funny little dance at the thought.

Then her joy immediately plummeted. There was every reason to believe she might be falling in love with Alex. And the more time she spent in his company, the likelier it became. Not the usual *tendre* preferred by the *ton,* and not the puppy love Kate felt for Lord Martin, but real love. True love. And what were the odds of finding true love? Dear God, what sort of calamity would she have to face to even out the good fortune of finding love? It was a terrifying thought.

In the end, her hesitation answered for her.

Alex dropped her hand. "When you are ready to explain your behavior, we will talk. Until that time, I'd prefer we keep separate company." He spoke in a cool voice that shot little darts of pain into her chest. "I suggest you think carefully on what you stand to lose, Sophie. And I suggest you do so quickly. My patience is nearing an end."

With that final warning, Alex gifted her with a stiff bow and left.

❉ Nineteen ❉

She spent the remainder of that night and all of the following day and night in her room, pleading a headache. She had attempted to allot herself only two hours for wallowing in sorrow, but for the first time in her life, her emotions refused to abide by her schedule. She'd fallen asleep that first night crying and woken with swollen eyes and a heavy weight determinately lodged in her chest.

She'd skipped breakfast and tried concentrating on her plans to save Whitefield, but that only resulted in another bout of weeping. Eventually, she gave up trying and returned to her bed, resolved to do better the next day.

She didn't feel particularly better then either. She'd awoken in the small hours of the morning, and after another cry decided she would enlist Evie's aid tomorrow at tea in fortifying her list. Then, before the week was out, she would pick one of the gentlemen, become engaged, and immediately tell Alex everything. She wouldn't need to wait until the announcement. Once she had a verbal commitment, Alex could neither offer his assistance nor convince her to go back on her word.

She had fallen back asleep wondering if Alex would forgive her, and what it might mean if he did. What sort of relationship could they have once she belonged to another man? She could never stray from her marriage vows, even in a union of convenience. But would that keep her safe from love? Her sleep proved fitful.

Morning dawned bright and clear, something Sophie was inclined to take as a personal affront in her current mood. The men went off to hunt, leaving the women behind to entertain themselves as they would. Sophie arranged a ladies' tea for her three friends that afternoon and gave the rest of the morning over to composing a letter to her father.

The girls met in a small second-floor parlor where they were unlikely to be disturbed. Evie was immediately filled in on Sophie's plans to marry and they had just begun casting out new names for consideration when the parlor door opened and a slightly mischievous-looking Whit entered the room.

"Good afternoon, ladies," he chimed jovially. "Imp."

"Whit!" Kate exclaimed, not looking entirely pleased to see him. "What are you doing here? I thought you'd gone hunting with the others."

"I stayed behind to assist Mother with some last-minute preparations for the next ball. Thought I might spare a moment to share a cup of tea with the ladies . . . and the imp."

"I caught that the first time," Mirabelle grumbled.

"The thing is, Whit," Kate began uneasily, "the thing is, this is a *ladies'* tea."

"Is it?" he asked innocently. "Well, I'll just drink mine quickly and be out of your hair then. Are those fresh biscuits?"

"Er . . . yes," Kate reached hesitantly for another cup.

Mirabelle turned to face Whit as he took the empty seat next to her. "I believe what your sister is trying to say—"

"I know what she was trying to say," Whit snapped. "Unlike some, I realize when I am not welcome."

Kate and Evie groaned. Sophie watched the pair trade insults in horrified fascination.

"And you still want to stay? I'd hate to see the great and mighty Lord Thurston lower himself to my level," Mirabelle drawled.

He took a bite of biscuit. "I thought there might be something in it I've been missing, like the pleasure of annoying someone. And don't concern yourself about my stooping too far, I couldn't invade your level with a shovel and pickax."

"You really are an ass, Whit. It's a wonder people still let you believe you're a gentleman."

"It is my gentlemanly nature that has kept me from killing you these dozen years or more. If I were any less a gentleman, or if you were a man, I'd have called you out by now."

"And if you were a man, I'd have accepted."

Sophie did her best to hide her amusement. Evie didn't bother. She laughed and raised her glass to Mirabelle in a salute. Kate managed to stifle her laughter well enough to issue a reprimand. "If you can't get along, then you'll just have to leave, Whit."

"Me?" Whit cried indignantly. "Why me? What about her?"

"She was invited," Kate answered primly.

"I was invited," Mirabelle repeated, just to be smug.

Sophie couldn't blame her.

"What about Alex?" Evie inquired out of nowhere.

Sophie choked. A small spray of biscuit sprayed from her mouth and landed on her lap. "Sorry," she choked out, wiping desperately at her skirts and glancing up with mortification to find Whit smiling serenely. "Sorry."

"And that, Kate, is why one does not talk with one's mouth full," Mirabelle stated succinctly.

"Sorry," Sophie said yet again. "But you surprised me. Alex isn't . . . that is, he doesn't meet my requirements."

"What requirements?" Whit inquired.

He was roundly ignored.

"True, but the way he looks at you . . ." Kate sighed.

"How does he look at me?"

"*What* requirements?" Whit repeated.

"As if he'd like nothing better than to drag you off into the nearest linen closet and ravage you," Kate explained with gleeful enthusiasm.

"For God's sake, Kate! You shouldn't even know about such

things, let alone talk about them," Whit admonished. "And what bloody requirements?"

"If you don't care for the conversation, Whit, you can leave," Kate answered haughtily.

Whit growled something about "bloody torrid novels" but otherwise kept his peace.

"He does seem fond of your company, Sophie," Evie offered. "I realize he has something of a rake's reputation, but it's talk mostly. He's a good man."

"He's friends with my cousin," she groused. *And at the moment he isn't speaking to me,* she silently added.

Whit shifted in his chair.

Mirabelle took a sip of tea and said, "It's not uncommon for a gentleman to be friendly with the family of a young lady he's courting. Even when he doesn't care for them."

Sophie wasn't sure if what she and Alex had been doing could be considered courting, but she couldn't very well say that with Whit in the room.

"And Kate's right," Mirabelle continued. "He does seem fairly eager to be in your company."

"Eager," Whit commented, "is too mild a word. He chases her around like some half-crazed lunatic."

"I think, by definition, a lunatic is fully crazy," Mirabelle stated.

Whit answered with what could only be described as a snarl.

"That's it," Kate announced. "I believe you're finished with your tea, brother mine."

"Actually, I've still more than half—"

"You're done."

Whit sighed and set down his cup. "If you weren't my only sister, I would strangle you in your sleep and blame it on your clumsy nature," he said fondly.

"Linen can be tricky," Evie supplied.

Mirabelle muttered something about murderous earls. Fortunately, it was too soft for the earl to hear.

Whit dropped a kiss on his sister's forehead and left.

The girls waited until the sound of his footsteps died out.

"Now, Sophie, about Alex . . ." Kate prompted.

She hesitated only a moment before deciding to share at least part of what was happening between her and Alex. "In complete confidence?"

There was a moment of silence, until Evie cried, "Why is everyone looking at me?"

Another moment of silence followed that.

Evie gave an affronted huff. "I have never betrayed a friend's secret. It just so happens that I haven't many friends."

"That's true on both accounts," Kate explained to Sophie. "Evie would take a friend's secret to the grave."

"We're not the best of friends yet, Sophie," Evie said, choosing her words carefully. "But I've every confidence we will be. You strike me as an intelligent woman, and you come with the highest of recommendations," she continued, indicating Kate and Mirabelle. "I give you the Cole word of honor that I shall keep your secrets safe."

"You can't ask for more than that," Mirabelle stated with confidence. "The Coles always keep their word. It's a point of pride for them."

Sophie accepted that. "Thank you, Evie."

"You may thank me properly by sharing your secret, and mind you make it a good one," she said good-naturedly. "I'd hate to think I went through all the trouble of clearing my good name just to hear how he sent you tulips and touched your bare hand."

Sophie grinned. "He has never sent me flowers. And he kissed me, or rather, we kissed."

There was a three-way intake of breath and then,

"When?"

"Did you like it?"

"See, I knew I'd like her. A real kiss or just a peck?"

Sophie wasn't sure whom to answer first, so she thought she might start with the last first. "It was a real kiss," she said, feeling her cheeks heat. "I liked it very much, and the first time was at the Pattons' ball."

"The first time?" Mirabelle croaked.

"It's happened once or twice since," Sophie replied evasively.

"Well, which is it?" Kate asked. "One or two?"

"Four."

"Oh, my." That came from both Kate and Mirabelle.

"Oh, now I know I like you," Evie declared with a satisfied smile. "But the first time is the most memorable, isn't it?"

"Evie's kissed one of the grooms," Kate explained with a roll of her eyes.

"Who *is* rather attractive," Mirabelle pointed out.

"He's a veritable Adonis," Evie said.

"Have you . . . that is, are you still . . . ?" Sophie wasn't sure how to ask whether Evie was carrying on an illicit affair with a member of the staff.

"Alas, it never went beyond a few kisses before he moved on to greener pastures. But enough about that, these two have heard all about it. Tell us about your Alex."

"He is not *my* Alex. And there isn't much else to tell. We kissed that first night and . . ."

"And . . . ?" All three prompted at once.

Sophie cringed. "And then he laughed."

"Oh, no," Evie murmured, sounding slightly more amused than dismayed. "Whatever for?"

"He said it was the situation."

"What the devil does that mean?" Evie asked.

"I have no idea. He did apologize, though."

"I should hope he did a great deal more than apologize," Mirabelle declared indignantly.

"Whatever he did, it should have involved flowers, candy, poetry, an enormous amount of flattery, and an even greater amount of begging," Kate added.

Mirabelle nodded her approval before adding, "A little punishment would not have gone amiss. Self-flagellation would have been appropriate in this case."

"And a horsehair shirt afterward," Evie suggested.

"But not before the salt," Mirabelle returned.

"Oh, naturally," Sophie laughed. "But none of them were necessary. Besides," she said sobering, "I'm not looking to Alex for a declaration, and I've received no indication that he's looking to give one."

"Are you sure?" Kate asked gingerly.

"Yes, on both accounts. I think it likely he is only playing the rake, and even if he were not, he would never allow me to return to my father."

"And you're certain that's what you want most?" Evie inquired softy.

Sophie nodded, but for some reason she didn't feel as confident as she had three weeks ago. This business with Alex was affecting her more than she realized. More than she could afford. "It's best to leave what's happened between me and Alex in the past. I need to concentrate on the gentlemen on the list. Speaking of which, Evie. . . ."

Several days later, Sophie had three new names on her list and had crossed out two. The three additions were middle-aged gentlemen without sons, but with nephews and male cousins they would be happy to see as their heirs. Her list thus fortified, she'd felt safe abandoning the chase of the two men she felt were the least suited to her needs, Mr. Johnson and Mr. Fetzer. The first made her skin crawl, and the second was so ancient and frail looking she felt guilty even contemplating dragging him into a loveless marriage.

Over the next three days she threw herself into the party, participating in almost every event scheduled. Unlike other house parties she'd heard about, which provided ample daytime pleasures for the men while the women were left to find their own amusements until evening, Lady Thurston had provided diversions for the ladies. There were morning rides, archery tournaments, dancing lessons, picnics, parlor games, a trip to the nearby village, and tea every afternoon.

Sophie tried everything to distract herself from her worries, playing the role of perfect guest by day and adorable debutante by night.

By the fourth day, she was on verge of tears. Nothing had succeeded in dislodging, even for a moment, the suffocating pain in her chest. She missed Alex with every breath. And to make matters worse, she had crossed off nearly every name on the list. Lord Verant had made a comment about the questionable wisdom of letting females travel to "such uncivilized lands" and had been the first to go. Mr. Carrow had then nodded vigorously, necessitating his own removal. Lord Chester had let it slip that he was courting a young woman of considerable wealth, and Mrs. Packard had made it clear that her son, Sir Andrew, was expected to do the same. Sophie looked over the remaining names and made a decision—she would ask Sir Frederick . . . soon.

When it was over and done with, she could explain everything to Alex. If he still wanted to be friends, then. . . . Well, somehow "friends" didn't sound appealing. She didn't want to be friends with Alex. She wanted so much more than that. She wanted everything—which was unlikely to happen, and would be a disaster if it did.

"Ugh. There's simply no winning. . . . I'll just marry Sir Frederick and hope for the best."

Her only other option was to marry Sir Frederick and fear for the worst.

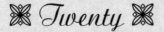

❈ Twenty ❈

The first ball had had no theme beyond a color scheme of gold and white, but the second ball was a masquerade.

Lady Thurston confided to Sophie that the mid-party ball was her favorite because the guests provided the most elaborate decorations. And she was right—some of the masqueraders had costumes that went past elaborate and straight into bizarre. The woman in the feather gown was certainly an odd sight. Most guests, however, chose costumes that were considerably tamer. Many, like Sophie, opted for an ordinary ball gown, but all of them wore masks.

The secretive atmosphere suited Sophie's plans perfectly. She needed to return to Lord Forent's study, since she had been unable to get into it on the night of his ball, and she needed to pay a visit to Sir Frederick. She would do both tonight.

London was less than two hours away. And who would miss one more partygoer in a pale rose dress with a demi-mask? Mirabelle and Evie might, but she intended to ask for her friends' assistance anyway.

Alex certainly wouldn't notice her absence. She'd been all but invisible to him for the entire week, receiving only formal greetings and polite inquiries when they met in the hall or were thrown together for a game of whist. And God help her, she'd been sorely tempted to find ways to be in a position for even those small scraps of interaction. But she couldn't do it. He had made his wishes known, and she would respect them.

She would engage herself to Sir Frederick tonight, sneak into Forent's office, return before morning, and then tell Alex everything first thing tomorrow.

First, however, she needed to find Mirabelle. Lady Thurston had mentioned that Mirabelle had returned to her room to fix a torn hem, and Sophie had immediately offered to seek her out and offer assistance. She couldn't sew two stitches in a straight line, but the opportunity to speak with Mirabelle about the best way to go about sneaking out of Haldon Hall was too good to pass up.

She made it to the stairwell landing in the west hall when she heard the first muffled cry for help, and she was halfway down the hall before she could hear the sounds of a struggle and pinpoint which room they were coming from. Sophie picked the lock in record time and barreled into the room.

Mr. Jarles had Mirabelle pinned against a bed, one hand covering her mouth and the other grabbing at her skirts. Mirabelle was clearly fighting him, but the man was a good three times her size.

"Let her up!"

Surprised by the intrusion, Mr. Jarles loosened his grip on Mirabelle long enough for her to give him one mighty, disgusted shove and scramble off the bed. Sophie pushed Mirabelle behind her, then reached down to her ankle and retrieved one of her knives.

Mr. Jarles climbed off the bed in the nonchalant manner of a man who had never been held accountable for his sins and had no intention of being subjected to that practice now.

Sophie watched him warily as he brushed off his coat and went through the motions of straightening his cravat.

Behind her, Mirabelle's breath came in ragged gasps. "I didn't want that," she whispered. "I didn't invite—"

"I know."

"We should go," Mirabelle urged.

Sophie didn't answer. She held her knife by the tip and brought it up for Mr. Jarles to see. "You will remove yourself from this house party before morning. You will give whatever excuse your little mind can manage in the next hour, and then you will take yourself off to some other estate where you can spend your time devising a way to never come within a hundred yards of Miss Browning again. Do I make myself quite clear?"

Mr. Jarles looked unconcerned. Completing the affectation of righting his appearance, he walked to a dresser and picked up a glass half filled with a dark liquid.

"I'll do nothing of the sort. The chit's undowered and unprotected. She'll only end up a mistress." He leaned against the wall carelessly and added, "Might as well be mine."

"And," Sophie continued, as if he had not spoken at all. "You will apologize to her."

Mr. Jarles made an ugly snort. "Apologize? To a whore?"

Sophie threw the knife at his head. It embedded itself in the wall two inches from his ear with a solid thump.

Mr. Jarles paled and dropped the glass.

Mirabelle let out a little squeak.

Sophie retrieved her other knife and held it up for him to see. "Apologize."

It took him a moment, but eventually he rasped out a terrified little, "Sorry."

Sophie wiggled the fingers on her free hand at him. "Nimble fingers," she reminded him. "Remember that while you're packing."

He didn't seem inclined to argue, so Sophie took Mirabelle by the hand and led her out of the room.

"Are you all right?" she asked, as they walked briskly down the hall toward the guest rooms in the east wing.

Mirabelle nodded shakily and smoothed the front of her skirt in a nervous gesture. "I'll be fine."

"We should find Lady Thurston."

"No."

Sophie was surprised by the vehemence in Mirabelle's voice. "But she needs to—"

"No," Mirabelle repeated firmly. Then she sighed and stopped to face Sophie. "Please understand, Sophie. Lady Thurston is like a mother to me. She has done more for me . . . she means more to me than I could hope to express. I won't say or do anything to upset her."

Sophie considered that for a moment. "Whit then—"

Mirabelle gave a humorless little laugh and resumed walking. "Whit wouldn't trouble himself over my concerns, except maybe to offer to buy the man dinner."

Sophie refused to believe that, but now wasn't the time to argue the matter. Mirabelle was understandably on edge, and a discussion of Whit's sense of honor, or lack thereof, would only upset her further.

"Someone needs to make sure he leaves," Sophie said instead.

"He'll leave," Mirabelle replied flatly.

It took a moment for Sophie to realize the full implications of that statement.

"This has happened before, hasn't it?"

Mirabelle nodded without looking at her.

Sophie cleared her throat. "Last time . . . did he . . . how did you . . . ?"

"I kneed him in the groin."

"Oh," Sophie replied, duly impressed. "Good thinking."

A whisper of a smile passed over Mirabelle's face. "Evie taught me. She learned it from one of the maids. Unfortunately, it's hard to use that trick on the same man twice."

Sophie had seen the effects of that particular maneuver once. It did seem the sort of thing a man would learn from quickly.

They stopped outside Mirabelle's door. Sophie waited while Mirabelle retrieved her key and turned it in the lock. She paused in the motion. "Thank you for what you did tonight, Sophie."

Sophie felt herself blush. She was uncomfortable in the face of such earnest gratitude. "It was nothing," she replied in a falsely bright voice. "You would have done the same for me."

Mirabelle gave a small laugh at that and finished opening the door. She waited until they were both inside, then turned back and relocked it. "I certainly would have tried," she said, moving to sit on the edge of the bed. "But I'm afraid I haven't your talent with cutlery."

"You could learn," Sophie offered, sitting down.

"I hesitate to ask after everything you've already done for me, but do you think you could teach me?"

Sophie grinned. "Absolutely. And if you're so terribly concerned over being in my debt—which is patently untrue, mind you—I have just the solution. . . ."

Mirabelle showed her a rarely used passageway out the back of the house. She agreed to spread the word that Sophie had the headache and should not be disturbed, then enlisted Evie's help in bribing the stable hands to hitch Sophie's team in secrecy, while Kate went in search of extra carriage lanterns. Sophie knew it would look silly, but she intended to have the carriage as brightly lit as safety allowed.

She was on her way to London within the hour.

Alex noticed Sophie's absence almost immediately. When he first entered the ballroom, he had caught sight of her, dancing with Mr. Johnson and looking decidedly unhappy about it. Of course, in his opinion she never looked overly pleased with the attentions of her admirers—despite her show of smiles and laughter—but this time her discontent was evident for everyone to see.

Interesting. Perhaps she had finally come to her senses. He meant to ask her that very question tonight—*have you come to your senses?* She damn well better have. He'd spent the entire week watching her every move from a distance, hanging on every word she spoke in conversations with other people, analyzing every expression, every wave of her hand, and every inflection in her voice. He'd even sent Whit on a scouting expedition. Clearly, he needed either to resolve matters with her soon or check himself into Bedlam.

He'd watched her dance next with Mr. Holcomb, looking only slightly less perturbed by the notion.

An excellent sign, he decided. He'd give her another hour or two to come to him, and failing that, he would devise a way to throw the two of them together, accidentally of course. He saw no reason for her to know the full extent of his mental decline.

He'd lost track of her for a while after that. The Earl of Efford had engaged him in conversation, then insisted he dance with his niece, Miss Mary Jane Willory—a stunning young woman whose attractiveness was greatly diminished by her malicious nature. Following the dance, the girl had insisted on introducing him to her dear friend, Miss Heins, a slightly pudgy girl who, even under a demi-mask, was clearly plain and clearly *not* a dear friend. But Miss Willory had cooed over the *poor dear girl* who hadn't danced all night, and if His Grace could only see his way to rectifying the matter, Miss Willory would take it as a personal favor.

Alex had done his best to aid the mortified Miss Heins, claiming that the favor would be hers to him, that he would settle for nothing less than a waltz, and that he could think of nothing better than to pass the time until then in her company. Miss Willory had been suitably abashed and taken herself off, leaving Alex to make stunted conversation with the nice but painfully shy Miss Heins.

Fortunately, a waltz was struck up almost immediately. His gentlemanly duty of dancing at least once a night with a wall-flower thusly dispatched, Alex had taken a turn about the room looking for Sophie. And came to the unsettling conclusion that she had disappeared. He'd searched the entire ballroom, the terrace, the garden, and finally sought Evie for the purpose of checking the ladies' retiring room.

Which is when Evie told him, "Sophie's headache returned, she's gone upstairs to her room."

Alex's eyes narrowed suspiciously. Evie had never been particularly good at dissembling. She always tensed one corner of her mouth slightly at the fib, causing her scar to pucker a bit at the edge. And now that he thought of it, he hadn't noticed her or Mirabelle in his search either. She must have just returned to the room.

"What aren't you telling me?"

Evie returned his searching look with an assessing one of her own, cocking her head slightly to one side and furrowed her brow. "You're in love with her, aren't you?" she finally asked.

Alex actually jerked in astonishment. Love? *Love?* He hadn't even thought about love. Was he in love with Sophie? He was fond of her of course, cared for her, admired and esteemed her. Certainly he desired her more than any woman he had ever met. But was he in love with her?

"I can see that you are," Evie murmured, and it took Alex a second to realize she was answering her own question, not his. "You'll want to check on her of course, and I think, in the end, she might like that as well. But don't bother requesting additional assistance in the matter. I've given my word."

Alex didn't bother asking for an explanation to that somewhat cryptic statement. Evie's pointed tone told him enough.

He reached Sophie's room as quickly and quietly as possible. She wasn't there, of course, but he'd had to look. He sent a maid for Whit, then began searching for clues to where she might have gone. With every item he encountered, a picture of Sophie entered his mind unbidden. Her dancing blue eyes peering over that fan. Strands of dark hair peeking out from under that bonnet. Her full and delightfully expressive lips smiling as she danced with him in that gown. Her slender hands in those gloves. The swell of her breasts . . .

"This is a very bad sign."

Alex looked up to find Whit in the doorway. "I don't think so," he said calmly. "All her belongings are here and . . . how did you know Sophie was gone?"

"I didn't. I was referring to the fact that you are rifling through a young lady's personal belongings. Have you *completely* lost your mind?"

"It's possible. At the moment, however, it is the least of my concerns. Sophie has disappeared."

Whit sobered immediately. "Are you certain?"

"Yes. Unless you ran into her on your way up here?"

Whit shook his head. "Any theories?"

"Evie knows something, and I think Mirabelle might as well. Question them, and Kate too if need be. I'll speak with the staff."

Mirabelle walked along the book-lined shelves in Haldon's library and let the smell and feel of aged leather and polished wood comfort her. She loved the library. She loved everything about Haldon actually, but the library was her favorite. The library at her uncle's estate, a paltry collection compared to Haldon's, had the added disadvantage of being connected to her uncle's study—a room she avoided like the plague.

Here, however, she could amble about to her heart's content. She could chose from thousands of books on every conceivable topic. She could read until her eyes gave out from the strain.

She ran her finger down the spine of a particularly large tome. This was what she needed to take her mind off tonight's events. She pulled the book from its space on the shelf and turned to leave.

"Hello, imp."

Mirabelle dropped her book and spun around with a gasp to find Whit leaning casually against the library door—watching her with an intensity that sent tingles up her spine.

"What the devil are you doing here?" she snapped in an attempt to hide her discomfort.

Whit shrugged and moved toward her with a careless grace. "Same as you, I imagine, just came in search of a little light bedtime reading."

He bent down and scooped up the book at her feet. "*Amphibian Wildlife in the New World*? Obviously we differ in our definition of 'light.'"

"Among other things," Mirabelle pointed out, snatching the book away. "What do you want?"

"Oh, I think you know what I want," Whit drawled, giving her a smile that held no warmth. "Answers."

Mirabelle didn't see any reason to pretend she didn't understand. With another man, she might have feigned innocence, or at least made an attempt to be reasonably civil. But this was Whit, he would never buy the former, and he wasn't worth the bother of the latter.

"Well, you'll not get them from me. Now leave before someone walks in here and—"

"I'm not leaving until you tell me where Sophie has gone."

"Why don't you ask Evie and Kate?" she asked scathingly. She could tell by his scowl that he had already explored that avenue and had met with similar reticence and she sent him a small mocking smile. "I see. Fine. *I'll* go."

Brushing past him, Mirabelle stalked to the door and grabbed the handle. It didn't turn. She tried again. *Locked.* She wheeled back to face Whit.

He dangled the key mockingly in front of her. "Perhaps I should have been a little more specific. *We're* not leaving until you tell me where Sophie has gone."

"You're mad! Any number of people may have keys to the library. You'll ruin me!"

Whit shrugged again. She stomped toward him.

"Give me that blasted key!" she hissed.

"Start talking, or we stay here till someone else lets us out. Your decision, imp."

"You bloody arrogant, heartless ass!"

"You have a rather colorful vocabulary, I dare say you don't limit your literary pursuits to the topic of zoology."

"For the last time, cretin. *Give. Me. The. Key.*"

"*Where. Is. Sophie?*" Whit stepped closer to her with every syllable until six feet of glowering male towered over her. It was a blatant attempt at intimidation, and another woman would have instinctually stumbled back in fright. Mirabelle didn't budge an inch. Instead, she gripped her book with both hands and smashed it squarely into Whit's face. The result was a thoroughly satisfying smack and a long colorful stream of expletives.

Whit stumbled back, howling and holding his nose. "What the devil is the matter with you?" he bellowed. At least, she thought that's what he bellowed. His voice was starting to sound a little funny. No question of the volume, unfortunately.

"Hush!" she whispered furiously. "Someone will hear you!"

"I thud bwoody well hope tho!"

"Quiet! You spoiled little . . ." A scrapping in the hallway cut her off. Dear God, someone had heard the noise. She glanced frantically around the room. Whit still held the key. He had it pressed against his face which he now held up toward the ceiling in an effort to stanch the flow of blood from his nose.

"Are you going to give me the key or not?"

"*No!*"

More noise from the hall. Voices. Mirabelle panicked. Fighting back wasn't an option this time. There was no place to hide in the library. The tables were too high, the chairs too low, and the lighting too good. Dropping her book, she ran to one of the windows and threw it open. It was a good drop down and there was some sort of shrubbery at the bottom.

"Whad are you doing, imp?" Whit still had his head tilted up and he was eyeing her down the length of what would normally be his nose, but was now two bloody hands and a key.

A rattle sounded at the door. "What the . . . It's locked. Simmons, give me your key."

Mirabelle sincerely hoped the hedge below wasn't rosebushes. She sat down on the sill and swung her legs over the edge.

"Miwabelle, no!"

With a whoosh she was gone.

❊ *Twenty-one* ❊

$\mathcal{A}$lex was having difficulty with the staff. He was certain several of them were hiding something, but no amount of bribing, threatening, or cajoling could break their silence. He was grumbling about the disadvantages of staff becoming too secure in their positions when he caught sight of a bedraggled-looking Mirabelle entering the downstairs servants' hall. She, in turn, was mumbling something about the advantages of staying in bed some mornings.

"Mirabelle!" he called to her back.

He thought perhaps she groaned, but couldn't be certain.

"Where is she?" he demanded immediately. There was a chance Whit had already spoken with her, or that he already knew, but—

She turned and offered him a strained smile. "I'm sure I don't know what you mean."

"Are you serious?" Alex wasn't referring to her guise of ignorance so much as her ridiculous use of the phrase, "I'm sure I don't know what you mean," when they clearly both knew she was lying.

"Of course I'm not serious," she responded calmly. "I am merely trying to be polite."

"What the devil for?"

"I rather like you, that's what for, and while I can't depart a secret that is not my own, I thought I might at least explain as much in civil terms."

Alex felt his fists clench tightly at his side. He took a deep breath and made sure his words came out even and calm. Mirabelle didn't respond well to intimidation or threats. "I like you very well too, Mirabelle. I'm also rather fond of Sophie. In fact, we're both fond of Sophie. So, why don't we—*why* are you shaking your head at me?"

"I'm not going to tell you where Sophie is. I can't. I gave her my word."

Alex decided a forward tactic might work best. "She may be in danger, Mirabelle."

That certainly caught her attention. She looked at him askance. "May?"

"*Is, is* in danger. I'm certain of it." Certain that she could be in danger, traveling alone. Absolutely positive she *would* be in danger once he got his hands on her. "So, please—"

"What sort of danger?" she asked, narrowing her eyes even further.

"The dangerous sort!" he snapped, suddenly beginning to see what Whit had been complaining about all these years.

She tilted her head suspiciously. "As in the 'female walking unescorted for half a block in broad daylight, in a respectable neighborhood' sort of danger, or 'the ship is sinking and—' "

"The second sort, Mirabelle!" Alex cut in, exasperated.

Mirabelle studied his face for an agonizing ten seconds, and Alex was torn between admiration for her loyalty to a friend and the nearly irresistible urge to shake her until she started talking. The latter was a mere second away from winning out when she finally sighed and said, "She's gone to London."

"What! Why?"

"Keep your voice down. You can ask her that yourself. There are only so many promises I'm willing to break in one night."

"Right." He turned to leave.

"Alex? You might consider waiting for her at her town

house. It's not the only place she could possibly be headed, but it seems sensible she might stop at her own home. Don't you think?"

Alex grinned—he couldn't help himself. He turned back and dropped a quick kiss on Mirabelle's forehead. "Thank you."

She smiled grimly. "Just bring her back safely. I'll not have broken my word for nothing."

He gave her a reassuring nod and then took off down the hall at a dead run.

Whit is an idiot, he decided. *Mirabelle Browning is a lovely girl.*

Alex and Whit saddled their horses themselves. Not only was it faster and quieter than asking for help, it also gave Alex something to do other than worry. He couldn't allow himself to think about all the harrowing things that could happen to a woman between here and London. All the things that could happen to her in London. All the added danger she might face being cousin to a suspected traitor.

Later he would let himself feel. For the moment, panic at her disappearance and self-recrimination at his failure to keep her safe and sound at Haldon would only serve to distract him.

"I can't believe she broke your nose," he commented. He couldn't conceive of a more effective, or enjoyable, way of distracting himself than tormenting his friend. "That must be a first."

"No ith nod," Whit grumbled. "Rememba da billiardth ball?"

"Good Lord, I had forgotten. Who would have thought the girl had such a fine aim?"

"Obwiously not I, or I woud hab mobed."

"Beg your pardon?"

"Mooobed. Em. Oh. Bee . . . you're endjoying dith, awent you?"

Alex adjusted a stirrup and smirked. "Immensely."

"Bathard."

"Come again?"

Whit responded with a vulgar gesture.

Alex moved to the other stirrup. "You shouldn't have let her jump out that window, you know. She could have been seriously hurt."

"I wood hab liked to thee you twy and thop her."

"She didn't know about the bookcase door?"

Whit shook his head, then groaned and gingerly prodded at his nose.

"Amazing, I would have thought she knew every nook and cranny of Haldon Hall by now."

Whit grunted noncommittally. "How did you find oud aboud Thophia?"

Alex grinned. "Mirabelle told me."

That elicited a string of vicious, if not entirely coherent, curses.

"She really is a lovely girl," Alex added. But as delightful a distraction antagonizing Whit was, Alex knew it was time to discuss more serious matters. He ran his eyes and hands one last time over the horse and tack. "Go to Loudor's. I don't think she'll be there, but I'd rather err on the side of caution. If she is, send word to me and do what you can. I want you to go to William's as well. Tell him what's happened and, if necessary, see he puts some men out to look for her. Drag him out of bed if you have to."

"Whad will you be doing?"

"I'll check her town house first."

"And if she's ad neider of dose pwaces?"

Alex swung up on his horse. "Then we'll contact everyone she's met since coming to London. If need be, we'll go door to door."

Whit nodded in understanding. "Anyding ewse?"

"Just one. . . ."

Sophie's plan was twofold. First and foremost, she would seek out Sir Frederick and propose a marriage of convenience. After that, she would make the short trek to Lord Forent's home on foot and take a peek at the contents of his study. With any luck—and she felt she really should have some coming her way by now—she'd be back at Haldon Hall before the first light of dawn.

She alighted from her carriage a half block away with instructions to the driver to return to her town house in four hours. She hurried down the sidewalk, reaching her first destination just in time to see Mr. Weaver being led in through the front door.

Damnation. She couldn't very well ask the man to marry her in the company of his lover.

She moved down the sidewalk until she could see around the house well enough to get a good look at the carriage and team parked by the mews. She scowled at both and swore under her breath. The horses pricked their ears in her direction, but appeared otherwise unimpressed with her temper.

Pulling her cloak tighter about her, she hitched the satchel she was carrying farther up her shoulder and headed off in the direction of Lord Forent's. She'd finish her business there first, and hope Mr. Weaver's carriage was gone by the time she returned.

The walk was a brief one, for which Sophie was exceedingly grateful. The streets of Mayfield were well lit, but the light failed to extend much past the pavement of the sidewalk. With the moon hidden mostly behind clouds, the houses loomed like giant mausoleums in the dark, and the expansive yards, with their perfectly trimmed hedges and silent fountains, reminded her of cemeteries.

She quickened her pace, hating to give in to her fears but knowing it was foolish to pretend they didn't exist. When she reached Lord Forent's, she stopped and stared at the house with resignation and dismay. Its yard was as dark and gloomy as the others. She really hadn't expected to find it lit the way it had been the night of the ball, but one could always hope.

She retrieved a small lantern from her satchel, lit it, and

quickly scurried around the side of the yard to the garden gate she had noticed earlier. It was dangerous to use a light, but she had no choice. She just couldn't walk through the garden in the pitch black. Good Lord, she couldn't walk through her own bedroom in the pitch black. Sophie draped her cloak over her arm and held it in front of the lantern to shield the light from view of the house.

Picking her way along the gravel paths—and studiously ignoring a certain gazebo—she made her way to the side wall of the house and counted windows.

. . . four, five, six, there!

It was a good seven or eight feet up, but the house was fashioned of rough stone that jutted out in some places and sunk in at others, perfect for climbing. She set the lantern between a bush and the stone and covered the foliage with her cloak to hide the light. Hitching up her skirts to tie them in a knot above her knees, she quickly, if not altogether gracefully, scrambled up to the window and slid it open with ease.

Thank God. She didn't know what the odds were of finding a window unlocked in Mayfield, but she had figured they were slim.

Twenty minutes later she was willing to entertain the idea that the open window hadn't just balanced her luck, it had tipped the scale too far in the other direction.

How could there be nothing? She'd dug through every drawer and cabinet, and she'd found not a single scrap of incriminating evidence.

Ready to tear her hair out in frustration, she sat behind the desk and opened a ledger. Maybe she was looking in the wrong places. Maybe men like these kept their secrets hidden in bedside stands or safes hidden behind large portraits. Or maybe. . . .

She paused in her mental rambling to stare at a familiar-looking set of numbers. She flipped back a month and found a similar entry. Then another month and another match. It went on and on. Nine of the last twelve months showed payments to Forent in amounts identical to the funds Loudor had stolen from Whitefield. She'd gone over those numbers enough times to have the exact amounts memorized. And there they were, down to the last shilling.

She trailed her finger along the entry line and found the entries were attributed to Lord Heransly, the earl's scape-grace son.

If they had been from her cousin, she might have attributed it to debts of honor. Lord Loudor was a notorious gambler. But these entries were from son to father. It made no sense.

She reached for supplies to copy down what she could of the entries but stopped short at the sound of movement in the hallway. She dropped the ledger, snuffed the candle, and raced to the window to throw her legs over the edge. She managed to crawl about a quarter of the way down, but in her haste and fear of being discovered, she made a misstep and lost her footing in the stone.

There was the rip of fabric, then falling, and then the hard impact of the ground.

Ummph!

It wasn't a far drop, but unprepared for it as she was, she landed fully on her back, and knocked all the air out of her lungs. For what seemed like an eternity, she lay prostrate, stunned and gasping like a fish on land.

Perfectly typical. She'd been lucky enough to have found a window unlocked, and unlucky enough to have fallen out of it.

When her breath finally returned, she managed, against the protest of every muscle and bone in her body, to roll onto her stomach and pushed herself up to her knees. Relatively confident she wasn't going to pass out, she climbed to her feet, grabbed the cloak and lantern, and ran.

She was almost to her house—having decided she would postpone her trip to Sir Frederick's until she could fortify herself with a cup of something hot and a change of gown—when the disturbing feeling that she was being watched first hit her. She stopped dead in her tracks and whirled to peer into the shadows, listening intently for sounds of pursuit. Nothing.

She stopped twice more, but each time she listened for footsteps behind her, she heard nothing but the still night air.

It was with immense relief that she mounted the front steps of her home and swung open the door.

"Aah! Oh God! Oh! A . . . Al . . ."

"Alex. My name is Alex."

"Yes! I mean, of course it is . . . Alex." Sophie closed the door and stood to face Alex. He was leaning against the stairwell banister—all muscle, tension . . . and anger. She dropped her satchel on the side table, made a token attempt to smooth her skirts, then having run out of things to occupy herself with, wrung her hands nervously. "Whatever are you doing here?" Her voice was bright and cheery. Much, much too cheery.

"I could ask the same of you," Alex replied.

"Oh, well . . . I live here."

The look he sent her was icy enough to make her cringe.

"In London, you mean?" she continued with forced buoyancy. "Right. Well, I . . . er . . . I forgot something . . . something rather important . . . and I came back to retrieve it."

"And that something would be?"

She really wished he would blink. That narrow-eyed stare was discomforting. "Ummm. Well, I'm afraid that's personal."

"I'm afraid you'll have to tell me anyway."

Well now, *that* was a bit much. She frowned at him, giving up all pretense of a normal conversation and said, "No, I don't."

"Yes, you do."

"No."

"Yes."

"No. Really, are we going to be doing this all night?"

He blinked, finally, but moved not a muscle besides. "That's up to you."

"Excellent. I vote we don't."

Alex snapped. In one quick movement he had her by the arm and was forcefully dragging her into the front parlor. Shoving her ahead of him, he whirled around and closed the doors. Sophie gave a quick thanks for the several lit candles in the room keeping the dark at bay. Alex looked ready to explode, which was terrifying enough in and of itself.

"You," he ground out, "will sit . . ." he lifted a small chair several inches off the floor before slamming it down again in front of Sophie, "*here*. I . . ." He lifted a second chair and placed directly in front of the first, ". . . will sit *here*. And *we* will continue sitting until I am completely satisfied that you have answered every one of my questions fully and honestly."

"Um . . ."

"Now!"

Sophie sat. She didn't care for his high-handed tactics, but now seemed an appropriate time to exercise a little verbal prudence.

"What in God's name happened to your dress?"

Sophie jumped in her seat, startled by the sudden rise of his voice. She looked down and barely managed to stifle a groan. Her dress was covered hem to waist in mud. She picked at it absently a moment, noticing several tears as well.

"I fell down."

"You fell down," he parroted slowly. He didn't believe her, which was rather ironic considering it was likely to be the only thing she told the truth about all night.

"Yes, I fell down. Honestly."

"Are you hurt?"

"No, I'm fine."

Alex looked her over, scanning the length of her with his eyes, and Sophie shifted uncomfortably in her seat. He nodded, apparently satisfied, and took his own seat. She squirmed again. The chairs were too close together and she had to maneuver her legs to the side to keep her knees from rubbing against his long legs.

"Where?" he asked.

"Where am I fine?" she asked a little incredulously.

"Where did you fall down?"

"Oh, here in London."

Maybe she could manage to avoid lying outright all night.

Alex scowled at her.

Maybe not.

"In Mayfield," she clarified.

Then again, maybe so.

"Sophie," he growled warningly.

"I'm sorry, Alex, but I am not going to tell you what I was doing tonight. It's not my secret to give away."

"Good Lord, why does everyone keep saying that tonight? Does anyone keep their *own* counsel?"

"I'm sure I don't know what you mean."

Alex felt his fingers digging into the arms of his chair. He took a deep breath and forced himself to relax. "Since we are on the subject of your attire—"

"Are we?"

"We are now. What in God's name are you wearing?"

"Er . . . a ball gown?"

Alex narrowed his eyes dangerously.

"I really don't know what else to call it," Sophie said honestly.

"It's indecent," Alex spat.

She gaped at him, insult warring with bewilderment. "It most certainly is not. I—"

"And you've been wearing gowns just like it for weeks now. Why is that, Sophie?"

"I like them," she replied indignantly. And it was true, once she'd gotten accustomed to the contemporary, less conservative cuts, she'd found she rather enjoyed the new experience of being fashionable. "And I don't see—"

"And," he cut in, "you've been flirting shamelessly—"

"That is *quite* enough, more than enough, actually. I have not behaved in any way that could be construed as indecorous, and my attire has not received so much as a disapproving glance," she paused and remembered something. "Perhaps one disapproving glance from Mrs. Willcomb, but that was only because her husband was leering at me most rudely, but I can hardly take the blame for that. He leers at everyone."

"Why are you doing it?" Sophie didn't respond, so he tried a different approach. "Why are you encouraging the attentions of these men, Sophie? I want answers this time. . . . Are you looking for a husband?"

He wasn't surprised that those last words should taste bad in his mouth, but he was surprised by the sheer violence of his reaction to the thought of Sophie in another man's arms.

"Aren't all women?" Sophie asked, interrupting his train of thought. And nicely sidestepping the issue as well, he noted grimly.

"Answer my question, Sophie. Yes or no. Are you looking for a husband?"

Sophie scrambled desperately for a suitable evasion, but she could think of no words, no excuse that wouldn't be so far-fetched as to not insult Alex's intelligence.

If she had any sense at all, Sophie mused unhappily, she wouldn't be concerning herself over the possibility of insulting Alex at the moment. God knew the man needed someone to take him down a peg or two. In fact, she ought to just toss him out. It was her house after all, and it would solve her current dilemma rather nicely.

She couldn't do it. For one thing, she'd have to find someone physically capable of performing the task, and it was highly unlikely Alex would excuse her long enough to accomplish that. And then, of course, there was the undeniable scene it would create. She and Alex had left a house party in the countryside in the dead of night. If they were discovered at her home alone, she'd be ruined, and her chance of saving White-field right along with her.

But neither of those reasons seemed nearly as significant as the simple fact that she didn't want him to go.

She had just spent the better part of two hours sneaking around in darkened London. She was quite terrified someone had been following her, and she was all alone in the house. She was frightened, confused, disheartened, and long past exhausted.

Alex, regardless of his present behavior, was a reassuring presence. She felt a little safer with him there. She felt a little less alone.

"Sophie?"

And, oh how she was tired of lying. Tired of avoiding and evading. Making up half truths because she was too afraid to tell him the whole. Tired of wondering what was to become of her, and of him. Of them.

Just tell him, she told herself. Just tell him and be done with it. He isn't going to let this drop anyway. It's only a few hours earlier than planned and—

"Sophie."

"I have to get married."

"I beg your pardon?"

"Yes," she said, and her voice sounded strange even to her, a little too hollow, like she was speaking through a tube. "I am looking for a husband. I have to get married."

There was a silence while Alex digested what she had said. When he finally spoke, his voice was low and calm, almost placating. "I understand most young ladies desire a family of their own, but—"

"I don't *want* to get married. I *have* to, and within a fortnight."

"A fortnight?" Alex's voice cracked a little on the word.

Sophie tried to stand up, but Alex caught her by the wrist in a gentle yet unyielding grasp.

"I'm only going to the desk. I have something I want you to see. It will help me to explain."

He kept hold of her wrist.

"You do still want an explanation, don't you?"

He seemed to think about that for a moment, scanning her

face. When he let go, she walked tiredly to the desk and retrieved the document responsible for all her troubles. Before she could think better of it, she grabbed her list of potential spouses as well. She returned to her seat and handed the former over to Alex.

He was on his feet before he had gotten halfway down the paper. By the time he finished reading, he was pacing and swearing.

Sophie let him fume. Her own reaction to her cousin's treachery had been similar, although Alex employed several choice words she hadn't thought of and a few she hadn't even heard before. She had calmed down eventually, and he would as well.

Only Alex didn't look ready to calm down. After several minutes his pacing showed no signs of slowing and his list of expletives was growing increasingly creative. He was angry. He was very, very angry.

Sophie couldn't regret showing him the document. There was something rather flattering at the sight of Alex so outraged on her behalf, or at the very least, at the injustice done to her. And comforting as well, because if Alex were this angry—

"You've sought legal counsel, I presume."

Sophie snapped to attention. He hadn't ceased his pacing, but at least he had stopped swearing.

"Yes, I went to three different solicitors, none of them connected in any way to my cousin. They all said the same thing. The contract, if one may call it that, may not be entirely legal given the method in which it was obtained, but it's close enough that it would take years in court to have it overturned. My father and I would be ruined by then. We don't have the funds to pursue the matter now," she stated bleakly.

Alex gave her a questioning look, and taking the hint and a deep breath, she told him the entire story—the stolen money, the forged letters, everything but her cousin's connections to a suspected French conspiracy.

Alex listened without comment, and without visible reaction

beyond his grim expression. When she finished, he nodded once and said, "And so you must marry before this contract becomes valid."

"Yes, before my twenty-fifth birthday. I have a little over a fortnight."

"To whom?"

There was no point in trying to pretend she didn't understand him. He'd get the information out of her eventually anyway. She handed him the list.

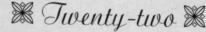

❋ *Twenty-two* ❋

*A*lex couldn't believe what he was seeing. It wasn't inconceivable that Sophie might have a list of prospective husbands; under the circumstances it seemed practical, reasonable even. And while a few of the gentlemen listed were far too old for her, they were mostly men Alex knew to be decent catches.

It wasn't that she had a list that bothered him, and it wasn't *who* was on the list.

It was the fact that he *wasn't* on the list that made his jaw clench and his stomach drop down to his toes.

He wasn't on the list.

He'd never been on the list. His eyes scanned the paper a second time. Several names had been written in and then crossed out. His was not among them.

He was not, and never had been, an option.

And his mind emptied save for that one disturbing fact.

He wasn't on the damnable, bloody, god-awful list.

"Why the devil am I not on this list?"

That question was immediately followed by a silent demand

to know where and when, exactly, he had misplaced his dignity.

"Oh, for heaven's sake," Sophie grumbled. "If I had known there was any chance anyone else might have seen that list, I would have been sure to include every unmarried gentleman in London and its surrounding counties. Lord knows I wouldn't want to prick anyone's vanity."

Alex shot her an annoyed look. He didn't care for her sarcasm, although it did provide a relatively dignified excuse for his otherwise embarrassing question. But he didn't feel relieved. He regretted having asked why his name was absent from the list in quite so pathetic a manner, but he was still desperate to know the answer. So he said nothing at all. Just continued to glare.

"Alex," Sophie said, attempting a more placating tone of voice. "The list is comprised of gentlemen I believe to be amiable to the idea of marriage, specifically with me."

"And you believe they're open to the notion of marriage to you because they. . . ." He cocked his head a little in a prompting fashion.

"Because they've engaged in the time-honored tradition of courtship. I believe you're familiar with the basics: flowers, compliments—"

"*I* compliment you." Alex heard the defensiveness in his voice but decided not to worry over it. He had already succeeded in completely unmanning himself, why worry over a little more lost pride?

Sophie snorted. "No," she stated emphatically, "you do not. At least, not in any manner that can't be easily followed by a wink, a nudge, and the directions to a discreet little inn."

Alex opened his mouth, pointed one finger at her and then . . . and then nothing. He just stood that way, frozen.

"Alex?"

His mouth opened a little wider. His finger came up a little higher.

"Alex?"

Finally, he dropped his finger, closed his mouth and—

Sophie groaned.

He was pacing again.

She couldn't *begin* to fathom why he was pacing again.

And she didn't really feel like trying. She was tired. Really, terribly tired. She wanted a hot bath, maybe a warm glass of milk, and a bed. She smiled at the thought. A big comfortable bed with a soft down mattress, lots and lots of fluffy pillows, and piles of thick blankets that had just come from the line. She could lay down, sink in, and—

"You'll marry me."

In the years that would follow, Sophie would blame her singularly unattractive reaction to that announcement on the fact that she was not fully awake when it was made.

Her jaw dropped. It didn't open; it dropped. Until her chin was very nearly resting on her chest. Her eyes squeezed shut tight in what could only be described as a desperate maneuver to save them from popping out of her head completely.

And then there was the sound.

An unnatural choking noise that she could only presume originated in her throat, but really could have come from anywhere since she didn't remember *making* the noise, just hearing it.

She tensed her whole body in an extraordinary effort to manipulate her mouth in such a way that a coherent sentence might be formed. Or a word even. Really, she'd settle for a word.

"You look positively ill," Alex grumbled.

She couldn't blame him. It certainly wasn't a flattering response to his suit.

"Is the prospect of marriage to me so bad as all that?"

"But you don't want to marry!" she blurted out, her eyes finally popping open and her whole body jolting then relaxing, as if she had been swimming under water too long and had finally broken the surface.

Alex eyed her curiously for a moment before asking, "And you do?"

No. She almost said it, stopping herself at the last moment when she realized it wasn't true.

She did want to marry. She just didn't want to marry any of the men on that list.

She wanted to marry Alex. She wanted that more than she had ever wanted anything else in her life.

Sophie remembered how her hands and heart had just itched to put his name on that list. At the very top. In big bold letters. All capitalized and underlined—twice. But her head hadn't allowed it for that very reason. He didn't want marriage, she'd thought, and she wanted him too much. She cared for him too deeply. She could fall in love with him so easily.

Members of the nobility who married the people they loved were lucky. Very, very lucky. Outrageously lucky. Sophie couldn't begin to imagine what luck like that would cost her.

"Sophie?"

"Right. Yes. Um . . ." Had he asked her a question?

"I asked you if you wanted to marry."

"Right." She paused, then said flatly, "No, I don't." She tried not to visibly cringe at the lie.

"Well then, that's fair."

"It is?" Sophie's mind was whirling. She wasn't at all clear on what Alex was talking about.

"Yes, it is," Alex said with a businesslike tone and a nod. "I'll procure the special license tomorrow."

"You will?" she asked dazedly. She blinked once and suddenly came to herself. "No, wait! I mean you won't! You won't procure a special license tomorrow because I am not going to marry you."

"Yes, you are."

"I believe I just told you I was not."

"Why not?" he demanded.

Because you won't let me return to my father.

Because I might fall in love with you.

Because I might be in love with you already.

Because I'll have to pay for it all later.

"Because I don't want to." Good Lord, she sounded like a five-year-old.

"You don't want to marry at all," he pointed out reasonably. "Unfortunately, it's clear you haven't a choice in the matter—"

"I have the choice of *who* I will marry."

"And you'll choose one of these?" Alex waved the list at her angrily. "One of these fops or old men? For God's sake, Sophie, Mr. Colton is seventy years old if he's a day!"

"He's three-and-sixty, and he has—" she cut off abruptly.

"Has what?"

She squirmed uncomfortably in her seat.

"And he has *what?*" Alex repeated.

"A very nice disposition," she offered lamely.

Alex didn't even bother acknowledging that pathetic attempt at evasion. "What does he have, Sophie? What does he possess that makes him such a fine catch?"

She really didn't want to embark on a conversation with Alex regarding her desire not to beget an heir. She couldn't envision it leading into anything that wasn't either vaguely insulting or blatantly embarrassing.

"One more time, Sophie—"

God, but he was stubborn.

"An heir," she snapped. "He possesses an heir. Almost all of them do. Are you quite satisfied?"

Alex didn't answer her at first. He just looked over the list again to confirm her statement, then said, "I see," in such a way that Sophie knew she would have to explain.

She took a deep, and she hoped calming, breath. "I wish to marry a gentleman who is not concerned with the production of an heir. I plan to return to my father."

She watched Alex's face for a reaction, but aside from the

muscle twitching in his cheek, which had been going on all night, his expression was unreadable.

"Sophie." Alex's voice was soft and calm, meant to lull. Naturally, it immediately put her on edge. "Do you really believe any of these men will be willing to abandon a pretty young wife to the other side of the world?"

"Yes," she replied firmly. "It is to be part of the marriage contract, or at least agreement. It will be a marriage in name only."

Alex set the list down and took a few steps toward her. "And is that what you really want? A marriage in name only?"

"Yes." Her voice was a little less firm this time around so she added, "I believe I've made as much clear."

Alex shook his head slowly. "No. What you made clear is what you need. I'm asking you what you want." He stopped in front of her. "What do you want, Sophie?"

He took one of her hands in his and gently pulled her to her feet. "Do you want to live the rest of your life alone?"

She wanted to tell him she wouldn't be alone. She'd have her father, Mrs. Summers, and Mr. Wang. She'd have her friends. But the words never reached her lips, partially because he was standing so close she could feel the heat of him, and partially because she knew that wasn't what he meant by alone.

"Don't you want a family of your own, Sophie? Don't you want children?"

She nodded. She couldn't help herself. She did want those things. She wanted them so much she could smell them, feel them, taste them in her mouth.

Alex gave her a small, sad smile and brought his other hand up to cup her neck and tilt her head toward him.

"And what about passion, Sophie?" he whispered, leaning closer. "Don't you want this?"

His lips met hers softly, gently, a question.

Sophie wanted to say yes. She wanted to marry Alex and spend the rest of her life kissing him. Just like this.

She wasn't sure how long they stood there. As always, when Alex kissed her, she lost all awareness of her surroundings, and when he finally pulled away she might have said only a minute had passed or she might have guessed an hour.

"What is your answer, Sophie?"

It took a moment for her to remember what he was asking. He still had his arms about her, and she still felt curiously warm and heady.

Eventually, she gathered her scattered thoughts well enough to ask, "Why?"

She wasn't certain why that question was so important to her at the moment, or even if she knew what response she wanted to hear. She only knew it seemed necessary to ask, and to know.

"Why should you marry me?" Alex asked.

She shook her head. "Why do you want to marry me now? You've never shown the least bit of interest—"

"I've shown an inordinate amount of interest in you." He pulled back a little to look at her in bewilderment.

"Yes, as a possible mistress—"

"What?" He dropped his arms in shock. "Where in God's name did you hear that?"

"I didn't," she said, growing a little confused herself. "I merely assumed—"

"Why would you do that?"

"Because you speak quite plainly to me, make advances of an intimate nature, and you were most emphatic about not sending flowers or writing poetry. I was under the impression that was how one wooed a mistress."

Alex stared at her for a long time, his expression unreadable.

"Was I wrong?" Sophie asked to make him talk.

"No." His voice came out a choked whisper. "No, you are right. That is how one treats a mistress. . . . God, that never occurred to me."

Unsure of how else to respond to that admission, Sophie just nodded. "And I'd heard you'd made a vow. A pledge not to marry until the age of forty."

"Forty," Alex repeated, remembering that ridiculous ruse. "Bloody hell." He stepped forward, taking her hands in his own. "I never intended to make you my mistress, Sophie. I am deeply sorry—"

"No, don't apologize," Sophie pleaded, hating to see him look so miserable. "You didn't do anything wrong."

"I've insulted you."

"No, you haven't," she insisted. "The role of a duke's mistress is a highly coveted position by many women."

"You deserve better than that."

"Why, because I was born a wealthy viscount's daughter?" Sophie asked, shaking her head. "I am not a better woman—"

"Yes, you are." Alex stated with quiet authority, capturing her chin with his fingers. "You're better than all of them. You are the most amazing woman I know. I didn't woo you in the traditional manner because I thought a different approach would prove more effective. I was under the impression that poorly written poetry would fail to impress you."

"Oh. Well, it doesn't impress me overmuch," she said honestly. "But a tulip or two wouldn't have gone amiss."

Every girl liked getting flowers after all.

Alex smiled. "I'll keep that in mind for the future. Does this mean you'll marry me?"

Sophie grimaced. "I'd like to, Alex."

He dropped his hand. "But you won't."

"You need an heir," she pointed out. "And I need to take care of my father."

"Well that's not so very difficult. We'll send for your father first thing and look after him together. You shouldn't bear the weight of that responsibility alone—"

"It won't work, Alex. My father will never return to England. There are too many memories of my mother and sister here."

"Then we'll—"

A muffled thumping noise in the back of the house cut him off.

"Stay here," he ordered, heading toward the parlor doors.

Sophie grabbed at his arm. "No. It's one of the servants, or the driver back early. If you're seen here, I'll be ruined. You stay here and I'll send them off to bed."

Alex looked torn. "It could be an intruder."

Sophie grabbed a nearby candlestick. "Then I'll scream for you," she promised in a hurried whisper. Then, realizing how little that seemed to console him, she bolted out of the room before he could stop her.

She hadn't gone far before remembering the eerie sensation of being followed she had felt earlier. Cursing herself for a fool, she pulled one out one of her knives and immediately turned back. It was quite likely that the only intruder was a member of the staff, but under the circumstances, it seemed wise to take Alex along for further investigation.

It was one thing to be ruined, quite another to be injured or dead.

She made it past the study doors when she heard them swing open behind her. She felt a blinding pain radiate down the back of her head. And then she felt nothing at all.

❈ *Twenty-three* ❈

*S*ophie woke to find her hands tied behind her, her feet bound, her mouth gagged, her muscles aching, her head pounding, and the whole of her moving.

They were in the back of a wagon. She eyed the small beams of sunlight sneaking through spaces between the boards and guessed she had been unconscious for at least four hours, maybe more. If she could see the sun's position, she'd know for certain, but there was some sort of tarp pulled tight over the top, allowing her just enough room to sit up.

Carefully wiggling her trussed form closer to the side of the wagon, she peered through the cracks between the wood and caught glimpses of passing countryside. They had brought her out of London. She sighed and closed her eyes, allowing her head to rest against the wood for a moment. She hadn't the vaguest notion who "they" might be.

Next to her, Alex moaned softly.

Dear God, Alex! She'd gotten him into this. She didn't know the identity of their kidnappers, but if the pain at the back of her head was any indication, they had few qualms about hurting their captives. Alex had been harmed because of her. He could be killed because of her. The thought set off a wave of fury and panic, prodding her to action.

She nudged Alex with her shoulder, leaned over and mumbled in his ear as loud as she dared, but he gave no further sign of waking.

She scooted until her back was against the roughened planks, then felt along with her bound hands until she found a particularly jagged piece of wood. Maneuvering herself, she felt the wood catch at the skin of her cheek, then, thankfully, at the gag. It took several painful tries but eventually she was able to pull the offending fabric out of her mouth.

Now the hard part. Sophie took several deep breaths and allowed her body to relax the way Mr. Wang had taught her. Then she bent forward at the waist. It was unfortunate that her remaining knife was strapped to the back side of her ankle for she'd never be able to reach it with her mouth. On the other hand, it had been immensely lucky that the kidnappers had tied her feet one on top the other. She could fold herself into a kind of cross-legged position that allowed her mouth to reach the insides of her ankles.

She lost all track of time pulling, gnawing, and tugging at the knots in the ropes. Her back and neck felt like they were on fire, but she didn't stop. She still had to contend with Alex's ropes. She'd like to be able to use her hands. It wouldn't be too difficult to maneuver her back to his feet and hands, but her fingers had grown completely numb and she probably wouldn't be able to manage anything more effective than a slap. She'd get their feet first. They needed their feet to run. Then she'd work on Alex's hands if she still had the energy. Or maybe she should get Alex's hands first and hope he woke up quickly. That way—

"What in God's name are you doing?"

Sophie's head snapped up at the sound of Alex's shocked whisper. "How did you ungag . . . *How did you untie yourself?*"

Alex reached over and finished untying her feet. "Sloppy knot at my wrists. Turn around."

Sophie began to turn but stopped at the sound of Alex sharply indrawn breath. "You're hurt."

"Of course I'm hurt. We were hit over the head, remember? Or, at least I was."

Alex reached up and touched her cheek. His finger came away bloody.

"Oh," she whispered. She hadn't realized the wood had cut her face that deeply.

Alex swore viciously, his face hardening into a savage mask. "Turn around," he ordered again.

She didn't take offense at his abrupt tone. He wasn't angry at her. Not yet, anyway.

He made quick work of her binds, then pulled off his cravat and handed it to her. "Hold it against your cheek."

He reached to the back of the wagon and prodded gently where the tarp met the wood. "Damn it, there's rope every two inches. They weren't taking any chances."

"They took some." Sophie handed him her knife. "They didn't bother searching me."

Alex looked as if he wanted to ask how she came to be carrying a knife but seemed to think better of it. He applied the knife to the fabric, cutting away a small hole closest to the floorboards. A crisscrossing of rope appeared on the other side and Sophie couldn't help feeling as if they'd been caged.

Alex motioned her closer. "I need you to hold the rope, Sophie. Drop the bandage and use both hands if you have to."

Sophie nodded and set aside the bloodstained cravat, grateful that her fingers were no longer numb. If they cut the ropes completely loose they might unravel, causing the tarp to shift or billow. It would give them away. Alex cut the first rope, then carefully tied the two loose ends to another strand two feet over. He repeated the process four times, making sure each time to connect the ends to a piece of rope that was still intact and taut. It seemed to take forever. But finally, they had an opening wide enough for a person to slip through. Sophie looked down at the road passing beneath the wheels and gulped.

"Not here," Alex whispered. "There's no cover. We need to wait."

Sophie forced herself to nod. She knew he was right. They were passing open fields where there was no place to hide. Knowing he was right, however, did nothing to stem the tide of panic that threatened to overwhelm her.

She wanted to leave *now.*

If she had to throw herself from a moving wagon to escape violent kidnappers, she wanted to bloody well get it over with. She didn't want to sit and wait, giving her fear an opportunity to grow to unmanageable proportions, and the kidnappers a chance to discover what they were about.

An eternity later, at least in Sophie's mind, the landscape began to change. The fields gave way to trees and rocky outcroppings.

"We'd better take our chances now." Alex held the tarp back for her. "The next time the wagon slows to take a turn, I want you to jump. Aim for the embankment. When you get to your feet, run to the trees. If anything happens just keep running. Head east."

"Why east?"

"Because it's not the direction the wagon is going."

"Oh."

"I'll be right behind you."

She nodded. She couldn't think of anything else to say. She felt the carriage begin to slow and her heartbeat speed up. She slipped her legs over the back of the wagon.

Alex gave her a quick but heartfelt kiss. "Bend your knees, keep your arms tucked about your head, and try to let yourself roll."

Sophie glanced down at the road flying past her feet. "Is not rolling even an option?"

"Just don't fight it. I'll be right behind you. Now go."

Sophie jumped. She tried to follow Alex's instruction, but after the initial jarring impact she lost all control of her body to inertia. She did manage a great deal of rolling though, and when she finally managed to clamber to her feet—ignoring the myriad of aches and pains that promised spectacular bruising—she contented herself with that knowledge.

Before her head could finish spinning, Alex was at her side, grabbing her hand and pulling her into the woods at a dead run. She was immensely grateful for his company at that moment. Not just for his calming presence, but also for his ability to move in a straight line, a skill she currently lacked.

"Did they see us?" she whispered between gasping breathes. It took an enormous amount of effort to keep up with him, and she suspected he was capable of moving much faster. She hated that she might be slowing him down, but she knew he would never leave her behind. Her only hope was that their escape had gone unnoticed.

"No. You don't have to whisper," Alex answered in a normal tone of voice and, she couldn't help but notice, a barely winded one. "The wagon picked up speed after it rounded the corner. They didn't suspect a thing."

"How do you know?"

"Because I waited to jump."

"You waited until it was going faster?"

"Not much, just enough to be sure they hadn't noticed you'd gone missing."

Sophie glanced around fretfully for any sign of pursuit. Then she stumbled over a tree root. Alex pulled her arm to right her without slowing. "But could they have noticed after you jumped?" she asked, whispering again.

"They didn't," he replied, and she could almost hear the confident smile he was wearing. It grated on raw nerves.

"Well, if they didn't see *me* and they didn't see *you*," she began caustically, "then why the devil are we running?" She considering digging her heels in for effect, but at the speed they were going, and with the death grip Alex had on her hand, she figured she'd probably end up with an injured shoulder for her efforts.

Besides, Alex was already slowing down to a brisk walk.

"Are you tired? Do you need to rest?" he asked. Concern laced his voice, and she immediately felt foolish for her outburst. And more than a little ashamed. After all, she was the reason he was in this mess.

"I'm fine," she answered in a small voice. It wasn't strictly true, she hurt to the roots of her hair, but she would live, and all because of Alex. She would run until she dropped if that's what he wanted. "Really, I'm fine, we don't need to slow down."

Alex shook his head. "We don't need to run anymore, either. We're far enough into the woods."

"Oh." She glanced at his profile. "You're not hurt, are you?" He looked well enough, but one could never be sure.

"Perfectly fit," he assured her, and with such confidence she took him at his word and walked along beside him for awhile in silence.

"Alex," she asked, once she'd more or less regained her breath and good sense. "How did you get out of those ropes so quickly?"

Alex flinched. He had gotten out by using tricks he'd been

taught by his father and William. Tricks Sophie clearly did not have. Dear God, she'd been trying to chew through her bindings. He was simultaneously horrified at the danger he'd put her in, and unspeakably proud of how well she was handling it. Untying knots with one's mouth wasn't the most efficient means of escape, but it was a damn clever solution for someone who, by all rights, should have been rendered senseless with fear.

"I'm proud of you," he said, giving her hand a little squeeze.

She blinked at him. "Um . . . thank you, I think, but I haven't done anything."

Alex stopped and looked at her. "You've been uncommonly brave, Sophie, and in circumstances you can't possibly understand—"

"Well—"

"Let me finish, please, I think this may be easier for me if I do it quickly."

She nodded. There didn't seem to be anything else for it, since she hadn't the slightest idea what he was talking about. He sounded as if he were about to pull out a tooth, or sever a limb.

Alex reached down and took her other hand in his. "I believe those men were either Napoleon sympathizers or hired by one. In fact I'm almost sure of it. I'm. . . ." Alex put a fist to his mouth and cleared his throat. He retook her other hand, increased his grip as if afraid she might try to bolt—and he was—and said, "I know because I'm an agent for the war office and I've been investigating your cousin's affairs. I am sorry, Sophie. I wanted to keep you safe. I never suspected they knew. I. . . ."

Alex didn't know what else to say, how to make things right, or even better.

At least she wasn't trying to run, although she did appear sufficiently shocked.

"You're a spy?"

Alex pulled a face. He'd never particularly cared for that word—spying was not considered by most to be an honorable means of warfare. He much preferred the term "agent." But probably now wasn't a good time to quibble over semantics.

"Yes, I'm a spy—"

"I thought you'd been a soldier."

"I was. I am whatever the war office asks of me. It's something of a family tradition. The Rockefortes have always been in the active service of the Crown."

"Oh," she said rather stupidly. But really what else *could* she say? *I'm a spy too. Goodness, what are the odds?* seemed hopelessly wrong.

"You're not angry." She was still gawking at him a bit, looking stunned, but not mad. It was immensely relieving . . . and a little odd.

"No, I'm not angry." How could she be? What a hypocrite that would make her. It was strange though, that they'd been working around each other all this time. It seemed awfully disorganized.

"What exactly were you suppose to do?" she asked.

"Initially, I was to ordered to keep an eye on you and Lord Loudor."

A uncomfortable prickly sensation started at the back of her neck. She narrowed her eyes in suspicion. "What does that mean, 'keep an eye on you'?"

"Just what it implies, I suppose. I was to develop an association with you and through you Lord Loudor—"

"What?"

He shifted his feet a little nervously. "You're angry now, aren't you?"

She ignored that. "You were spying on me?"

"Only for a few days, a fortnight at most—"

"A fortnight. . . ." Memories of those first two weeks in London came flooding back. Alex laughing with her, Alex taking her to the opera, Alex kissing her . . . all lies?

"Yes, only a fortnight, ten days to be specific, not so very long if you think about it. After that, my mission was just a convenient excuse to court you—"

"You needed an excuse to court me."

Her voice was very, very calm. Disturbingly calm.

"Yes. No! I mean, not under normal circumstances, but—" Alex stopped and glanced down at his feet. He couldn't help it. Surely to God there was some visible evidence of the hole he was digging himself into. "You must understand, I had a duty—"

"A duty," she repeated ominously.

How deep was it now? Three feet, maybe four?

"An assignment. I couldn't very well—"

"Now I'm an assignment?"

"No. I did *not* say that."

Six feet. Definitely six.

"Sophie."

Surely that, at least, wouldn't get him into any more trouble.

She glared daggers.

Apparently, it wasn't enough to get him out of any either.

He tried again anyway.

"Sophie."

"How much of it was a lie?" she asked quietly.

Alex blinked in confusion. "I beg your pardon?"

"Those first ten days, and all the days after that . . ." She swallowed audibly. "How much of what you . . . what we did was a lie? All of it? Did you even want to be with me?"

"What? No, Sophie, don't." He reached out for her arm to stop her from turning away. "Look at me, sweetheart." He put his fingers under her chin and titled her head up. "Look at me," he repeated softly. "I have wanted to be with you since the moment I saw you. You took my breath away. The first moment we spoke, you stole my heart."

"Alex—"

"Nothing we have shared has been a lie," he insisted.

"Nothing. The reason for seeking you out was a pretense, yes, but I could never counterfeit the pleasure it brings me just to be near you."

His fingers left her chin to wipe a tear off her cheek. "Please, believe me, Sophie," he pleaded. "I will always want to be with you."

Even as he said the words, Alex knew they were true. He simply couldn't imagine a future without her. Couldn't imagine waking up each morning alone, or worse, next to a woman who wasn't Sophie. Couldn't imagine not hearing her laugh, seeing her smile, tasting her lips. . . .

"I believe you."

Sophie's voice shook him out of his reverie and he let out a breath he hadn't realized he'd been holding. "Thank God."

He took her hand and resumed walking. "If it makes you feel any better, I knew immediately *you* weren't a spy."

Sophie made a strange noise that was part laugh, part groan, and part choke. He stopped again and looked at her questioningly.

"As to that . . ." The words came out a nervous squeak.

He dropped her hand. His stomach did a slow roll before plummeting to his feet.

It couldn't be.

"Oh, don't look at me like that. I'm not a French spy."

"What sort of spy are you, then?"

"Besides an inept one," she grumbled, "an English sort of spy. The Prince Regent hired me to look into the affairs of my cousin and several of his associates."

"Prinny hired you?" he asked, unsure if he were more relieved, confused, or angry. "Prinny doesn't hire agents."

"Well, he didn't do it personally."

"Of course not, Prinny doesn't do anything personally, except make an ass of himself. I meant he always looks to the war office when he wants someone watched. We try to keep him out of the more important affairs, but. . . ."

"Maybe he figured that out and decided to circumvent you?" she offered.

"Maybe, but I doubt it. We've never actually denied him anything." He looked at her for a moment. "How long have you been in the business of espionage?"

"About as long as I've been in London," she answered with a wry twist of her mouth. "A man approached me on the boat over, and I wasn't in a position to refuse. He offered a great deal of money."

"Good Lord, I can't believe I didn't figure this out," Alex muttered.

"Maybe I'm a better spy than I realized."

"And I can't believe you had the audacity to become angry with me—"

"You were spying on *me*."

He pretended not to hear her. "When this is over, I'm going to wring Prinny's neck."

"I'll thank you to wait until after he's paid me."

"Your espionage days are over, Sophie."

Alex picked up her hand again and resumed walking.

"Not quite yet, they're not," she retorted, struggling to keep up with his brisk pace. "I still haven't found the proof they want. Although there is the matter of Whitefield's missing funds, and I did come across some interesting letters in Lord Calmaton's desk drawer."

He shot her sideways glance. "How did you get into Calmaton's desk drawer?"

"I picked the lock."

"Picked the . . . ?"

He stopped and turned abruptly.

She barely avoided running into his chest. "We are never going to get anywhere like this," she mumbled.

"How, in God's name, did you come by that talent?"

"We'll be out here for days."

"I'm waiting for an answer, Sophie. You said you'd never done this before. So where did you learn to pick a lock?"

"Mr. Wang taught me," she said impatiently. "May we start moving now?"

"Not yet. Why the devil would he teach you such a thing?"

Sophie sighed in the manner of one much put upon. "If you must know, I can't play the pianoforte."

An expectant silence followed.

"And . . . ?" Alex finally prompted.

"*And* Mr. Wang decided my talents might lie elsewhere. I'm not at all musically inclined and the more I practiced, the more frustrated I became. Eventually, Mr. Wang took me aside and explained that everyone has their own unique set of gifts. He gave me a few options to try and I chose the ones that sounded the most interesting."

"And how to effectively open a door without a key was one of those options?" he asked incredulously.

"Yes, and Mr. Wang was correct. I took to it right away and felt immensely better about myself."

"You couldn't have just attempted the harp, or the flute?"

"I told you, I have no skill with music. Besides, we were in the Cape Verde Islands at the time and there were no harps or flutes readily available."

Alex looked at her a moment longer, shook his head in disbelief, then started off again.

"Finally," she muttered.

❊ Twenty-four ❊

$\mathcal{B}$y the time they came across an old hunting box in the woods, Sophie was ready to weep with exhaustion.

She was also ready to push Alex off the nearest cliff. She was hot, tired, frightened of the coming dark, and very, very annoyed.

Over the last few hours she had attempted to broach the subject of her continuing work for the Prince Regent several times. *Her* arguments had been all that was rational and sensible. Alex had responded with a spiteful obstinacy that made her want to scream. She was not to risk herself any further, and that, it would seem, was that.

She didn't actually need his permission. In fact, at the moment, she didn't much care about his opinion on the issue one way or the other. It was his high-handedness that infuriated her. No one cared to be ordered about, particularly herself. Particularly by *him*.

Fuming, she watched as Alex tested the door to the cabin. It swung open on squeaking hinges.

"You see," he said in a jovial voice that made her want to slam the door shut on his fingers. "Your skills are not required."

She glared at his back. She'd been forced to do that all day, as the path through the woods had become too narrow for them to walk side by side, and it wasn't at all satisfying.

"The Prince Regent disagrees," she retorted, moving past him to go inside.

"I suggest we let the matter drop."

"You began it." She headed straight for the meager kitchen and began searching for candles, too tired and too worried to care they were bickering like children.

"Well, now I'm finishing it."

"Fine," she snapped.

"Excellent."

A few minutes passed while he watched her moving restlessly about the kitchen. "What are you looking for?"

"Candles, I can't find them," she answered distractedly.

"Probably there aren't any."

She didn't bother looking at him, but continued her search with a kind of manic desperation. "Of course there are. Why wouldn't there be candles? Everyone has candles."

"Apparently not the everyone who owns this cottage."

"Don't be obtuse. There have to be candles, have to be. . . ."

"For God's sake, Sophie, you've searched every drawer and cupboard in this place. Surely it hasn't escaped your notice that our little abode is in serious disrepair. There's no food, no bed, a broken fireplace, and what is here is covered in dust. I doubt anyone else has been inside this place in years."

"Well, we'll just have to use the fireplace, surely—"

"It's in shambles. We'd be smoked out. Will you sit down?"

"No! I want—"

"Candles. Yes, I know." He gave up and watched her open a cupboard she had searched twice already. She reached up and patted the recesses of the shelves, groping blindly with her hand. Her cheeks were flushed, and her eyes held a wild glint to them. She looked positively furious. Positively beautiful, actually, but he wasn't in the mood to pay compliments.

"Of the multitude of disasters we are currently facing, you're in a tizzy over some missing tapers? Good Lord, you have a skewed sense of priorities. Why do you need them so badly?"

She had difficulty answering. The panic that had been nibbling away at her nerves as evening progressed was beginning to take increasingly large bites. The sun was almost down, and in a few moments it would be dark, completely black. And Alex was right, there were no candles, no fireplace. Nothing to hold the night at bay.

There would be no light.

The certain knowledge of that sent an icy coldness prickling along her skin and sinking into her muscles. It squeezed her chest until her heart pumped too hard and her lungs seemed barely to work at all. It crept into her mind, gleefully pushing aside reason and courage.

In a daze, she looked past Alex to the window.

"There's no moon," she whispered. "It's cloudy and there's no moon out."

His brow knit in confusion and concern. "Why does that matter?"

"I . . ."

He walked around a counter to cup her face in his hands. He'd been wrong, he realized. It wasn't anger that lit her face. It was something else entirely. "Sophie?"

"It'll be dark. Completely dark."

"Yes," he said slowly, carefully. "It's better that way. We'll be harder to . . ." His voice trailed off as she shook her head vehemently.

His thumb traced a gentle path along her jaw. "What is it? What are you afraid of, sweetheart? Is it the dark?"

"I . . ." For a brief moment, shame was nearly as powerful as the fear. She wished it would overwhelm her entirely. Humiliation would be worlds better than this slowly creeping madness. But with each passing second, the light in the room grew dimmer. And simple fear quickly stepped aside for terror.

"Sophie?"

"Yes," she admitted in a mortified whisper. "Yes, the dark. I can't . . . I can't . . . things happen."

"What? What happens, Sophie?"

"Things . . ."

Death. Death happened in the dark.

When her eyes filled with tears, Alex scooped her up in his arms and carried her to the window. Questions would do her no good now. Later he would ask them. Later he would find the source of her pain.

And do everything he could to kill it.

"Here now, love. Look at the sunset. It's dipped below the clouds now. See the way the light passes through the trees? When I was a very little boy, my mother would take me for walks in the evening. When we passed through light like that, she would tell me we were touching the fingers of God. It's beautiful, isn't it?"

"Yes." Her voice was hardly more than a whisper, but it was enough.

"Take a good look, Sophie. Hold the picture in your mind. Can you do that?"

Her nod was jerky against his shoulder.

"Good, now close your eyes and—"

"No! I can't! I have to watch. I have to see."

"Watch for what, sweet?"

She shook her head, but he had a terrible suspicion he already knew the answer. "All right, I'll watch. How's that? I'll watch over us tonight, I promise. Now close your eyes. There's a girl."

He sat down against the far wall, settling her in his lap.

"You won't fall asleep?" Her voice was mumbled against his chest but he heard the fear, and the hope. And it broke his heart.

"No, love, I promise. I won't fall asleep."

Good to his word, Alex kept guard throughout the night.

He held her while she trembled, stroked her hair and rubbed gentle circles along her back. He spoke to her of the sun that would fill the forest just outside the door, of long golden summer days and the soft blue light of winter evenings. Anything and everything he could think of to ease a terror he didn't understand.

When the first rays of light broke across the horizon he

whispered for her to open her eyes. Sophie took one look, sighed raggedly and closed her eyes again. Alex laid them both down and let himself follow her into sleep.

The sun was high into the sky when Sophie woke. She felt stiff, groggy, and miserably ashamed.

"How are you feeling?"

One look at Alex standing over her added a generous heaping of guilt. His clothes were rumpled, his hair a mess, and there were circles under his beautiful green eyes. Because of her.

"I'm fine," she mumbled. "Did you sleep at all?"

"I did, yes." He sat down beside her and pulled a hankerchief out of his pocket. "Blackberries," he supplied. "I found a patch almost outside our front door."

Though her system was still reeling from the nightmare of last night, Sophie accepted a few of the juicy black berries. She hadn't had a meal in over a day.

"Won't you have some?" she asked when he made no move to eat.

"I had my fill while I picked," he explained. "Go ahead."

Feeling uncomfortable under his watchful eye, she nonetheless ate every last berry and licked her fingers clean.

"There's a bucket of rainwater outside if you like."

She nodded and rose, avoiding looking him in the eye.

She took her time cleaning up, letting the sun warm her face, and settle her mind and body. She'd spent the night in a man's arms. Alex's arms. She wasn't at all certain how she felt about that—touched that he'd taken such care of her, amazed that his presence, his voice, his smell, the feel of his strength, had kept the worst of the fear at bay.

And she felt embarrassed. Mortified, really. She'd spent the whole of the night crying and shivering like a frightened child. What must he think of her?

He'd want an explanation, of course. He deserved one.

She tilted her head back and let the sun shine on her a moment longer then went back inside.

Alex watched her cross the small room to stand in front of him. He remained quiet as she took a deep breath and closed her eyes.

"It was dark when my mother and sister died," she whispered.

He brought a hand up to rub the path of freckles across her nose. She was still so pale, he thought. He'd seen the echoes of last night's fear in her clear blue eyes before she'd closed them.

"You don't have to explain. Not until you're ready. I can wait."

She let out an enormous sigh of relief and her lids fluttered open. "You don't think me a coward?"

The hope in her voice broke his heart. "Sophie, of course not. How could you think that? How could anyone think that?"

"*I* think that. You saw me last night." She laughed without humor. "I was fully mad, wasn't I?"

"*No.* You were terrified. I've seen men in the grip of madness and men in the grip of panic. They may look similar, but I assure you, they are two very separate states."

Sophie was momentarily taken aback by his reasoning. She had never thought of it that way. She had always viewed her terror as a kind of transient insanity, a weakness she couldn't fight.

She looked up at him with gratitude, with longing.

If only he would agree to go with her to China. If only, for once in her life, she could just be lucky without having to pay for it later. If only Alex loved her and nothing else in the world mattered.

And when "if onlys" were pound notes she'd hire a team of lawyers and send her cousin to debtors' prison on his way to hell.

At least the sun was shining, Sophie mused as she climbed over yet another fallen tree. They'd hiked across the countryside all morning and well into midday. It was hard going, but she could only imagine how much worse the trek would be if they had foul weather rather than a clear fall day.

Alex seemed to have some idea of where they were headed, insisting that they were following some sort of trail after she pointed out that they were no longer traveling east. She tried in vain to detect any sign of an intentional path through the roots and brambles, but eventually abandoned the effort in favor of simply putting one foot in front of the other. He'd never given her any reason to doubt his navigational skills, and England was a fairly well-populated island. How long could they possibly travel before finding civilization?

Three hours later, Sophie was beginning to consider the possibility that they had left England behind—and were now well into Scotland—when they stumbled out of the thick woods and onto a road.

"Thank God," she panted, letting her legs collapse ungracefully beneath her until her rump was settled comfortably—relatively speaking, of course—in the dirt. She very nearly leaned down and kissed the gravelly earth, she was so delighted to see it.

"You sound awfully pleased for someone sitting in the middle of a rural road with no help in sight," Alex commented suspiciously.

"Just thrilled to be out of the woods," she replied. And so very, *very* relieved that he had actually found a road. Even if it was in Scotland.

Alex didn't look convinced, just gave a "hmm" and turned to take in their surroundings.

"Should we just wait here for someone to come by then?" she asked hopefully and was more disappointed than surprised when he shook his head. The road was in terrible shape, with large ruts and grass growing down the middle. Clearly, it wasn't a major thoroughfare.

"We could be here for weeks," Alex answered. "Which direction would you like to go?"

"I beg your pardon?"

Alex pointed down one end of the road and then the other. "North or south? Your choice."

"My . . . ? Don't you know which way to go?"

"How on earth would I know that?"

Confused, she stared at him a moment before speaking.

"Well . . . you knew which way the road was."

"I can follow a trail, not see across miles."

"Oh." She probably would have thought of that if she hadn't been so tired. She looked down both directions and frowned thoughtfully. "It's silly, of course, but this road looks familiar to me somehow. It can't be the one to Haldon, I know, but. . . ."

"You're tired," Alex said sympathetically taking a seat next to her. "It's perfectly understandable—"

"Please don't patronize me, Alex," she said without any real anger. She simply hadn't the energy for anything more than a token annoyance at his tone.

"My apologies. I'm tired as well."

She sighed. "I'm sorry, too. We've been at each other's throats for almost a full two days now, haven't we?"

He gave her a small smile. "We haven't argued the whole time," he pointed out.

"Yes, and thank you for last night Alex, and this morning," she said sincerely. "I should have thanked you earlier. I . . . what you did for me . . ."

"It was nothing."

"It was something to me."

He crouched down and squeezed one of her hands. "Then it was my pleasure. Now, pick a direction while we're still in each other's good graces. With any luck, we'll find assistance before I learn firsthand if you know how to use that knife."

"Oh, I'm a master," she said baldly, knowing he wouldn't believe it and finding a kind of perverse amusement in that. "Best you keep it with you, lest I feel compelled to prove my skill."

"An excellent suggestion." He held his hand out and helped her to her feet. "Shall we try the north route?"

"Oh, no, south. Definitely south."

To England.

❋ *Twenty-five* ❋

$\mathcal{S}$ophie couldn't shake the feeling that she had been on the road before. There were no definitive markers to either support or dispel the suspicion, but every now and then they would pass a meadow that looked familiar, or come upon a bend and she knew, just *knew,* there would be a steep incline on the other side.

As the sun began to lower in the horizon, however, she lost interest in the peculiar feeling. If they didn't find shelter soon, they would be stuck outside at night, in the dark. Sophie didn't think she could take another night like the previous one. *Don't borrow trouble,* she admonished herself silently. The sky was clear. If it stayed that way, and if the moonlight was bright enough, she would be all right. Just keep moving, she told herself. Just keep moving. She fixed her eyes on the horizon and forced her protesting legs into longer and faster strides.

"That tree is enormous."

Sophie snapped out of her self-imposed trance and followed Alex's gaze to a towering elm, its thick branches shading where they stood.

And she suddenly realized why everything seemed so familiar.

She made a slow turn in the road.

She knew this road, this spot, that tree.

Alex, who had moved on, stopped and turned back. "So-phie?"

She didn't answer him. She couldn't speak at all, just stare at the tree. Numbly at first, as memories flooded her so fast she couldn't sort one from another. And then with a kind of growing wonder she would never have expected to come from this place.

"Sophie?" Alex said again, reaching her side. He followed her gaze to the elm. "It's impressive, I know, but we need to keep moving if—"

"I *have* been here before," she whispered.

"Are you sure?"

"I know where we are. This road leads to Whitefield," she said still looking intently at the tree.

"That would explain a great deal," Alex commented, thinking that it didn't do much to explain her odd fascination with the tree. "What is it, Sophie?"

"This is where it happened."

Her voice was so soft. So soft, he had to lean down to catch the words. "Where what happened, sweetheart?"

"This is where they died."

Feeling helpless, he brought a hand up to stroke soothingly down her dark locks. "Your mother and sister, you mean?" he asked gently.

She nodded, but there was more than sadness in her eyes. There was a quiet awe. And, he realized with dawning horror, there was memory.

"Were you there, Sophie? Did you see it happen?"

She nodded again and pointed at the tree. "I remember that tree."

Alex felt as if someone had punched him in the gut. No one had told him she had been in the carriage. "I'm sorry, darling. I'm so sorry."

"We lost a wheel, I think, or maybe we just slid off the road. I don't remember. I don't remember much of anything except that tree and how cold it was."

And the dark. Oh, how she remembered the dark.

"They said later that the driver had died instantly. Mama must have known, because she got out of the carriage for a bit, and when she came back she said we just needed to be patient until Papa came to get us. I thought everything was fine. . . ."

"Your mother got out? I thought . . ."

She turned to look at him for a moment. "That the accident had killed her?" She shook her head and looked back at the tree. "Mama and Lizzie weren't hurt at all, that I know of."

He waited a minute for her to resume talking. When she didn't he said, "I don't understand, Sophie."

"It was snowing," she said softly. "It was a blizzard, and Papa's men couldn't get through to us until morning. Mama and Lizzie fell asleep."

"But you didn't," he guessed. "You stayed awake, didn't you?"

A sad smile tugged at one corner of her mouth. "It was the tree," she said, motioning toward the massive elm. "I could just make out its outline through the snow and darkness. I was old enough to know better, but every time I tried to close my eyes all I could see was its gnarled branches reaching out for me, and the vision would scare me awake. I watched it the whole night—I thought it was a monster."

Alex regarded the tree with something akin to gratitude. It had saved her life. "What do you see now?" he asked.

She turned and caught his eye. "I see life," she said simply. "I don't know why that is. Perhaps, it's simply because I'm older now, or perhaps because it's so different in daylight."

Alex took her face in his hands and kissed her. Kissed her with the desire he felt every time he looked at her. Kissed her with the gratitude he felt but couldn't express to a tree. Kissed her with the sorrow he felt for the loss of two people she loved so dearly. But mostly he kissed her with the joy he felt of being alive.

When he was done, she looked suitably dazed.

"We need to get moving," he said, placing one last smack on her forehead and dropping his hands while he still had the strength of will to let her go.

"Right," she croaked.

He smiled smugly. He couldn't help himself. He loved knowing he could do that to her, loved thinking of all the things he would do to her as soon as they were married.

"Are we close to Whitefield then?" he asked over his shoulder as he headed down the road.

Sophie hadn't moved yet. "Sorry, what? Oh!" She jogged a bit to catch up. "Whitefield. Right. It's not far, I think. Two to three miles? My memory of the area is a little fuzzy."

The portly man eyed the two miscreants in front of him with open disgust. "How did you let her get away?"

"Best we can figure, the chit 'ad a knife. Ain't that right, Sam?"

"That's what we figured all right. A real clean cut——"

"Did I not specifically instruct you to check her for knives!"

"And so we did guv, the both of 'em. We found one on the toff, and the one the girl was holdin' when we grabbed 'er, but she weren't carrying one of 'em bags fings . . . what'd you call 'em, Sam?"

"Reticules," Sam offered knowingly.

"And on her person?" Portly man ground out.

The men looked taken aback. "You did'n say nofink abow stickin' our 'ands up a lady's skirt!" the first man cried accusingly, his accent becoming more pronounced in his indignation.

"We was hired to kidnap the girl, not paw her," Sam pointed out.

"An the toff weren't suppose to be there a'tall," the first man grumbled. "We'll be wantin' double for that."

The portly man was struck dumb for a moment with shock

and fury. Finally, he found his voice and began bellowing. "You're common criminals, thieves, murderers—!"

"I ain't newer killed no one in my life," the first man stated promptly.

"I have," Sam admitted sadly. "But it were in the army. I suspect the good Lord might see fit to forgive me for it, if I spend my days repentin' for what I done."

The first man gave his friend a reassuring pat on the back. "True enough, Sam, true enough." He turned a hard eye on the portly man. "He can't rightly maul a girl and atone for what he done at the same time, now can he?"

"You kidnapped her!"

"Aye, we did," Sam replied in that same resigned tone. "Got mouths to feed at home, don't we? 'Spect God'll see fit to forgive me that too."

"Some of those mouths be wives," the first man commented pointedly.

"And daughters," Sam added, "and sisters."

"Nieces."

"Got a grandbaby on the way, might be a girl—"

"Yes, I get it! For the love of God, where does he find you people? I can't decide if you're mad or merely stupid!"

Two sets of eyes narrowed at that comment, but the portly man was too intent on his own anger to notice the danger he was in. "It's a damned good thing Heransly had the foresight to hire another set of men!" he yelled. "They'll have no trouble cleaning up the job you two idiots—"

"Don't seem right he set competition on us, does it, Sam?" the first man asked quietly.

"Not right at all," Sam replied.

The first man began cracking his knuckles. "Someone might 'ave gotten 'urt in the mix-up, eh Sam?"

Sam rolled his shoulders. "Aye, they could have."

The first man clenched and unclenched his hands. "Seems like backstabbing to me."

Sam twisted his neck from side to side, effectively emitting a loud popping noise. "Aye, and me."

The portly man watched the antics of the two ruffians with dawning apprehension. Perhaps he had been a little free with his comments. That happened on occasion when he'd had too much to drink. He gulped nervously and eyed the distance to the door. "Remember your immortal soul, Sam," he croaked. "What would the good Lord think?"

"Expect he'll understand," was Sam's only reply.

Whitefield was deserted. Sophie wasn't surprised to find the old manor house devoid of residents, but it was disturbing to see that it had been stripped of most of its contents. No doubt her cousin had sold everything of value. She wondered about the tenants. She knew some worked the land. The estate was highly profitable, but who did they look to for guidance, or in time of need? She hated to think what state their homes might be in. She couldn't imagine Lord Loudor was a generous or responsible master.

Sophie wandered the halls and rooms in a kind of stupor. There were so many memories, so many of them lost to her until now. . . . The nursery where she and Lizzie had done their best to torment their first nanny, that priggish Mrs. Carlisle. And the orangery where her mother could most often be found in her spare time, lovingly tending her myriad roses and orchids. Sophie smiled fondly at the memory. For all the enjoyment her mother took in the work, she had never been a particularly adept gardener. More than once, her father had replaced dead or dying plants in secret to avoid seeing his wife disappointed.

And Sophie had forgotten that window seat in the library, where she and Lizzie used to sit for hours, curled up in blankets on cold winter days, reading to each other, speaking of their plans for the future. Lizzie was going to marry a foreign prince and spend her time writing scandalous novels.

Often they would just sit in comfortable silence watching the snow fall, needing no words to communicate their happiness.

"Is it difficult to return after so long an absence?" Alex asked, coming up behind her with an armful of blankets and pillows.

She turned away from the window. "A little," she replied. "But I'm not sorry to be here. Where did you find those?"

"The beds are gone, but the linen closets are still intact," he answered. "I noticed there are quite a few candles left in the dining room, and a positively enormous table."

"A gift from King George," she explained, following him out of the library. "I suppose its regal origin wasn't incentive enough to convince a buyer to invest in the cost of its removal."

Alex set down his burden a little way from the dining room fireplace, and arranged the blankets into a makeshift bed. "This fireplace is the only one in the house that looks reasonably clean," he explained. "I doubt we'll need it, but one never knows, and I'd hate to have gotten this far only to burn Whitefield down around our heads."

"Especially after all the work I've put into saving it," Sophie muttered to herself as she began to light the candles randomly about the room. The sun had already set, and she wanted the place well lit before night set in.

Alex walked to the windows and began pulling the curtains closed to keep the light from announcing their presence to the outside world.

"After we're married," he commented offhandedly, "I assume you'll want to spend some time here, refurbishing, getting to know the tenants, that sort of thing."

Sophie stared at him with a kind of awe. "You are, without doubt, the most tenacious human being I have ever met."

"Was that a compliment or an insult?"

"I'm not quite certain," she replied honestly. "Alex, we've discussed this. I am not going to marry you. I am flattered by your offer, and I . . . like you very much. I respect and admire you, and I know we have a certain . . ."

"Mutual passion?" he offered helpfully.

"Affinity," she stated primly. "But we simply will not suit."

Alex pulled a chair out from the table. "Sit down."

"No, thank you. I'm perfectly comfortable as I am." She wasn't the least bit comfortable. She was tired and sore, and she had run out of candles to light, but he was telling her what to do again.

"Sophie, please, have a seat. I am exhausted, but good manners dictate I not sit in a lady's presence while she is yet standing."

She wasn't entirely sure she believed that, but at least he was trying.

She took the proffered chair and watched as he pulled out another and turned it to face her. Sitting down, he leaned forward and captured her hands in his.

"Sophie," he started gravely. "We disappeared, at night, from a house party attended by half the *ton*. We have since spent two full days and nights together, alone. Surely it has occurred to you that you have been compromised?"

Sophie paled. "I hadn't . . ." She swallowed hard. "With everything else, I hadn't given it any thought."

"I'm sorry."

She pulled her hands from his and crossed the room in a futile effort to give outlet to the panic beginning to well up inside her.

Alex stood, but made no move to follow her.

"It's not your fault," she mumbled.

Dear God, compromised. She searched her memory for what Mrs. Summers had told her of girls who had the misfortune of becoming compromised. She'd only half listened at the time. It simply wasn't a concern when you were often the only English-speaking woman within hundreds, even thousands of square miles.

"I've been compromised," she repeated thoughtfully. "But

not ruined. I need only marry to set things right, and to my knowledge there's no rule stating *whom* I must marry. I'll simply ask Sir Frederick when we return."

"Sir Frederick?" Alex was too surprised to point out the glaring holes in her plan.

"Of course. He's perfect."

"Of course," Alex mimicked.

"He can give me Whitefield, and I can give him a respectable marriage . . . to a woman."

Alex didn't pretend to not understand her meaning. "How is it you know about Sir Frederick?"

"Mirabelle told me. It was her idea to put him on the list. Although, I believe it was Evie who came by the information originally."

"Good Lord," Alex muttered. "William should have hired those two girls. They would have ferreted out Loudor's secrets months ago."

"Undoubtedly."

"Sophie, Sir Frederick will not agree to marry you. He wants a bride who will repel scandal, not invite it, and a young woman who has been compromised by another man does not fit the description of a respectable bride."

"Well, beggars can't be choosers."

"Unfortunately for you, Sir Frederick isn't a beggar. He's wealthy and immensely popular. He'll have no difficulty securing some open-minded widow in need of the financial security a union with him would provide."

Sophie thought about that for a moment, then—"Damn it!"

She returned to pacing the room, ranting in a language Alex didn't understand. He let her rave a while, which he felt was rather good of him, considering it was a reaction garnered from his marriage proposal. What he really wanted to do was clamp a hand over her mouth. Finally, when he felt she had cooled off sufficiently, he took a deep breath and tried reasoning with her again.

"We must marry." Very well, it wasn't reasoning, but she was so blasted stubborn and—

"No."

Alex had used up his store of patience. "Why the hell not?"

"Don't swear at me."

"You must be joking. You swore at me not five minutes ago."

"I wasn't swearing at you. I was swearing at. . . ."

"The situation?" he offered caustically.

She answered him with a scowl.

"Answer my question: Why not?"

She wanted to shout, *Because I love you!* And then she wanted to cry. If he ever loved her in return, the price to be paid would be too high.

If he ever loved her. *If* he ever loved her. That was a fairly enormous "if." She knew he cared for her, and it was possible, if they were together for many years, that he might grow to love her. But it wouldn't be love as she knew it. It wouldn't be this all-encompassing emotion that made her want to simultaneously throw her arms around him and kick him in the shins. He wouldn't be *in* love with her. The sort of love she felt for him was very rare indeed, and to have it returned was even rarer.

What she felt for him was surely . . . unrequited love. The thought of it had the oddest effect on her. She felt a fierce pain in her chest . . . and she felt relieved. She didn't think unrequited love could be considered balanced in and of itself, but she was absolutely certain it could never be mistaken for good fortune. Since he would never love her back, she wouldn't be at risk to suffer the inevitable payback of an equal dose of misfortune.

"Sophie."

She would be safe. She *was* safe. She could marry Alex—*if* he allowed her return to her father. She groaned inwardly. So many ifs!

"Sophie! Either you marry me, or you don't marry at all," Alex declared, having given up on his earlier question.

She stopped pacing and looked at him. "One of us was insulted by that remark, but I'm just not sure which one."

"Do I get a vote?" he grumbled.

"No."

"I thought not. Be reasonable, Sophie."

"I am being reasonable. All I want is to be able to return to my father."

Alex considered that for a moment. "Very well."

"I beg your pardon?"

"I said 'very well.' We'll marry and you can be reunited with your father." He held his hand up to forestall any comment from her. "*After* you give me an heir." Alex was reasonably certain he could convince the viscount to return to England by then.

She narrowed her eyes suspiciously. "What if I can't have children? Or what if I only have daughters?" she asked.

"I would be delighted with daughters," Alex said honestly. Little dark-haired, blue-eyed imps just like their mother. He reconsidered that. Little dark-haired, blue-eyed angels sounded better. His daughters were not going to spend their days learning how to pick locks and throw knifes. Nor were they going to engage in dangerous activities of any sort.

"You're scowling," Sophie remarked, not sounding particularly concerned. "But what of an heir? And what if I can't have children at all?"

Alex sighed. *Then I will thank God every day for having you all to myself,* he thought. What did it matter? They'd find a way to be happy together. Lord knew he couldn't be happy without her.

"We'll set a time limit," he said. "If we are unable to produce an heir in, say . . ." he waved his hand about a bit, "ten years, then—"

"Ten years!"

"Well, we don't want to be too hasty. Lady Thurston had Kate fairly late in life, you know."

"Three years," Sophie countered.

"Seven."

"Five."

"Done."

And that was that.

❀ *Twenty-six* ❀

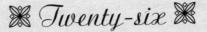

*S*ophie blinked.

Alex grinned.

"Well then," she gulped.

"Well then," he repeated, smiling wolfishly and moving toward her in much the same manner. "How shall we celebrate our engagement?"

"Er . . ."

"Come now, you don't mean to renege do you? It's considered very bad form, you know."

"I'm not going to renege," she said a little defensively, glad to focus on something other than the feral way he was eyeing her.

"Delighted to hear it."

He advanced toward her and Sophie instinctively retreated until her back was pressed against the wall. Alex leaned forward and pressed his palms on the wall at either side of her head, neatly boxing her in. His eyes raked over her as if she were a feast set before a starving man and Sophie felt the heat of it, the thrill of it, race along her skin.

"I think we've tried this once before," she said, wondering at her nervousness, and the excitement that came along with it. It wasn't as if she had never kissed him before. Of course, she didn't recall him ever before looking quite so . . . hungry.

Alex's eyebrows shot up. "Betrothal?"

"No, kissing to celebrate an agreement. It involved a hat pin, remember?"

"Ah, yes," he murmured, bringing his face closer to hers. "The hat pin. If I recall correctly, I suggested we kiss to seal a pact that day. Now we are celebrating our engagement. It is entirely different, I assure you."

"If you say so." Really why should she argue? Were she nervous or not, he was going to kiss her and they were going to be wed.

Sophie felt a weight lift from shoulders. She was going to marry Alex and not some old man who treated her like an adorable bonbon. Whitefield was safe, her father was safe, and she got Alex. Perhaps not forever, but for a while at least, and that was considerably more than she had allowed herself to even hope for.

She no longer had to fight down every desire, the longing she felt every time she looked at him, thought of him. Alex was hers now. She could kiss him to her heart's delight.

She threw her arms around his neck and did just that.

Alex may have been a little bewildered at her sudden enthusiasm, but it came nowhere near his delight. And that didn't come anywhere near to the overwhelming lust that started in his groin and expanded to encompass every nerve ending in his body.

His hands traveled up her back, into her hair, down her shoulders and to her waist. He reached around and cupped her bottom, bringing her tight against the proof of his desire.

She groaned into his mouth, and the sound made him a little crazed. Easing away from her, he hooked one arm beneath her knees and lifted her high against his chest. He made slow progress to the makeshift bed, finding it difficult to remember where he was going. She was doing the most amazing things with her mouth. Nibbling on his lips, nipping at an earlobe, trailing wet kisses down his neck. They were untutored caresses, but they elicited a response from him the most skilled of courtesans could not have managed.

"My God, Sophie," he breathed, finally finding the linens on the floor and lowering them both until she lay beneath him.

"I should wait," he mumbled kissing his way down to one still-clothed breast. "You deserve a real bed, a—"

"I don't want to wait," was her breathless reply.

"Thank God." Alex pulled the fabric of her dress down to expose a single taut nipple. He lightly trailed his tongue over it in experimentation. She gasped. He grinned against her skin and did it again, teasing her endlessly, lapping, circling, blowing gently against the damp nub, until her gasps became moans. Then he latched on and suckled. She cried aloud and threaded her fingers through his hair.

Alex could have stayed there for hours. Well, maybe not hours exactly, he was more than a little eager to explore other parts of her. But he could have stayed there for a good deal longer if the weatherworn fabric of her dress were not scraping at his chin, a reminder that it was an obstacle to what lay beneath.

"This has got to go," he said, giving the nipple a final kiss before sitting her up and helping her unbutton the back of her dress.

They undressed each other in stages. His coat, shirt, and waistcoat. Her gown and stockings. All the while stopping to kiss, to caress, to explore.

Sophie was fascinated by every inch of him. He was all hard angles and muscle.

"Amazing," she whispered.

Alex chuckled. He unfastened his breeches but left them on. He'd never made love to an innocent, but he rather thought they might frighten easily. God knew their mothers did them no favor by keeping them in ignorance. The thought gave him pause.

Sophie, still in her chemise, was watching him undo the

buttons on his breeches with a mixture of excitement and trepidation.

Suddenly, he stopped and looked at her a little worriedly.

"Sophie?" he said in that way people have when they're about to ask a question but aren't quite sure how to go about it. "Sophie, we're . . . that is . . . do you know what we're doing?"

She blinked. She would have though that was fairly obvious. Then a terrible thought occurred to her. "Did I . . . do something wrong?" she asked in a horrified whisper.

"No, sweetheart, no. You've done everything right, better than right, perfect." He reached out and gently tucked a lock of hair behind her ear. "I just don't want to frighten you."

"Because I haven't done this before," she explained, not quite over the scare that she may have committed some horrible faux pas.

"Yes, I know, and I can't tell you how ridiculously pleased I am by that. But do you know what to expect?"

"Oh . . . Yes?" She sounded more hopeful than certain.

Alex didn't think that was a very promising sign.

"I have a general idea," Sophie explained. "But I'm a little fuzzy on the specifics."

He considered that for a moment. "Why don't you tell me what you do know," he suggested.

Sophie pursed her lips. "Well . . . I know it involves kissing."

"There is that," Alex drew his thumb along her bottom lip. "Have I mentioned how partial I am to your lips? Lush, ripe . . ." The tip of his finger dipped inside, back out again. "Perfect."

A shiver traveled up her spine and he pulled his hand away.

"What else, Sophie?"

"Um . . . touching . . . I know it involves touching," Sophie managed.

"That is also true," he said, trailing a finger down the length of her cheek.

"And . . ." He was making this awfully difficult. "The removal of clothing is necessary."

Alex's hand slid down to rest at her hip. "Certain pertinent articles, at any rate."

"You mean it isn't necessary?" She rather liked the idea of being able to do this without having to be completely naked.

"It is tonight," he growled, gripping her other hip and pulling her onto his lap. He leaned over to trail slow hot kisses down the side of her neck. "What else, Sophie?"

It took a moment for his words to seep into her passion-clouded brain. "Are you really determined to talk about this?"

"Talking about it can be almost as much fun as doing it," he murmured.

"Really?"

"Almost," he clarified.

He straightened a little and gently tugged on her ear with his mouth. Her senses were humming.

"What else?" he prompted.

"Um . . . I know . . . er, I know . . . I know you're making this terribly difficult."

He didn't stop.

"I know that . . . that you and I are . . . different."

He snaked one arm around her waist to hold her in place, while the other hand came up to fondle a breast.

"We have different parts," she said on a gasp.

"Thank God for that. What else, Sophie?"

What else? Sophie couldn't think of what else. She couldn't seem to think at all. She wrapped her arms around his shoulders.

Alex stilled suddenly, and then let out a long breath against the damp skin of her neck. "That's it, isn't it?" he asked.

Sophie tensed. He didn't have to sound so put out about it. And that wasn't it, thank you very much.

"I've seen cats do it," she blurted out quickly, then clamped her eyes shut in mortification.

Cats?

Cats?

She felt the muscles in his arms tighten and shake and forced her eyelids open. He straightened and looked down at her, his own eyes dancing with merriment.

"Cats," he repeated in an amused and slightly patronizing tone that prompted an explanation from her.

"Yes, cats." In for a penny, in for a pound. "I was very young, and I thought they were fighting. Mrs. Summers told me to look away, but I only pretended to, of course, and . . . well, she tried to pull them apart but only got scratched for her troubles. She still has the scar on her hand," Sophie rambled nervously, simultaneously wondering if it was possible to bite off one's own tongue, and how much it might hurt if one tried.

"I'll wager that scar makes for some interesting dinner conversations," Alex said, grinning—in Sophie's opinion—like an idiot.

"I've quite ruined the moment, haven't I?" she grumbled.

"On the contrary, this is the most delightful moment I've had in years. I shall remember it always."

Sophie cringed, very much afraid he would.

"Any other animal husbandry lessons you—?"

"No." Several actually, but at this particular moment, no force on heaven or earth could force her to admit to that.

"I do understand the basics, Alex," she said instead. "I've heard enough talk when people didn't know I was listening. Some of the cultures we visited were very open about . . ."

She flipped her hand about helplessly. Just because he was comfortable talking about it, didn't mean she ever would be.

"Making love?" he offered.

"Yes, thank you. I'm aware of the, er . . . mechanics involved. I know you . . . that is, we . . ."

More hand waving followed until she finally said, in a much smaller voice than she would have preferred, "er . . . join."

That was good enough for Alex. He reached for her.

"I'll show you the rest."

He pulled off her chemise and laid her back down against the blankets.

He took his first look at a fully unclothed Sophie and sucked in a tortured breath.

"Lovely," he whispered dropping down to lightly kiss one nipple. "Beautiful."

Sophie moaned and drew his head up to kiss him until they were both panting. He used the distraction to disrobe completely, thinking it best to do it while her eyes were closed and thereby accustom her to his body in stages.

Finally, *finally,* when they were both naked, he gave himself over to the task of pleasuring the both of them. His hands and lips wandered over her restlessly until she was writhing beneath him.

One hand slid down between them to tease the curls at the apex of her legs.

Sophie tensed immediately.

"Shhhh," he crooned. "Let me, sweeting. Trust me."

She did, relaxing as his hand continued down to tease at the hidden folds. Slowly, he slid one finger deep inside her. Watched her face as her breath hitched and her mouth opened in a silent moan.

"So wet. So perfect," he murmured, leaning down to feast on one breast. If he kept watching her, he would be finished before they even started.

Patiently he moved his finger in and out, listening as the sounds of her desire grew higher in pitch. He wanted to take her right then. He wanted to bury himself to the hilt in one solid stroke and never leave. But even more than that, he wanted to make this good for her.

"Alex, I can't. . . ."

"You can. Let it happen, sweet."

She arched her back and cried out, her muscles tensing around his finger.

Alex would have grinned in triumph if his own desire

hadn't swallowed up every other thought. He settled between her thighs and groaned when she instinctively brought her legs up to wrap around his own and caress his calves with her feet.

"Perfect," he whispered again, pushing persistently deeper into her with each slow stroke. "You're perfect."

Again and again he pressed into her, until he reached the proof of her innocence.

Alex grimaced and kissed her lightly. "This will hurt, Sophie."

"I know," she replied with quiet understanding. "It's all right."

Alex lunged once, sheathing himself fully inside her.

"Dear God," he groaned. She felt like heaven, and every instinct screamed out for him to move, to pound into her until he reached blessed relief. But he held still, waiting for her to accustom herself to his invasion, praying she would do so quickly. The last remnants of his willpower were slipping away quickly.

"Sophie," he murmured kissing her lips, her nose, her forehead. "Sophie." He reached between them and rubbed gently at her most sensitive spot until finally she relaxed, then moaned and began to writhe beneath him.

Silently thanking every deity he could think of, Alex began moving in shallow strokes, reveling in every gasp of her breath, every lift of her hips until his resolve to go slow and be gentle was lost to the all-consuming desire to spill his seed deep inside her and mark her as his.

He thrust harder, faster, silently promising to gentle his movements at the first sign of her distress, and wondering how he could manage it. He could hear her cries growing louder and higher in pitch. Her hands grabbed frantically at his back.

She was so close. If he could just hold off a moment longer—

She screamed. Her muscles rippled around him and pulled him over the edge.

He made one final shove and let out a hoarse shout of his own.

When he regained some semblance of control, he wrapped his arms around her and pulled them both to their sides.

"Are you all right?" he whispered worriedly as she buried her face against his chest.

She bumped his chin when she nodded.

"Are you certain, because—"

"I'm fine," she whispered. "Better than fine. I. . . ."

"Then why are you hiding from me?" he asked, trying to work a hand down to her chin to bring her face up. "Sophie? If I hurt you—"

"It's not that, truly. I'm just a little . . ."

Alex smiled. "Embarrassed?"

She nodded again.

He wrapped his arms around her tighter. "Sweetheart, don't be. What we did was perfectly natural."

She snuggled closer. "I know. I'm simply not used to it."

"Well, we'll just have to work on that," Alex answered, sliding a hand down her hip.

"Now?"

"No," he chuckled, although he certainly wouldn't have minded accustoming her to the joys of lovemaking right away. "You're new to this yet, and we've had a long day. You need to rest. Sleep now, and I'll find something for you to wash with when you wake."

She yawned hugely. "Stay with me?"

"Always."

Sophie decided to worry about "always" tomorrow.

❋ Twenty-seven ❋

$\mathcal{I}$t was night when she awoke in a tangle of bedsheets and Alex's arms. For a while she lay silently with her face resting against the muscled expanse of his chest, watching the candlelight dance about the room, and reflecting on what had happened that evening.

She'd made love with Alex. Incredible.

Sophie had heard tales of what it meant to share a bed with a man. Whispers of the pleasures that could be found with the right man, but she had always been more interested in learning the specifics of the act than the possible results.

Now she wished she had paid more attention to the other details. Had she reacted appropriately? Had she moved too much? Not enough? Made too much noise? She didn't recall having much choice in the matter, but maybe there was a trick to being subdued, something young ladies learned before their wedding nights from the women in their families.

Sophie smiled a little at the thought of prim Mrs. Summers educating her on proper conduct in the marriage bed. And decided she didn't want to learn what was proper and what was not. Tonight had been perfect as far as she was concerned. Alex certainly hadn't complained.

She must have smiled even broader at that thought, because Alex stirred and reached up a hand to stroke her hair. "Are you awake, sweet?" he whispered.

"A little," she mumbled.

She felt the soft rumble of his chuckle against her ear. "Well, see if you can manage a little more. It's time to get up."

She tilted her head up a bit for a better look out the windows. "It's still fully dark outside."

"Western windows," he informed her. "It's nearly dawn. How far is the nearest village?"

Sophie snuggled deeper into the blankets. "Three, maybe four miles I think. Not too far. We can wait until it's light at least."

"It'll be light on the other side of the house soon enough. I want to get you safe to London and find out who's behind our attempted kidnapping. And for that we need horses."

It'd been a bit more than *attempted* kidnapping, Sophie thought, and he wasn't going to be looking into it alone, but she didn't feel like arguing with him. Nor was she going to be able to go back to sleep, she realized. Her mind was spinning now with thoughts of her upcoming marriage to Alex, their kidnappers, her cousin, her work for . . . whoever it was she was working for. Which reminded her . . .

"Alex?"

"Hmm?"

"The man at the war office, the one you work for, what is his name?"

"William Fletcher. Now rise and shine."

She bolted straight up.

"Stocky man with a bulbous nose and a love of brandy?"

"You know him, I take it?" Alex asked.

"I know a Will Fetch, as a solicitor! He's my contact for the Prince Regent!"

"Was," he corrected automatically, reaching for his breeches.

She ignored him and grabbed her chemise. "Why would he lie to me, to both of us? And why bother with such a minimal change in name?"

He pulled on his shirt. "I don't know."

She wiggled into her gown and strained to reach the buttons in the back. "Does this mean I work for the war office or—"

"As of yesterday morning, neither." He reached for his boots and she resisted the urge to pick up one of her own and toss it at his head. She was tying the top bow on the second boot when she realized he had finished dressing and was now pacing. It would be a bit then, she thought, before they left. She settled back on the blankets and watched him for a moment longer before losing herself in her own thoughts. She had spent weeks picking locks, climbing in and out of windows, and rifling through the personal articles of several prominent members of society—all on the assumption that she was doing the bidding of the Prince Regent himself. Now that the identity of her employer was suspect, she wondered if she was nothing more than a common thief.

Good Lord, had she traveled all the way to London to become a criminal debutante?

Sophie hastily dismissed the notion, only partially because the idea was so unpalatable. Clearly the war office knew of her activities, and their involvement provided at least some measure of validity. Why then, had they made a point of keeping their involvement a secret? And why had they not wanted her to work with Alex? Things would have been a great deal easier if she'd had someone to create distractions, watch outside of doors, read letters written in French.

Sophie smiled a little at the picture of Alex in the role of assistant spy.

The sound of shattering glass in a distant part of the house broke the fantasy.

Alex was pulling her to her feet before she had time to fully register what the sound meant. He bustled her toward a large nearby storage closet, his expression cold.

She balked at the door. "I can't," she whispered. "It's dark."

"There's a window, Sophie," he answered. He pulled back the curtains to allow the light of the setting moon into the little room. It was just enough to keep her terror at bay.

"Stay here," he ordered, pressing the knife she had given him earlier back into her hand. She wanted to tell him to take it, he was certain to need it more than she, but he was gone before she could open her mouth to speak.

He left the door cracked open several inches. It took her a moment to realize he had done so on purpose—nothing looked quite so suspicious as a closed door—and then she noticed the way the light from the dining room began to dim. He was blowing out the candles. Sophie gripped the knife tighter and huddled into the far corner of the closet. It was going to be very, very dark in that room.

The sound of splintering wood reverberated into her little hiding spot. Sophie pulled her knees up tightly against her chest. She heard masculine voices. Then the telltale sounds of a scuffle. Shouting, swearing, the sound of bone meeting flesh. How many were out there? How outnumbered was Alex?

Get up! she ordered herself.

Can't. Too dark.

Get up!

I can't!

Something smashed. Someone yelled, then grunted in pain.

Death was out there.

Alex's death. He was out there fighting for his life, for her life, while she sat cowering in a closet.

Get up, damn you!

Alex was going to die, and if she didn't move, she was going to let it happen.

Something inside her snapped at the thought. She gripped the knife in her hand and slid from her hiding spot to crouch against a wall of the dining room. It took a minute for her eyes to become accustomed to the dark, and in that minute she felt the terror threaten to overwhelm her. She battled it with every ounce of courage she owned. But it wasn't enough, so she thought of Alex instead. The fear abated. Her eyes focused.

Someone moved to her right. A faint outline of someone

short and stocky betrayed itself against a beam of moonlight that had snuck around the edges of a curtain. He wasn't watching her. He hadn't seen her.

She saw his arm raise and point a pistol at the struggling forms at the far side of the room. Without stopping to think about it, she sprung up and threw the knife.

He screamed and lurched. Glass shattered. The pistol fired. Someone else screamed, but it wasn't Alex and that was all that mattered.

A heavy silence followed, broken only by the sound of heaving breathing across the room.

"Alex?" she whispered.

"Sophie!"

She heard him move toward her. Then he had her by the shoulders in a brutal grip.

"What the hell did you think you were doing?"

Sophie couldn't answer him. Now that the danger had passed and Alex was safe, she was beginning to feel the darkness weigh in around her.

"Do you think . . . ?" She licked dry lips with a dry tongue. "Can we light a candle now?"

Alex swore viciously, then grabbed her hand and pulled her from the room. They crossed the foyer swiftly and headed out the front door. Sophie relaxed considerably at the sight of the first hints of dawn in the eastern sky. Alex pulled her along until they reached a small shadowed recess against the house. Abruptly, he pushed her into the little corner.

"Stay here," he ordered, holding her against the wall. "Do you understand me? Stay *here*. Do not move from this spot."

She nodded.

"I will have your word, Sophie." His face was an unfamiliar mask of stone.

"I promise," she whispered.

"Don't *ever* break your promises to me."

"I won't."

She watched him until he disappeared around the side of

the house, then took in her surroundings. The darkness in her little corner didn't extend much past the tips of her toes, and she could make out the expanse of the side lawn clearly. It was enough.

And she felt stronger now, besides. She would probably always be afraid of the dark, but tonight she had fought that fear and won. Maybe now, she could control it well enough to keep from truly panicking, from losing herself like she had at the cabin.

Someone yelled in the distance.

She instinctively took a step toward the sound.

No. She'd promised. She forced herself back into the corner, balling her hands into impudent fists at her sides. Damn that promise. And damn Alex for insisting on it. What good did it do either of them if he died for it?

What good would she be able to do if she broke it? She no longer had her knife, and she wasn't confident she could bring down a fully grown man with her fists. She was better at fighting then most women, yes, but probably not better than most hardened criminals, certainly not the homicidal type.

Of course if she found a weapon of some sort . . .

Sophie's eyes scanned the yard. She'd just settled on a particularly sturdy-looking stick, deciding that she would rather have Alex alive and hating her, than Alex dead and she hating herself for allowing it to happen, when he appeared from around the corner of the house leading two horses.

She waited diligently until he reached her side, then said, "Are you hurt? Were you followed?"

"No."

"Thank God," she breathed, then narrowed her eyes at him. "Don't you ever, *ever* ask me to promise something like that again."

He shot her a look that would have made her fear for her safety if she hadn't already been overwhelmed with fear for his. "I cannot believe you would make me wait here while—"

"Get on the horse, Sophie."

"—you run off to certain danger. You could have been hurt or—"

"Now!"

Every instinct screamed at her to run at the horse and vault on top.

Sophie was more than a little sick of her instincts. He was not going to witness her jumping to do his bidding like a cowed servant. She tilted her chin up and walked, not ran, toward the horse. She had briefly considered arguing with him, but she was aiming for brave, not stupid.

Apparently, Alex didn't feel she was being brave quickly enough. He reached over, picked her up by the waist, and fairly tossed her into the saddle.

They rode in silence for the first quarter of an hour, never setting the horses at more than a trot for fear they might stumble into a rut on the shadowed road.

Sophie spent that time searching for an advantageous opening to the argument she felt was coming. She was weighing the pros and cons of simply sidling her horse up beside his and giving him a healthy shove, when suddenly he was next to her. He grabbed her horse's reins and brought them both to a stop.

"You're angry with me," she stated quickly, figuring she might as well get in the first word, even if it wasn't particularly brilliant.

"I told you to stay in the closet," he snapped.

"I'm not a child or a soldier to be ordered about, Alex."

"No. You are my betrothed. Very soon you will be my wife, and you will not put yourself in harm's way again. Do I make myself clear? It is my duty to protect and—"

"You were worried about *me?*"

He shot her the sort of disbelieving look usually reserved for the terminally stupid or criminally insane. "Have I not been making that clear?"

"No. What you've made clear is how much you dislike being disobeyed. But I'm warning you now, Alex, I have no intention of standing aside if your life is in danger—"

"I wasn't in danger of dying," he snapped. "You, however—"

"I saved your life!"

"You did nothing of the sort. I saw the pistol. I intended to pull my attacker into the line of fire."

As it happened, Sophie's knife had caused the shooter's arm to jerk wildly, sending the bullet into Alex's assailant's leg rather than his head. Alex had been obliged to knock the man unconscious.

"Oh," Sophie whispered. "Oh. I thought . . . I thought I'd saved your life. I thought . . ."

She thought she'd fought death in the dark and won. But she hadn't. Alex was alive, yes, but what of the other men? She'd killed one herself. She'd heard the knife hit, seen the shadowy figure fall. She hadn't beaten death at all. She'd lent it a helping hand.

Disgusted with herself and uncertain what to say to Alex now that her anger had turned to shame, she nudged her horse forward into a slow walk, intending to think the matter through.

Alex followed suit, bringing his mount beside hers. One look at her crestfallen expression and he felt all his anger drain away, promptly replaced by remorse.

He was a heel. An absolute heel. She'd been proud of what she'd done tonight. And if he hadn't been so furious with her for putting herself in danger, so consumed with his fear for her safety, and (and he hated to admit this), his wounded vanity that a woman should feel it necessary to come to his rescue, he would have realized he was proud of her as well.

He cleared his throat awkwardly and did his best to swallow his ocean of pride. "It *is* possible you did save my life," he offered. "It was very dark, and I may have miscalculated where the bullet would hit. And you did dispose of that last man very effectively."

There, that should make her feel better.

She stared vacantly at the trees. "I killed him."

Alex frowned. Clearly, she was not feeling better. He reached over and grabbed the reins of her horse, stopping them both.

Sophie groaned. "Not this again."

He ignored that. "No one died tonight, Sophie."

She stared at him in bewilderment for a moment. Then shook her head as if to clear it and began babbling. "What? Are you sure? Because . . . you . . . and my knife . . . and then he—"

Alex cut her off before she confused the both of them. "Your knife caught him in the arm. He fell into the window and it knocked him out."

"You're certain?"

"Absolutely. The first two men I managed to render unconscious, the third you hit with your knife, and the fourth took the bullet in the leg, and I knocked him out afterward."

The implications of what he was telling began to seep in. "No one died," she said slowly.

"Nary a one," Alex replied, immensely relived to see the light returning to her eyes. He couldn't see it very well in the semidarkness of early morning, but he knew, knew by the sound of her voice, it was there. "In fact," he continued, "you may very well have saved the last man's life. I had intended to aim his head at the bullet."

"I saved his life," Sophie repeated, smiling now and sitting a little straighter in the saddle.

"Little as he deserved it, yes, you did."

"No one died," she repeated yet again. She couldn't help it. It felt so good to say it, so good to hear it. Maybe too good. . . .

"I heard a scream," she said quickly. "When you went to get the horses."

Alex's expression darkened. "Ah yes, the boy they left behind to watch the horses. Lad couldn't have been more than ten. I was soundly tempted to take him over my knee. You needn't worry. I frightened him into submission merely by showing up. He very nearly tied himself up for me."

"Thank God." She'd done it, then. She'd conquered death this night. Not one of those men had died. Not one. Which meant . . . Dear God, which meant—

"Should we be sitting here? They're likely to wake up at any moment—"

"Relax, Sophie," Alex said, but let go of her reins and allowed the horses to begin moving. "I cut the straps on their saddles and scattered the horses. If they're chasing us, which I doubt, they're doing it on foot."

Dawn came and went well before they reached London. By the time they reached William's house, the sun had worked its way fully up, and Alex had worked himself into a full fury.

The lies William had told them both had put Sophie in danger. She could have been hurt, or killed, or God only knew what else. The thought was enough to make him see red.

He pounded loudly on the front door.

Sophie shot him a nervous glance. "Maybe we should wait—"

"No. We finish this now."

The door opened and a young man appeared.

"Your Grace."

Alex grabbed Sophie's hand and barreled past the youth and into the front foyer.

"Where is he, Sallings?" Alex demanded.

"I'm terribly sorry," Sophie offered.

"Mr. Fletcher is in his study, but . . . wait, please, Your Grace, not again!"

Sophie allowed herself to be dragged down the hall, followed closely by the young man.

"He's rather young for a butler," she commented to Alex.

"He isn't the butler," Alex answered. "There is his butler."

Sophie gaped at the man coming down the hall. "That's my butler!"

"Yes, I know." Alex stopped before a set of French doors. He dropped her hand, gripped the handles, and pushed the doors wide open.

"William!" Alex roared.

"Ah, Alex, my boy."

"Sophie, dear."

"Mrs. Summers!"

"I'm sorry, Mr. Fletcher, sir."

"His Grace, the Duke of Rockeforte!"

And then all hell broke loose.

❋ *Twenty-eight* ❋

$\mathcal{A}$lex let mayhem reign for about two minutes. It seemed fitting in his mood, and he rather felt Sophie had the right to rage a bit. Of them all, she had been the most ill-used.

Eventually, however, he grew impatient to find out just *how* ill-used she had been. That, and she had begun sliding in and out of a foreign language. Insults were always less fun when you couldn't understand them.

"Sallings!" he snapped in his best officer's voice. "You're dismissed!" Then, "James!" he barked in his best ducal voice. "Bring tea for the ladies and make sure we are not disturbed." And finally, "Sophie," he cajoled in his best husband-to-be voice. "Sit down, love, and let us get some answers."

He turned to Mrs. Summers, intending to use his best future-employer voice but stopped short at the raising of one supercilious eyebrow.

"Do not attempt it, young man," she warned in her best governess voice. "I have seen the best and the worst this world has to offer, and you are neither so terrible nor sufficiently wonderful as to hold me in your awe."

Feeling uncomfortably like a chastised boy, Alex held his tongue and offered her a chair in a gesture of truce.

Mrs. Summers nodded regally and accepted the seat. "Tea would be lovely. Thank you for thinking of it."

"My pleasure," Alex ground out. "Now," he declared turning to William, who had wisely taken his own seat, "start explaining."

"It's a bit of a long story actually," William hedged.

"Shorten it," Alex advised grimly.

William took the hint. "Right. Well the shortest possible version, I suppose, would be to say . . . ," he took a fortifying breath. "There was not originally a suspected plot of treason. You were both led into what was intented only as a ruse in order that I might fulfill a deathbed promise I made to Alex's father." His words tumbled out like a well-rehearsed speech—which, as it happened, it was.

"What promise?" Alex demanded.

"Your father was a spy?" Sophie asked in surprise.

"I'll explain later," Alex assured her.

"They prefer 'agent,' dear," Mrs. Summers commented.

William slumped in his chair. His plan for revealing the truth hadn't gotten any further than that last little recitation. The rest he would have to improvise. William hated improvising.

"What promise?" Alex repeated. "I thought you told me everything my father said the night he died."

"I did, save the final vow I made, and to be honest, he fairly tricked me into it. I promised to make certain you as well as several others . . ." and at this point the head of the war office actually blushed a little, "find love."

"What?" Both Alex and Sophie cried at the same time.

"Yes, well, that was very near to my own reaction, I assure you. But a promise is a promise, especially one made to a friend on his deathbed. He wished for his son the happiness he had with his beloved Anna."

"My mother," Alex explained to Sophie before returning his attention to William. "You still have a good deal of explaining to do."

William nodded. "For many years, I watched you flit from actress to opera singer without evincing the slightest interest in a woman of good breeding. Had you shown a particular preference for one of your paramours, I might have searched for a woman for you amongst the *demimonde*—I agreed to help you find love after all, not a wife—but you went through mistresses the way some dandies go through cravats . . . Terribly sorry, Sophie dear."

Sophie shrugged. "I've already heard the gossip. Don't censure yourself on my account."

"So you took it upon yourself to find me a life mate, is that it?" Alex asked incredulously.

William nodded.

"Why Sophie?" he asked, then, feeling it might be wise, quickly added, "Not that I oppose your choice."

"Mary . . . that is, Mrs. Summers, gave me the idea. You wouldn't remember me, Sophie, but I met you the day Mary arrived at Whitefield to be your governess. I was responsible for her obtaining the position."

"I'm sorry, I don't—"

"No, no, quite all right. You were very young and, if I recall correctly, rather preoccupied with several stitches you received on your arm from a dog bite. You were quite proud of them."

Sophie smiled at that. "Harry. We became the best of friends after that little misunderstanding. But how is it you knew Mrs. Summers?"

"She and I met in this very office."

Sophie whirled on her companion. "You're a spy?"

"Of course not, dear. Espionage is not a suitable occupation for a lady," she said pointedly. "My husband, however—"

"You said your husband died in the Terror," Sophie said accusingly.

"And so he did. His job required he spend a considerable amount of time in Louis' court. To the mob, he was just another courtier."

"Oh," Sophie murmured. "I'm terribly sorry."

"It's quite all right. It was a long time ago, and William was a great support to me. Even convincing your father—an old Eton friend of his, before you ask—to hire a governess with no experience. We have kept in contact for years."

"She often wrote to me of your adventures," William said with a smile. "She was concerned you would not be able to find a respectable husband, one you would not drive to distraction within a year. I, in turn, was worried I would not be able to find a young lady who could hold Alex's interest for more than a fortnight. Mary suggested the two of you might suit."

Sophie considered that for moment, then said, "I can understand the rationale of that, I suppose, but why the elaborate ruse? Why not simply introduce us in the normal manner, at a ball or a dinner?"

William shook his head. "Mary and I agreed that both of you were too stubborn to take kindly to blatant matchmaking. You would have been bored by the formalities and indignant over the mechanisms. So I formulated an alternate means of bringing the two of you together."

"I'm still indignant," Alex pointed out. "Sophie?"

"Oh, rather."

"Yes, but it's too late, isn't it?" Mrs. Summers stated pertly. "You're already in love."

Sophie had no intention of having a discussion on that theme. "But why lead me to believe I was working for the Prince Regent?" she asked. "Why not team us together at the start?"

William looked at Alex. "If I had suggested you look into a

French conspiracy with a young woman of no experience, who didn't speak French—"

"I would have been suspicious," Alex admitted reluctantly.

"There you go," William declared. "The plan was to have Alex catch you, Sophie, in the act of sneaking—"

"Why all the other gentlemen?" Sophie demanded. "You could have sent me to spy on Alex alone and left everyone else out of this. For that matter, you could have left me out of it. All you needed, apparently, was for Alex to seek me out."

Sophie looked to William for an answer. William looked to Mrs. Summers. And Mrs. Summers, very pointedly, did not look at Sophie when she said, "You needed something to do."

"What does that mean?"

Mrs. Summers heaved a dramatic sigh. "Really, dear, how long do you suppose you would have been content running about town, playing the debutante?"

"I—"

"You would have had us both packed and headed for parts unknown within days, unless you were given something to keep you occupied . . . and in town."

"That is not true!" Sophie declared firmly. "Not necessarily," she added, a little less firmly. "Oh, very well," she concluded, in defeat. "You're probably right."

Alex leaned over and patted her knee, but wisely kept his opinion to himself. "Prinny has nothing to do with this, has he?" he asked William.

"Not a thing," William replied.

"Why didn't you simply send me to spy on Alex?" Sophie asked, still hopelessly confused.

This time, Mrs. Summers looked to William, who very pointedly looked at Alex. "It was assumed that Alex would catch you too quickly. It was *assumed* he would catch you crawling in and out of people's homes eventually, of course, but by then it would be clear whether or not you would suit. Perhaps you'd join forces against Loudor and—"

Alex coughed into his fist uncomfortably.

"My cousin," Sophie murmured. "He isn't a Napoleon sympathizer then, is he?"

"No," William responded. "Most of the men the two of you were investigating were never suspected of treason. They are either old school chums of mine or they owed me a favor or two. The exception would be Lord Heransly, whose involvement in this has come as a late development. As for Lord Loudor, his love for the French doesn't extend past his brandy and the cut of his waistcoat. His interest in Whitefield, however, was very real."

"Oh." Sophie felt a wash of disappointment come over her. For a moment, she had hoped Loudor could be redeemed. She didn't have enough family left not to grab at the chance to keep a cousin.

Alex gave her shoulder a reassuring squeeze. "I assume he was responsible for the men who attacked us last night."

William nodded. "Whit and I went to your town house yesterday, Sophie, and found the documents detailing the conditions of Whitefield's transfer—documents you should not have kept to yourself, by the way. We proceeded to Loudor's last night to confront him with that evidence. That, along with your disappearance, was enough to have me worried. We found him in the midst of a rather heated argument with your failed kidnappers—rather reasonable chaps as it happens. Loudor decided he would rather give us a full confession than spend further time in their company. They sent their apologies, by the way, Sophie. Seems they have large families and were rather desperate—"

"They hit her over the head!" Alex roared.

"Yes, well, I said they were reasonable, not clever. At any rate," William continued, wisely changing the subject "Loudor admitted to becoming quite nervous as your popularity with several gentlemen began to grow. He sent your erstwhile kidnappers to the Thurston house party with instructions to keep you hidden away until time ran out for you to take a husband and cancel the contract on Whitefield."

"They followed me to London," Sophie guessed.

"Well, they really more chased you to London, as it took them a bit of time to realize you'd snuck away. Found you walking just by your house and opted to abduct you inside."

"But Alex and I escaped."

"So you did. Unfortunately, you went to Whitefield, which was the original destination for your captivity."

"Yes, that would be my luck," Sophie muttered.

Alex just growled.

"And that," William continued saying, "is where you were attacked by the group of men Lord Heransly insisted on hiring to follow the first two men. They had instructions to, shall we say, finalize matters should such extreme measures become necessary."

Sophie gulped.

Alex growled louder.

"Where is my cousin now?" Sophie asked.

"On his way to Australia."

"I see. But I found entries in Lord Forent's ledger that matched the sums stolen from Whitefield. They were attributed to his son, Lord Heransly."

"Ah, yes. I was curious myself as to how Loudor could steal so much money and have so little to show for it. Lord Heransly held a great many of your cousin's vowels, you see, and Heransly owed his father a great deal of money for the support of numerous by-blows. The earl reminded his son the estate was entailed, but not the funds to sustain it. Its worth is at least four times that of Whitefield, no offense, my dear."

"None taken."

"But—and this is the one case in which treason has been committed—Heransly quickly tired of delivering the funds straight from Loudor to his father. With a few clever excuses, he held back some of the payments and used them to finance a smuggling adventure. The arms and information sort, I'm afraid."

"You didn't know of this?" Alex inquired.

"The operation, as I said earlier, was a recent development. Hernasly's ship hadn't yet made its maiden voyage. Thanks to the two of you, it never will. He too is being packed off to Australia."

"Oh . . . good." Really, what else could she say? Except maybe, "Your plan is the single most *ridiculous* thing I have ever heard."

Mrs. Summers sniffed and took a sip of tea. "I told you it was a bit much, William. Too many details, you know."

Insulted, William straightened in his seat. "Worked, didn't it? God is in the details, after all."

"It's a wonder we aren't overrun with the French," Sophie muttered.

"Are there any other questions?" William asked, ignoring her completely, and with the clear hope that his job was now done.

Sophie effectively squashed that hope. "What of the letters I found in Lord Calmaton's study?"

William's face suddenly broke into a large grin. "It would seem that my dear friend Richard is a talented poet with a romantic bent. The letters were submissions to the small but rather popular publication, *Le Journal de Prosateur*. He was quite delightfully embarrassed when I returned them to him."

Mortified, she groaned and dropped her head into her hands.

"Now, now my dear, no need for that. The man knew you would be snooping about the room. He should have taken better care to hide his little secret. He has only himself to blame and holds no grudge against you. Wanted to know what you thought of them, actually."

"What did you tell him?" she mumbled into her hands.

"The truth, that you can't read French. I'm still not certain if he was more relieved or disappointed. Is there anything else?"

"You might want to explain the butler to her," Alex advised.

"James, right. After Lord Loudor's removal from your home, I thought it best to put a man in place until I worked out exactly what your cousin was about. Penny was most instrumental in seeing him placed—"

Sophie's head snapped up. "Penny? Penny's a spy?"

"No, dear," William stated. "Just the granddaughter of a retired comrade, who needed a little extra money. Every precaution was taken to see you safe and well settled in London. Mr. Wang insisted upon it—"

"Mr. Wang, too?" This time her voice came out a choked whisper.

"He did work for the war office for a few years. How did you think he came by the peculiar skills he's passed on to you? He's been mostly in London since your arrival. He insisted on being readily available should we, or you, need him. But then he thought you'd be safe enough at Haldon Hall, and went to see his friends in Wales."

Sophie wanted to say that she had asked Mr. Wang how he came to know how to pick locks and throw knifes, and that he had given her the vague, but still satisfactory, answer that his grandfather had taught him. But her mouth seemed strangely disconnected from her brain and all she managed was to repeat, "Mr. Wang?" in that same strangled voice.

Alex reached over and took her hand. The small contact served to bring her back to the present, and in a much healthier voice she demanded, "Is everyone a spy?"

"No one's a spy, dear," William assured her. "They are simply acquaintances and friends of mine who either owed me a favor, or—"

"I'm a spy," Alex pointed out reasonably.

"Well, yes," William conceded. "But only on the rare occasion that—"

"I thought you preferred 'agent,'" Sophie commented distractedly.

"You needn't make it sound like a hobby," Alex said by way of replying to William's remark.

William groaned and ran his hand down his face. "*Yes*, Alex performs the role of agent for the Crown from time to time. It is his duty to his title. However, it is not and will not be an occupation he pursues on a full-time basis, at least not until there is an heir to the dukedom."

"Not even then," Sophie muttered.

William ignored her. "No one else, however, is a spy."

"I can't believe this," Sophie murmured.

Alex stood. "I can. You!" he snapped at William, "Outside. Now."

"Alex, don't," Sophie pleaded, eyeing the older gentleman with concern.

"Let them go, dear," Mrs. Summers advised.

"How can you say that?" Sophie demanded as the two men left the room.

Mrs. Summers appeared unmoved. "It is the duke's right. I should be concerned if he didn't at least make a show of retribution. Deathbed vow or not, if one puts one's nose where it doesn't belong, one should expect it might come out the worse for wear."

"You're guilty as well," Sophie pointed out.

"Yes, but not to the same degree. And I am a woman. He can't very well break my nose. You, however, may choose not to speak to me for several days, if that is your wish."

Sophie rolled her eyes. "Generous of you."

They sat in awkward silence for a full minute, Mrs. Summers sipping her tea and Sophie's mind still racing over the events of the day. Then—

"I would never have left!" Sophie cried, nearly before she had even completed the thought in her head. She turned to her companion in a combination of outrage and confusion. "You know very well I never would have dragged you out of London merely because I had gotten bored, not with you visiting old friends and so clearly enjoying yourself. How could you think I would be so selfish?"

Mrs. Summers set down her drink, sighed, and, unless Sophie

was mistaken, cringed just a little. "I don't believe you to be selfish, dear. I know you are not, but . . . oh dear, I had rather hoped you would be too distracted with everything else going on to question my excuse overmuch. I'm not very good at lying, you know."

"You were lying?"

"Perhaps, a little. There was a last-minute change of plan, you see," Mrs. Summers explained. "We had to . . . shuffle things about a bit. William knew your cousin was pilfering from your father's coffers, but didn't realize the extent of his treachery, or the damage it had caused, until after we had left China. There was a letter waiting for me at one of our stops, detailing the condition the estate was in and . . . well, I knew you would never take the money from me, but if you thought it was coming from the prince—"

"It was *your* money?" Sophie demanded. "Your twenty thousand pounds?"

"Don't be silly, dear. How on earth would I come to have twenty thousand pounds? . . . It was to be ten thousand."

"Ten. . . ."

"Without proof, you would have been given ten thousand pounds for your troubles."

She *had* found proof, but it seemed to Sophie a relatively minor point at the moment. "But that money is yours, Mrs. Summers. You—"

"It most certainly is not," Mrs. Summers snapped, slapping one bony hand angrily against her thigh. "Honestly, child, am I family, as you are so fond of saying, or am I not?"

Sophie blinked, taken aback at the vehement tone. "Of course, you are, but—"

"Very good. There is no reason, then, to have been paying me an enormous fee these last twenty years, and there is no reason you cannot accept assistance from a family member."

Assistance was no longer needed, of course, but that fact could not hope to dim the generosity of Mrs. Summers' offer.

Sophie took her friend's hand and enclosed it in her own. "You have gone through a great deal of trouble. For me, for my father, for all of us. Thank you." She gave her a peck on the cheek. "I love you very much."

Before the tears shining in Mrs. Summers' eyes could began to fall, Sophie added, "But should you ever again take it into your head to manipulate me like a puppet on a string, I shall indeed break your nose."

William followed Alex into a side yard with a tall wall that afforded some measure of privacy.

"Before you commence with the breaking of any bones," William stated calmly. "May I point out that Sophie was never in any real danger from my plans? . . . Also, I am an old man."

Alex hit him on the nose.

"You may have taken precautions against physical harm, William, but Sophie could have been ruined," Alex snapped. Then, with a sigh, he reached down and offered William a hand up. "And you're not a day over forty-five." Alex blinked as if just realizing something. "My God, you must have been a mere boy when you began working with my father."

William pulled out a handkerchief and used it to stop the flow of blood from one nostril. "I was fourteen years old on my first assignment, sixteen when I met your father. He used to call me old man," he chuckled. "Thought it was funny, his being a solid decade my senior."

"I'm sure he did," Alex murmured distractedly. "William, was there anything else you haven't told me about the night he died?"

"No."

"The rest was true then? He died in France saving a compromised agent?"

"The agent wasn't compromised, Alex. He wasn't even in play. It was the last years of the Terror. A person only had to look at their neighbor askew to be denounced. But yes, he was an agent, and yes, he was going to die, and your father died saving him. We made it all the way to the coast before running afoul of the local authorities. It was just rotten luck."

Alex accepted that with a small nod.

Neither man spoke for awhile, Alex lost to his thoughts and William patiently dabbing at his nose as the blood flow slowed to a small trickle.

Finally, William said, "You'll need a special license. I suspect you won't run into much trouble there, being a duke."

"It's already been handled. I sent Whit for one the night we came to London."

"Before Sophie was compromised," William stated with obvious approval. "Excellent."

Alex threw him a disgruntled scowl. "This was damn humiliating, you know."

"But worth it, eh? Sophie will make you a very happy man."

"She already does," Alex admitted, before adding, "I agreed to let her return to her father after an heir is born or, in the event that proves impossible, after five years' time. I hope to convince her father to return to England by then, or convince her to stay."

"Won't be necessary. He's already on his way. Before leaving China, Mary accused the viscount of jeopardizing Sophie's future happiness with their nomadic way of life. Lectured and chastised the poor man no end, I'm sure."

"She *is* formidable," Alex agreed. "Come on then, let's get you back inside before the ladies begin wondering if we've run each other through."

William gave his nose one more dab and eyed the ruined handkerchief. "I appreciate your not breaking my nose. Quite charitable of you, really."

Alex just shrugged and held open the door. William was halfway through the threshold when Alex stopped him with a hand on his shoulder.

"Who are they? The others you promised my father to help?"

"Can you not guess?"

A slow smile spread across Alex's face.

"May I assume your silence on this matter?" William asked continuing on his way.

"Only if you allow me the pleasure of assisting in Whit's downfall. Any candidates in mind?"

"Miss Mirabelle Browning."

"Good Lord!" Alex cried, and then promptly shut his hand in the door.

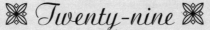

❊ *Twenty-nine* ❊

*T*hey were married the next day. Alex wanted to hunt down a vicar and have the ceremony performed that very afternoon, but Sophie insisted that they wait until Kate, Mirabelle, and Evie could arrive from Haldon Hall. She wished her father and Mr. Wang could be present as well, but Alex was already put out with just a day's postponement. She didn't think he'd be willing to wait the several weeks it would take for them both to arrive.

She received the news of her father's move from China with mixed emotions. She was delighted at the prospect of seeing him after so long a separation, and truly overjoyed that she now had nothing to stop her from spending the rest of her life with Alex.

Except that she loved him.

She had no idea what the odds were that he might one day fall in love with her in return, but she thought they might be dramatically improved if she was actually around. It was a wonderful and terrifying thought. And one that she doggedly refused to dwell on. She was getting Whitefield and marriage to a man she loved. Alex would have an heir, and marriage to a woman he cared for. That would have to be enough. Especially on her wedding day.

Mirabelle, Kate, and Evie were delighted to be a part of the celebration. And they were positively enthralled at Sophie's accounting of her adventures. Per Alex's request, she left out all mention of Mr. Fletcher's involvement and focused instead on relating the full extent of her cousin's treachery. She felt a little guilty not sharing all the details, but she wouldn't risk spoiling Mr. Fletcher's future plans.

She rather liked the idea of Mirabelle and Whit.

The wedding was a subdued affair. The only excitement occurred at the conclusion of the ceremony when Lady Thurston burst into tears, necessitating Alex's and Whit's immediate and adorably awkward attention. It had been rather sweet, watching two otherwise self-assured men hover helplessly over the woman.

"The last time Mother cried was at Papa's Funeral," Kate whispered in her ear. Sophie couldn't help noticing that the younger woman's voice was a bit tight as well.

"Is she that upset?" Sophie whispered back in horror.

Lady Thurston dispelled that notion before Kate had the chance to respond.

". . . what I have always wanted for you, Alex . . ." Lady Thurston hiccuped, having gotten over the worst of her sobs. ". . . couldn't have made a better match myself. Your mother would be so happy."

Sophie beamed a smile at her. Alex leaned down and whispered something in Lady Thurston's ear that brought a fresh round of tears before she finally managed in a tremulous, but joy-filled voice, ". . . and you have always been a second son to me."

The newly married couple settled into Alex's town house that afternoon, opting to postpone the honeymoon until after Sophie's father arrived and preferring to stay in town to reinforce their story. Lady Thurston had agreed to spread the word that the new Duke and Duchess of Rockeforte were madly in love, had been secretly engaged for weeks, and had decided to elope to Gretna Green before reconsidering and marrying by special license. It was still a scandal, but it was romantic, and provided a happy and, more importantly to some, respectable conclusion. Society was enchanted, and Lady Thurston, already popular, was thrilled to find herself one of the most sought-after guests in town.

Alex and Sophie were completely unaware of her bliss for two full days. Despite their intention to be seen as a united couple in public as soon as possible, they spent forty-eight solid hours ensconced in their bedroom instead. For her birthday, Alex took her sightseeing at all the places they'd avoided on their last outing. But most of the fortnight following the wedding they spent in idleness about the house. Taking breakfast on the terrace, reading to each other in the library, but still preferring to spend most of their time in the bedroom.

Alex took the opportunity to learn all the little habits and preferences of his new bride. He found that she liked lilies more than roses, that she always sneezed twice, never more and never less, that she liked her eggs scrambled dry, and that she never snored in her sleep, but did occasionally drool.

He was watching her do that very thing at the moment, marveling at the sweetness of it, at the wonder of her lying asleep beside him, when it finally hit him.

His wife was drooling all over her pillow, no make that *his* pillow, and he thought it enchanting. Nothing about this woman could ever bore him.

He loved her.

There could be no other explanation. And frankly, Alex didn't need one. He liked being in love with Sophie. Liked the way he missed her a little when she was in another part of the house. Liked how just the thought of her made him smile at odd times of the day. Mostly, he just liked being happy. And Sophie made him very, very happy.

He'd tell her tomorrow, he decided, carefully sliding a dry pillow beneath her head. He figured a man could never go wrong telling a woman he loved her. Leastwise, not if he were being truthful.

And he'd tell the staff to bring more pillows.

Sophie eyed Alex furtively over the top of her book.

He'd been acting strangely all day.

At breakfast, he'd poured cream into his juice without even noticing his error. Sophie had only barely managed to warn him in time. They'd gone riding in the park afterward where she made several attempts at conversation, but gave the effort up when he failed to answer her after the third try. Then, to her annoyance, she caught him mumbling to himself instead.

Now it was late afternoon, they were in the library, she was reading aloud, and he was clearly not paying the least bit of mind to what she was saying.

He was just staring at her.

Sophie closed the book with a decisive clap. "I do wish you would tell me what is wrong," she said impatiently.

He blinked twice. "Wrong?"

"Yes, wrong. You've been behaving as if you're . . . I don't know . . . distracted."

Alex rubbed the palms of his hands on his trousers. "Likely because I am."

"Care to tell me why?" she asked in a more sympathetic tone. Alex was more than distracted she realized, he was nervous.

"I've been meaning to . . . that is to say, I should like to tell you something, but it seems getting the deed done is somewhat more difficult than I anticipated."

Now *she* was nervous. "What is it?"

He stood abruptly and hauled her to her feet.

"I love you," he said clearly, albeit quickly.

Sophie heard herself make an audible gulping noise.

No. No. *No.*

Alex must have been feeling rather optimistic because he seemed to take her response as a good sign and continued in a more confident voice.

"I could give you a million different reasons for why I love you, or how I love you. I could even tell you when I began loving you, and when I finally came to my senses long enough to realize I love you, but it all seems inconsequential next to the simple fact that . . . I just do. I am completely, madly, deliriously in love with you."

Sophie opened her mouth, let out a small squeak, and ran.

Alex watched her go in stunned amazement.

Over the last twelve hours, he had mentally played out every scenario he thought might occur after professing his undying love to his wife. Sophie laughing with joy followed by passionate lovemaking. Sophie crying with joy followed by passionate lovemaking. Sophie being struck mute with joy followed by passionate lovemaking—although he rather thought this one to be the least likely. Not once, however, had it occurred to him that she might become upset and run away, completely forgoing the joy and lovemaking the situation warranted.

Eventually, he regained the use of his muscles and took the steps two at a time.

"Sophie!"

Damn it, why had she run?

He reached the door and tried the handle. It was locked. He pounded on the wood.

"Sophie! Open this door!"

"No," came the answer from the other side. "Not yet. I need to think."

He could hear her pacing the floorboards. "You can damn well think while I'm in the room, and after you explain to me what this is about."

She didn't answer. Alex raised his fist to pound some more, but stopped midswing, a horrible thought occurring to him.

"Sophie?" he called through the wood. His voice sounding a great deal less confident than it had a minute ago. "I . . . you don't owe me anything, you know."

She stopped pacing, so he forged ahead. "What I mean is, while I should like to think that you care for me, and perhaps might one day love me in return, I didn't tell you of my own feelings with any expectation that you return them." Hope, yes. Lots and lots of hope. And perhaps even a touch of suspicion, but not a definite expectation.

"That isn't it," she replied, and he could tell she was standing on just the other side of the wood.

"Well then, what the bloody hell is it?" Alex roared, losing patience.

She moved away from the door.

"Sophie, will you open this door, or I will have Mansten bring the key? Either way, I—"

"Who is Mansten?"

"The butler," Alex ground out. "Either way, I am coming in, the choice is yours."

He heard the lock slide on the door. "That's no choice at all," Sophie muttered as he shouldered his way past her to stand in the center of the room.

"Tell me what is going on here," he demanded.

Sophie closed the door and turned to look at him. "I don't know how to explain it, Alex."

He leveled one long cold stare at her. "I just informed you that I love you, to which your reaction was to look horrified, run away, and lock yourself in our room. 'I don't know how to explain it, Alex' is not an acceptable response."

Sophie winced. That had been more than a little badly done. "I am so sorry," she murmured guiltily. "I panicked."

"Shall we go through your entire repertoire of lame excuses tonight?"

"I said I was sorry and I meant it," she said a little indignantly. "You have every right to be hurt and angry with me, but don't throw my apology away as if it means nothing."

"I accept your apology," he said in a slightly more conciliatory voice. "It's the reason for its necessity I find hard to swallow."

"Well, I did panic," she pointed out reasonably. A deaf and blind man would have been hard pressed to argue with that.

Alex ground his teeth together in frustration. "*Why* did you panic?"

Sophie grimaced in the manner of someone desperately trying to find the right words, and failing in the endeavor.

"Is the prospect of my love so disagreeable?" Alex asked.

"No!" she burst out. Suddenly all the words she was searching for seem to come to her at once, only she found it immensely difficult to get them out in the right order. "It isn't *your* love or *my* love I fear, it's the combination that scares me. If you just loved me, or I just loved you, everything would be fine. Well, not fine exactly, one of us would be fairly miserable," she conceded. "But now, one or both of us will be so much worse than miserable. I'm not sure what that might be, but *dead* might be a reasonable assumption, or at least grievously wounded—"

"Sophie, stop. You're not making any sense."

She threw her hands up in defeat. "Well, I told you I couldn't explain it, didn't I?"

Alex walked over to stand in front of her. He searched her face with his eyes, then crushed her to his chest. "So, you do love me?"

She could hear the smile in his voice, and knew he wasn't asking a question. Groaning, she leaned into his embrace, and spoke into his shirt. "Caught that part, did you?"

"It did seem the most pertinent."

She immediately pulled back from him. "Well, it's not," she informed him. "That we love each other is what matters."

"You are right of course," he conceded happily.

"You're missing the point!" she cried, pushing herself away from him entirely. "This is disastrous!"

Alex considered snatching her back into his arms, but thought it might be best to wait until they worked through whatever was bothering her. He didn't want her to think he would ever take her concerns lightly.

Of course, she wouldn't be able to see the loopy grin on his face if he held her, and that should be taken into consideration. She loved him.

He was hard-pressed to find anything but the greatest of joy in the moment.

"Sophie, come here."

"No," she stated resolutely, taking another step back. "Not until you listen to what I have to say."

Alex gave a sigh of resignation. "Very well, explain to me why our having fallen in love spells certain doom."

She scowled at him. "If you're not going to take this seriously—"

He held his hands up in a conciliatory gesture. "I am sorry, you are right, and I am listening." He schooled his face into a reasonably sincere expression. It was damned hard work.

She eyed him warily.

"Please, Sophie, talk to me."

She searched his face for a moment longer, then nodded. "Have you not stopped to consider," she began, "how very odd a great many of my experiences have been. . . ."

As she spoke, Alex found he no longer had to concentrate to keep from smiling. He could scarcely believe what he was hearing. Sophie had gone her whole life in what Alex could only imagine would be a state of constant anxiety. Never being able to enjoy a bit of good fortune without wondering what calamity must follow. Always waiting for the other shoe to drop.

Alex didn't believe in fate. He firmly believed that, outside of birth and death, life was what you made of it. But Sophie clearly held to a system of checks and balances he found baffling and cruel.

"How can you live like this?" he asked in sad wonder.

"Believing that every good thing that happens to you comes with a price?"

"I've never concerned myself with the little things," Sophie explained. "Everyone has good days and bad days. I'm not unique in that. It's the really monstrous events that require my attention."

"You aren't allowed something wonderful for free, is that it?"

"Yes, but you needn't sound so appalled. It works both ways. More often than not, the terrible occurs first, and then I know I have the wonderful to look forward to."

Well, that was something, he supposed. A very little something.

"Except for death," she amended with a grimace. "Death plays by a set of rules I am not privy to."

Rules, costs, balances. It was mind boggling.

"Who put this notion into your head?" he demanded. He rather thought it might have been that Mr. Wang. Any man foolish enough to let a rash and headstrong child (and he just knew Sophie had been rash and headstrong as a child) play with knives was likely stupid enough to fill her ears with the sort of tripe an imaginative girl (and she was still imaginative) would sop up like a sponge. Besides, Mr. Wang was the only suspect Alex had besides Mrs. Summers, and he was rather inclined to think well of Sophie's matchmaking chaperone.

"I don't suppose it occurred to you that I might have figured it out on my own," she replied.

It had, actually, but he hoped it was otherwise. He was looking forward to taking up the issue with the thoughtless bastard responsible.

"Well, I did," Sophie continued without waiting for his response. "But it's universally accepted as fact."

"Define 'universal.'"

"Oh, my father, Mrs. Summers, Mr. Wang, and a few others who have known me for a while."

Well, he could pummel Mr. Wang, at any rate. He'd have to see how old her father was.

"I know you don't believe it Alex, but—"

"What I believe is not an issue at present," he stated with a swiftness that amazed her.

He was willing to put aside his own beliefs in order to better understand her own. The selflessness of that small act humbled her.

"Unless I am mistaken," he continued, "and please correct me if I am, you believe that falling in love comes with a price of misfortune equal to its worth. Am I correct?"

"Yes!" she cried, relieved that he appeared to comprehend how serious the matter was to her. "And because this is the best thing, the absolute best thing that could ever happen to me, or anyone, imagine what the cost will be! I don't know that I could afford it. Something must be done."

Alex didn't care for the sound of that.

He closed the distance between them in two long strides. Cupping her face between his strong hands, he leaned down until their foreheads rested against each other.

"What are you proposing, Sophie? Will you leave me?" The question came out rather strangled.

She flinched. "I don't know," she choked out.

He brushed his thumbs along her temples. "I love you. I love you with my heart, my body, my every breath. If I lost you, my life would be nothing, an endless waking nightmare. You said you loved me too. Is it not the same for you?"

She nodded. "Yes."

"And if you walked away from this, what would be a sufficient compensation for that kind of pain, Sophie? What could make up for the loss of what we have?"

She was silent for a moment, lost in thought. "Nothing," she finally whispered with a touch of surprise in her voice. "Nothing could make up for losing you."

"So why go?"

She didn't appear to hear him. Her head turned to the side

and her eyes darted back and forth across the room unsee-ingly. She was still mulling over what he had said. "It couldn't be balanced," she said with growing wonder. "It couldn't even itself out."

"Perhaps love is like life and death," he suggested. "Maybe it has its own rules."

"Maybe, I—" As quickly as her face had begun to lighten, it dimmed.

"What?" Alex prompted urgently. Dammit, they'd been so close. "What is it?"

"It can balance out if I stay," she whimpered in disappoint-ment. "If I stay . . . I could lose you."

Alex groaned. She was not going to lose him. Anymore than he planned on losing her.

"I don't know what to do, Alex."

"I know darling, I know, but we'll figure something out. Just—"

Alex's head snapped up suddenly. "What is the average life span for a gently reared British woman?"

She blinked at him. "What? What are you—?"

He dropped her face and began pacing the room. "Never mind, doesn't matter, let us say fifty for now. Sound reason-able?"

"I suppose. . . ."

"Right. Fifty. And you are now, five-and-twenty, correct?"

"Yes," she said slowly, having no idea where the conversa-tion might be headed.

"Excellent. That gives you a quarter-century to live, give or take a couple months. With your history you're bound to live right up to the average, wouldn't you say?"

"I suppose so."

"Excellent. Excellent. That, in turn, gives you twelve years, six months with me, and twelve years, six months without."

He stopped and at looked at her expectantly. She just stared back.

"As I see it, Sophie, you have two options. You could stay

and give me the pleasure of making you deliriously happy for the next twelve and a half years, believing there could be twelve and half years of heartache to pay for it. Or, you can forgo the happiness altogether and spend the next five-and-twenty years alone and miserable, with the knowledge that you have made me miserable as well."

She still didn't speak, but she no longer looked quite so confused.

"Can you think of an alternative, Sophie?"

Finally she swallowed and spoke. "You could leave me," she answered.

"That is not going to happen. Besides, the results for you would be the same, wouldn't they?"

She nodded, looking torn.

"Stay," he urged, taking a step towards her.

She searched his face with her eyes, and then searched her own heart. What he said made sense. A decade and more of bliss followed by a decade of misery was a damn sight better than a lifetime of pain with nothing to show for it.

"Stay, Sophie," he pleaded taking another step. Then another. "Give me the twelve years."

A small smile tugged at the corner of her mouth, before blooming into a full-fledged grin.

"And six months," she reminded him.

He gathered her into his arms. "And six months," he agreed.

❀ Epilogue ❀

$\mathcal{S}$ophie sat on the stone garden bench and tilted her face to the sun. If Mrs. Summers could see her now, no doubt she'd launch into a diatribe regarding the perils of freckling. But her friend was busy inside the Rockeforte country manor happily chatting with Mr. Wang and the visiting Mr. Fletcher.

With Alex busy attending the estate business he had neglected over the last few months, Sophie had taken the opportunity for a little quiet solitude to think over the last few weeks of her life.

She was happy. Absolutely, blissfully happy. But she was hard-pressed not to dwell on the fact that it might very well prove temporary.

"Why the sigh, Sophie?"

She turned to find Mr. Wang standing not three feet behind her. "You move like a cat," she said without rancor. She had never noticed that before.

"Old habit," the man replied. "I could teach you, if you like."

Sophie smiled at him and waved for him to take a seat next to her. "I would, although it might be best not to mention it to Alex. He seems determined not to like you, I'm afraid," she said honestly.

Mr. Wang just chuckled softly. "He holds me responsible for some notion you have about things going terribly wrong in twelve years."

"And four months. He mentioned that, did he?"

"He did. I am surprised at you, Sophie, to hold to such silliness."

Sophie was taken aback. "You've never called it that before."

"I hadn't thought it necessary. I assumed you knew all that talk of luck and misfortune was merely for fun."

"How can you say that?" she demanded. "Knowing everything that has happened?"

"How can I not, knowing *how* it all happened? You are a willful and sometimes rash young woman with a propensity for finding trouble. That tiger came after you because you had recently come from the butcher's. You got lost in that jungle because you wandered off to inspect an interesting bloom, rather than stay with your guide as you should have, and—"

"Even if what you say is true, though I reserve the right to disagree, how do you explain my narrow escapes?"

"By pointing out that although you are a troublesome young woman, you are also rather clever and levelheaded when the occasion requires it. If you had panicked, that tiger would have pounced on you before I could intervene, and you came across that jungle tribe by following running water with the knowledge that it was your best chance of reaching civilization."

Sophie thought about that for a very long time. What Mr. Wang was implying threatened a concept she had held as irrefutable truth for most of her life. It was not something she could simply accept out of hand.

"It doesn't explain everything," she finally said in a soft voice.

"No, but then we are all subject to the whims of fate now and again. You are not alone in that."

Mr. Wang stood up and tugged gently at the hem of his coat to straighten it. "Think on what I've said. Neither your father, nor Mrs. Summers, nor myself ever meant our little jests about your luck to be anything more than that, little jests."

Sophie nodded, silently agreeing to consider the matter further, but unable to promise more than that.

Mr. Wang must have understood her reticence. "If you find you cannot bring yourself to see the matter differently, at least consider this. You do not have twelve years and four months with Alex, you have five-and-twenty years . . . half your life with him, and half without, hmm?"

And with that revelation he took himself off, following the gravel path deeper into the garden.

Sophie sat stunned for a moment.

He was right.

Five-and-twenty years.

They had five-and-twenty years!

She shot up and headed toward the house at a dead run.

She had to tell Alex!

Then she had to go back and thank Mr. Wang properly. He'd given them five-and-twenty years.

And he'd given her hope.

The feud between them has scandalized the *ton* for years. But what happens when Whit and Mirabelle are forced to put their differences aside? They just might be…

Tempting Fate

by

Alissa Johnson

Read ahead for a sneak peak.

_____

"What else is it you wanted, Whit?" Mirabelle asked.

"It isn't a matter of what I want, but of what my mother has…requested."

"Your mother?" A tickle of unease formed in her throat.

"She's asked that we set aside our differences for a time—call a truce of sorts." He twisted his lips in thought.

"I…" She paled. "Is she very angry with me?"

"She's not—" Whit broke off with a curse and stepped forward to take her arm. "Sit down. You look half ready to faint."

"I don't faint," she argued unconvincingly, but let herself be guided back to the settee. "What did she say to you, Whit?"

"Nothing that warrants this sort of reaction," he replied, but his words were gentled by a soothing pat on her arm, and by the good sized glass of brandy he poured and pushed into her hand. "Drink it down."

She made a face at the amber liquid. She didn't think spirits would settle well in her stomach at present. "I don't want it. I want to know what your mother—"

"And I'll tell you, after you have a drink." He tapped the bottom of the glass to nudge it closer. "Go ahead."

She scowled at him, but drank the contents of the glass in one quick swallow. She coughed, wheezed, and spluttered her way back. "Oh, ack!"

He searched her face. "Feeling better?"

"No." Which she really wasn't. "There was nothing wrong with me to begin with." Which there really was.

"Huh," was his inarticulate and—she was forced to admit—diplomatic reply. He straightened and looked down at her. "I forget sometimes how much you care for her."

"Lady Thurston? I love her, with all my heart."

"I know you do. But I forget." He patted her arm again. "She's not angry with you in the least. Nor with me. She… Are you looking for a husband?"

"Am I…?" She gaped at him, wondering if the inquiry had really come from nowhere, or if the brandy had begun working much faster than anticipated.

"Imp?"

She held up a finger. "A moment—I'm trying to ascertain if there's an insult in the question."

He straightened his shoulders. "I assure you, when I insult you, you'll know it. Just see your way to answering the question. Are you looking for a husband?"

"No," she said clearly. "I most certainly am not. Does this have something to do with your mother's request?"

He leaned forward a bit and searched her face, much as he had done almost moments ago, but it wasn't concern in his blue eyes now, it was the inexplicable heat of temper. Why ever would he still be irritated, she wondered. She'd answered the question, hadn't she? Of course, Whit was irritated with her as a rule—her presence alone was sufficient to spark his ire. But there was something different this time. Unable to put her finger on just what, she watched him in return, fascinated as the fire was banked, if not entirely extinguished.

He straightened once more with a quick nod, as if coming to some decision. "Mother is under the impression that you're seeking marriage, and that our disagreements could hamper your attempts to find an eligible gentleman."

"That's absurd," she scoffed. "She knows very well I've no interest in chaining myself to a husband."

"Chaining yourself?" He pulled a chair over to sit across from her, close enough that their knees almost brushed as he sat. "That's a rather grim view of marriage, don't you think?"

"No," she replied with all sincerity. "And I doubt you do as well, given that you're past thirty and still unwed."

"Taking a wife is an entirely different matter. It's a responsibility that requires a great deal of forethought, planning, and—"

"I had no idea you were such a romantic," she drawled.

He shot her a hard look. "My wife, when I take one, will want for nothing—including romance."

She sighed, suddenly tired and a little fuzzy from the brandy. "I know," she reached over and patted his knee congenially. "You'll make some fortunate girl an excellent husband one day, Whit."

Whit shifted slightly in his seat. He wasn't about to let her see how her brief touch, her nearness, was suddenly, surprisingly, interfering with his train of thought.

She laughed at his wary stare. "No insult. I'm in earnest. You're a catch, and not just because of your wealth and title, though I can't imagine that's a detriment."

"Will you admit to having said this tomorrow, in front of witnesses?"

"Oh, I'll suffer the tortures of the damned first."

"Thought so. You're just a bit foxed, aren't you?"

She thought about it, but having never before been foxed, she decided she couldn't quite say for certain. She'd had a glass or two more champagne than was wise in the past, however, and rather thought she felt now as she had on those occasions.

"I believe I'm a bit tipsy," she admitted. "It's your own fault, pushing that brandy on me."

"I hadn't expected you to down it in one gulp," he pointed out.

It occurred to her that she should probably be offended by the laughter in his voice. And she would be, she decided—later. When it would be easier to concentrate on the matter. For now, she needed to turn her mind to Lady Thurston's request.

"I don't think it's necessary to postpone this," she said, attempting to instill a touch of sobriety in her words. "I'm a bit worse for wear, I'll admit, but I can follow the conversation well enough. Your mother has asked us to call a truce, correct?"

"Yes," he replied, and she decided to ignore the twitch of his lips.

"Very well. For how long?"

"Until…" He frowned thoughtfully. "I've no idea. If my mother had been right, I'd have suggested we keep at it until you were comfortably settled with a husband."

"Ah, so it would be a permanent sort of arrangement. That might be asking a bit much for the two of us."

"I agree. I suggest we do the thing in stages." He leaned back in his chair and steepled his fingers in front of his chest. "We'll start by agreeing to remain civil for the duration of this house party and any events hereafter in which my mother—or someone likely to report to my mother—is present. Should we find the task to be accomplishable without any great hardship, we can reevaluate and decide at that time if we wish to make it a permanent arrangement."

"That sounds immensely sensible." She bobbed her head good-naturedly before tilting it to study him. "You've great gobs of sense in that head of yours, don't you, Whit?"

"It's true," he agreed with another twitch of his lips. "I am all that is good and wise. And my astounding intellect tells me now that it is past time for you to crawl into bed and sleep off the brandy—not that I don't like you this way," he added.

"And what way might that be?"

"Inebriated," he supplied with a grin. "And pleasant."

She made a face at him. She wasn't sure what sort of face it was, exactly, as she was experiencing some numbness about the nose and lips, but she was relatively certain it was some form of scowl—possibly even a haughty glower. "I'm not pleasant…that is…I'm not inebriated. I'm only—"

"Tipsy, I know." He stood and took her hand. "Up you go, then."

She allowed herself to be pulled to her feet.

"Do you really think we can—" She broke off when she realized he wasn't listening to her. He wasn't even looking at her.

Well, he *was* actually, and quite intently. But his gaze was clearly focused below her face. A breathlessness stole over her, and her skin seemed to prickle and warm as he did a slow sweep of her figure, his expression one of…

What did one call that? Irritated bemusement? Reluctant interest?

"Is something the matter?" she asked in what she hoped was a cool tone. Tucking her chin for a better view of her gown, she trailed her fingers along the neckline. "Have I a spot?" Oh dear, what if she'd dribbled brandy down the front of herself without realizing? "You might have mentioned earlier, you know," she grumbled.

She looked up when he didn't respond and found his gaze focused on where her hand rested against her chest. He looked just as intent as he had a moment ago—standing absolutely still, with his brow furrowed and his jaw clenched. But he didn't look half as reluctant. And she suddenly felt twice as breathless.

"Whit," she snapped, a little amazed she'd found the necessary air.

His eyes snapped up to hers. "What? Yes. No. I beg your pardon?"

"Whatever is the matter with you?"

"Not a thing," he offered, waited a beat and added, "I'm checking for swaying."

"For…oh." The logical explanation made her feel silly. What else would he have been doing? "Right, well, I'm not. Swaying that is." She quietly slid her right foot out a little.

"So I can see," he said with enough lingering amusement that she was reminded of the question she'd meant to ask.

"Do you *really* think we can manage to behave civilly to each other for the whole of the week?"

"Of course. Nothing to it—for me, at any rate. You'll need to employ your skills as an actress." He gave that some thought. "Or perhaps we should just keep you in brandy."

She merely lifted an eyebrow, which had him swearing, which, in turn, had both her eyebrows lifting.

"From insulting a lady, to swearing at her." She tsked at him. "You're beginning very badly, you know."

"We'll start tomorrow."

She turned her head pointedly—if a little wobbly—toward a clock on the mantel. Its hands indicated that it was well past midnight.

"We'll start," he ground out, "at sunrise."

"You see? Gobs and gobs of sense."

Read more at www.alissa-johnson.com.

JADE LEE

A new, stand-alone novel from the *USA Today* bestselling author of *Dragonborn* and *Seduced by Crimson*

THE DRAGON EARL

Revenge. It poisoned everything he'd learned, everything he'd done, and yet every fiber of Jacob Cato burned for it—just as he burned for the beautiful but very English Evelyn Stanton. Long ago, the conspiracy to kill his family had stranded Jacob in the exotic East and made him unrecognizable to his countrymen...and women. In far-off China, Jacob had found sanctuary. In a Xi Lin temple he learned to be strong, but now he had a grander goal: to reclaim his English heritage as the Earl of Warhaven and the woman he'd left behind.

ISBN 13: 978-0-8439-6046-4

✂

☐ **YES!**

Sign me up for the Historical Romance Book Club and
send my FREE BOOKS! If I choose to stay in the club, I will
pay only $8.50* each month, a savings of $6.48!

NAME: _____

ADDRESS: _____

TELEPHONE: _____

EMAIL: _____

☐ I want to pay by credit card.

☐ VISA   ☐ MasterCard.   ☐ DISCOVER

ACCOUNT #: _____

EXPIRATION DATE: _____

SIGNATURE: _____

Mail this page along with $2.00 shipping and handling to:

Historical Romance Book Club
PO Box 6640
Wayne, PA 19087

Or fax (must include credit card information) to:
610-995-9274

You can also sign up online at **www.dorchesterpub.com**.

*Plus $2.00 for shipping. Offer open to residents of the U.S. and Canada only. Canadian
residents please call 1-800-481-9191 for pricing information.

If under 18, a parent or guardian must sign. Terms, prices and conditions subject to
change. Subscription subject to acceptance. Dorchester Publishing reserves the right to
reject any order or cancel any subscription.